MW00579704

THE CTHULHU CASEBOOKS

SHERLOCK HOLMES
and the Highgate Horrors

ALSO AVAILABLE FROM
JAMES LOVEGROVE AND TITAN BOOKS

THE CTHULHU CASEBOOKS

Sherlock Holmes and the Shadwell Shadows
Sherlock Holmes and the Miskatonic Monstrosities
Sherlock Holmes and the Sussex Sea-Devils

THE NEW ADVENTURES OF SHERLOCK HOLMES

The Stuff of Nightmares
Gods of War
The Thinking Engine
The Labyrinth of Death
The Devil's Dust

Sherlock Holmes and the Christmas Demon
Sherlock Holmes and the Beast of the Stapletons
Sherlock Holmes and the Three Winter Terrors

FIREFLY

Big Damn Hero
The Magnificent Nine
The Ghost Machine
Life Signs

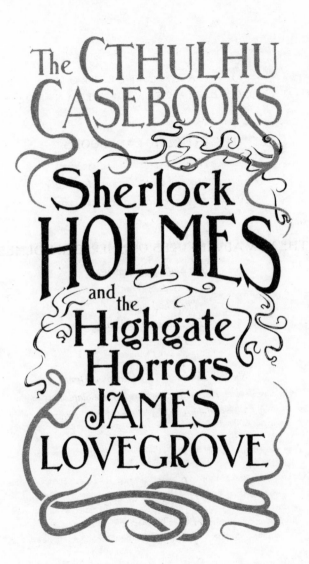

The CTHULHU CASEBOOKS

Sherlock HOLMES

and the Highgate Horrors

JAMES LOVEGROVE

TITAN BOOKS

The Cthulhu Casebooks: Sherlock Holmes and the Highgate Horrors
Hardback edition ISBN: 9781803361550
Electronic edition ISBN: 9781803361574

Published by Titan Books
A division of Titan Publishing Group Ltd
144 Southwark St, London SE1 0UP

First edition: October 2023
2 4 6 8 10 9 7 5 3 1

A CIP catalogue record for this title is available from the British Library.

Printed and bound CPI Group (UK) Ltd, Croydon, CR0 4YY.

PREFACE
BY JAMES LOVEGROVE

IF YOU'VE READ THE *CTHULHU CASEBOOKS* TRILOGY, particularly the last volume of the three, then you'll know that, for me, preparing those books for publication turned out to be a terrible ordeal. The strain of toiling over Dr Watson's typescripts for months on end wore me down, and I ended up having some sort of psychotic break. Consequently, for my own wellbeing and that of those around me, I was detained under Section 3 of the Mental Health Act and sent to an NHS facility for treatment.

The place was situated deep in the heart of the East Sussex countryside, not far from the town of Crowborough, and was called Providence House. The associations between "Providence" and H.P. Lovecraft are not lost on me, although in this instance the name was surely chosen to evoke a sense of destiny and supernal protective care rather than the capital city of the state of Rhode Island, that author's birthplace and hometown. Nor does it escape me that the celebrated Sir Arthur Conan Doyle, who among his many accomplishments served as Dr Watson's literary agent, spent the last couple of dozen years of his life in Crowborough at his house, Windlesham Manor, where he lies buried. There's even a statue of the man in the town, at the central crossroads (it's not life-size and makes him look very short when in fact he was tall). In all, then, Providence House would seem an ironically appropriate location for someone whose condition had been brought on by exposure to a confluence of Lovecraft and Sherlock Holmes.

I'd love to tell you that the building was a rambling Gothic mansion with elaborate wrought-iron gates and ivy crawling up its sides like a host of demonic dark green claws, and that the skies above it were perpetually overcast and threatening rain. In fact, Providence House was a linked set of modern low-rise blocks nestling among neatly cultivated grounds – more Premier Inn than Arkham Asylum – and during my time there, which lasted six months, the weather was largely pleasant, England in all its temperate glory.

The care I received within the walls of that establishment was second to none. Through a mix of counselling, group therapy sessions and pharmaceuticals, I was able to come to terms with the things I'd seen, or thought I'd seen, and the unusual behaviour patterns I'd exhibited, in particular crouching on a beach as though in prayer and incanting the phrase *"Ph'nglui mglw'nafh Cthulhu R'lyeh wgah'nagl fhtagn"* over and over. It was made apparent to me that, doubtless through stress and working too hard, my imagination had overridden the logical part of my brain and I'd lost the ability to distinguish delusion from reality. This is a commoner occurrence with authors than you might think (or perhaps you might not). We live in our heads so much that sometimes we get stuck inside them and can't find our way out.

Towards the end of my spell of treatment the staff took some of us inmates on a day trip to nearby Groombridge Place, to give us a bit of an airing. As is the case with many a stately home these days, the grounds of the house have been turned into a tourist attraction, with various fun activities on offer and the inevitable gift shop and tearoom. But Groombridge Place also has special resonance for Sherlock Holmes fans, since it appears, thinly disguised, in *The Valley of Fear*, Dr Watson's account of the events surrounding the seeming murder of John Douglas.

While roaming the gardens I got talking to someone who worked at the property, an archivist, and when he learned that I had a Holmes connection and had edited the three *Cthulhu Casebooks*, he got quite enthused.

"I have something I think you'd like to see," he said, and once I'd obtained permission from one of the nurses, I went off with the man to the manor house itself, which is a private residence and not open to the public. We crossed the moat via a conventional stone bridge – not a drawbridge as Watson has it – and soon we were in a large library and the archivist was opening a locked cupboard, from which he took out an old, very scuffed and battered box file. The artefact exuded age and neglect, right down to the layer of dust that seemed ingrained in its cardboard and the splotches of mildew along the edges.

He placed the box file reverentially on a table and raised the lid. Inside lay a sheaf of brittle foolscap, bound with a ribbon. The paper may have once been white but it was now a pallid mushroom grey. Handwritten across the top page, in faded blue ink, were these words:

The Highgate Horrors

*Being an account by Dr John H Watson MD
of a series of ghastly eldritch adventures
that befell myself and Mr Sherlock Holmes*

NOT FOR PUBLICATION

I felt a little shivery thrill. "Is that what I think it is?"

"What do you think it is?" the archivist said.

"Well, 'eldritch' suggests it isn't a conventional Holmes chronicle."

"Quite."

"It's another *Cthulhu Casebook*."

"That's my own conclusion."

I was both excited and apprehensive. "How come it's here?"

"Conan Doyle used to visit Groombridge a fair amount," said the archivist. "The story goes that one day, late in his life, he brought this manuscript along and asked for it to be looked after. He was Dr Watson's agent, as you know. He said Watson had sent it to him recently and he wanted the thing out of his house and kept away from prying eyes. He especially didn't want his executors to find it among his effects. This was a year or so before he died, and clearly notions of posterity were weighing on his mind. He spoke of the manuscript as though it was diseased, something rotten and dangerous."

"'Cursed', perhaps?"

"If you're being fanciful, then yes, maybe. Doyle expressed a wish that nobody should ever read it. There was some curiosity about this at the time within the family. Understandable, given how popular Watson's works were."

"And still are."

"But when a gentleman of Sir Arthur Conan Doyle's stature makes a request, it's respected," said the archivist, "and so the manuscript has sat in this library ever since, locked away and more or less ignored, becoming just a scrap of odd family folklore. That's how it stayed for nearly a century, until I came along. The current owners of Groombridge hired me to sort through their papers and their book collection, and when I chanced upon this thing, stashed in a cupboard, I couldn't help but take a look and find out what I could about it. And now – lucky me – I've run into you, Mr Lovegrove. Someone who knows a fair bit about Dr Watson's more esoteric output."

"Too much for my own good," I said, mostly to myself.

"Having read it myself, it seems of a piece with the other *Cthulhu Casebooks*, the same mix of straightforward sleuthing and outlandish supernatural shenanigans. Parts of it, in fact, made me somewhat uneasy even as I was leafing through. That 'glancing over your shoulder' feeling. You must know what I'm talking about."

"I do."

"And it occurs to me – just a thought – but now that I've met you, I'm wondering whether you might be willing to read it yourself and authenticate it for me."

I shook my head, not so much a "no" as an "I'm not sure".

"There'd be a fee involved," the archivist said. "I can arrange that. And perhaps, if you do decide the manuscript is the genuine article, we could look into getting it published. I mean, the *Cthulhu Casebooks* have sold well, haven't they? If this is another of them, it makes commercial sense to get it into readers' hands. There's always a market for newly discovered Dr Watson works, isn't there?"

None of this I could argue with. I was hesitant only because the existing three *Cthulhu Casebooks*, although they'd benefited me financially, had cost me in other ways.

"You'll consider it at least?" the archivist said, handing me his card.

I gave a noncommittal nod and slipped the card into my pocket.

A couple of weeks later I was discharged from Providence House with a clean bill of mental health. I went home, and I tried not to think about the archivist and that greyed, brittle manuscript. But the title had stuck in my brain – *The Highgate Horrors* – and I couldn't help wondering what was contained within those pages. What story did Dr Watson have to tell that was so alarming, so unsettling, that he had designated it "NOT FOR PUBLICATION"? What was it about the manuscript that had compelled Sir Arthur Conan Doyle to ditch it at Groombridge Place like so much literary toxic waste?

In the end I called the archivist. I just couldn't not. The compulsion was too strong.

A few days later a parcel arrived.

It took me a few further days to get around to reading the manuscript, and within a couple of chapters I knew that I was on familiar ground. The writing style was unmistakably Watson's. More to the point, I could see that the material matched that of the existing three *Cthulhu Casebooks*. The narrative, in fact, dovetailed around the events in the trilogy. This was the real deal. The only difference was that the book was handwritten rather than a typescript, for reasons explained in Dr Watson's covering letter to Conan Doyle.

So now, with the permission of all parties concerned, I'm presenting the work to the world, slightly retitled as *Sherlock Holmes and the Highgate Horrors*. I've deciphered Watson's sometimes very shaky penmanship as best I can. I've cut several sections for length and pace. I've worked long and hard over it, and I'm hoping that this time there'll be no negative repercussions for me.

Fingers crossed. Because, I tell you, after everything I've been through lately, I really don't need any more bad stuff to happen.

J.M.H.L., EASTBOURNE, UK
September 2022

A NOTE

Paddington
May 1929

My dear Sir Arthur,
For many a year now, you have served faithfully and
diligently as my literary agent. We have both profited
from my histories of Sherlock Holmes's investigations
and, furthermore, we share the distinction of both
being medical men, even if you retired from practice
far younger than I. On several occasions, we have
consorted convivially together in social circumstances.
In short, I like to think that we have, over time, become
more than colleagues; we have become firm friends.

By means of hints I have dropped, you are aware
that the various narratives which I have produced
pertaining to Holmes, and which you have sold on my
behalf, are fictions. You may not be privy to the full
facts that lie behind them – and for that you should
be thankful – but you have at least some notion that
while they purport to be reportage, each instead
glosses over a true incident. The impressions of that
incident may still be glimpsed beneath – "grinning

through", as it were, like the skull beneath the skin –
by those with an eye for such things.

What you cannot know, for until now I have
not told you, is that I spent the last year enshrining
much of the real story behind Holmes's and my
adventures in three volumes, these going by the titles
The Shadwell Shadows, *The Miskatonic Monstrosities* and
The Sussex Sea-Devils. Feeling that the public need
not be apprised of the shocking information they
contained, I dispatched all three by transatlantic post
to my American correspondent and fellow author
Howard Phillips Lovecraft, for his safekeeping. He is
as conversant as anyone in the subject matter they
allude to and therefore less apt to be appalled and
alarmed by it.

I have since compiled this fourth volume, *The
Highgate Horrors*. The arthritis in my hands is now
so bad that I can no longer manage the typewriter,
hence I have resorted to the pen once more, the tool
I used back in the days when I was a fledgling writer.
Holding it pains my old gnarled knuckles still, but not
as much as the repeated striking of keys.

I am sending the manuscript to you, rather than
to Lovecraft, merely because I feel it is high time
you understood more clearly what Holmes and I
had to face over the course of our thirty-and-more
years together. You will see that the narrative spans
the entirety of that period and is comprised of a
number of discrete-seeming sections which, *in toto*,
constitute a single unit, rather as the segments of an
orange form the whole. You will see, too, that certain
familiar names and situations crop up throughout,
albeit in unfamiliar contexts. I trust it will not be
too disconcerting to learn how, in the past, I have
ameliorated – one might say bowdlerised – some very

dark and sinister personages and occurrences, and altered others, so as to be more or less unrecognisable. Likewise, I trust that the exploits contained herein will not seem too grotesque to a man such as yourself, who has, in both his life and his literary works, shown himself to be open-minded when it comes to the fantastical and the extraordinary.

I am not asking you, Sir Arthur, to submit this work to Greenhough Smith at *The Strand* or to whomever the current editor of *Collier's* is (Chenery?), as has been your wont. Indeed, even were you minded to do so, I forbid it. I ask merely that you read the manuscript, digest its contents, and perhaps as a result feel more sympathetically disposed towards a frail old man, nearing the end of his life, who has done much and suffered greatly. Then, in whatever manner you deem fit, you may dispense with it.

I remain respectfully and amiably yours,

JOHN H. WATSON

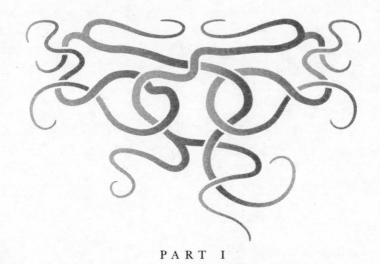

PART I

Autumn 1888

MANY A SCOTLAND YARD OFFICIAL CROSSED THE threshold of 221B Baker Street during Sherlock Holmes's tenure at that address. The majority came to consult him on some police matter or other and benefit from his expertise as a criminalist. A few wished to applaud him after he had aided them in foiling a felony or catching a culprit. Very rarely one might seek to upbraid him for involving himself in business that was not considered the rightful province of the amateur, or else to trumpet a perceived triumph of his own, the which, later, Holmes would invariably prove to be erroneous.

None, however, had any awareness of the investigations which comprised the bulk of Holmes's life's work, those forays into otherworldly mysteries where ghastly, ravening monsters and ancient, inimical gods were a prominent feature. None, that is, save Tobias Gregson. The unfortunate Inspector Gregson was drawn, against his will, into the murky supernatural waters in which my friend and I secretly swam; and indeed, many years after the events of the narrative I am about to relate, the man would perish in heroic yet tragic circumstances while assisting us in our endeavours, saving our lives at the expense of his own on an occasion when those same metaphorical waters threatened to drown us.

Of the rest, there was a single individual who may have developed some inkling about Holmes's more esoteric pursuits, and that was Inspector Athelney Jones. Readers of my published works will recognise his name from *The Sign of Four*, a heavily amended account of a case involving a four-pointed version of the mystical sigil known as an Elder Sign. He also features in "The Adventure of the Red-Headed League", although in that tale I mistakenly refer to him as Peter Jones, a slip of the pen for which I was often derided by him, and deservedly so.

"It isn't even as though Athelney and Peter sound similar," he once said to me. "Could it be you have got me confused with the Sloane Square department store?"

The events behind *The Sign of Four* were too macabre and extraordinary for Inspector Jones to remain oblivious to their true origin, much though we tried to hide it from him. Perhaps, like many a Welshman, with both a devout Methodist upbringing and an innate Celtic superstitiousness coexisting within him, he was already highly attuned to the mystical side of life, and thus had less difficulty than most reconciling himself to the existence of powers and entities beyond normal human ken. Now, at any rate, whenever he stumbled upon something with a whiff of the weird or uncanny about it, Sherlock Holmes was always his first port of call.

So it was that on a brisk late-autumn afternoon in 1888, not long after the above-mentioned escapade, the man in question walked into our sitting room and heaved his burly, plethoric bulk into the basket-chair, which emitted several small protesting creaks as it accommodated his weight. Gratefully he accepted the offer of a cigarette and a snifter of brandy, and then, peering at us with eyes that glittered from within their puffy pouches like twin trinkets sunk deep in the velvet lining of a display box, he proceeded to inform us about certain recent nefarious goings-on at Highgate Cemetery.

Little did he, or we, realise, but the horrors in which he was to embroil us were the start of an enterprise that would occupy Holmes's and my attention, off and on, over a span of some thirty years.

*

"Graves, Mr Holmes," began Jones in that distinctive voice of his, which contrived to be both husky and mellifluous at once. "Graves," he repeated. "Three of them."

"What about these graves?" asked Holmes.

"Well, that's the thing, isn't it? That's the thing. Dug up they've been, sir, and the bodies that lay inside exhumed and absconded with."

"Gone?"

Jones nodded. "Gone without a trace. Or no, perhaps not entirely without a trace."

"What on earth do you mean?"

"Let me tell it to you in order," Jones said, "and then we shall see what sense you can make of it all. Early this morning, a report reached us at the Yard concerning three graves at Highgate that had been interfered with."

"A report from whom?"

"An undertaker, name of Dole, who was visiting the cemetery in preparation for a burial this weekend. Mr Dole spied the fresh excavations and knew straight away that there was something amiss, not least because he was recently responsible for laying to rest one of the graves' occupants. He looked closer, found all three graves empty, and went to the nearest telegraph office to wire us."

"Bodysnatchers?" I offered.

"Of course the notion crossed my mind, Doctor, even as a cab drove me to Highgate. 'Jones-bach,' I said to myself, 'could we be dealing with some latter-day Burke and Hare types here?' But then you, as a medical man, know as well as I do that bodysnatching just doesn't happen any more, thanks to the Anatomy Act of 1832."

"Yes, true. There simply isn't a black market for dead bodies these days. By law, any unclaimed corpses go straight to the anatomists, with the result that they have all the cadavers they need, and more."

"Quite so, Watson," said Holmes, a measure of condescension in his tone. "Bodysnatching is highly unlikely to have been the motive for such a desecration, for the very reason you and the inspector have just stated. You really should have thought before you spoke. I can only assume you are so distracted by your forthcoming nuptials that your faculties are not as acute as they might otherwise be."

"Ah yes," said Jones, "the wedding isn't so far off now, is it? And how fares the lovely Miss Morstan?"

"Full of plans," I replied. "Every day, it seems, she has something she wishes to consult me about – the guest list, the wedding breakfast, the table decorations. I myself was hoping for a small, discreet ceremony, but Mary's ambitions for the occasion just keep growing. I find myself saying yes to whatever she asks for, regardless of my own feelings or, for that matter, the welfare of my wallet."

"And that is excellent practice for married life. Take it from someone who has been a husband for nearly a decade, Doctor: saying yes to your wife is the surest route to contentment. Besides, given your fiancée's undeniable charms, how could you in all conscience say no?"

Jones appended his remark with a throaty chuckle, which I joined in with, albeit circumspectly.

"If we could perhaps return to the matter at hand…?" Holmes prompted.

"Yes. Of course. Quite," said Jones. "Well, there I was at the cemetery, and bless me if there weren't three graves, fully opened up. Each was in fairly close proximity to the others, and each contained a vacant coffin whose lid had been forcibly dislodged."

"You said that Dole the undertaker had recently been involved in the funeral for one of the deceased."

"I did."

"How long ago did the interment take place?"

"A week, no more."

"Which would indicate that the soil was newly turned, making the act of unearthing that much easier."

"Which in turn," I said, "makes the bodysnatcher theory that little bit more conceivable, don't you think? A set of fresh corpses, readily accessible…"

"But what for, Watson?" said Holmes. "Why go to significant risk and effort to wrest three bodies out of the ground when, at least as far as illegitimate medical usage is concerned, there's no chance of financial gain?"

"A prank, maybe?"

"A very unsavoury one."

"Just for the sheer, perverted joy of desecration, then. How about that?"

"If so, it is suggestive of a very sick mind. More plausibly, we could be looking at grave robbing. The three deceased may have been buried with certain valuables on their persons, which others have sought to plunder. In that instance, though, why not simply grab the loot and have done with it? Why make off with the bodies as well?" Holmes turned back to Jones. "That said, Inspector, I am yet to be convinced this is anything more than a commonplace crime. No question, any right-minded individual would be repelled at the thought of disturbing the dead in their final rest, but I do not doubt the capability of Her Majesty's constabulary to hunt down the perpetrators and bring them to justice."

"Well now," said the police official, his eyes twinkling all the more brightly, "in that respect I would agree with you, Mr Holmes. But here's where it gets interesting."

"By which I take you to mean unusual."

"Exactly."

Holmes leaned forward in his seat. "Do tell."

"I ascertained from the cemetery's records the home address of each of the deceased whose grave had been violated," said Jones. "Then, back at the Yard, I sent constables to break the news to the relicts. It seemed better that they should learn what had happened to their dearly departed from someone in authority rather than read about it in the newspapers or hear of it by word of mouth – or, for that matter, witness the situation for themselves should they happen to visit the grave."

"Such thoughtfulness is greatly to your credit," I said.

Jones acknowledged the remark with a small bow. "One of the constables returned with a tale. He had gone to see a Mrs Thisbe Pickering, of Lanningbourne Common, whose husband Everard, an actuary with a Chancery Lane insurance brokerage, died less than a fortnight ago. Mrs Pickering was in a dire state when my man called, pale and trembling, and at first he thought that somebody must have got there before him and conveyed the dreadful news already. It turns out, however, that Mrs Pickering had seen her husband just last night."

This was Jones's coup, the bait with which he hoped to hook Holmes, and it worked. My friend was all at once a-quiver. Were he a cat, his ears would have been pricked, his tail twitching, his hindquarters swaying from side to side.

"Not in a dream, I take it," he said. "Not as some imaginary phantasm conjured up by a grieving woman's anguished brain."

"From an upstairs window," said Jones. "Lurking at the rear of the house. Her husband, standing there amid the shrubbery between her garden and the common behind the house, visible in the moonlight, gazing up at her. She caught only the briefest glimpse of him before collapsing in a swoon, but she would be willing to swear on the Bible that it had been he. So she said to my constable. Block, he's called, and he's as solid and dependable as his surname suggests, if also somewhat lacking in imagination."

"In that respect, he is a fairly typical example of his species. Present company excepted."

"Thank you, sir. I shall take that as a compliment. Constable Block, at any rate, was not persuaded by the widow Pickering's claim. 'If she saw her late husband, sir, I'm a Dutchman,' were his words to me. 'Yet for all that,' he added, 'she seemed quite certain about it. There was the light of utter conviction in her eyes as she related the incident. I can tell when a person is shamming, Inspector, and she was not. It may not have been true but neither was she making it up.'"

"Intriguing."

"So I thought myself, Mr Holmes, and that is why I have come to you." Jones held out his hands, palms upward, as though presenting a gift. "I know how fond you are of the outré and the inexplicable. You have rather a sweet tooth for it, I've observed. You enjoy confronting the irrational and rationalising it, and what could be more irrational than three missing corpses, one of which has, if Mrs Pickering's account is to be believed, regained the power of locomotion and visited his erstwhile home?"

"It is certainly a singular conundrum," Holmes replied in a careful manner, "and naturally I am curious to know more. What say you, Watson? A short trip up to Highgate? How does that strike you?"

*

Accordingly, Holmes, Jones and I made our way northward to that elaborate and rather wonderful necropolis known as Highgate Cemetery.

Anyone who has visited the place will know it to be full of winding alleys, imposing mausoleums and proud, ornate obelisks. It has avenues lined with vaults and lawns dotted with toweringly tall cedars, all set on a hillside with sweeping views across London. There is about it an atmosphere of gloomy, hushed grandeur. Those who have been laid to rest in its grounds seem to lie in a state of solemn splendour, as though death, for them, is a privilege. Here and there one finds headstones fashioned in shapes denoting the trades or hobbies that preoccupied the deceased in life – a hammer, a violin, a tennis racquet, a horse, an accordion – while, whichever way one turns, one is greeted by hosts of carved angels and cherubs, looking majestically downcast, their wings drooping in sorrow.

On Swain's Lane, the narrow, walled thoroughfare that bisects the cemetery, our hansom deposited us at the gates to the graveyard's eastern half. This is the more modest portion of its near-forty acres, where a plot may be secured for as little as £2 10s, and Jones led us along its pathways to the location of the first of the three ravaged graves. He had posted a constable here to stand guard, and the fellow saluted his superior officer as we arrived.

"Constable Gorham," said Jones. "You know Mr Holmes, do you not?"

"By reputation only. An honour, sir."

"And this is, of course, Dr Watson."

Gorham touched forefinger to forehead. "Sir."

"Anyone been by since I left you here?"

"A few random folk nosing around, curious. I've steered them off. Also that gravedigger chap. Coker?"

"Roker."

"That's him. Wanted to know when he could set to straightening things up again. I told him what you told me to say: not until Inspector Jones gives the word."

"Good man."

The grave itself was a pitiful sight indeed, a deep, ragged-edged cavity surrounded by heaps of scattered soil. At its head was a discreet wooden marker bearing the name of the person supposed to be interred beneath, one Marcus Knightley. This was a temporary token, there to serve as a placeholder until the ground had settled and a permanent memorial could be installed. The marker lay flat, clearly having been uprooted when the grave was disturbed.

Holmes fell to a squat and embarked on a close survey of the hole itself and the soil around it. Then he leapt down nimbly into the pit, landing in the open coffin, where he continued his examination, with much use of his lens on the coffin's rim and lid. When he was done, he gestured to Jones and me, and we each took one of his extended hands and hauled him out.

"Next," he said, and with Jones showing us the way we

proceeded to the site of the second despoiled grave, leaving Constable Gorham at his post.

The second grave stood some thirty yards from the first, just within Gorham's view, and there Holmes conducted a similar study. The marker identified the absent occupant as Miss Amelia Throckmorton. The third grave, a few dozen yards further on and also visible to Gorham from his vantage point, had belonged to Everard Pickering, and was in a similar condition to the previous two. Holmes scrutinised this one no less thoroughly.

At last, brushing dirt off his sleeves and trousers, he said, "There are certainly a number of singular elements worth noting here. For instance, I'm sure you will have spotted, Inspector, that all three of the deceased perished within the space of a week. So the dates on the grave markers attest."

"I had not noticed that," Athelney Jones admitted. "The three were all buried recently, that much we already knew, but the closeness of their death dates escaped me. Do you think it significant?"

"It may be. We have passed five other newly dug plots on our journey through the cemetery – none of them, of course, disturbed the way these three have been – and the dates on the markers of those display a considerably wider span of time. The oldest goes back nearly four months."

"I believe it can take anything up to six months before a headstone may be laid," I averred. "The ground is not stable enough until then."

"The salient point, Watson, is that our trio of missing corpses met their ends a few days from one another. That may well be coincidence, but I am willing to bet there is something more to it. Then there is the matter of— Oh ho, who's this?"

Holmes's attention had been caught by the rapid approach of a fellow in labourer's clothing. The man strode towards us with the air of one who had a territorial right to be in the grounds of the cemetery, and the spade he carried slung over his shoulder seemed to justify this, affording as it did a clear indication of his profession.

"That," said Jones, "is Jem Roker, the cemetery's head gravedigger, as mentioned by Gorham. I should warn you," he added, dropping his voice so that only Holmes and I could hear, "he is an irascible sort. Best not to antagonise him." Turning, he hailed Roker. "Good day to you again, Mr Roker."

"Good day indeed," said the gravedigger. He was broad-backed and raw-cheeked, and his bearing was none too cordial. "Inspector Jones, you told me this morning that I and my men were to leave these three particular graves as they are, and we have done as you asked, all obliging like, out of respect for your rank and position. Now I'm telling you that they must be filled in and neatened, as soon as possible. We pride ourselves on keeping things all shipshape at Highgate. We've already received complaints from folk wanting to know how come there's such a mess in this particular corner here and why there's a uniformed policeman on duty. They don't want to see dirty great holes yawning in the earth or bluebottles standing around."

"It was, alas, unavoidable, Mr Roker," said Jones. "I promise you, you and your men shan't have to stay your hands for much longer. I needed the graves untouched so that my colleague here, Mr Sherlock Holmes, would have a chance to view them as is."

"Ah yes," said Roker, pivoting towards Holmes. "You. Didn't I just see you clamber out of this very grave? I was looking on from up yonder, and I could swear I spied you ferreting around inside it."

"Guilty as charged," replied Holmes. "I was doing my best to determine what manner of foul play has occurred."

"And jumping in and out of graves is how you go about that?"

"If you can think of a better method for gathering evidence in a case like this, I would be happy to hear it."

"You don't consider your actions might be disrespectful to the dead? Not to say downright ghoulish?"

"Given that the dead are not themselves present at this moment in any of the graves I have ventured into, I am not particularly concerned on that front."

Roker's eyes narrowed. "You have a pretty answer for everything, don't you, sir?" He swatted irritably at a wasp that was buzzing about his face. "Well, let me tell you, I don't take kindly to folk treating my cemetery as their personal gymnasium." He flapped a hand at the wasp again. "Pesky jasper," he growled. "Leave me be." The insect seemed to get the message and flew away. Roker jabbed a forefinger at Holmes. "Tramping around inside graves like that – it's not proper, not even with a copper's say-so."

"If an apology will placate you, Mr Roker," said my friend in his suavest tones, "then by all means, I am sorry."

"Yes, well…" The gravedigger harrumphed. "You just mind yourself. Who are you anyway? What's your job?"

"Mr Holmes is a much-respected consulting detective," said Jones.

"Consulting detective? Never heard of such a thing."

"Perhaps because I am one of a kind," said Holmes. "And in that capacity, I was wondering if you'd mind answering a few questions for me, Mr Roker."

"Mind? Yes, I do mind, as a matter of fact. I have work to do. Proper work, unlike some."

"I shan't detain you long."

"You shan't detain me at all." Roker spun on his heel and began to walk away at a brisk pace.

Holmes made after him. "Really, it will only take a minute or so," said he. "As head gravedigger, you must be privy to all kinds of—"

He broke off because Roker had abruptly rounded on him. Unshouldering his spade, the gravedigger thrust it in Holmes's direction, like a soldier attempting to impale his enemy with a bayoneted rifle. Had my friend not sprung smartly backward in the nick of time, the tip of the implement's blade might well have penetrated his abdomen.

Roker thrust the spade again, but once more Holmes was too quick for him. This time, though, he not only evaded the blow but was able to catch the spade's haft with both hands. With a sharp, powerful twist of his wrists, he yanked the tool free from Roker's grasp.

The gravedigger, thus disarmed, appeared to weigh up his options. Should he fight or flee? He plumped for the latter, and all at once he was sprinting off at impressive speed, hobnail boots pounding the earth.

Tossing the spade aside, Holmes gave chase, as did Jones and I. I had no idea why Roker was so keen to avoid interrogation by Holmes. Perhaps it could be accounted for by his basic ill-temperedness: he resented my friend's enquiries as an impertinence, a personal affront. It seemed more likely, however, that he had something to hide.

We pursued him along the mazy pathways of the cemetery, Constable Gorham joining the chase after a shouted summons from Jones. Holmes already had a head start over the rest of us, and he rapidly widened the gap, by dint of being fleeter of foot. Roker, alas, was swifter yet, for he soon vanished from sight. Holmes likewise disappeared ahead, and eventually Jones, Gorham and I stumbled to a halt. The heavily built Welshman was wheezing hard and in urgent need of a breather. The constable, similarly, was panting and red-faced, and as for me, it was either take a rest or else pass out from pain. Certain events in a cavern in the wilds of Afghanistan some eight years earlier had weakened my constitution and left me in a state of permanent physical debility. My shoulder was the principal source of enfeeblement and caused me no small discomfort whenever I overtaxed myself.

Once we three had recovered from our exertions, Jones suggested we split up. "Better chance of finding Roker that way," said he. "Should anyone come across him, seize hold of him and don't let go, and then yell and keep yelling until the rest of us arrive. I've no idea what the rascal thinks he's up to, but we can have him up for assault on Mr Holmes, if nothing else."

Alone, I picked my wary way through the necropolis. Now and then I heard oncoming footsteps and tensed up, only to encounter some innocent visitor wandering by, perhaps bearing a bunch of flowers to lay upon a grave.

I passed through the tunnel that ran under Swain's Lane, connecting the two halves of the cemetery, and entered the older western portion. Here lay such noted landmarks as the colonnaded Circle of Lebanon, the imposing Egyptian Avenue, and the Terrace Catacombs with their tall, arched entrances. Here, too, was proof that death's reputation as the great equaliser was unfounded, for only the wealthy could afford to be entombed thus, in such funereal high style.

I trod along sloping paths and up and down stone staircases, all the while keeping an eye out for Roker. I was nearing the cemetery chapel, and ready to give up the search altogether, when a hand seized my elbow from behind. I whirled round, fist clenched, all set to deliver a swingeing uppercut – until I realised that it was not the gravedigger waylaying me.

"Holmes!" I declared. "You should not sneak up on a fellow like that. I nearly hit you!"

"Apologies for startling you, Watson." Holmes's face bore a sheen of perspiration, and two livid dots coloured his gaunt white cheeks. "That was not my intention. I assumed you heard me coming."

"Then you are stealthier than you think. I take it you have failed to apprehend our friend Roker."

"He evaded me," Holmes said ruefully. "He is faster than he looks, and, understandably, possesses an intimate knowledge of the cemetery's layout, which he used to his advantage."

At that moment, Athelney Jones lumbered into view, with Constable Gorham not far behind. "There you two gents are," the inspector said. "No luck? Us neither. Seems Mr Roker has given us all the slip. He's obviously mixed up in this business somehow, isn't he? Why else would he be so aggressively uncooperative? My guess is he dug up the corpses himself."

"But whatever for?" I said. "His own benefit?"

"Or another's."

"You mean someone paid him to exhume them?"

"That's precisely what I mean, Doctor. After all, if you want that sort of work done, who better to employ than a gravedigger? A head gravedigger, no less."

I nodded. "And he was agitated about filling in the graves because he wished to cover up any evidence of his own complicity. It wasn't about professional pride at all, not really. Yes, that makes sense."

"Well, he shan't get away with it," Jones stated through clenched teeth. "You mark my words. I am going straight to Scotland Yard and I will have half the force out looking for Mr Jem Roker. We'll find out where he lives, and if he isn't there, we'll scour London until we've unearthed him. No pun intended. Come along, Gorham."

With that, the two policemen departed, leaving Holmes and myself to our own devices.

My friend had a familiar sly expression on his face.

"What is it, Holmes?" I said. "I know that look. You think Jones isn't quite on the money, don't you? He's missing something – some clue, some angle on the case that you yourself have identified."

"Am I quite so easy to read?" came the reply. "Well, you're not wrong. I don't believe our Mr Roker is as guilty in this affair as the worthy inspector does. I believe someone has bribed the fellow for some purpose, that much is certain. But I am not so sure it was to dig up the three graves."

"Care to elaborate?"

"Gladly, on condition that you are willing to repair with me to a nearby pub first, where we can refresh ourselves after all this haring about."

"More than happy to," said I.

*

As we slaked our parched throats with pints of porter, Holmes shared with me his thoughts regarding Roker.

"You noted, of course, the watch poking out of his waistcoat pocket? Ah. Your blank look is all the answer I need. It was a thing of beauty, that watch. Enough of it protruded that I could identify it as a gold-plated half hunter with blued steel hands. The casing was well polished, likewise the part-glassed lid. It was of European manufacture, a Junghans if I don't miss my guess. What a contrast a watch like that made to the worn, threadbare nature of its immediate setting, and indeed, to the general coarseness of its owner. You really did not observe it?"

"Holmes, after eight years together, you surely know by now that my eye for such details is far inferior to yours."

"But it stood out like the proverbial sore thumb. Well, regardless, one must ask oneself how the likes of Jem Roker, on a gravedigger's salary, could afford a timepiece of such quality."

"A family heirloom?"

"This was no scuffed, much-handled object that has been passed down through the generations. It was quite clearly new and in nigh-immaculate condition."

"So a gift."

"It was certainly given to him," said Holmes, "and not long ago, I would wager, since he has not yet gone to the trouble of purchasing a chain for it. No, all in all, I think the watch was more in the nature of a bribe."

"A bribe to dig up the graves?"

"But that's just it, Watson. Roker did not do the digging."

"To turn a blind eye, then, while someone else did?"

"Perhaps I am not making myself clear. There was no digging involved whatsoever. No spadework, at least." Holmes frowned at me. "A blank look again. Really, it is becoming a bad habit. I see I shall have to explain as straightforwardly as I can."

"Since you have so far been rather obtuse, that would be welcome."

"My survey of the gravesites yielded three signal facts," my companion said. "Firstly, the soil was not dug out with a spade. If it had been, it would surely have been piled up more neatly, or at any rate in a series of heaps rather than scattered any-old-how. In addition, the inner walls of the graves showed none of the flat, scraping impressions one might expect if a spade had been used. Secondly, the coffin lids were not jemmied off, otherwise I would have found marks around their rims in the squared-off shape typical of a jemmy's tip. Thirdly, graverobbers might have taken the trouble to replace the earth they had dug up, in order to make their crime less readily detectable."

"As to the last," I said, "perhaps the perpetrators were pushed for time. Dawn was coming and they feared exposure."

"That is possible, I grant you, but is undermined by the fact that, as I have been at pains to establish, no spades were used, nor jemmies, nor any other kind of tool."

"But all that leaves is bare hands."

"Precisely, Watson! Precisely!" Holmes took a long draught of his beer. "The disinterment was done with bare hands. I saw with my own eyes, inside the grave pits: plainly visible fingermarks. They presented clear evidence of a scooping action."

"I cannot imagine graverobbers, bodysnatchers, resurrection men, whatever you wish to call people of that ilk, choosing to use their hands."

"I should add that the scooping action tapered in such a way as to indicate it came from below rather than above."

I mulled this over for several seconds before realising what he was getting at.

"It can't be," I murmured.

"Oh, but it must be," replied Holmes. "The only reasonable inference one can draw from the data is that no external agency was involved. In other words, the three bodies were not dug up. On the contrary, *they dug themselves up*."

Now it was my turn to take a long draught of my drink. "This is no longer one of your common-or-garden, bread-and-butter cases, is it?" The pub was none too busy, but I had lowered my voice, as had Holmes his, for fear of being overheard. "This carries the whiff of the supernatural."

"Indeed. Athelney Jones has brought us something both sinister and anomalous. He really has a knack for it, doesn't he?"

I shook my head. "The dead coming back to life and hauling themselves out of their graves…"

"The coffin lids were pushed up from within," said Holmes. "The looseness of the soil above would have allowed that. Then the corpses clawed their way out into the open air, casting dirt all around them and in the process practically emptying the gravesites. Their movements thereafter are hard to discern. I found numerous footmarks in the vicinity of the graves, going in various directions, but they could have belonged to anyone: Jones, Roker, the undertaker Dole, Constable Gorham, and who knows how many others besides."

A thought struck me. "Could we be looking at cases of premature burial?"

"You know as well as I do how unlikely that is," Holmes replied. "Premature burial is rare enough, but three such, in immediate propinquity to one another? And even if it were so, our untimely-interred trio, having struggled their way up out of the ground, would not simply have disappeared without trace. At the very least they might have languished beside the graves, exhausted from the effort of liberating themselves, or else they might, if recovered sufficiently, have gone to seek medical attention or the aid of a policeman, whereupon the plight from which they had just escaped would quickly have become common knowledge. I wonder, moreover, whether anyone has actually ever survived premature burial. Surely suffocation within the airless confines of the casket would soon turn the error made by coroner or doctor into awful reality. We must consider, too, the sheer strength required to lever up a screwed-down coffin lid, especially with a significant weight of earth on top."

"In panicked desperation, a man is capable of supreme physical feats."

"True. But a reanimated dead body, immune to pain or terror or fatigue, would have the stamina to conduct a patient, sustained effort at freeing itself, much more so than would a living person. You seem eager to dismiss the notion of ambulatory corpses, Watson, yet this would not be the first occasion you and I have encountered the phenomenon. Remember the crypt beneath St Paul's Shadwell?"

"Only too well," I said, with feeling. "I was rather hoping never to repeat the experience."

"Far be it from me to dash your hopes, my friend," said Holmes, "but I fear I have no choice. Now, sup up."

"Why? Where are we going?"

"Lanningbourne Common, to pay a call on the widow Pickering, of course." Holmes rose from our table. "She has alleged that her late husband put in an appearance at his former home, the selfsame night he emerged from his grave. The least we can do is confirm, or otherwise, the veracity of her claim."

*

Lanningbourne Common perched atop one of north London's many hills and was a modest acreage of semi-wild public land with only a handful of streets backing directly on to it. Finding the residence of the lady in question, therefore, was easier than anticipated. By dint of knocking on a few doors in the neighbourhood, Holmes was soon able to glean her address. Nonetheless, by the time we stood outside her house – one of a terrace of bow-fronted red-brick buildings – the afternoon was starting to wane, the shadows lengthening, a chill creeping into the air.

Thisbe Pickering proved to be a woman in late middle age with tightly pinned grey hair and a bony, compact frame. The paleness of her complexion was accentuated by the dress of sombre black bombazine she wore, yet there was more to it than that. She had the blanched look of one who has lately suffered not just bereavement but a terrific shock. Her voice, accordingly, was a thin, reedy thing, and her every gesture was timorous and restrained, as though she did not trust herself to speak or move with vigour lest the effort induce further reaction.

Holmes, who could exercise a powerful influence over the fairer sex when he wished to, charmed his way across her threshold. Inside the house there were signs of mourning etiquette all around, over and above Mrs Pickering's widow's weeds. Pictures had been turned to face the wall. Black crepe ribbons had been draped on doorknobs. Clocks had been stopped.

Presently we were ensconced in the parlour and Holmes had inveigled the woman into telling us about the sighting of her husband some twelve hours earlier.

"I chanced to get up in the middle of the night," said she. "I have not been sleeping well this past fortnight, not since my Everard… Not since he, you know, *succumbed*. I was crossing the landing and happened to glance out of the window, and there he was, at the far end of the garden, plain as anything. I know it was him. I'm sure of it. A moonbeam caught his face, and it was a face I know as well as my own. After nearly three decades of marriage, how could I not? Even with the recent disfigurement – or indeed because of it – I am in no doubt that it was my husband's face."

"Disfigurement?" said Holmes.

"Yes, alas. Everard was always a handsome man, but the disease which killed him ravaged his features."

"What did he die of, may I ask?" I said.

"Cancer, sir. A terrible cancer that stole his health, his looks, his vigour, everything, and eventually his life."

"I am sorry to hear of it."

"Evil illness," said she. "Not six months ago, he was in fine fettle. Then the cancer took hold, and it spread fast. He became riddled with tumours, including some within the flesh of his face, which left it distended and frightful to behold. His end was protracted and gruelling. I would not wish such a death upon my worst enemy. Everard suffered the torments of hell in his last few weeks, and it was a blessing, truly a blessing, when finally it was all over. I did my best to console him throughout and ease his pain, but it never seemed enough."

"Rest assured, my good woman, you have the condolences of us both," said Holmes. "Now, if it's not too much trouble, might you be willing to show us where in the garden, exactly, your husband happened to be standing?"

"Of course." Mrs Pickering sniffed hard and dabbed a handkerchief around her eyes. "You said you are with the police, am I right?"

"Affiliated."

"Well, at least you seem to be taking me seriously. That constable, the one who came this morning to inform me that Everard's body had been taken from his grave – what was his name? Block. He all but laughed in my face when I told him I had seen Everard myself during the night."

"I like to think I am more open-minded than the average bobby," said Holmes, "and sharper of intellect, too. Where the police are a rusty handsaw, I am a scalpel."

Mrs Pickering invited us to follow her. We exited the house via a set of French windows at the back and traversed a well-kempt lawn. Halfway across, the lady halted. "I shan't go any further. I do not feel comfortable approaching the spot. You carry on. There, just beneath the cherry tree – that's where Everard was. In life, he used to like to sit beneath its boughs, of an evening. It brought him peace." So saying, the widow turned and, her shoulders sagging as though burdened with a great weight, went back indoors.

The garden and the common behind it were separated by bushes and rough undergrowth, so that the division between the two was not clearly demarcated. The cherry tree itself was a splendid thing, just coming into blossom, tiny flowers emerging from their buds all over it like little pale pink exclamations of joy.

Holmes fell to his usual practice of investigating a scene minutely. He studied the bark of the tree trunk. He prowled on all fours through the long grass at its base. He pored long and hard over broken stems and snapped branches and over every small declivity or impression in the ground that his eye fell upon. For a time he ventured out into the common, casting this way and that along its footpaths and greenswards.

"Well," he said when he returned, "Constable Block – or should that be Blockhead? – passed up a prime opportunity to do some proper police work. Rather than scoffing at Mrs Pickering's account of a nocturnal visitation, he should have troubled himself to follow it up, whereupon he would have found ample substantiating evidence."

"In his defence, his task was merely to deliver bad tidings. He could not have suspected that there is more to those empty graves than meets the eye."

"Negligence is never excusable, Watson. At any rate, Everard Pickering was definitely here last night. See there? And there? Footmarks made by a man wearing size eleven shoes. There are several pairs of shoes and boots lined up in the hallway of the house. We passed them on our way in. The masculine pairs are size elevens and can only be Pickering's. Furthermore, the spacing between the footmarks suggests a man of around six feet in height. A topcoat hanging from the coat rack in the hallway would fit someone just that tall."

"It's a good thing that Pickering's death is still so recent that his widow has not yet got round to throwing out his personal effects," I said.

"For our purposes it is fortunate indeed."

"All the same, might it not be possible that the footmarks belong to another man who just happens to have the same physical proportions as Pickering?"

"But with the same facial disfigurement?" said Holmes with a dismissive flap of the hand. "Now then, let us consider the tale the footmarks tell. We see that Pickering entered the garden from the common and stood beneath the cherry tree for some while. The depth of the indentations when he was stationary suggest as much. He then departed, back the way he came, out onto the common. However, he did not depart alone. There is a secondary trail, made by a man with much smaller feet, size eights. In several instances that trail crosses Pickering's as it comes in from the common, partly obliterating his footmarks when it does so. Thus we know that the other man was a subsequent arrival. Both sets of footmarks, though, leave the spot in tandem, side by side. From this we may infer that the second man came to fetch Pickering and either led him away or accompanied him. The trail then goes cold, I regret to say. The footpaths on the common are too dry for clear prints. Would that it had rained lately!"

"Could the second individual have been another of the three reanimated corpses?"

"A fair assumption, I suppose," said Holmes, "but there is a notable difference in character between the two sets of footmarks. Pickering's exhibit a dragging, clumsy gait, such as one might expect of a walking dead man – such, indeed, as we ourselves have witnessed in the past. The other person's, by contrast, are footmarks of the type any ordinary living human being might leave."

"So the mystery deepens," I said. "Who is this other? Might it be Roker?"

"The second set of footmarks betray that their owner is not only short but pigeon-toed. Roker is neither."

"Clearly, though, whoever it is, he has some connection with Pickering, and perhaps also a connection with the other two missing corpses."

"The former is indisputable," said my friend, "and the latter plausible."

I chuckled mirthlessly. "You know, Holmes, sometimes I wonder at us. Here we are, talking about reanimated corpses as though they are an everyday, mundane occurrence. The type of thing that the rest of the world relegates to the realms of fantasy or myth, you and I treat as routine."

"In a sense it is, to us. It has been eight years since my 'dream-quest'." He was referring to the drug-induced mental journey he had undergone on Box Hill near Dorking, which had served as his initiation into a terrible secret: the existence of ancient godlike entities bent on subjugating and destroying mankind. "It has been slightly longer since your expedition to the lost subterranean city of Ta'aa, where you fell foul of the last remnants of a race of human-reptilian hybrids. Following those discrete revelatory episodes, you and I have had many grotesque and terrifying experiences together, and we now know, beyond a shadow of a doubt, that hideous dark forces swirl around mankind, lurking at the periphery of things, utterly inimical in nature, ever ready to sow havoc and harm. This has become our norm, we are accustomed to it, and hence it is no surprise if we should discuss such matters and related topics between ourselves with the same dispassion as you, I imagine, discuss case histories and the latest surgical techniques with your medical colleagues."

"You might say we have taken the sane approach when dealing with insanity."

"Well put," said Holmes. "You really have a way with

words, Watson." He clapped his hands together. "Anyhow, it is getting dark, and we have accomplished as much as we can here. Let us pay our respects to the widow Pickering and be on our merry way."

Indoors, Holmes thanked Mrs Pickering for her hospitality and said we would not impose upon her any longer.

"Mr Holmes," the lady said, "tell me this. Did I truly see Everard? Or am I mad? Forgive my asking, but you must understand, he was not just my husband, he was my everything. We were not blessed with children and we lived only for each other. To think that he may not be dead, that we may be together again… It is inconceivable, yet I am filled with hope nonetheless."

"And it is a hope," my friend said stiffly, "that I am obliged to dash. Your husband has not returned from the grave. You were, I'm afraid, sorely mistaken in thinking you saw him."

Mrs Pickering's face fell. "But I was so sure. He seemed so real. And then when the constable said his grave was empty, I dared to believe the unbelievable."

"I detect the smell of laudanum on your breath."

"Well, indeed. Over the past few days I have been resorting to the drug in order to keep my nerves in check, as anyone might in my situation. What of it?"

"It is a concoction known to cause hallucinations in even the most well-ordered mind," Holmes said. "Is that not so, Watson?"

I mumbled a few words of assent.

"All you saw last night, Mrs Pickering," Holmes continued, "was a mirage brought on by a heady cocktail of laudanum and grief. You wished very much to have your late husband back, and at an ungodly hour, in a half-sleeping state, with a quantity of opium in your bloodstream, you glimpsed a shape in the garden which you took to be him. I put it to you that a shaft of moonlight happened to strike a clump of cherry blossom in a particular way; your imagination, aided by the laudanum, did the rest."

Mrs Pickering looked wholly crestfallen now. A sob escaped her, and she turned away from us with a forceful gesture that indicated she wished us to depart.

We did as bidden, and while we were walking away from the house, I said to Holmes, "Could you not have been a tad more tactful? You left that poor woman crushed."

"What would you have had me do instead? Tell her the truth?"

"Some version thereof."

"Watson, whatever has become of Everard Pickering, it is safe to say he is no longer the man Thisbe Pickering was married to. There is to be no happy reunion for the pair, at least not in this world. If Pickering were as he used to be, if somehow he has been not just reanimated but restored to his full former glory, would he not have gone to her rather than merely loitering at the end of the garden? Would he not have rapped at the door and then swept her up in a loving embrace as soon as she answered his knock? Whereas he was drawn away from the scene by the owner of the second set of footmarks, much like a small child surrendering himself to the stewardship of a parent. That suggests his corpse is possessed of only the dimmest spark of sentience – enough to have got him to the house in the first place, but no further – and is incapable of independent thought. I could not in all conscience pretend to Mrs Pickering that she will ever have her husband back, and it seemed better to quench the flame of optimism rather than kindle it. Does that make me cold, my friend, or compassionate? Do tell."

"A bit of both, if I'm honest," said I.

Sherlock Holmes shrugged his shoulders. "So be it. I can live with that."

*

The next morning, a telegram arrived from Inspector Jones. Mrs Hudson brought it up to our rooms as we were breakfasting, and Holmes paused from his neat evisceration of a boiled egg in order to read it.

"Ah," said he, "now here is an interesting development, Watson. It transpires that the irascible Mr Roker has been found."

"That's good," I said. "Jones has him in custody, I presume, and you may now question him at your leisure."

"No, you misunderstand. When I said 'found', I meant 'found dead'."

"Oh. That rather puts a new complexion on things. Dead how?"

"The inspector, somewhat disobligingly, has declined to specify. He has, however, furnished us with Roker's address, with an invitation to meet him there. Finish up those last few mouthfuls of kedgeree, why don't you? The salubrious delights of Camden await us."

Roker's lodgings were situated above a butchers on a busy street of that northern borough of the capital and consisted of a cramped, sparsely furnished living room and an even smaller and barer bedroom, along with a bathroom down the hall shared with the various other tenants of the house. The gravedigger may have boasted of "keeping things all shipshape at Highgate", but the same principle did not apply to his domestic arrangements. The windowpanes were cloudy with filth, cobwebs clung in every corner, and empty beer bottles, many bearing a patina of dust, cluttered every available surface. Unlaundered clothing lay around in foetid piles, and the floor was liberally festooned with tiny black droppings, denoting an infestation of mice or rats or both.

Roker himself, at least, would no longer have to worry about the squalor of his living conditions, if it had ever bothered him. He lay sprawled on his back, quite still, next to an overturned wooden chair. His face was purple and puffy, his tongue protruded from between his lips, and his eyelids were half closed, as though he were narrowing them against a bright light.

"I'm glad you have been able to attend too, Doctor," said Athelney Jones. "You can confirm what I believe: that the cause of death here was asphyxiation."

I knelt to examine the body. "The face appears congested and cyanotic," I said. "There are numerous petechiae in the skin – tiny haemorrhages – resulting from high intravascular pressure." I peered at the thin slivers of sclera revealed by the eyelids. "Likewise in the whites of the eyes. These are all signs of hypoxia. I don't see any bruising to the throat, so I would say he was not strangled. Absent a coroner's report, then yes, I would lay good money on this being a case of asphyxiation, Inspector, just as you say."

"But if not by strangulation then by what other means?" said Jones. "That is the question. The house is not connected to the gas main, so some mishap with the jets cannot have been responsible. The fire in the hearth was not lit, so he did not die of smoke inhalation either. Burning charcoal is a possibility – it can remove the breathable air from a room in no time – but there is no indication of that to be found here. Besides, with so many chinks in the walls and gaps around the frames of the windows and doors, the place is hardly airtight, so the very idea of suffocation due to fumes may be safely discarded, I feel. Moreover, I was the one to discover the body – I and the constable who came with me – and neither of us smelled anything untoward when we entered."

"The rooms are themselves none too fragrant," Holmes pointed out. "That may have disguised the last lingering odour of toxic fumes, which have since entirely dispersed."

"True, true. For what it's worth, my constable ventured that Roker might have had a fit of some sort and swallowed his own tongue, suffocating that way. But as you can see, his tongue is more or less where it ought to be."

Holmes knelt beside me, put his nose close to Roker's inert face, and sniffed.

"I don't detect the lingering scent of cyanide," said he, "nor of any other poison."

"It is baffling," Jones said. "Dead as a doornail, but not a trace of evidence to suggest how it might have occurred."

"Not quite, Inspector," Holmes said slowly. "Have you marked this?"

He pointed a long, thin forefinger at Roker's neck. There, in the skin above the left levator scapulae muscle, was a tiny raised bump, at the centre of which lay a barely perceptible puncture wound, little more than a pinprick.

"Goodness me," declared the police official. "No, that escaped my attention. It looks rather like a bee sting, does it not?"

"And the venom in bee stings," I interposed, "is known to trigger anaphylaxis, which in its acutest form can cause the throat to swell and the airway to become inhibited. Could that be our culprit, an innocent bee?"

"If a bee, where is its body?" said Holmes. "Bees famously perish when they sting someone. The stinger is wrenched from the abdomen, taking much of the innards with it. I see a fair few dead flies around us, and a number of living ones as well, but not a single dead bee. By the same token, where is the stinger? Should it not still be embedded in Roker's flesh?"

"A wasp, then. Unlike a bee, a wasp does not disembowel itself when it stings and may sting multiple times with impunity."

"A valid notion, but I refer you to our brief and rather intemperate audience with Roker yesterday at the cemetery. At one point a wasp assailed him and he swatted it away without apparent concern. A man who knew he was dangerously allergic to wasp stings would not have been so nonchalant."

"What if he did not know? What if this, here, was the first time he discovered he had that allergy? The first and, as luck would have it, the last."

"I find it hard to believe that a man who worked outdoors all day long, surrounded by vegetation and thus insects, would not have been stung by a wasp at least once. But while we should not discount the idea altogether, we should also consider the possibility that death was induced by means of a fatal injection. Could this puncture wound, Watson, to your expert eye, have been made by the needle of a syringe?"

"Why, yes, I suppose it could."

"Then that is our wasp theory partway dismantled. Furthermore, would a wasp, having successfully envenomed and slain Roker, then have taken his watch?"

Holmes indicated Roker's waistcoat pocket. The gold-plated Junghans half hunter which he had spotted during our meeting with the gravedigger — and I had failed to notice — was not present.

"I put it to you," he continued, "that whoever donated the watch to Roker is the same person responsible for his demise. Once Roker was dead by his hand, the murderer decided to retrieve said rather expensive item of property."

"An opportunistic thief might have done the same," Athelney Jones offered.

"But would an opportunistic thief have availed himself of a syringe filled with some lethal substance in order to subdue his intended target? Customarily the cudgel, the knife or the sidearm is such a person's weapon of choice. Nothing so subtle and sophisticated as poison."

The inspector nodded. "That is a fair point."

"Watson, would you do me the courtesy of opening Roker's mouth?"

"Whatever for?"

"So that I may peer inside his throat, of course. Don't tell me you are squeamish."

I must admit I have never found it pleasurable touching dead bodies, nor is it something I have ever become accustomed to. I know of coroners, pathologists and embalmers who are able to switch off the natural revulsion most of us feel towards a cadaver and can handle one with detachment and even a certain respectful tenderness. I am not among that fraternity.

With a grimace that I did my best to mask, I pinched Roker's upper and lower lips between forefinger and thumb of each hand and prised apart those two lumps of cold, pliable flesh. Then, moving his tongue to one side, I delved both sets of fingers into the buccal cavity and held his maxilla stationary with one hand while gently but firmly levering his jaw downward with the other. Both temporomandibular joints creaked as I worked.

At last his mouth gaped, and stayed that way after I let go, thanks to rigor mortis.

Holmes produced his lens and squinted through it down into Roker's mouth. Presently he let out a soft "Hum!" and passed the magnifying glass to me.

"Take a look for yourself. What do you see?"

Deep in Roker's gullet, just past his uvula and tonsils, I spied a swelling. It was purplish-black in colour, and it originated in the wall of his oesophagus, expanding all the way across so as to obstruct that passage entirely.

"There is the source of asphyxiation," Holmes said.

"What is it?" asked Jones. "What can you see in there?"

"Watson? What does it look like to you?"

"A fleshy protrusion, roughly the size of a plum," I said. "A growth of some sort. I would suggest a vocal cord polyp, but it is not the right colour, not even for a haemorrhagic one, and also it is far too large. Likewise, for much the same reasons, it is not an abscess."

"A tumour?"

"Quite possibly. Some form of lesion for certain."

"Would you be so good as to take a sample of it for me that I might examine back at Baker Street?"

He handed me a penknife and a small envelope.

While I set about the grisly business, Holmes said to Jones, "For the record, you and your constable found the body as we see it?"

"Just so. I checked for a pulse, but otherwise touched

nothing. As soon as I realised Roker was dead, I knew I would be calling you in, and I know you're pernickety about things at a potential crime scene being left as they are."

"And at what time was this?"

"Just gone seven. We would have pinned down Roker's whereabouts sooner, but his employment records at Highgate Cemetery are not up to date. Or rather, he moved around a great deal. He was not, I am given to understand, the ideal tenant."

"The beer empties and the overall condition of his lodgings attest to that," Holmes said.

"Nor was he always forthcoming with the rent," Jones added. "He left a string of debts and disgruntled landlords behind him. But we followed the trail and caught up with him eventually."

"Eventually, yes, but too late for Roker. Had you found him sooner – yesterday, say – he would be in a holding cell at the Yard now, and alive, rather than lying dead on this floor. I mean that as a statement of fact, not a criticism. Was the door unlocked when you arrived?"

"Yes. I knocked, there was no reply, so I tried the handle and it turned."

"That accords with my thinking. Sometime last night Roker received a guest, a person with whom he was already acquainted. He invited him in. They shared a drink. You see the unfinished bottle of whisky on the table? I believe the guest brought it with him. It is a fine single malt, not Roker's usual tipple – ale seems his preference – and not something he could normally afford. When Roker was in his cups, with his guard lowered, the guest whipped out a syringe and attacked. Whatever was in the syringe created the growth in Roker's throat that stopped up his windpipe. Then the guest took his watch and his leave."

"Fiendish," said Jones, adding, "I don't suppose you have some inkling as to the identity of this individual?"

"At this stage I cannot even conjecture," Holmes said. "Watson, how are you getting on?"

"Just a moment." It was fiddly work and Holmes's penknife was not the best tool for the job, but I had managed to excise a small slice of the lesion. Balancing the bloody morsel on the tip of the blade, I carefully extricated it from Roker's mouth and popped it into the envelope.

"Excellently done." Holmes took the envelope from me and sealed it. "Inspector? Would you or one of your men do me the kindness of asking the other tenants in the building if they saw anyone enter or leave Roker's rooms last night?"

"Of course."

"I suspect the answer will be no. This strikes me as the kind of dwelling where nobody is any too curious about the comings and goings of others, and where minding one's own business is prized. We may get lucky but I am not pinning my hopes on it. By contrast, this" – he held up the envelope with its little gory piece of cargo – "may prove very instructive."

"I don't suppose you'd care to give me some idea how."

"Not now. Not yet."

"You are ever the enigma, Mr Holmes," said Jones, with a wearily resigned shake of the head.

"And you would not have me any other way."

*

I had my practice to attend to for the rest of the day, but afterwards, around teatime, I repaired to Baker Street, where I found Holmes at his microscope. A handful of telegrams lay scattered on the acid-scarred chemistry bench at which he was working.

"A profitable day's work?" I enquired.

"Very much so," replied Holmes, glancing up from the microscope's eyepiece. "Tell me, old friend, how fast do cancers grow?"

"That depends on several factors: the age of the sufferer, his overall state of health, the particular type of cancer. There are no hard and fast rules."

"Let me rephrase. The lesion in Jem Roker's throat was big enough to obstruct his throat completely. Could such a growth occur overnight?"

"I hardly think so."

"Or, for that matter, instantaneously?"

"Definitely not."

"I thought as much. I am of the opinion that the lesion was artificially induced and that it manifested so swiftly, it killed Roker on the spot."

"That is impossible."

"Surely, Watson, if we have learned anything over the past eight years, it is that nothing is impossible. I have been studying the sample of the lesion under the microscope." Holmes tapped the scientific instrument with a certain affection. It was a handsome brass thing made by H Crouch of Barbican which I had bought second-hand and given to Holmes as a gift one Christmas. "What I have discerned is that it is riddled with cancerous cells. I have compared these with illustrations in my biology textbooks and there is no doubt in my mind as to their nature. I have also found, apart from the cancerous cells, a host of other particles which I have been able to identify as spores."

"Spores?"

"Fungal spores, to be precise. Again, my biology textbooks have come in handy."

"And you are telling me there is an association between those spores and the cancer?"

"A close one."

"You believe them to be the agency by which the cancer has been generated."

"I can draw no other conclusion," Holmes said. "The spores attacked the cells of otherwise healthy tissue and turned them cancerous with an unnatural speed and aggression. Result: a lesion which would normally have taken weeks or even months to develop, occurring in a matter of seconds."

"How ghastly," I said. "So we can infer that the substance injected into Roker's neck was a solution containing the fungal spores."

"We most certainly can."

"But what kind are they? What plant do they belong to?"

"There, I am stumped. The biological literature contains many that are similar but none identical."

"May I have a look?"

"Be my guest."

I put my eye to the microscope's eyepiece, adjusted the focus, and saw a multiplicity of shapes ranged beneath the objective lens. The cancerous cells were easy to distinguish. They were distorted and corrupted versions of healthy cells. Dotted around in their midst were clusters of brownish-green spheres. Each of these was fringed with what resembled tiny hairs and each also sported a single, thicker extension of itself, somewhat reminiscent of a sucker on an octopus's arm. They could only be the spores.

The more I peered at them, the less I liked the look of them. They exhibited a certain sponginess which I found, for some indefinable reason, repellent. They were just minuscule insentient organisms, invisible to the naked eye, and yet somehow I was glad that they were stuck between the slide and the cover slip, fastened in place, unable to escape, and moreover that they were dead and inactive.

All at once, the spores pulsed. A spasm passed through them, in uncanny unison, as though each was shuddering in a sudden cold breeze. The little hairs waved, and the sucker-like extensions extruded and retracted.

Startled, I withdrew my eye from the microscope.

Holmes gave a low chuckle. "Did the spores move?"

"You knew they were going to."

"They have been doing it regularly, once or twice every minute."

"You could have warned me."

"And spoil the surprise?"

"Spoil your fun, more like. They are still alive."

"It is hard to know what constitutes life in something so infinitesimal and basic," said Holmes. "Is an amoeba alive? A bacterium? The spores are still functional, unquestionably, yet they lack any purpose, now that their deadly work is done. They have fulfilled their role, infecting the cells around them with cancer. All that remains is for them to sit in a kind of torpor, dormant, twitching occasionally in their sleep. Who knows how long they might stay in that state, without decaying. Indefinitely, perhaps."

With a certain pardonable cautiousness, I returned my eye to the microscope. The next time the spores pulsed, I was prepared for it. That made it only slightly less disconcerting.

"We should destroy them," I said, going from the chemistry bench to the sideboard and pouring myself a shot of whisky. It seemed ridiculous that my nerves were so unsettled by the spores and their little seizures, but there it was. To my mind, the things exuded a strange smugness, even a malevolence, as if they were aware they were being watched and wanted the observer to know how noxious they were and how much they should be feared.

"All in due course," said Holmes. "But before that, I would like to study them a little further." He waved a hand at the telegrams. "I have wired a description of them to several eminent mycologists. Their replies uniformly state that no such spores are known to exist. A couple of them have requested I send samples so that they can examine them for themselves."

"I don't think you should."

"I don't think I should either. I shall subject the spores to a battery of tests, with a view to garnering as much information as I can about them, and then I shall incinerate every last scrap of the lesion sample. In the meantime, you and I have a visit to make."

"Where?"

"Not far," said Holmes. "To a medical practice just off Harley Street. Virtually around the corner."

*

As we made our way along Marylebone Road through the late-afternoon crowds, Holmes said, "I have not spent the entire day hunched over a microscope. Some of it I devoted to ascertaining who treated Everard Pickering in his final days. We know, after all, that Pickering died of cancer and that a cancerous growth caused the death of Jem Roker, and this surely cannot be coincidental. In both instances the cancers appear to have been of a rare, unnatural virulence, and this surely cannot be coincidental either. Given a clear connection like that, it seemed worth my while making enquiries in that direction. With the assistance of Inspector Jones, who sent a man on my behalf to speak to the widow Pickering, I learned that her husband was tended to by Ulrich Felder, a German-born cancer specialist. I don't suppose you know of him?"

"The name is unfamiliar."

"Perhaps not surprising. Herr Doktor Felder is, by all accounts, something of a black sheep in the medical flock. That is according to one Dr Ross Moore-Moffatt, whom I prevailed upon to grant me a brief audience earlier this afternoon."

"Oh, I've heard of *him*," I said. "He is pre-eminent in the field of oncology. Second to none."

"Dr Moore-Moffatt was good enough to fill me in on the subject of cancer generally and, more specifically, Felder. He was of the view that the fellow is little better than a quack. He described him as a wealthy dilettante who has been making a name for himself lately in the profession, but not a good one. 'Banging on about developing a treatment for cancer utilising naturally occurring substances,' he said. Felder even claims to be working on a form of radical therapy that doesn't simply retard the progression of the disease but might even provide a cure. 'All sounds like so much flummery to me,' was Moore-Moffatt's opinion, 'an attempt to drum up custom for himself among the desperate and the gullible. I mean, he has the qualifications – University of Heidelberg School of Medicine, if I remember rightly – but nobody in our line takes him seriously.'"

"He sounds like one of those unscrupulous types who offer spurious cancer cures using electricity, mesmerism and so forth," I said. "The truth is, cancer can't be cured except by surgery, and that brings with it a host of complications and is seldom wholly successful. In the vast majority of cases, the condition can only be managed and palliated. Almost invariably, barring rare instances of spontaneous remission, it is a death sentence, and anyone who says otherwise is deluded or a liar. What were these 'naturally occurring substances' of Felder's? Did Moore-Moffatt say?"

"He did, if vaguely. 'Lichens, mosses, something like that,' he said."

"'Something like that'," I echoed. "Such as, perhaps, fungi?"

"Exactly, Watson. You have hit on it. Might Felder's radical therapy involve fungal spores? If so, it would tie him to Everard Pickering as well as to Jem Roker. Then there is another correlation."

"Namely?"

"The half hunter temporarily owned by Jem Roker. Who did I say the manufacturer was?"

"Junghans."

"A German watchmaker, from the Rottweil district."

"And Dr Felder is German."

"Indeed."

At that point we had turned off Harley Street and were hastening down a narrow side-street which ran perpendicular to that prestigious thoroughfare upon which countless medical practices were situated. We arrived at a building where, among the several brass plaques on the portico bearing the names of the businesses within, there was one inscribed "Ulrich Felder, MD". His surgery was on the second floor, and we climbed the stairs to find a young woman on the landing outside who was in the process of closing and locking the door behind her. She was dressed in bonnet, gloves and gabardine, with a gladstone bag hooked on her arm, and was evidently an employee of Felder's, leaving work at the end of the day.

"Madam, if I may intrude," began Holmes.

"Sir?" said she. "Can I help you?" Her face was appealing if unremarkable, with a certain rounded, slab-like quality. Her accent betokened the Midlands.

"You work for Dr Felder, I presume."

"I am his receptionist. If you wish to book an appointment, might I ask that you come back tomorrow? I have already overstayed my hours, and I must not miss my train."

"Naturally I would not wish to hold you up," Holmes said. "It is a lengthy journey to Northampton."

The receptionist gave him a searching look. "I am not surprised that you can tell I am from the Midlands, but I am surprised you know precisely where."

"The Northamptonshire accent is unique, in so far as it contains a mixture of both northern and southern pronunciations. More to the point, it involves much pursing of the lips, particularly over the long vowels, which you have amply exhibited. Just as I can tell where you hail from, I also know that you are a wholly admirable young lady."

"What makes you say that?"

"Well, it is plain to me that you have an invalid father at home who is waiting for you to come in so that you can cook supper for him and your mother."

Now she was taken aback. "Have we met before, sir?"

"We have not," said Holmes. "I have merely applied my powers of analytical observation. You are unmarried, judging by the fact that there is no wedding ring visible on your left hand through the fabric of your glove. Therefore it is more than likely that you live with your parents. You have taken a job some distance from home since jobs tend to be better paid in London. From this I infer that you are the sole breadwinner of the family because your father is incapable of work, owing to some infirmity, and your mother is obliged to spend her days tending to him. The extra income which a job in the capital earns you is necessary in order to purchase the medicines he requires for his condition. As for the supper part, a bulge in your gladstone bag is suggestive of the outline of a pie, doubtless purchased earlier in the day. Steak and ale, if my nose does not mislead me. The pie is large enough to feed at least three." Holmes spread out his hands. "Each link in the chain of deductions reinforces the rest."

"A pretty parlour trick," said the receptionist. Her tone was disdainful, but her eyes suggested she was impressed all the same.

"I take it that Dr Felder has himself already gone home," he said.

Now, briefly, the young woman looked evasive. "That's right. As I say, if you come back tomorrow, I can make arrangements for you to see him. Although," she added, "I cannot guarantee how soon that might be."

"He is busy?"

"In a manner of speaking."

"Ahhh," said Holmes. The syllable was a low, satisfied purr. "From that, one might take you to mean the opposite. After all, if he were really so busy, would you be locking up the surgery alone? On the contrary, it is probable that a busy physician would be heading homeward at least at the same time as his receptionist, if not later."

The girl was becoming flustered. "I really must be going. My train will not wait."

"Just a moment more of your time," said Holmes. "Your

employer has been absent from his place of work lately, has he not?"

"He has been…" She searched for the appropriate word. "…indisposed."

"Come, come, young lady," Holmes chided. "You can do better than that. I realise you are trying your best to cover for him. You are a conscientious employee, just as you are a dutiful daughter. Dr Felder did not come in today at all, did he?"

She sighed. "To tell the truth, sir…"

"It would be greatly appreciated."

"You are right, he did not come in today, nor yesterday, and I have no idea what has happened to him. All I know is that I arrived here yesterday morning to find a note on my desk from Dr Felder instructing me to cancel that day's appointments and all appointments for the coming week. Since then I have been expecting him to reappear, or at any rate send a message explaining his absence. I would have left for home earlier but I've been hoping all day for some news. I'm beginning to worry about him. He is normally so reliable."

"Hah! Incommunicado since yesterday morning," said Holmes. "It fits."

"You are not a prospective patient after all, are you?" said the receptionist. "I can be forgiven for thinking you were, because you are very thin and pale, and those traits are common among the people who come to see Dr Felder. You have a vitality, however, not usually found in a cancer sufferer. Might I ask what your purpose here is, you and your colleague's?"

"We seek Herr Doktor Felder's assistance on an urgent matter. It is related to a patient of his, Everett Pickering."

"*Everard* Pickering," she corrected him.

"Then he *is* a patient of Felder's," declared Holmes. "You have inadvertently just confirmed it."

The receptionist realised she had been wrongfooted. "Gracious. That was clumsy of me."

"As, likewise, are Marcus Knightley and Amelia

Throckmorton," Holmes said, hazarding the names of the occupants of the other two vacant graves. "They, too, were treated for cancer by Dr Felder. Am I right?"

"What if I deny it?"

"I think we are past that stage, my dear."

Her shoulders slumped in a capitulatory fashion. "There is not much point me hiding anything further from you. You seem to know what you need to know already, and you see through my attempts to dissemble. Who are you gents anyway? I don't believe you are the police."

"Would the police have cause to be interested in Dr Felder?" Holmes enquired.

"They would not," came the forthright reply. "He is a respectable man. There are some in his profession who consider him unorthodox. He has been relegated to the fringes and has been known to complain about it from time to time, calling it unjust and prejudiced. For all that, he is sincere in what he does. He honestly tries to make his patients well again, and within my hearing he has stated, more than once, that he is on the verge of a great breakthrough, perhaps even a cancer cure. I do not pretend to understand the science he is using or the methods involved in his treatments. I can assure you, however, that Dr Ulrich Felder would never do anything unethical or illegal. It is not his way."

"I shall take your word on that. Two more things, before I let you go and you can catch your train. It would be of no small assistance if you were able to supply me with Dr Felder's private address."

The receptionist studied each of us in turn. Finally she said, "Perhaps it would be no bad thing if someone went to check on him. His note yesterday morning was strange. It had been written in haste, I could tell, and he is usually so precise and methodical about everything. He has been running himself ragged over the past few days, coming in each morning looking tireder and tireder, doubtless having lost sleep in his pursuit of that breakthrough I spoke of. Can I trust that you mean him no ill?"

"None whatsoever," Holmes said. "Our primary concern is the late Mr Pickering."

"Why?"

"That, I'm afraid, I am not at liberty to divulge. Suffice to say, I wish to ensure that he rests in peace."

After some further deliberation, the receptionist gave us Felder's address, which lay in Muswell Hill. "And the second thing?" said she.

"Dr Felder – is he by any chance of slight stature and pigeon-toed?"

She gave a bemused nod.

"Thank you," said Holmes. "That will be all."

The young woman hurried off downstairs.

As the front door thudded shut below, Holmes turned to me, his eyebrows arched, his grey eyes agleam. "That clinches it, Watson. All three of our mysteriously revived corpses were being treated by Dr Felder, for cancer obviously. He is at the heart of this affair, there can be no question. And now, to Muswell Hill!"

*

Night was falling as we drove northwards, and it was fully dark by the time we alighted outside Felder's townhouse in the heart of the genteel northern suburb of Muswell Hill.

"Holmes," I said as the cab rolled away, "it's just occurred to me. Ought Inspector Jones not be here with us? If I'm not mistaken, we are at the dénouement of the case, and it was he who brought it to us in the first place. Does that not give him the right to be present at its resolution? More to the point, it would be good to have a policeman on hand, should an arrest need to be made."

"You and I are perfectly capable of detaining someone under our own auspices," Holmes answered. "As for inviting along the redoubtable Jones: if my suspicions are correct, then the inspector is best left out of it. I do not think he will benefit from witnessing the things we are about to witness, not if he values his reason. Think of Gregson, who has become, whether he likes it or not, our brother-in-arcana. To this day he is haunted by his experiences in that cavern beneath St Paul's Shadwell, when he and Mycroft were almost sacrificed to Nyarlathotep. While he continues to function as a police officer, he has never been quite the same man since."

"Jones strikes me as better equipped, psychologically, to cope with exposure to the preternatural."

"But why put that to the test if we do not have to?"

Just then, there came from within the house the crash of breaking glass.

"Hark!" said Holmes. "What's that?" He thrust open the gate, darted across the small front garden and hastened up the steps, I following close behind. He tried the bell pull, then the knocker. There was no response to either.

Through the door we heard further noises. There was a loud clattering, and a cry of alarm. There was also, just discernible, an eerie, inhuman groaning.

"A struggle, it sounds like," I said. "Whatever is going on?"

Holmes tried the door, but it was locked. He cast around. "That window there. Watson, give me a leg-up."

Squatting, I interlaced my fingers to create a stirrup for Holmes and hoisted him up until he was abreast of the window. He braced one knee on the ledge to relieve me of some of his weight. Then, taking out his penknife, he slipped the blade between the sashes and levered the catch aside. He shoved up the lower half of the window and wriggled through, after which he turned, leaned out, and hauled me in after him.

We found ourselves in a smartly appointed dining room. The commotion was coming from the hallway adjacent. There, we found a scene of chaos and horror.

A small, dapper-dressed man was cowering with a walking

stick in both hands, which he was using to fend off a monstrosity. The creature was human, but barely. Dressed in a filthy, mud-stained suit, its face bore a sickly yellow pallor and was grossly misshapen. It lunged at the small man again and again, uttering a series of low groans that spoke of anguish and despair. Ropes were tied around its wrists and ankles, with loose ends flapping. A side table lay overturned on the tiled floor, the remnants of a shattered crystal vase beside it. A hatstand had been toppled.

Every time the creature went for the small man, he repelled it with a blow from the walking stick. The thing would cringe and moan, then resume the attack.

"*Halt! Ich befehle dir anzuhalten!*" the man barked at it, but the imprecation fell on deaf ears. The creature would not be commanded to stop; it was relentless in its assault.

"Dr Felder!" said Holmes sharply.

The small man shot a surprised look over his shoulder at us. "Who are you? How did you get in?" he said in heavily accented English. "You should not be here. Go away!" With that, he returned his attention to the marauding thing in front of him, delivering yet another blow with the stick.

"I rather think you need our help, Doctor," Holmes said. "Unless you reckon you can corral that undead man by yourself, and frankly, you don't appear to be having a great deal of success on that front."

Felder sized up his predicament and realised he had little choice. "Very well. Help if you must."

Holmes beckoned to me, and together we closed in on the rampaging creature. "You grab one arm, Watson. I'll grab the other. Between us we can wrestle it to the ground."

Easier said than done. The thing was possessed of a maddened, unholy strength and resisted us with all its might. Up close its body exuded a rank stench – the odour of decay and putrefaction, powerful enough to make one retch.

Nonetheless Holmes and I, by dint of much pulling and

striving, were able to bring it down. We held the creature prone on the floor, pinning it beneath our combined bodyweight, and although it writhed strenuously in our clutches, it could not get up. It alternated between snarling savagely and letting out strings of garbled syllables that, though unintelligible, could still almost be taken for speech. The gusts of breath that accompanied these inarticulate ejaculations were foul-smelling in the extreme.

"Make yourself useful, man," Holmes told Felder, who had just stood there gawking. "Fetch more rope."

Felder scurried off, returning with a bundle of the requested item. Holmes secured the creature's arms behind its back, then fastened its legs together tightly. Now all it could do was wriggle impotently like a landed fish. Bit by bit its guttural protests subsided to a sullen mewling.

"I suppose thanks are in order," said Felder, a grudging note in his voice. "I had matters under control, of course."

"That is not how it looked to me," said Holmes.

The little German straightened out his lapels and the hem of his jacket. I noted that, when at rest, he stood with his feet turned inward towards each other. "I shall ask again. Who are you gentlemen?"

Holmes introduced us. "And you are the oncologist Dr Ulrich Felder."

Felder gave a small bow. "At your service."

"And this," Holmes went on, waving a hand towards the bound creature at our feet, "is Everard Pickering – or should that be *was* Everard Pickering? As things stand, the fellow exists in a state of being and not-being, present tense and past tense. All courtesy of you, Doctor."

"You seem inordinately well informed, Herr Holmes."

"It is something I pride myself on."

"Possibly I should be asking what has brought you to my home…"

"But I feel it is rather obvious."

"*Ja*. Much though I hoped I had everything under control, it seems otherwise."

"You have certainly been ruthless in your efforts to contain your little problem," said Holmes. "Not least with your unusually callous treatment of one Jem Roker, gravedigger."

The German's head drooped. "Would that it had not been necessary, but Roker was proving a liability."

"Where are they?" Holmes said, glancing around him. "The other two undead? Mr Knightley and Miss Throckmorton?" His gaze fell upon a door that was set beneath the stairs to the first floor. It stood slightly ajar, and through the narrow aperture another flight of stairs was visible, descending into darkness. "The cellar, I would hazard," he continued. "That's where you have been keeping all three of them. I see smears of mud on the door jamb. Grave dirt, I should imagine, that chanced to rub off their clothing as they passed through."

"It is clear that nothing escapes you. The jig, as you British say, is up." Dr Felder's attitude was one of total resignation. He could have lied or prevaricated, but he seemed to have accepted that Sherlock Holmes had command of the situation and that anything other than full compliance was futile.

"Shall we return Mr Pickering whence he came?" Holmes suggested. "He can re-join his fellow ex-corpses down below, and this time, perhaps, we can make sure he is tied up more tightly so that he doesn't break free again to menace you or anybody else."

"That," said Felder, "would be a very good idea."

*

Holmes and I hauled Pickering to his feet and manhandled him down to the cellar, with Felder leading the way.

At the foot of the stairs Felder lit a pair of oil lamps. Their glow revealed not only the extent of the cellar – its dimensions were sizeable, matching the entire footprint of the house – but also, more unpleasantly, two further reanimated corpses positioned against one wall. Each was bound to a wooden chair, while broken pieces of a third chair were strewn across the bare brick floor. One could only assume Everard Pickering had strained at his bonds so intently that the chair's joins had weakened and it had fallen apart beneath him. Thereupon he had stumbled up the stairs, only for Felder to confront him in the hallway.

Our arrival in the cellar set the two seated corpses mumbling and squirming. Marcus Knightley, who wore a frock coat and a cravat and sported a few wisps of white hair pasted across his sallow, peeling scalp, gnashed his teeth at us. Amelia Throckmorton, who in life must have been a respectable elderly spinster type, would have gnashed her teeth too, but all she had was bare gums; her dentures had not, it would appear, been buried with her, or else had fallen out since her interment. Like Pickering, each of this pair was a withered, emaciated shell with sunken, cloudy eyes. Also like Pickering, each was peppered with lumpen subcutaneous growths, which showed both on their exposed skin and as unsightly bulges beneath their clothing.

We lay the still squirming Pickering down next to them, on his side, and Holmes trussed him further with another length of rope so that he was unable to move whatsoever. Pickering wailed his discontent, which the other two undead echoed, a keening, wordless chorus. Horrifying and revolting though these creatures were, there was something pitiful about them too. I could not help but feel that they had not asked to be raised from the dead and were appalled to find themselves in this state.

The necrotic reek from the corpses permeated the air, mingling with another, more sharply pungent smell: that of chemicals. The cellar boasted a couple of workbenches that were laden with test tubes and condensers, retorts and tripods, scales and balances, flasks and droppers, along with rack upon rack of stoppered phials containing compounds, tinctures and reagents. The copious array of scientific paraphernalia gleamed in the lamplight, and I caught Holmes running an eye over it with, I fancied, a hint of jealousy in his gaze, for his own collection of such equipment, while substantial, was nowhere near as comprehensive.

In addition to all this apparatus, which was in immaculate condition, I spotted various cages of the sort designed to hold small animals. They were empty and stacked tidily on top of one another in a corner. There were also a number of journals and sheets of foolscap lying around. The handwriting and diagrams on the latter looked fastidiously neat, and I recalled Dr Felder's receptionist referring to her employer as "precise and methodical".

"So," said Felder, brushing his palms together. "Here we are. What now, gentlemen? I take it you plan on turning me in to the authorities."

"That is certainly our intent," said Holmes. "But first, let me tell you everything I know, and you can then supply a few further details. I have the bricks. What I need from you is the mortar to bind it all together."

"Very well. Seeing as it appears I have no alternative." The corners of Felder's mouth twitched drolly. "Perhaps you might like to tie me up, like these three, lest I attempt to escape."

"That won't be necessary. Unless you make it so."

"I shall not."

"I'm glad to hear it," said Holmes. "Now then, if I am correct, this all started when you subjected three individuals to a form of cancer treatment, one of your own devising. The treatment somehow involves fungus, in a manner that I am not quite able to fathom."

"That is the case," said the oncologist. "My aim was to create a fungus-based preparation that can consume cancers. Many fungi are saprophytic, after all, meaning they feed on dead matter, whether it be plant or animal material. Others are parasitic. I thought that if I could breed a form of fungus that lives off cancerous tissue and inject a solution of it into human sufferers, this would provide the cure for cancer that the world has been crying out for."

"And you believed you had succeeded."

Felder nodded. "A certain rare form of fungus came my way which seemed to fulfil that very role. Initial experiments on tumours provided to me by anatomists offered very encouraging results. The fungus spores flourished in the medium of the cancerous tissue, devouring it eagerly until none was left. The next step was to try it out on living test subjects."

"None other than these unfortunates," said Holmes, indicating the trio of undead corpses.

"To call them unfortunates makes them sound as though they were reluctant participants. They were anything but. The three of them – Herr Pickering, Herr Knightley, Fräulein Throckmorton – were my patients already and were in the end stages of the disease."

The three undead seemed to recognise their names as Felder uttered them. They were roused to a kind of mournful chattering, like agitated birds.

Oblivious, Felder carried on. "The prognosis for each was a matter of weeks. One by one, I offered them a proposal. I made it clear that this remedy of mine was untried and its possible side effects uncertain. They, even knowing that, gave enthusiastic consent."

"I can understand why," I said. "What was the worst that could happen? The treatment would kill them?"

"The risk, they felt, was worthwhile," said Felder. "I did not guarantee them full remission. I made no promises at all. I simply told them there was an outside chance they might be cured."

"But things didn't go as you, or your patients, might have hoped. In fact, the outcome of injecting them with your fungal preparation was the reverse of what you anticipated."

"That is self-evident, Watson," said Holmes with asperity,

the tone he customarily adopted towards me whenever I failed to meet his exacting standards.

Felder himself acknowledged my remark with a rueful shrug. "The fungus spores, it transpired, did not merely consume cancerous tissue. They facilitated its spread throughout the host body. Where initially there had been just one tumour, or a few, all at once there were dozens. I can only assume that individual spores attached themselves to clusters of loose cancerous cells and then were carried elsewhere through the bodily systems by natural processes. The cancerous cells propagated themselves in healthy organs, generating fresh tumours. It is even possible that the fungus and the cancer developed some form of symbiotic relationship. The fungus wanted to increase its sources of nutrition, and it is in the nature of cancer to proliferate, and so together, like farmer and crop, the two found a way to prosper, mutually beneficial to both. The world of microbiology really is quite fascinating, you know. Tiny organisms that you might think lack any form of intellect are able, collectively, to accomplish amazing feats. It is almost as if they can communicate among themselves in ways you or I could never understand."

I recalled, with a shudder, the spores I had seen through Holmes's microscope the previous day – how alive they had seemed, how *knowing*.

"At any rate," Felder continued, "it was soon clear to me that I had failed dismally. One after another, in quick succession, the three patients passed away."

"And all three were buried locally, at Highgate Cemetery," said Holmes. "At which point, gravedigger Jem Roker entered the picture. But before we get to him, I feel, Dr Felder, that there is something you haven't told us. A moment ago you said that the next step, after trying your fungus out on tumours, was living test subjects. Any scientist worth his salt would use animals for that purpose before human beings, and I see cages here – cages that would have once held rats or rabbits or small monkeys.

What became of them? Why have you omitted mention of them? Could it be because you did resort to experimenting on animals first and the results were discouraging?"

"You are asking me whether I knew, in advance of giving the fungal preparation to people, that it might cause harm?"

"I am not asking, I am telling you. You tried it on animals, and it had dire consequences, and in spite of that you still went ahead and administered it to humans."

Felder shook his head wonderingly and with a touch of exasperation. "There truly is nothing I can hide from you, Mr Holmes, or so it would appear. In my defence, I am trying not to make myself seem monstrous. I want you to understand that everything I did, I did with the best of intentions. The preparation was not fully ready, I admit, when I dispensed it to these three here. It could have been refined more, I don't deny that. Perfected, even. What can I say? I was excited. I got ahead of myself."

"What did it do to the animals?"

"Killed them. Killed them, then brought them back to life." The matter-of-factness with which Felder said this gave me a chill. "Or at least to a semblance of life. In this respect my fungus resembles *ophiocordyceps unilateralis*, a tropical mould discovered by your own Alfred Russel Wallace back in 1859. That great naturalist found that *ophiocordyceps unilateralis* infects ants, taking over their bodies and altering their behaviour. It might even be said to control them, mastering them from within. The infected ants leave their colonies and go in search of a moist, warm place, the ideal medium for fungal growth, where they promptly die. Thereupon the fungus sprouts fruiting bodies from the ants' corpses and continues its reproductive cycle. My fungus did something akin to that with mammals. Every time, the animal would perish within twenty-four hours or so of being injected with the spores. Or rather, it would appear to perish, whereas actually it entered a state of inactivity indistinguishable from death. A while afterwards, it would emerge from that state, giving an impression of being alive once more. The animal would mimic the common behavioural patterns of its species but was no longer, to all intents and purposes, a living creature. You might instead call it a fleshly vehicle for the fungus, a carriage transporting its occupant from place to place."

"I presume you destroyed these abominations."

"*Natürlich*. I killed them humanely with chloroform, then dissected them, after which I consigned the remains to the garden incinerator."

"My God," I breathed. "You gave the same fungal preparation to your patients as you did to animals, in the full knowledge of what it would do to them."

"*Might* do to them, Dr Watson," said Felder, wagging an admonitory finger. "*Might*. My thinking was that the fungus ran rampant in healthy animals, yet also consumed cancer tissue. If introduced into people with cancer, would it not focus its attention on the diseased parts to the exclusion of all else?"

"I doubt you warned your patients of the effect it had had on the animals. I'll wager you kept that piece of information very much to yourself."

"Why frighten them unnecessarily?"

"To summarise your narrative so far, Dr Felder," said Holmes, "you injected three unsuspecting patients with a substance which you had reason to believe might be fatal to them but might also alleviate their cancer."

"That is hardly responsible doctoring," I interjected hotly, glaring at Felder. "You are a disgrace to your profession."

The oncologist held my gaze evenly. He appeared impervious to guilt or shame.

"And when their respective cancers grew exponentially worse and all three died," Holmes went on, "you were perhaps not surprised. Furthermore, you knew the three might well manifest the same result as your test animals – in other words, they might return to life. In anticipation of that eventuality, you enlisted the aid of Highgate Cemetery's head gravedigger. You tasked him with reporting to you if the soil of the graves showed signs of disturbance. You offered him a decent sum of money, and Roker accepted and dutifully kept a weather eye on the graves, doubtless thinking your request peculiar but choosing not to question it too hard, not when it afforded him extra income. Then, not so long ago, he alerted you to the fact that the graves were indeed starting to look as though there was undue activity below ground. I imagine he found this more than a little disconcerting and could only be mollified with the offer of more money. When that would not suffice, you presented him with your watch, the rather splendid gold-plated Junghans half hunter that is currently nestling in your waistcoat pocket, back where it belongs. Probably Roker had taken a shine to it and remarked upon it admiringly at some point. You gave it to him, and thus was his full compliance once more assured. Do tell me if I am wrong on any count."

"You are not, Mr Holmes. Not as yet."

"Now that you had a good idea your patients were coming back to life and apt to dig their way out of the earth," Holmes continued, "you began staking out their graves at night, leaving Roker to maintain his watch on them during the day. This I infer from your receptionist telling us that you looked as though you had not been sleeping well lately. Your plan was to intercept the undead corpses at their moment of emergence and bring them back here, where you might keep them out of sight and study them at your leisure. Dissection? Was that on the cards?"

"In due course. It will be necessary, so that I can learn more about where my treatment went astray and try to make improvements in future. For the time being, though, I have been content with merely observing them as they are and taking notes. I have been seeing how they respond to stimuli — speech, bright light, food, music and so on. It has been... most interesting. In certain instances they react quite normally. The response to pain, for example, is much as it is in any living thing. In other respects, however, they are senseless. It is as though vestiges of their old selves remain but buried deep. At this stage, I must point out that I have taken to calling them 'fungal reanimates'. Since they are neither living creatures, nor dead ones, I feel that some new classification is required."

"Why not?" said Holmes equably. He resumed his elucidation. "As chance would have it, all three of these fungal reanimates of yours sprang forth from the ground on the same night, the night before last, right before your eyes. I can only speculate how perturbing a sight that must have been; but also, to you, perhaps thrilling, in some perverse way. You managed to round up two of them, Mr Knightley and Miss Throckmorton, and guide them back here, but not the third. He, Mr Pickering, temporarily eluded you."

"Fräulein Throckmorton was first to emerge," said Felder. "By the time I returned from escorting her hither, Herr Knightley was just worming his way out of the ground, and Herr Pickering was starting to make his presence known. I thought I had time to deal with Knightley and get back for Pickering, and I was as quick as I could be, but too late. He was already gone."

"Yes. Pickering became quite the wild rover. He wandered the darkened streets of north London, finding his way through some dim instinct back to his own house, where his widow spied him loitering dumbly in their back garden. Later that same night, you located him there, having correctly surmised where he might be. Soon enough you had him stowed in this cellar with the others. But now we return to Mr Jem Roker, who became, in your own parlance, a liability."

"Ja. Roker."

"Blackmail, was it? Threatening to expose you? Demanding yet more money?"

"All of the above," said Felder. "Roker may not have understood exactly what I had done, but he was no fool. He came to me yesterday evening, to my own front door, and started accusing me of witchcraft and blasphemy and saying he would report me to the police and the newspapers. He was quite inebriated. I told him to go home. I would come to him there, I said, bringing with me something which would placate him once and for all. Those were my exact words: 'placate you once and for all'." The German chuckled as though at his own cleverness. "Roker, in his drunken greed, was most amenable to the idea. He already had my watch, and clearly believed I was going to bestow on him some item of even greater value."

"Whereas what you actually brought along was a hypodermic syringe," said Holmes, "containing a mixture of your fungal preparation and some cancerous cells drawn from the body of one of your three captives. Am I right?"

Felder's top lip drew upward, exposing his upper set of teeth. This, I realised, was his smile, although it could easily have been mistaken for a sneer. "You are."

"You also took an expensive bottle of whisky along with you, which you and Roker drank together. You knew he had a penchant for alcohol and would not be able to resist such an alluring offering. You knew, too, that he would imbibe more of the whisky than you, until his guard became lowered. And that was when you struck. In went the needle, into the unwary Roker's neck. Your special concoction did its wicked work. The dose of spores and cancer cells was highly concentrated. A tumour swelled in Roker's throat. He was dead within a matter of moments."

"It worked better than even I had expected, and that is just as well, as I had no wish for him to suffer unduly."

"He was a nuisance," I growled, "and you murdered him." I had taken a profound dislike to Dr Ulrich Felder. I don't know which irked me more about him, his smugness or his utter lack of conscience. I had not made the provision of bringing my service revolver with me to his house, for Holmes had not suggested I might need it, and I invariably took my lead from him in such matters. I mention this simply because, had I had the gun with me at that moment, I might have been tempted to use it.

"So judgemental, Dr Watson," said Felder. "Had I given in to Roker's blackmail, it would not have ended there. He would have kept coming back for more, and yet more. He was that kind of man. He was putting my career in jeopardy, my research, everything I had worked for."

"Still, you put him down with no more compunction than if he had been one of your laboratory animals."

"Will you not at least acknowledge my brilliance? I disposed of Herr Roker in such a way that his death would appear to have been through natural causes. Nobody could have known otherwise. Nobody except, it seems, your friend here. Him I did not reckon with."

"Many a criminal has failed to reckon with me," said Holmes, "to his cost."

"So I am learning, although I resent being called a criminal."

"What are you, then?" I said.

"A man of science who is prepared to do whatever it takes for the advancement of knowledge and medicine."

I snorted.

"However you choose to regard yourself, Doctor," said Holmes to Felder, "you are inarguably a ruthless, coldblooded individual. Proof: having done away with Roker at his lodgings, you calmly collected your watch and made your exit."

"What use was my watch to him any more?" said Felder. "The dead do not need to tell the time. Besides, it is mine. I paid good money for it."

"And its presence on Roker's person might have connected you to him."

"That never occurred to me. The watch carries no personalised inscription, nothing to show whom it belongs to, but I suppose for an astute fellow such as yourself, Herr Holmes, it might be all you needed to forge a link between myself and Roker."

"It absolutely was," said Holmes. "And now I believe we are up to date. I am satisfied with my deductions, which you have confirmed in all aspects, Dr Felder. Unless, that is, you have anything to add?"

"I do not think so. This is the point at which you and your colleague forcibly restrain me and hand me over to the police, *nicht wahr*? You are both of you bigger and stronger than I, and I do not rate my chances against you. I suppose I must come quietly."

"That would be by far the easiest thing for all concerned."

"But I am afraid I cannot allow it. I will not be hanged for murder. I have too much to offer the world."

That was when Felder sprang into action.

*

Two things happened pretty much simultaneously. First, Felder snatched up one of the lamps and hurled it at the workbench nearest him. The lamp shattered, oil splashed from its reservoir, and flame erupted all around. This, though, was merely a distraction, for in more or less the same instant the oncologist's hand dived into his jacket pocket and drew out a syringe. Brandishing it over his head, thumb poised on the plunger, he threw himself at Sherlock Holmes.

I was too astonished by the suddenness of these actions to respond straight away. I saw the syringe flash downwards, on course to pierce Holmes's chest. There was a murky green fluid inside its glass barrel which I could only think was the selfsame substance Felder had used to kill Jem Roker. Holmes was about to meet a similar grisly end to the gravedigger.

This appalling prospect galvanised me out of my frozen stupor, and I propelled myself forwards to intercede between Felder and Holmes.

Holmes's reflexes, however, were superior to mine. Even as the little German brought the syringe down, my friend raised a forearm to block the thrust. Felder's wrist collided with the edge of Holmes's arm, and he yelped in thwarted frustration. He drew back his hand for a second attempt with the syringe, but this time Holmes was more than ready for him. With lightning swiftness he seized Felder's wrist with both hands, twisting the German's arm at the same time. The momentum of Felder's swing, assisted by Holmes, carried the syringe in a downward arc, straight towards his own stomach. The needle penetrated his clothing and embedded itself in his flesh. His thumb inadvertently depressed the plunger part way.

For a few fleeting moments Felder stood staring down at the syringe protruding from his midriff. About half of the green fluid remained in the barrel. The rest was inside him, already coursing through his body.

His head came up, and his eyes were bulging, his features a mask of dread and horror.

"*Nein*," he croaked. "This cannot be. *Nein. Nein! Gott hilf mir!*"

Holmes stepped back. "God cannot help you, Doctor. Nor, I suspect, will He have mercy on you in the hereafter."

The fire started by the broken lamp was spreading fast. Already the entire surface of the workbench was alight, with trails of burning oil snaking across the floor in all directions. Chemicals in the rack on top of the workbench were contributing to the blaze. Phials exploded in the heat, spilling their volatile contents.

Felder, by the light of the flames, gasped and staggered. He was clutching his belly. The syringe had fallen out onto the floor. He reeled towards the other workbench and grabbed it for support.

"I can feel them," he gasped in a tone that was half wonderment, half horror. "I can feel them inside me, growing, multiplying. They are in my stomach. Oh, now in my lungs." His breathing grew rapid and stertorous. "This is what it is like. This is how it feels."

He coughed wetly, and blood bubbled at his lips. Next moment, he bent double and a whole torrent of blood came gushing forth from his mouth. He collapsed, still vomiting crimson.

By this stage, flames from the first workbench were licking at the ceiling beams and acrid smoke had begun to fill the cellar. Felder, meanwhile, lay curled on the floor, his body wracked with convulsive spasms, blood now issuing from every facial orifice. He was scarcely recognisable as the dapper, prissy little man he had been. He was a shuddering, blood-soaked shambles.

"Come, Watson." Holmes plucked at my sleeve. "We can't stay."

I nodded agreement. My eyes were starting to stream from the smoke, while the heat of the fire was ferocious. We stood no hope of extinguishing the flames, and retreat was the only sensible option.

"What about them?" I said, meaning Felder's fungal reanimates.

The three undead corpses were recoiling from the fire, moaning, their eyes rolling. They heaved at their bonds with animal desperation.

"We cannot help them, any more than we can help the man responsible for making them what they are," Holmes replied. "We don't have time to untie them and shepherd them out of the building, not without risk to life and limb, and even if we did, what good would it do? What kind of future awaits them, save more of this terrible twilight state in which they exist now? This condition which is neither life nor death but the worst of both worlds?"

I tried to gainsay his argument, but could not. I looked to the trio of fungal reanimates, and their gazes met mine. They ceased their thrashing about, and I could see that they had reached a shared understanding. They were well aware they had nothing to look forward to, just as Holmes said. They accepted that the best thing for them was to be consumed by the holocaust and their torment brought to an end.

So I thought, at any rate. So I told myself then, and still tell myself to this day. The fungal reanimates were resigned to their doom and did not wish to be rescued. I have to believe that was the case.

Dr Ulrich Felder lay in an expanding pool of his blood, motionless apart from the occasional twitch of limb and head. There was no saving him either, but I had far fewer qualms about that.

Holmes shoved me towards the stairs, and as I began to ascend I spied him, out of the corner of my eye, grabbing one of Felder's journals. He stuffed the book into his pocket as he followed me up to the ground floor.

Outdoors, in the street, we set up a hue and cry. "Fire! Fire!" Then, in the darkness, we made good our escape, even as neighbours emerged inquisitively from their homes and the crackle of the inferno in Felder's basement grew ever louder.

*

There were several articles in the following day's papers about a fatal house fire in Muswell Hill. The conflagration gutted much of the property but thankfully, through the brave efforts of the fire brigade, was extinguished before it could spread to the adjoining buildings. Four bodies were found in the basement, charred to the bone, and it was believed that one of them belonged to the man renting the townhouse, an oncologist from Heidelberg by the name of Felder. The other three were yet to be identified. The fire was presumed to have been caused by accident, perhaps somehow related to scientific equipment, of which certain badly damaged specimens were discovered in the basement, including the remnants of phials

SHERLOCK HOLMES *and the* HIGHGATE HORRORS

of chemicals. Generally, the whole incident was felt to be little more than tragic misadventure.

Inspector Athelney Jones came to call at Baker Street that same afternoon, to see what progress Holmes had made on the matter of the three corpses missing from Highgate Cemetery and Jem Roker's death. With a shrewd look, he mentioned the Muswell Hill fire and mused aloud, with every appearance of airiness, whether that and the other events were in any way associated.

"I cannot lie to you, Inspector," said Holmes, and promptly did just that. Or rather, he gave Jones a heavily edited account of our exploits. Dr Felder, he said, was a rogue medic experimenting illegally on the corpses of his own patients, in order to test certain outlandish theories he had about cancer. He bribed Jem Roker to dig them up for him. The two men had a falling out, and Felder killed Roker using a poison of his own devising. Holmes tracked him down to his home in Muswell Hill and, together with me, challenged him there. Felder retreated to the basement and set fire to it, and himself, and the corpses, rather than face justice.

"And that is the truth, the whole truth and nothing but the truth?" said Jones.

"Upon my honour as an Englishman," answered Holmes.

"And you, Doctor, will corroborate everything Mr Holmes says?"

"To the letter." I was not even half the thespian my friend was, but I did my best to bluff it out, and it seemed to do the trick.

"Very well," Jones decided. "That all makes reasonable enough sense, and I will frame my report accordingly. I just wonder…" He lofted an eyebrow. "You wouldn't by any chance be keeping something back, would you, gents? Something you think I'm not ready to hear? Something, shall we say, out of the ordinary?"

"Nothing, my good man," said Holmes. "Not a thing."

Jones hummed to himself. "I don't suppose, even if there was, I'd ever manage to winkle it out of you. I know the two of you stand firm against evil in all its forms, be they manmade or otherwise, and that," he said with dignity, "is sufficient for me."

*

As a brief postscript to this section of my narrative, I must relate that Holmes spent several days studying the journal he took from Felder's basement. He did this with a view to learning all he could about the doctor's cancer treatment and the experiments he undertook.

"Damnably unrewarding," was his conclusion. "I have been through the text over and over, and I am little the wiser. My German is good enough that I can make sense of it. There just isn't much that is revelatory or illuminating. It is simply a day-by-day explication of procedures and findings, offering little more than Felder himself told us. I wish I had had the opportunity to gather up more of his notes. The only point I have found that is of any interest is that the fungus he used was donated to him by a certain benefactress, whom he neglects to name. He refers to her just once, and then only as an '*Amerikanische Frau*'."

"An American woman," I said.

"There are no other clues to her identity, just that single, infuriatingly vague mention. Who can she be? And why did she give him a fungus? And why that particular fungus, whose effects proved so strange and extraordinary? There is something going on here, Watson. I can feel it." Holmes lifted both hands as though he were holding an invisible object in them, caressing it, examining its texture and contours. "My every instinct is telling me that a deeper mystery lies beneath all this. I cannot grasp it. I cannot even descry the outline of it. But it is there. I swear to God, it is there. And I shall get to the bottom of it, whatever it takes, whatever the cost."

These were to prove prophetic words indeed.

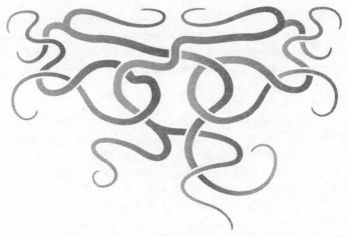

PART II

Winter 1888

I HAVE IT ON GOOD AUTHORITY THAT ONE OF THE most celebrated lines in my entire published oeuvre is this one: "To Sherlock Holmes she is always the woman."

The subject of the sentence is, of course, Irene Adler, the adventuress and contralto whom Holmes first matched wits with in an episode I have chronicled under the title "A Scandal in Bohemia". The events of that tale took place a short while after the events of the foregoing section of this manuscript and constitute, for once, a more or less exact rendering of the incident as it actually occurred.

The one instance where my published account veers from the truth lies in the story's later stages. Therein I describe a brief encounter with "a slim youth in an ulster" who passed Holmes and myself while we were stopped at the entrance to Baker Street and bade us good morning. The fellow moved hurriedly on and neither of us caught more than a fleeting look at him. I assumed he was some acquaintance of Holmes's unknown to me, while Holmes averred that he was not unfamiliar but his identity remained a puzzle.

The next day, Holmes received a letter from Miss Adler – Mrs Godfrey Norton as she was by then – in which the lady confessed that it was she, in masculine dress, who had greeted us on our doorstep. "I have been trained as an actress myself," she wrote. "Male costume is nothing new to me. I often take advantage of the freedom it gives."

What I omitted to mention in the story is that, even though I had only the briefest glimpse of the aforementioned "slim youth", the person concerned was unquestionably a man. The size of the hands, the timbre of the voice, the squareness of the jaw, and especially the Adam's apple, were all features which no actress, however skilled, could have mimicked.

In this, Holmes agreed with me. There was only so much, he said, that could be accomplished with padding and stage makeup and alteration of one's posture and gait.

"Naturally she could be lying in her letter," he concluded. "The fellow was an operative of hers, and she is merely pretending he was she in order to bamboozle me further. Because otherwise, if he truly was Irene Norton, née Adler, in disguise, then her powers of impersonation border on the miraculous."

Holmes's fascination with her went beyond her physical allure, which was all too apparent in the photograph of her that he accepted in lieu of payment by the King: that fulsome mouth, those spirited eyes, that irrepressible voluptuousness. In fact, I would submit that Irene Adler was beguiling to him *in spite of* her beauty. She was his intellectual equal, of that there is no doubt, and he was impressed to have been thwarted by her so charmingly and with such aplomb while pursuing the King of Bohemia case. Yet I am willing to suggest that he was captivated by her in no small part because of the possibility, remote though it was, that she genuinely did boast abilities beyond normal human ken. Holmes might not have had an eye for the ladies but he did have a nose for the anomalous.

*

The above serves as preface to what occurred well over a year later, towards the tail end of 1888, when Holmes and I received a summons from his brother Mycroft to attend a meeting of the Dagon Club.

This I learned of when Holmes called round at my house in Paddington one evening, just as Mary and I were settling down to dinner. We had been husband and wife for scarcely a month and were not long returned from our honeymoon in Bournemouth, about which I shall say nothing other than that it was a week of perfect happiness, marred not at all by the chilly weather.

No sooner had the maid shown Holmes in than he bowed to Mary and said, "A thousand pardons, Mrs Watson. Far be it from me to ruin this picture of newlywed domestic bliss, but I need to borrow your husband."

"I cannot help but think that you would not be calling at such an hour if it were not a matter of urgency," said Mary.

"You read me like a book, madam."

I looked at my wife. "I have your leave?"

She gave a gracious nod. "I saw, though, that mournful glance you just threw at your serving of game pie, John. Would it help if I asked the maid to prepare you a paper of sandwiches to take with you?"

"It would help very much, my dear."

"And for you too, Mr Holmes? Mrs Hudson is an excellent cook, but you are still as thin as a rake, so I suspect you of skipping meals from time to time."

"A sandwich would not go amiss."

"Do you like sliced tongue?"

"Delicious."

As our cab circumnavigated Hyde Park, Holmes and I ate our impromptu repast.

"Where are we bound?" I enquired between mouthfuls.

"Pall Mall."

"The Diogenes?"

"Not exactly. Think of a circle within a circle."

"Ah. The Dagon Club."

"I'm afraid so."

Disembarking outside the Diogenes, we entered and passed straight through to the Stranger's Room.

An august assemblage awaited us.

The Dagon Club had been established back in 1880 by Mycroft Holmes following the unpleasantness at Shadwell, in which he had become unwillingly embroiled and which had nearly cost him his life. This secret conclave gathered in the Stranger's Room at irregular intervals, as and when necessary, with its membership composed of seven notables, each pre-eminent in his sphere. Its stated aim was to suppress knowledge of certain specific arcane matters – anything pertaining to the Great Old Ones, the Outer Gods, and sundry related beasts that were less cosmically awesome but no less monstrous. While Sherlock Holmes fought these enemies of mankind through the sweat of his brow and the might of his fist, Mycroft Holmes and his confrères went to great pains to keep all mention of them out of the public domain, thus protecting the innocent in their own way.

On that evening a quorum of four was in attendance. Their number comprised Mycroft himself, his second-in-command Lord Cantlemere, the financier Milton Goldsworthy, and Sir Alexander Chalfont-Banks, the high court judge.

"First things first," said Mycroft Holmes, dispensing with any preamble. "You, Dr Watson."

"Me?" said I.

"Are you planning to write any further books?"

The question caught me on the hop. "I… I don't know… That is to say…"

"Heavens, man," barked Sir Alexander Chalfont-Banks. "It's a simple enough query. Are you or aren't you? Pull yourself together and give us an answer."

I reminded myself that I was a campaigner, a physician, as respected in my own way as any of these august individuals; I should not be browbeaten by them.

"I am contemplating the possibility," I said. "There are numerous of Sherlock Holmes's cases which might lend themselves to—"

"Yes, yes," said Mycroft, overriding me. "All we want is an assurance that you will send any manuscripts to us before submitting them to a publisher, just as you did last time with… what was it called again?"

"*A Study in Scarlet.*"

"That's it. Florid, melodramatic title."

"I was originally intending to call it *A Tangled Skein*."

"Is that any better?"

"I'm not sure."

"Selling well?" enquired Lord Cantlemere. With his hatchet-like nose and drooping whiskers, he had one of those faces that looked irascible all the time, even when its owner was not. Having said which, His Lordship was seldom not irascible.

"None too badly," I replied. "I, regrettably, struck a poor deal. Twenty-five pounds for the full rights, so I shan't see a penny in royalties."

"Ah. Foolish," said Milton Goldsworthy, who was a man of few words and not all of them courteous. "Bad business brain."

"I have learned my lesson and shall endeavour to do better in future." I was conscious that, in speech and bearing, I had been reduced to a state of embarrassingly earnest obsequiousness. I felt like a schoolboy who had been called before not one but four stern headmasters and asked to account for his poor performance in his exams.

"What we can't have," said Mycroft Holmes, "is you revealing certain unpalatable facts that the world is better off not knowing."

"I would never do so on purpose."

"But you might inadvertently. So here I am, Doctor, reminding you. Every single word you ever publish must be scrutinised by the Dagon Club before it sees print. Understood?"

"Understood."

I glanced sidelong at Sherlock Holmes, who was having trouble masking his amusement at my discomfiture.

"We are at war," said his elder brother. "War with eldritch forces that dwell on the borders of reality and mean us nothing but harm. And in war, one strategy is the control of information. We cannot have society at large learning about the existence of Cthulhu, Nyarlathotep, Azathoth or any of their ilk, nor about those humans who offer obeisance to these entities and actively incite them to spread their malign influence over the

Earth. If the truth were to become widely known, there would be panic, chaos, insanity, anarchy on an unprecedented scale. Civilisation would falter, and the so-called gods would find mankind an easy mark. They are bent on our destruction, and there must not be a single chink in our armour, else we shall surely succumb."

His three colleagues murmured agreement.

"That is why I founded the Dagon Club," Mycroft went on, "and that is why we are monitoring your activities closely, Doctor. Yours and Sherlock's. But anyway. To the subject at hand."

He charged a wineglass from a bottle of what appeared to be a rather fine Burgundy, and took a long, slurping sip. I looked on with envy. The other three club members were all enjoying alcoholic beverages too, while Holmes and I had not been offered so much as a cup of tea.

"Extortion," Mycroft said. "It is an ugly word and an uglier deed. Uglier still is the peculiar kind of extortion I have come across lately – and I use the word 'peculiar' advisedly."

"Peculiar how?" asked the junior Holmes.

"I shall come to that in a moment. It all began just over a month ago, when Sir Martin Tideswell sent out a memo proposing that the Royal Navy be reduced in strength by a third."

"The First Naval Lord said that?"

"He did. The memo was not widely circulated and I have managed to keep it under wraps, so that the press have not got their grubby hands on it. Privately, however, Sir Martin came in for plenty of criticism, both from within the Admiralty and in the top echelons of government. It was a significant misstep in an otherwise unblemished career, and I fear that his days as commander of the fleet are numbered. Then, a week later, came the Marquess of Beecherston's letter to the *Times*."

"Yes. I recall reading it and being surprised by its sentiments."

"Not half as surprised, I'll bet, as the Queen was," said Mycroft. "Beecherston had been widely tipped to be the next Viceroy of India, and there he was, stating openly in a national daily that the Raj was an oppressive colonialist regime and that Britain should not – and I quote – 'continue to plunder the subcontinent for its wealth and resources, like a band of pirates in pith helmets'. Until then, His Lordship had been a staunch proponent of greater social intervention in India as a means of reinforcing Her Majesty's dominion over her subjects there, so it was something of a volte-face on his part."

"To put it mildly."

"Needless to say, the Queen was unamused, and the viceroyship is no longer on the cards for Beecherston. He'll be lucky if he keeps his seat in the Upper House. It wasn't long before I became aware of similar antics from four other equally prominent individuals, every instance so alike that it formed an unmistakable pattern. Each man displayed a sudden, radical change of heart which would seem to undermine his own position and possibly the fabric of the nation. It was as though, all at once, these pillars of the establishment had crumbled."

"Very queer," opined Sherlock Holmes.

"Naturally I took it upon myself to interrogate the persons in question," said Mycroft. "I spoke to the six of them one-to-one, and each defended his stance with gusto and talked about experiencing pangs of conscience and wishing to do what was right. None showed regret for his decision, nor could any be convinced to recant it. Beneath all their protestations and self-justifications, however, I noted a common denominator. To a man, they were clearly frightened. Frightened to death."

"Of what?"

"I could not persuade them to say. The further I pressed them, the more they retreated into prevarication and bluster. I presumed that agents of some foreign power must be threatening their personal safety or the safety of their close kin. It was the only explanation that made sense. Spies abound in this country of ours and are getting more ruthless by the day. There are also anarchists and the Fenians to consider. They, too, will stop at nothing to undermine the fabric of this great nation. Certainly my thinking was running along those lines. That was until one of the six, in an unguarded moment, let slip something. 'I must keep quiet,' he said, 'or it will come again.' Those were his exact words. 'It will come again.'"

"And did you get him to expand on that remark?"

"No, Sherlock." Mycroft Holmes gave a sombre shake of the head, which set his jowls wobbling beneath his chin. "Try as I might, I could not. But mark the pronoun. 'It'. Not 'he' or 'they'. Not even 'she'. '*It* will come again.' Now what do you think that might signify, brother?"

"Without further data, I would be loath to speculate."

"But if we factor in the fear shown by all of them, it hints at something abnormal, don't you think? Something outside the mundane sphere. Something belonging to the preternatural demimonde that you and Dr Watson – and we Dagon Clubbers too, in our way – now inhabit."

Lord Cantlemere fixed a gimlet eye on Holmes. "Sounds to me like exactly the sort of knotty, arcane problem that you revel in unlocking."

"Don't you mean un*Sher*locking?" said Milton Goldsworthy, and immediately started sniggering at his own pun, as though it were a witticism of the highest order. Sir Alexander Chalfont-Banks chimed in, and together the pair chortled and snorted in their shared mirth. Meanwhile Mycroft Holmes sat patiently by, essaying the thinnest of smiles. As for Lord Cantlemere, he did not go so far as smile, but then humorousness did not fit comfortably on his austere face, any more than a rose might flourish on stony ground. He did, however, tilt his head to one side as though catching strains of a distant, haunting music.

Once the outbreak of jollity – if that is the right term for it – had run its course, Mycroft fetched out a folded sheet of paper from inside his jacket. He handed it to his younger sibling.

"Here is a list of the people concerned, with notes on each."

Holmes unfolded the paper and, glancing at it, whistled. Over his shoulder, I read the half-dozen names. Including Sir Martin Tideswell and the Marquess of Beecherston, they constituted as illustrious a roll call as ever there was.

Holmes waved the sheet of paper at his brother. "What do you want from me, Mycroft?"

"What I want, Sherlock, is for you to do what I could not: find out what has terrified these men so. You might need this." Mycroft produced a sealed envelope. "A letter of authorisation, signed by me. It will guarantee you an audience with any of the names on the list and access to almost anywhere you might desire."

"I'm sure I can manage, even without your imprimatur."

"Take it anyway."

Holmes did as bidden, stowing the envelope, unopened, in an inside pocket.

"I wish you luck," said Mycroft. "Report to me as soon as you learn anything useful."

He batted a hand in the air, dismissing us. There were no goodbyes. The meeting had been adjourned, just like that, and Holmes and I were expected simply to leave.

As we made our way out onto the street, I felt compelled to voice my disgruntlement. "Really, those men in there are among the rudest I have ever met. They seem to have forgotten that manners exist. Your brother is the exception, I suppose. He may be curt but he is not actively impolite. As for the others, they truly believe that the majority of folk are lesser beings, to be disdained and disparaged."

"I have often found that those deemed 'the great and good'," said Holmes, "have relinquished goodness on their way to greatness. We just have to accept that the Dagon Club are there to help and that whatever minor indignities they inflict upon the likes of you and me are worth enduring in the name of allyship. Now then." He flourished the list of names. "I have some other 'great and good' to interview. You probably shan't see me for a few days."

"Let me know how you get on."

"Of course."

*

A week passed, with no sign of Sherlock Holmes. I expected him to drop by at any moment, or else to wire me. A further few days went by, still without any word from him, but I wasn't especially worried. Holmes had a tendency to throw himself wholeheartedly into a case and would disappear from view for however long it took, before re-emerging at the end, brimming with new intelligence, like a diving bird coming to the surface with a beak full of fish.

Then, on a bitterly cold Sunday afternoon, I received a visit from his brother. I answered the knock at the door myself, for it was the maid's day off and Mary was out. I could not disguise my amazement when I saw who was on my front doorstep. Mycroft Holmes seldom strayed from his Whitehall stamping grounds. His immense physical bulk seemed to anchor him there, where he was in constant demand for advice and policy-making, and only under exceptional circumstances did he bestir himself to venture elsewhere. With that in mind, my thoughts immediately took a dark turn.

"Not that this isn't an honour and a pleasure, sir," said I, ushering him to the drawing room and taking his coat, gloves and scarf from him, "but might I ask if all is well? You are not, I trust, the bearer of grim tidings."

"You mean about Sherlock?" Mycroft lowered his corpulent self into an armchair and held out his hands to the fire to warm them.

"That is what I mean. I cannot for the life of me imagine why you might be calling, not least on a Sunday, unless something dire has happened involving your brother. Pray tell me I am wrong."

"Could it not be that I am simply here for social reasons?"

"With all due respect, no."

Mycroft nodded, the roll of fat beneath his chin bulging outward with each inclination of the head, much like the vocal sac of a croaking frog. "True. We are not friends, you and I, Doctor. Associates, yes, even brothers-in-arms, but not friends. Tell me, how would it feel if you learned that Sherlock had met with some great misfortune?"

My heart was racing now. "I should be destroyed. It would be the worst calamity I could imagine, apart from if it was Mary."

"Ah yes. The fragrant Mrs Watson. Is she home?"

"Playing bridge at a friend's house. But never mind her. Right now, it's your brother that concerns me. If you have something to say about him, for God's sake say it."

"You look shaken, Doctor."

"I am very shaken. Come on, out with it. What has happened to him?"

At that, Mycroft started chuckling. His belly shook and his eyes creased up, disappearing into the folds of his face.

"This is no laughing matter," I said heatedly. "We are talking about your own flesh and blood! Your closest living relative! Is he injured? Comatose? Dead? What?"

"Oh, my dear Watson," said Mycroft, in tones both higher-pitched and clearer-sounding than before. "Your face. It is a picture!"

"Holmes?" I breathed.

"One and the same," said my interlocutor. It was still Mycroft Holmes, to all outward appearances, but the voice was unambiguously that of Sherlock Holmes.

"My goodness! You absolute fiend!" I shook my fist at him. "What a horrible trick. I hope you're ashamed of yourself."

"I didn't plan it in advance," said Sherlock Holmes. "I admit that part of my reason in coming here in guise of Mycroft was to hoodwink you. It never fails to entertain me when at last you penetrate my masquerade and realisation dawns in your eyes. 'Good grief, it is you, Holmes!' But when you started showing fretfulness as to the reasons for my brother's presence and were so obviously fearing the worst… I'm sorry, but I just couldn't help myself."

I poured a glass of sherry to steady my nerves. "Never do it again. You had me thinking… well, you know what you had me thinking."

"And it was touching, how upset you got. Nothing can be more gratifying for a man than to see the devastating effect that news of his death has upon his best friend."

"Nothing can be crueller than to purport to be conveying such news."

"And I apologise for doing so. The Devil took me. Say you forgive me."

"Grudgingly," I replied.

"Demonstrate it by giving me a glass of that sherry."

"That really is a quite brilliant impersonation," I said, handing him the drink. "Even by your standards. I'd never have known you weren't Mycroft."

"In truth, passing myself off as my own brother is not so difficult," said Holmes. "After all, we grew up together. I know his every tic and mannerism intimately. Added to that, we are the same height and have many physiognomic characteristics in common. The size was the thing." He clapped his bulbous stomach with both hands. "I am carrying dozens of pounds in padding, and I have used up half the theatrical putty in London fleshing out my face. Walking around with all this additional ballast – being so large and ungainly in general – is profoundly uncomfortable. Frankly, I don't know how Mycroft can bear it."

"He does not move much. That's how he bears it. Am I to

take it that the purpose of all this is to facilitate your interviewing the men on the list he gave you?"

"Spot on, Watson. The letter of authorisation Mycroft handed me gave me the idea. I thought, rather than wave that under people's noses and have to come up with various pretexts for meeting them, why not simply *be* him? He had spoken to each of them already. All I needed to do was claim that he wished to follow up that conversation with a few supplemental enquiries. Nobody refuses when the mighty Mycroft Holmes asks for a chat. In his world, to do so is practically a capital offence."

"Were you not concerned that, your brother already having drawn a blank with these men, you yourself, as he, might not get any further with them? Anything they had been reluctant to tell him the first time, they might be even more reluctant to second time around."

"But I am not Mycroft. I have my own wiles, and I would say they are superior to his."

"Fair enough. So, what have you discovered?"

"Plenty," said Holmes, "and much of it worrisome."

"Very well," I said. "But before we continue, I'd be grateful if you would shed that disguise. It's disconcerting to see Mycroft but hear Sherlock."

"I would happily oblige," replied he, "but unpicking all this putty and divesting myself of the padding is an arduous process. I would prefer to leave it until I get back to Baker Street, when I can do it at my leisure."

"Very well. Go on then."

"My first interviewee was Sir Martin Tideswell," said Holmes. "I went to his office at the Admiralty. To be Mycroft Holmes in the halls of power is to be like a god. Doors open as if by magic. Flunkies kowtow. Even Sir Martin himself, lord of the oceans, was deferential. We fell to discussing his memo, and midway through the exchange I ambushed him. I asked, apropos of nothing, if he had ever seen a monster.

There was a momentary hesitation before he replied roundly in the negative, but that hesitation spoke volumes. Sometimes a man pauses because he does not understand the question. Other times he pauses because he does not want to answer the question. This was indisputably the latter case.

"'You mean at sea?' he said. 'During my days as a naval officer? No, sir. Not once. Not a mermaid, not a sea serpent, not a kraken. I do not believe in such creatures.'

"'I am not talking about years ago,' said I. 'I am talking about recently, in the past month. Something horrifying, something your mind could scarcely encompass.'

"Sir Martin was thoroughly discombobulated now. His face grew red with indignation, even as his eyes darted hither and yon in panic. 'This is an absurd line of enquiry,' he said. 'What on earth has got into you? I never thought you the sort to entertain such a ridiculous notion as the existence of monsters. Mycroft Holmes is famously a repository of logic and reason.'

"'Whatever you encountered,' I said, 'it has scared you so much that you have begun acting against your own best interests and those of England.'

"'Preposterous!' he snapped.

"'You would not be the first person whose grip on sanity has been loosened by a confrontation with the unnatural.'

"He rose to his feet, looking fit to burst. 'That is quite enough,' he thundered. 'I don't care that you are who you are, Mr Holmes. I don't care that you have the ear of the prime minister and the Queen. I will not tolerate this rank idiocy one minute longer. Get out. Go!'

"I knew I had pushed him as far as I dared. Also, I had no wish to tarnish my brother's reputation as a subtle operator. I made my excuses and left. Nonetheless, I was now inclined to believe that Mycroft's suspicions were correct and that there was an element of the uncanny involved here."

"Sir Martin protested too much," I said.

"Quite. It seemed at least possible that he had been surprised by some weird and – to him – inexplicable entity, and either was afraid to talk about it or had been constrained not to by someone. What I next had to do was find out whether the same held true for the other five names on the list."

"And did it?"

"Indeed so," said Holmes. "Refill my sherry glass, would you? That's a good fellow. My second interviewee was the very man who confessed to Mycroft that he must stay silent or 'it will come again'. This was the munitions manufacturer Sir Stockton Spaulding, whose company has supplied our nation's military with armaments and ammunition for over a quarter of a century. Up until last month Spaulding Ordnance Ltd was busy developing a successor to the thirteen-pounder gun, currently the gold standard for field artillery. Sir Stockton himself promised to deliver a weapon of far greater accuracy, lighter so that it requires fewer horses to pull it, and with an effective firing range of four thousand yards. Then, abruptly, he cancelled the project and ordered all of the blueprints and prototypes destroyed. He has since put his company up for sale. The only explanation he has given is that he no longer wishes to be responsible, however indirectly, for countless deaths on the battlefield."

"One can't blame him for that, perhaps. Remorse is a powerful motivator."

"But after twenty-five years of faithful indenture to the Crown, and with so much government money invested in his operations, for him to turn around like that and toss it all on the dustheap? Churlish, to say the least."

"Self-destructive, too. How did your meeting with him go?"

"Sir Stockton is renowned as a man of steely resolve," said Holmes. "Business rivals fear him. He drives the hardest of bargains. It's said you are as likely to get a concession out of him as you are to get a hungry lion not to eat you. Yet the fellow I encountered at his palatial residence in the leafy depths of the

Surrey countryside was as timid as anything. Far from being the grizzled old brute of his reputation, he looked frail and broken. Odder still, it was broad daylight and he had every single shutter in the mansion closed. Inside, the place lay in perpetual gloom. I made some cursory remark about this, and he said, 'Yes, you mentioned it last time you came, Mr Holmes. I will tell you now what I told you then: my eyes have developed an unusual sensitivity to sunlight.'

"'Is that the real reason,' I said, 'or is it the case that your eyes do not wish to see something on the outside looking in?'

"'Whatever can you mean?' said he tremulously.

"'What *thing* is it out there that you fear so much? What are you screening yourself against, Sir Stockton? Describe it.'

"'I can hardly find the words to—' he began, then stopped himself. 'There was no *thing*, sir, as you put it. I repeat: my eyes have become sensitive to sunlight. That is all. I cannot abide it. It gives me a headache.'

"'You are afraid of seeing it again, this creature,' I persisted, 'and you were told that you would, unless you did as ordered and abandoned your plans for the new artillery piece. In the event, you went further than that and decided to sell your company as well. Who orchestrated all this? Who is wielding such influence over you?'

"At that, Sir Stockton let out a cry and swooned. I revived him with some brandy, and as he came round I spoke to him soothingly and solicitously. I said he should make a clean breast of it. He would not find me a sceptical audience, and anything he revealed, I would treat with the utmost discretion.

"At last he said, 'If one cannot trust Mycroft Holmes, whom can one trust?' Whereupon, with the relief of a sinner in the confessional, he told all.

"The long and the short of it, Watson, is this. Late one evening last month, as Sir Stockton was smoking a cigar on the terrace before turning in for the night, a figure loomed out of the dark. It came loping across the lawn towards where he stood, and at first he thought it merely a man, perhaps one of his domestic staff, the gardener or the gamekeeper, fresh from some nocturnal errand. That was until he perceived that the figure had curving horns on its head, talons on its fingers, and a spiked tail. It had wings, too, leathery and membranous, like a bat's. It was thin and long-limbed and seemed as much to dance on tiptoe as to walk. Its black, glossy hide glistened in the starlight.

"As it approached ever nearer, Sir Stockton was overcome with terror. 'I could not move,' he said. 'I thought I must be dreaming, for this was an apparition that could only belong in a nightmare. It had no face, Mr Holmes. No eyes, no nose, no mouth, just a smooth, hideous blankness. It stepped up onto the terrace and halted a few feet away, and I would swear it then set to studying me. It canted its head from side to side, appraising me as a cat might a mouse or a dog a juicy steak.' He wanted to run, but felt that even if he had been able to stir his numb legs into motion, he could not have escaped. He sensed that the beast in front of him, whatever else it was, was a consummate predator and would bring him down before he had gone three steps.

"'What happened then?' I asked him.

"'After several interminable moments,' came the reply, 'the thing did a smart about-turn and left me there. Why, I could not fathom. I had been convinced I was going to die and my last few moments on earth would be spent screaming in agony as that hellish, faceless entity tore me to shreds. Instead, I was spared. Long after it had gone, vanishing into the darkness, I remained rooted to the spot. I was shaking all over, light-headed, utterly unmanned.'

"Eventually Sir Stockton's valet came out of the house looking for him. It was past his customary bedtime and the fellow was wondering where his master had got to. He could see Sir Stockton was in a state of shock and helped him indoors. When the valet enquired what the matter was, Sir Stockton could not say. Words failed him. He did not sleep a wink that night. Then, the following morning, the woman came."

"The woman?" I said.

"According to Sir Stockton, she turned up at the mansion gates, unannounced. She never gave a name. She told the butler that she had a message for Sir Stockton which she must deliver in person. It concerned the events of the previous night. Learning this, Sir Stockton felt he had no alternative but to agree to see her. He could only assume this woman had knowledge of the monstrosity that had menaced him on the terrace. Perhaps, he thought, she could explain what he had seen. Perhaps she could reassure him that it had just been some phantasm, a trick of the mind."

"What did she look like?"

"She was in her twenties, petite, pretty, well presented. She had long, curling blonde hair and one of those pert, uptilted noses that, as Sir Stockton put it, 'speak of intelligence and vivacity'. She reminded him, indeed, very much of his late wife, as she had been in the bloom of her youth.

"'Sir Stockton,' the woman said, "I shall keep this brief. Last night you came face to face with a creature known as a nightgaunt. It is as deadly a beast as ever walked the planet. If you wish never to meet it again, here is what you must do.' And she proceeded to list her terms.

"'Which were that you must give up work on the new gun,' I said to Sir Stockton, 'and not tell a soul why.'

"'It was as straightforward as that,' replied he, with a nod. 'I was still dazed and trembling from my encounter with that thing she called a nightgaunt. Exhausted, too, after my sleepless night. I could scarcely think straight.'

"The woman told Sir Stockton that he had three days to comply. If he had not commenced dismantling the project by then, he should prepare for a return visit from the nightgaunt.

"'It will come to you,' she said. 'It will find you wherever you are. No door can be barred against it. No gun can harm it.

Trust me on that. And this time it won't be content merely to look at you. Imagine those talons rending your flesh. Imagine it lingering over your slaughter, savouring every second of it. That is all. Good day!'

"So saying, she departed. The whole exchange lasted no more than a couple of minutes, and Sir Stockton described her as being bright and cheery throughout, as though it was all just some pleasant social occasion. He was left to ponder her words, but really he could see no option other than to do as she demanded.

"'You have no idea, Mr Holmes,' he said, 'how appalling the nightgaunt was. That featureless face. The supple rubberiness of its hide. The way it moved across the grass – so light-footed, so silent, so sinister. Even recalling it now, I feel my stomach churning and my pulse starting to race. Oh God! I can't bear to leave the house any more. I don't dare look out of the window, in case the nightgaunt should be there, peering in. I wonder constantly if it is lurking in the woods at the edge of the estate, or in one of the hedgerows, biding its time. I have done everything the woman asked, and more, and yet I remain in a state of, as it were, paralysis. Is this my life from now on? Am I never to be free of this abiding, sickening dread? Am I to be a prisoner always – a prisoner of fear?'

"With that, he put his head in his hands and wept. This hard-nosed captain of industry, this esteemed, knighted millionaire – sobbing in front of me like an admonished infant. I tell you, Watson, it was pitiful to behold.

"I felt that I had gathered all I usefully could from him, and so, with a few words of consolation, I left him in peace."

"In pieces, rather," I said.

Holmes chuckled dryly. "Alas, too true. At least I now had two salient facts. One: there had indeed been monstrous visitations. Two: there was human involvement."

"What else do we know about nightgaunts?" I asked. "I must confess, the name alone gives me the shivers."

"The arcane literature does not tell us much, but what it does tell is bad enough. Nightgaunts are baleful, feral abominations with no love for human beings. They seem to relish the terror they cause by their appearance alone, and will attack without provocation and kill without compunction. In short, Watson, we can count ourselves blessed if we go through life without ever falling foul of one."

"Amen to that," I said.

"I shan't bore you with a full account of my meetings with the other names on the list," Holmes said, resuming his thread. "They went much as the one with Sir Stockton Spaulding did. By applying the right mixture of probing, cajoling and sympathy, I was able to break down each man's resistance and get him to tell his story. In every instance the details were similar to those of his peers' stories, but not the same."

"How so?"

"Where Sir Stockton was terrorised by a nightgaunt, the others encountered a range of different monsters. One man, it was that slobbering winged hybrid known as a byakhee. Another, it was a guttural, subterranean, cannibalistic humanoid known as a ghast. Yet another, a shoggoth – protoplasmic, many-eyeballed, covered in slime. A whole gruesome bestiary of abominations. I looked them up in my copy of Von Junzt's *Unaussprechlichen Tieren*. The title might translate as *Unnameable Beasts*, but Von Junzt nonetheless succeeds in providing a name for almost every creature he alludes to."

"For your interviewees it was a unique monster on each occasion," I said. "I wonder why."

"That is certainly one of the more singular aspects of the whole affair. That and the fact that somebody appears to have mastery over these various entities, who are not known for being tameable, let alone governable. But listen to this. Each man also received a subsequent visit from an anonymous woman."

"Sir Stockton's petite blonde."

"No, that's just it. In one instance, it was a rather buxom

redhead. In another, a tall, slender brunette. In a third, a young lady of Latin heritage, with dark, flashing eyes, who spoke in heavily accented English."

"Not just a regiment of monsters but a monstrous regiment of women too."

"Ho, Watson! Pawky as ever. A different woman in each instance, but all of them delivered the same message: 'Change your ways in the manner I stipulate, or else the next time the creature you encountered comes calling, it will be the last thing you ever see.' The result was invariably capitulation on the victim's part. What is interesting, however, is that every time the woman resembled a significant female from the man's life. Remember what Sir Stockton said about the blonde?"

"She reminded him of his late wife."

"The same held true for the rest of them, more or less. For one man, the woman took after his daughter, who had married a Canadian and moved to Toronto and whom he missed terribly. For another, she brought to mind his long-lost mother, who died when he was a boy. For yet another, she was not dissimilar to his first love, whom his parents had considered an unsuitable match and forbidden him from pursuing a relationship with. This cannot be accidental. And hence, by such a means, through a combination of fear and sentimental appeal, six great men have been brought to their knees. A law proposing stricter ratification of existing international treaties will now not be passed in the House of Commons. The police, due to be given broader powers when it comes to investigating sedition and treason, will now not get them. And so on and so on. It is a subtle, concerted campaign to undo much of what makes this country of ours – this empire of ours, for that matter – indomitable."

"As Mycroft put it, pillars of the establishment have crumbled," I said. "How many more would it take for the whole edifice to come crashing down? We must stop this before it goes any further."

"Of course we must. These half-dozen men are, I am sure, only the beginning. There will be more. Those behind the scheme, having been successful thus far, will feel emboldened to carry on. But how do we find them and curtail their operations? That is the question."

"You must have a plan."

"I have the germ of one," said Holmes. "There is one man among the six who is made of sterner stuff than the others. He is Professor Avery Mellingford."

I recalled seeing his name on Mycroft's list. "The chemist. A Fellow of the Royal Society."

"For some time now, Professor Mellingford has been working on a form of poison gas that may be used on the battlefield against enemy troops. It is an innovation which, if implemented, could tip the balance of future wars in our favour. He was dissuaded from continuing his researches after a run-in with a formless spawn on a beach near his home in Rye."

"A formless spawn?"

"Not one of Von Junzt's more inspired nomenclatures. A formless spawn is, well, formless. A better adjective might be 'protoplasmic'. In its basic manifestation it resembles a pool of tar, but it can assume any shape that suits its purpose. Most often it has insect traits, with tall, stilt-like legs, but it is apt to extrude tentacles too, of the kind you might see on a squid or octopus."

"It sounds delightful."

"Now, the professor being a man of science, he takes a level-headed approach to life," said Holmes. "There is no denying that the formless spawn put the frighteners on him and the extortion has worked, in as much as he has got rid of his notes on his poison gas and locked up his laboratory. I think, however, that he may be amenable to changing his mind about that. During my conversation with him, he talked about 'childish superstition' and 'the necessity for empiricism at all times', and he seemed half-inclined to think he had been the object of an elaborate hoax, for which he chastised himself more than once.

He is a bachelor, moreover, and a loner, with few attachments to other people, women least of all, giving him a certain independence of thought and freedom from conventionality."

Holmes could almost have been describing himself. "If women do not feature greatly in Mellingford's life," I said, "then I'm curious to know what sort of woman was deployed to deliver the extortion threat to him."

"A matriarchal figure," Holmes replied. "Not tall, rather portly, in her sixties, imposing, dressed in black, probably a widow, with an aristocratic voice and a certain regality of bearing…"

"Akin to his grandmother, perhaps?"

"No, Watson. Try again."

"An aunt?"

"You are being really quite dense. Must I spell it out?"

"Well, otherwise you would appear to be describing our very own queen."

Holmes clapped his hands. "There we have it! Even someone who has little affinity for his fellow countrymen feels an intrinsic, patriotic loyalty towards our monarch. It is in the British blood. If Victoria, or someone very like her, makes demands of us, we are apt to obey."

"And you think Mellingford might be persuaded to begin work again on his gas?" I said. "Even if it puts him at risk of another, potentially fatal brush with the formless spawn?"

"I do," said Holmes, "not least when I tell him I can guarantee his safety."

"Can you?"

"I believe I am capable of defending him against the depredations of a formless spawn. But only provided I have the dauntless John Watson by my side."

I mustered a stoical sigh. "I had a feeling you might say something like that."

*

The next week, I found myself travelling to Sussex. I caught a train to Eastbourne and changed there for the spur line towards Rye. The track for this last leg of the journey ran alongside the coast, with my compartment window affording views of sea and shingle beach practically the entire way. The weather had turned blustery. Shreds of silvery cloud streaked across the sky, while the English Channel was in a fractious mood, all heaving grey-green waves marbled with froth.

Past Hastings, with just a couple of stops remaining, I drew from my pocket the letter from Holmes which had coaxed me out of London. It went as follows:

Watson,
Matters are coming to a head and you are needed.
Bring your wits, your courage and your service
revolver.
Holmes

This terse missive had come with a newspaper clipping attached, a short article that had appeared in one of the broadsheets the previous day. It read:

NOTED SCIENTIST RESUMES
IMPORTANT MILITARY RESEARCH

Professor Avery Mellingford announced yesterday that he is to begin work again on a weapon vital to our nation's interests.

The nature of said weapon remains top secret but it is believed to possess the capability to alter the face of warfare radically. The professor recently suspended his researches, citing personal reasons. He has since rescinded that decision and is pleased to claim that his labours are proceeding apace.

> Professor Mellingford is one of Britain's foremost chemists, credited with numerous innovations regarding chlorine compounds and the atomisation of liquids. His speech last year at the Royal Society on the topic of the fixation of atmospheric nitrogen and its potential for use as an agricultural fertiliser drew considerable acclaim.

I had in fact spotted the article in the paper and had immediately discerned the hand of Sherlock Holmes in it. Doubtless he had organised its publication, most likely via Mycroft and the Dagon Club, one of whose members was a press baron. It was a deliberate provocation. Those responsible for the campaign of extortion, whoever they were, would surely see it and respond accordingly.

I disembarked at Rye, that cluster of houses which sits atop a hill overlooking Romney Marsh and the River Rother. During its heyday as a port town, Rye had been a thriving centre for trade and commerce, until the river silted up and became unnavigable to large ships. Thereafter, in the seventeenth century, it turned to fishing and pottery for its economy, although smuggling flourished as well. Now it had settled into genteel respectability as a market town, yet it still seemed very much on the periphery of things, an isolated outpost of civilisation with emptiness all around.

Holmes met me at the station and ushered me towards a four-wheeled trap waiting outside. We headed eastward out of town, across the river, and thence into the flat, desolate expanse of the marsh. Here, sheep grazed on rough fields amid drainage ditches and outcrops of scrubby, stunted trees. The lanes we drove along were muddy and deeply rutted, and the earth itself looked perpetually sodden, as though in a losing battle with the sea. The further we went from Rye, the more I felt as though the landscape was fraying around us, giving itself up piece by piece until eventually it would disintegrate altogether.

"You have remembered your pistol, of course," Holmes said to me.

I patted my pocket where the sidearm lay. "And plenty of rounds, too. It did occur to me that I might need your specially adapted bullets, the ones daubed with the Seal of Unravelling. Have you prepared some?"

"No."

"But we face a foe of supernatural origin. Standard ammunition might not suffice."

"We shall see."

"What do you mean by that?"

"Our formless spawn, should it put in an appearance, may not be all that we are expecting," said Holmes.

"There is more to it than meets the eye, then?"

"Or less."

"Less?"

He smiled at me, damnably enigmatic. "Worry not, Watson. Sit back. Enjoy the scenery. We haven't much further to go."

At last we reached our destination, a largish house of Elizabethan vintage that seemed not so much to rise from the ground as teeter unsteadily on top of it. Diamonded windows were set into crumbling brickwork, much of which was overgrown with various kinds of creeper. A single-storey outbuilding squatted alongside.

Professor Mellingford greeted us at the door, and I quickly gathered that Holmes had been staying as his guest for the past few days. During that time the two men had achieved an easy-going familiarity, to the point where Mellingford, as he shook my hand, said, "Welcome, Doctor. Make yourself at home. If my friend Holmes vouches for you, that's good enough for me."

The professor was tall and slender, with a bald pate surrounded by a curtain of slightly too long hair. He wore a brocade waistcoat, a wing-collared shirt and a cravat secured with a ruby-topped pin, and struck me as rather raffish-looking for someone who pursued such a sober-minded vocation. He had an amiable air, though, and I took an immediate shine to him.

Soon enough we three were sitting down to lunch, where the conversation was cordial but serious. Mellingford spoke a little about his poison gas, disclosing that it was a colourless, odourless compound which raised blisters on the skin and, when inhaled, in the lungs. "My aim," he said, "is to create something sufficiently noxious to disable the enemy but not kill. If their soldiers are hospitalised in great enough numbers, then our soldiers will have an easier time of it. There are other factors to bear in mind, such as wind speed and direction and the rate of dispersal during deployment, but strength of toxicity is the main one."

"Wouldn't blistered lungs pose a risk of pulmonary oedema?" I said.

"Potentially. That is why I have to be careful when calibrating the composition of the gas. I am keen for it to be non-lethal."

"I was led to understand that you destroyed your notes on the gas. If so, how are you going to be able to recreate it?"

"The notes may be gone," said Mellingford, "but everything is still up here." He tapped his head. "I am not starting over from scratch, and it shouldn't take me long to get back to where I was."

"But who is to say that the military brass won't take your compound, when it's ready, and develop a more concentrated, deadly version?"

He spread out his hands. "That, Doctor, is beyond my control. All I can do is present them with a humane deterrent and hope for the best."

Talk then turned to the incident that was Holmes's and my reason for being at his house.

"It was hair-raising, and no mistake," Mellingford said.

"As I've told both Holmes here and his brother, it happened as I was walking home from Rye one evening, where I had just dined at the Mermaid Inn. Dusk was settling, and in the half-light I spied something out of the corner of my eye, a dark silhouette on the horizon. At first I thought it was a cow but, from the way it moved, I soon perceived it was not. It both crawled and slithered, if that is possible, and I became aware that it was getting closer, on a course to intercept me. I quickened my pace, and the thing accelerated too. I broke into a run, but it was faster and in no time it was upon me. It reared up, a mass of legs and tentacles, looming over me. It opened a vast maw, fringed with countless teeth. At that moment I feared I had lost all rationality. This was like nothing I had ever seen, nothing *anyone* had ever seen. No Linnaean taxonomy could account for it. No academic textbook bore its image. I am not ashamed to say that I fainted. When I came to, the thing was gone, without a trace. What it had gained by harassing me but leaving me unscathed, I had no idea. Not until the following day, when that woman called. Then it became all too apparent what was going on, and unfortunately, I gave in to duress. Thank God that the Holmes brothers have been able to convince me to see sense."

"You do not fear the return of that creature?"

"I would, Doctor, if for one moment I thought it was real."

"You think you imagined it?"

"Not at all," said Mellingford. "It existed. It had physicality. It was, however, a confection. Someone went to great lengths to construct a monster costume using all manner of theatrical artifice – rubber, paint, wires, levers and so forth – which was then unleashed upon unsuspecting me. The fact that it manifested at twilight is surely no accident, for during that liminal period one's eyesight is at its least sharp. Nor would I be surprised if, in order to enhance the effectiveness of the illusion, some form of hallucinatory substance was used on me as well. An opiate could have been slipped into my drink at the pub. It is easy to say all this with hindsight and be phlegmatic about the experience, but in the immediate aftermath I was profoundly unnerved. Little wonder that I acceded to the woman's ultimatum. I am now resolved to continue as before and damn the consequences. These villains can try to intimidate me again, but I am wise to their game. Besides, I have Holmes – and now you as well, Doctor – to protect me. I feel perfectly safe."

Later, privately, I asked Holmes if he thought Mellingford was correct and the formless spawn was just someone in a costume.

"That at least would explain why you don't feel we need your 'magic bullets'," I said.

"Mellingford has accounted for the creature in a way that satisfies his sense of logical propriety," Holmes said. "Whether or not it is the truth, I have done nothing to dissuade him. As long as he no longer fears the formless spawn, he will not hide or cower."

"I see. You mean to put him out there, do you not? Dangle him as bait to draw the formless spawn into the open?"

"You make it sound as though I am using him to ensnare our adversary."

"Aren't you?"

Holmes gave a dry chuckle. "Guilty as charged. But I would not do it if I wasn't confident that we can keep him safe from harm. At any rate, I have already outlined a plan of action to him and he has consented. This very evening, Mellingford is going into Rye for dinner and returning just as darkness falls."

"Alone?"

"So it will seem to any observer," said Holmes. "In fact, he will have a pair of guardian angels watching over him."

*

In the early evening, as planned, Mellingford set off on foot to Rye. Holmes and I accompanied him until we were within sight of the town, whereupon he and we parted company. While Mellingford carried on, Holmes and I repaired to a spinney of hawthorn beside the lane. Holmes had selected this beforehand as a suitable place of concealment.

We lurked within the spinney for an hour or so while the daylight waned. A breeze soughed across the marsh, rattling a nearby clump of bullrushes. Sheep bleated to one another at intervals, an oddly mournful sound. The world quietened and darkened, even as lights came on one by one in the windows of Rye until the place bristled with illumination. A half-moon hung in the purpling sky, low and pallid.

Holmes was adamant that, if the formless spawn were to attack, it would do so in a lonely spot, away from potential eyewitnesses. Mellingford would therefore be safe while in Rye itself, and once he left the ambit of the town, he would have us with him as bodyguards, albeit at a remove.

Presently we heard footfalls, and here came Mellingford, striding forthrightly down the lane. Even though he knew where Holmes and I were, he gave no indication of it. He marched past, and once he had gone some hundred yards further, Holmes tugged my sleeve.

"Now we follow," he whispered.

I drew my revolver, and together Holmes and I stole along the lane in Mellingford's wake, crouching low. I was on the alert, my every nerve end tingling. I scanned ahead and to the left and right, searching the gloaming for any sign of the formless spawn. Every now and then my attention was caught by a patch of darkness moving, but it always proved to be something innocent: a shadow, a wind-shivered tree and, in one instance, a black ram.

Mellingford made it back to his house without incident. No formless spawn appeared. I cannot say I was unhappy about that.

We regrouped in his drawing room.

"Disappointing," Holmes declared, "but it was just a first

attempt. Our foe will show up, I am sure of it. He needs to make good on his threat, otherwise what is the point of threatening?"

And so we did the same thing the next evening. Mellingford sallied forth to Rye again, and Holmes and I took up our position in the hawthorn spinney and waited.

"I must say, Mellingford is being incredibly brave," I murmured to Holmes, "voluntarily exposing himself to danger like this."

"Like any good scientist," my companion replied, "he is putting a theory to the test."

"Not all tests involve personal peril."

"He has assessed the odds. He firmly believes he is up against charlatanry. He is challenging our foe's determination with his own pragmatism."

"That does not diminish my admiration for him."

"His admirability is all the more reason why we must make sure his life is preserved."

Shortly after this exchange, Mellingford came back down the lane. As before, his demeanour exuded confidence. Holmes and I slipped again into our roles as shadowers, I with my gun drawn. We skulked along a fair way behind him, and he continued onward, seemingly blithe to our presence, not sparing us so much as a backward glance, for all that he was well aware we were there. He was playing his part impeccably.

All proceeded as it had the previous evening, save for the fact that near Mellingford's house, Holmes and I were accosted by a farmer. The fellow emerged in front of us from a gateway, quite unexpectedly. We halted, shrinking towards the edge of the lane, but he spotted us and gave a start. Mellingford, meanwhile, was turning a corner ahead, so that he was temporarily lost from view.

"Why, bless me!" the farmer declared in a thick Sussex burr, his hand on his heart. "What are you two gents doing there, acting all furtive like? Affrighted me something terrible, you did." He was a plump, jolly-looking sort, dressed in a well-worn tweed jacket and a collarless shirt with a kerchief tied loosely around his neck.

"Our apologies," said Holmes, straightening up, while I hid my revolver behind my back. "My friend and I are playing a game with another friend. We are seeing whether we can reach his house before he does, without him catching sight of us. It's silly, I know. A childish whim, cooked up over a pint of beer. But there is money riding on it."

This sounded fairly plausible to my ears, and certainly seemed so to the farmer. "The things you toffs get up to," said the rustic, with a cheery laugh. "You do so love your little japes. Well, far be it from me to stand in the way of a wager. I shall bid you good evening and good luck, sirs."

We continued on our way, and he on his, and I prayed that this interruption, brief as it was, had not left Professor Mellingford unchaperoned for too long.

As it was, Mellingford was fine. Holmes and I hastily recovered the ground we had lost, bringing the chemist within our sights again, and saw him to be unmolested. The rest of the journey was uneventful, and once more we convened in Mellingford's living room.

"This will work," Holmes insisted. "We simply have to be patient."

Mellingford spent the next day, as he had the last, ensconced in the outbuilding next to the house. It was a stables which had been converted into a laboratory. He busied himself therein, starting first thing in the morning and carrying on well into the afternoon, while Holmes and I passed the time in our own way. Remote though its location was, Mellingford's house was snug and comfortably appointed, and his cook was skilled. He had an extensive library, which I availed myself of, and there were pleasant rural walks to be had in the vicinity. Under other circumstances, if we hadn't been there on urgent, possibly life-or-death business, I would have called our sojourn pleasant. I missed Mary terribly, of course, and kept hoping the current situation would be resolved soon so that she and I might be reunited.

The third evening passed much as the previous one had, even down to another encounter with the farmer. This time, he surprised Holmes and me just as we had secreted ourselves in the hawthorn spinney.

"Goodness!" we heard him say from outside our hiding place. "Hello! Is it you two again? I saw you sneaking in there, and I thought to myself, 'Can it be them same pair as I saw last night? Why, it surely can!' and I felt I ought to investigate. What is it now, gents? Are you lying in wait? Planning on leaping out at your friend and giving him a scare?"

Holmes shouldered his way out of the hawthorn to stand before the farmer. I could just make out the both of them through the tangle of branches.

"Listen, my good man." Holmes adopted the same amenable approach as before, although there was a tetchy edge to his voice. "I'm delighted that what amuses us amuses you too. I do rather wish, however, that you would leave us be. Our friend is liable to come along at any moment, and we'd be grateful if you didn't give our position away."

"Oh no, sir. I'd never dream of doing that. Wouldn't want to ruin your fun."

"Here," said Holmes. "Here's a half-crown. Now do us a favour and run along, would you?"

The coin disappeared smartly into the farmer's pocket. Then, touching finger to forelock, the man strolled off. I heard him humming to himself as he went and I recognised the tune as the folk ballad "Early One Morning". Still just within my earshot, he started to sing the words of the chorus:

> *Oh, don't deceive me*
> *Oh, never leave me*
> *How could you use*
> *A poor maiden so?*

For a coarse son of the soil, he had a surprisingly melodic singing voice.

Holmes resumed his place at my side, muttering something about meddlesome locals, and together we waited for Mellingford to appear.

Sure enough he did, and we tailed him all the way to his house without incident.

"I am beginning to think," I said to Holmes once we were all three indoors, "that the formless spawn is never going to put in an appearance. Could it be that our adversary failed to note the article in the paper?"

"I doubt it. We are dealing with people of great resourcefulness and thoroughness."

"Then why have they not acted yet?"

"Be patient, Watson. The moment will surely come."

We went to bed, only to be awoken at daybreak by a loud, bloodcurdling scream.

*

The scream came from outdoors, and I leapt from my bed and ran to the window, which afforded a clear view of the garden and also of Mellingford's laboratory. I threw open the curtains and saw, to my horror, Mellingford kneeling on the stretch of lawn between the two buildings while a great black monster hulked over him.

The thing stood some seven feet tall, supported by a pair of long, backwards-bent legs. Its spindly arms were capped with pincers, and numerous tentacles whipped and writhed about its head and torso like snakes. Its mouth yawned so wide, it could have engulfed an entire football. Two bulbous eyes, positioned asymmetrically, glared down at the cringing chemist, each of them sulphur-yellow and slitted like a cat's. Its skin glistened blackly and seemed to have the consistency of crude oil.

Mellingford was in a state of helpless, quailing terror, and who could blame him? Even in the dim dawn light it was obvious that the formless spawn could not be a manmade artefact. Everything about it, from the sinewy musculature of its legs to the supple fleshiness of its tentacles, was organic. The thing lived, and Mellingford could see that for himself now, beyond dispute. His scientific brain could no longer explain away its existence in terms of cunningly wrought theatrical costuming. His eyes bulged. His jaw gaped. He was moaning incoherently. Everything about him betokened a man whose mind was rapidly unravelling.

I knew I had only seconds to act. The formless spawn looked set to rip Mellingford to shreds. I scooped up my revolver and dashed downstairs, calling out for Holmes in the meantime, in case my friend had not already been alerted to the crisis by Mellingford's scream.

He had, for as I reached the hallway he was there ahead of me, making for the front door. He paused just long enough to snatch a furled umbrella from a stand, and then he was outside, with me following hot on his heels.

We ran across the grass barefoot, in our pyjamas, and rounded the corner of the house just in time to see the formless spawn grasp Mellingford's throat in one pincered claw. Holmes did not hesitate. He raced towards the creature and, reaching it, adopted a fencing stance. Then he lunged, jabbing the umbrella tip into the formless spawn's torso.

The creature recoiled, letting Mellingford go. Holmes lunged again, delivering a second jab, and the formless spawn took another backward step. He repeated the action a third time, and a fourth, with similar results.

I would never have credited the idea that a mere umbrella could prove so effective against a large, horrifying abomination such as that formless spawn, but Holmes was demonstrating otherwise. An expert fencer, he was wielding the implement with aplomb, as though it were genuinely a rapier or foil. He was offering the creature no quarter, and his efforts to repel it were proving absurdly successful.

Yet I wondered how long he could maintain this intensity of exertion and how soon it would be before the formless spawn saw an opportunity and counterattacked.

"Holmes!" I cried, raising my revolver and cocking the hammer. "Stand aside!" I had no idea whether a plain Eley's No. 2 round could wound a formless spawn, let alone slay one, but I was more than willing to give it a try.

"No," cried he in return. "Don't!"

"All I need is a clear shot."

"I have this, Watson."

Holmes beleaguered the formless spawn a few moments more, then paused. There was a brief lull, during which he and the monster regarded each other. The formless spawn seemed to be looking at him curiously, almost quizzically, as though it could not fathom what sort of being this was, this human who did not fear it and was so determinedly resisting it.

I held my revolver steady, braced to fire should the formless spawn so much as twitch in Holmes's direction.

Then, to my surprise, the creature turned around and shambled away.

To my greater surprise, Holmes said to it, "Fontaine's on the Strand. This Saturday. Eight o'clock."

The formless spawn glanced back at him, before continuing its slouching retreat.

"Don't be late," Holmes added.

I kept my revolver trained on the monster until it was out of range, and even then I did not lower the weapon until it was gone from view altogether. Thereupon I decocked and pocketed the gun and went to Mellingford's side.

The man was a wreck. He blubbered and sobbed like a babe, and was so limp and incapacitated that it needed both Holmes and myself to bring him to his feet. We all but carried him back into the house, where, having lain him down on the sofa with his head propped up, I attempted to ply him with brandy, to no avail. I tipped the liquor between his lips but he appeared to have forgotten how to swallow. I am not sure I have ever seen a man so completely and abjectly broken, and I feared it would be a while before he regained his wits, if he ever did.

"You hardly need me to tell you he is in a bad way," I confided to Holmes, out of the prostrate Mellingford's hearing. "I shall send for his usual doctor. With time and professional care he may recover, but brain-fever is likely, and possibly a complete nervous collapse."

"I am at fault here," Holmes said, pursing his lips ruefully. "I should have seen this coming. Our enemy must have studied Mellingford's routine and known that he is wont to go to his laboratory at dawn every day. It was a moment of vulnerability and they exploited it. I have been outwitted, Watson, and I do not like that."

"At least Mellingford is alive. You saw the creature off before it could do him any physical hurt – and with an umbrella, of all things! And then you had the bravado to invite it to dinner." I grinned at the recollection of Holmes calling out the name of one of London's top restaurants to the formless spawn, along with a date and hour. It had been a deliciously impudent verbal *coup de grâce*. "What gall! As if you hadn't already shown it how little you were scared of it."

"Gall?" said Holmes. "Oh no, Watson. The invitation was genuine."

I frowned. "I don't understand."

"There's no reason why you should. All I can say is that I need to book a table at Fontaine's on Saturday night. I am hoping that I will have a charming guest for dinner and that it will be a pleasant and, if all goes well, revelatory occasion."

I looked at him to see if he was joking.

He was not.

*

Fontaine's was at that time the best French restaurant in town. Its head chef had studied under Escoffier, no less, at the Faisan d'Or in Cannes, while its pastry chef had been trained by Alphonse Gouffé, the Queen's own pâtissier. Its wine cellar was said to be second to none, and its gourmand menu ran to eighteen courses and had famously defeated the gastronome and food writer Nathaniel Newnham-Davis, who in spite of his battle-hardened stomach could not cope with the sheer quantity of dishes on offer but nonetheless praised the meal as "an embarrassment of riches that leaves one wanting more even when one has had ample". It was a place of swagged, tasselled curtains and rich red flock wallpaper, with plenty of brightly lit tables where a beau might entertain a lady he wished to impress – and be seen to be doing so – but also the odd dark niche where a married man might enjoy a discreet tryst with his mistress. It was a favourite haunt of wits, aesthetes and socialites, and indeed of Oscar Wilde, who was all three, as well as of grandees and nabobs of every stripe. Booking at least three months in advance was recommended.

Happily for Holmes, he knew the maître d', Georges. Better yet, the fellow owed him a favour.

"You recall the affair, don't you, Watson?" he said. "The case of near-fatal food poisoning at the restaurant where Georges previously worked? The substitution of spoiled beef for good? The malefactor who gave himself away by arranging the forks the wrong way round? No? It was one of those pettier problems that might make a nice little story for you to write someday. At any rate, Georges vowed he would never forget the help I gave him, and now, as if by a miracle, there has been a cancellation at Fontaine's and a table for two is mine."

"But who are you meeting there?" I asked. "More to the point, how does using a formless spawn as a messenger even work? As far as I could tell, the thing was mindless and speechless as well as formless."

"The average formless spawn may be that, but ours was not."

"You are speaking in riddles."

"All will be revealed, my friend. It is possible, of course, that I am wrong, and then I face the mortification of turning up at Fontaine's only to sit across from an empty chair all evening. But I do not think I am wrong. Let us meet up on Sunday morning, you and I, when I can regale you with everything that occurred."

I duly returned to Baker Street that Sunday, to find Holmes in a strange mood. He seemed enervated, bemused and whimsical all at once, and a smile kept playing at his lips, which, in one so habitually straight-faced as he, was a perturbing mannerism. I could see he had much to relate, for he was puffed up with anticipation, like a ripe peapod. At the same time, it was apparent that he did not know where to start, and he spent many minutes making sure that I was sitting comfortably and that my coffee cup was filled and that the fire was stoked in order to alleviate the autumnal chill pervading the room.

"Well now," he said, settling down in his chair at last, "what a night that was."

"You dined well?"

"Oh, excellently! The reputation of Fontaine's is richly deserved, and Georges could not have been a more punctilious host."

"And your guest? I presume he made it."

"She did."

"She?"

"And what congenial company she was, too," said Holmes. "Given that she and I had hitherto exchanged only a few words, we discovered we have a great deal in common and are highly sympathetic. Her physical attractions are manifold, for those with an eye for such things, but her mind... What a mind! And what talents she has, withal."

"Who are you talking about?" I said.

"Who do you think?"

"If pushed, I would say Irene Adler. She is the only woman about whom you would ever speak so rapturously."

Holmes nodded. "And she it was who joined me at Fontaine's. She who dined with me, drank with me, conversed with me at length, provided me with much valuable information, and in the end, as is becoming her custom, outplayed me."

"I am intrigued, to say the least," I said. "Tell me all."

*

I record the events at Fontaine's here just as Sherlock Holmes reported them to me, with a few added authorial inferences and interpolations of my own.

He sat down at his table at eight p.m. precisely, but it wasn't until a quarter past that his guest arrived.

"Mrs Norton," said Holmes, rising.

"Mr Holmes," replied she, settling into the chair which Georges the maître d' had drawn back for her. She offered Holmes a gloved hand across the table, which he shook before lowering himself back into his own chair.

"Madame's outer garments?" prompted Georges.

Irene Norton, née Adler, doffed her cloak, scarf and gloves and passed them to him. Then, after he had whisked them away, she and Holmes faced each other for a silent minute. Their table was in prime position, away from the main entrance and any draughts that might come in when the door was opened, and convenient for the kitchen but not so close that waiters would be constantly brushing past.

"I did ask you not to be late," said Holmes.

"And if you knew anything about women," came the rejoinder, "you would know that it is our prerogative to do as we please, which includes, if we so wish, being late."

"Wine?"

"Don't mind if I do."

Holmes had ordered a bottle of white Bordeaux, an 1870 Sauternes, per the sommelier's suggestion.

Even as he reached for the bottle, however, Georges was there, plucking it from its ice bucket and charging Irene's glass, then topping up Holmes's. The maître d' was as attentive as this all evening. He had an almost preternatural knack for knowing what his customers needed before they did and would glide into action whenever required and melt into the background straight after.

"Now then, Mrs Norton—"

"Shall we order first?" said Irene, interrupting.

"I've taken the liberty of doing that already."

"How very forward of you."

"Georges made recommendations from the *à la carte* menu. I'm certain that every course will be top-notch."

"Even so, that isn't how we do things in the States." Irene's New Jersey accent thickened as she expressed her disapproval. "A woman is entitled to her say in all aspects of life, including choice of food."

"But we are not in the States," Holmes pointed out.

"And another thing. It's not 'Mrs Norton'."

"Forgive me. I should have realised. You do not have a wedding ring on."

"I am not divorced. I simply prefer to go by my maiden name, which is also my stage name."

"Yet the absent wedding ring implies that all is not as it might be in the Norton household."

"If I'm honest…"

"Do be."

"I am not finding marriage to my liking."

"Why not? By all reports Godfrey Norton is a good man."

"That's just it. He is. Kind-hearted. Handsome, what's more. But also…"

"Uninteresting?"

"I thought it would suit me, being the wife of a lawyer," said Irene. "A man who is respectable, decent, reliable, with prospects. I thought it would bring stability to my life, and it did, for a while. But it turns out that it is also rather dull. The dinner parties, the Bar functions, the endless shop talk about this trial or that legal precedent – not my thing at all. And that cramped, fusty flat at the Inns of Court we have to squeeze ourselves into…! So Godfrey and I are trying to negotiate a way in which we can continue to coexist as spouses while each enjoying a degree of freedom. Until we have worked out a suitable compromise, I stay at Claridge's and my wedding ring stays in its box. But we are not here to discuss my marital status."

"Indeed not," said Holmes. "We are here to discuss your involvement in a scheme to cripple Britain by means of extortion, terror and intimidation."

Irene arched a perfectly plucked eyebrow. "When you put it like that, Mr Holmes, it sounds so shabby."

"How would you put it, Miss Adler?"

"A job," said she.

"A performance too."

"Performing *is* my job."

At that moment, a waiter appeared with two small plates. Like Georges, and all the staff at Fontaine's, he was French. "Madame, monsieur, an *amuse-bouche*. Compliments of the chef."

Each plate held a disc of toast topped with foie gras and a sprig of parsley. These canapés were no bigger in diameter than a florin and vanished in a single, flavoursome bite.

"So you do not deny you are part of an anti-British conspiracy?" said Holmes.

"Is it ever worth denying anything to Mr Sherlock Holmes?" came the reply. "Mr Sherlock Holmes always seems to know everything anyway."

"Not everything, Miss Adler."

"Oh, do call me Irene."

"In most instances," Holmes continued, "I know enough to form a concrete theory, but still there remains scope for conjecture. For the sake of completeness, I like to have the blank spaces filled in. Hence, we are here."

"Well, that may be why you are here. Perhaps I am here

simply because a man has invited me to Fontaine's, and who would turn down a free meal at Fontaine's?"

"I put it to you, Miss Adler—"

"I told you. Irene."

"I put it to you, Miss Adler, that as part of the aforementioned conspiracy you have applied your acting skills and passed yourself off as an array of women, each of whom has conveyed a message to a noteworthy Englishman, asking him to desist from a certain course, or else to act against his own best interests and those of the nation. You have then told him that the consequences of failing to do so would be quite literally monstrous."

"That certainly sounds like something I could do. I am highly versatile on the stage. I have been Rosina in *The Barber of Seville*, Maddalena in *Rigoletto*, Cornelia in *Giulio Cesare*, among others. I have played a few 'breeches roles', too, such as Maffio Orsini in Donizetti's *Lucrezia Borgia*."

"Is it not the case that contraltos are usually saddled with the part of the female villain?"

"Better to be that, surely, than some winsome soprano who sings interminable arias about some man she loves and can't have."

"The remarkable thing about the women I have mentioned," said Holmes, "is quite how unalike they were."

"I said I was versatile."

"Their heights, their complexions, their figures – all wildly varying. Yet I suppose a consummate operatic actress could adjust her appearance in such a way that she could look like almost anyone. Each woman, too, bore a passing resemblance to a woman who had some influence over the victim in question."

"Generally speaking, I'm the sort who does her homework. I like to be thorough."

"I do not doubt it," said Holmes. "Researching your intended target beforehand, seeking out a photograph or portrait of a female he loves or reveres in order to model yourself on her… Such things are well within the capabilities of one as resourceful as you."

"You honour me, sir, with this praise."

"I think you'll agree that everything I have just enumerated lies safely within the bounds of reason. What I find not so reasonable is how you could also alter yourself to become something inhuman."

"Inhuman?" said Irene.

"I refer, Miss Adler, to a shoggoth. To a byakhee. To a ghast. To a nightgaunt."

"You have stopped speaking English."

"I refer, also, to a formless spawn."

"Still not making much sense, Mr Holmes. How much of this delectable wine have you drunk?"

"There, there," said Holmes in mild rebuke. "The coquettish naïf? It ill behoves you. You know the words I am saying, or, even if you don't know the names, you are at least cognisant of the distinctive physical appearances of the monsters I have enumerated. You have been not merely the agent through which the extortion demands were imparted, you have been the medium of extortion. Convincingly impersonating others of your own species is one thing. Convincingly impersonating loathsome unearthly creatures is quite another. How you accomplished it is a mystery to me, one I would be delighted for you to clear up. Your move, Miss Adler."

*

Irene Adler paused for a moment. Around her and Holmes was the clink of cutlery on crockery and the thrum of idle conversation. Her eyes graced him with a look that carried both appraisal and approbation.

"My move, Mr Holmes?" said she. "Is this a dinner or a game of chess?"

"Perhaps it is a game of chess, in a manner of speaking," said Holmes. "Two minds vying across a table."

"Very well then. Let me offer a riposte to your challenge. If I were a conjuror, would you ask me how I pulled off a certain trick?"

"Not at all. I wouldn't have to. Conjuring tricks are easily penetrable. I have yet to see one I cannot parse. Whereas the ability to turn into monsters is nowhere near as explicable."

"Some would say it was impossible."

"Impossible to do perfectly. Your formless spawn, for instance, which is the only one I have had first-hand experience of… Traditionally a formless spawn is protean, changing shape almost continually. If threatened or attacked, it will retreat into the aspect whereby it is least susceptible to injury, namely an oozing liquid. Yours, however, maintained the same shape the entire time it was at Professor Mellingford's house, a blend of human, insect and cephalopod. This confirmed to me that it was a formless spawn in name only."

"Sherlock Holmes the logician," said Irene in an arch tone. "The paragon of rational thinking. The no-nonsense nonpareil of all that is practical and verifiable. Such is your reputation. And now you speak of monsters as if they were real?"

"Whether they are real or not," Holmes said carefully, "you yourself have given them corporeality. I should like to know how you did it."

"I should like to know why you think it was me."

"Because you too are protean, Miss Adler. More so than any ordinary actress – any ordinary human being, for that matter. I first suspected it some weeks ago, on the occasion when you addressed Watson and myself outside Baker Street in the guise of a young man."

Soup arrived, a veal consommé Breton garnished with julienned leek and celery. Holmes and Irene tucked in.

Between spoonfuls, Irene said, "This might be a good time for me to ask whether you intend to have me arrested. I mean, what is to prevent me standing up right now and walking out of here? You could grab ahold of me, sure, but then I would scream blue murder and accuse you of all manner of depravity. I am very capable of causing a scene, as you can well imagine, and I could do it in such a way that every red-blooded male in this room would set upon you in order to prove his masculinity and defend the honour of little old helpless me. By the time the dust had settled, you would be bruised and battered and I would be long gone."

"A fascinating scenario," said Holmes, "and a plausible one. In counterargument, I offer you this. Call it my version of the Sicilian Defence in chess. The Sherlockian Defence, if you will. There are a dozen people in the restaurant who are in my employ. I have salted the place with paid agents, among both diners and waiting staff, and all of them are poised to spring into action should anything untoward occur at this table. They are watching us closely, even if it appears they are not. For instance, that lady of a certain age over there, behind you, dining on her own."

Irene cast a subtle glance over her shoulder. "I see her. The one with the hatchet face and the string of pearls. The wealthy-dowager type."

"So she would have you think. In actual fact she is Molly Upshaw."

"Should I know the name?"

"Why would you? Mrs Upshaw runs a refuge for waifs and strays on the Isle of Dogs. She is as tough as old boots but has a big heart. Children in the East End know they can go to her if they are in trouble and she will shield them from harm. She and I have collaborated in the past, and she is happy to help me out now in exchange for a modest donation to assist with her cause. Then there is that youthful pair billing and cooing over by the window."

"Love's young dream."

"Pinkerton agents whose speciality is posing as infatuated lovers."

"Ah, that rare thing, a female Pinkerton," said Irene.

"Following in the footsteps of the great Kate Warne, who uncovered the Baltimore Plot to assassinate Lincoln. If this one is half as gutsy as Mrs Warne, then she's my kind of girl."

"She and her partner are pursuing a corrupt Chicago union boss who has fled to England to escape charges. The trail has led them to London, but they have agreed to take time out from their investigation to work for me. There are yet others who are in my employ. The old married couple three tables away. The sandy-haired fellow with the outmoded four-in-hand necktie, and his companion in the loud check suit. That waiter with the curly hair."

"The Adonis?"

"The one just passing, with the salver perched on his fingertips."

"I didn't notice any salver. Too busy admiring his looks."

"Those are just some of my allies," said Holmes. "You will be under close surveillance the whole time you are here. Remember that."

"Well, you've certainly taken precautions," said Irene. "I'm flattered. Am I truly that dangerous?"

"Let's just say I am leaving nothing to chance."

"But what if I, too, have taken precautions? What if, for argument's sake, I were to reach into my handbag – this handbag here – and pull out a loaded Derringer? I could do it in a trice. One shot, straight to your heart, and then flee. I predict that, paid agents or not, in the confusion following the gunshot I would stand good odds of making a clean getaway."

"An eventuality I have foreseen," said Holmes. "The moment I detect a hint of trouble from you, I shall give a prearranged signal. Produce your Derringer by all means, but all it takes is a gesture from me, and you will suddenly find a host of guns pointing at *you*. You might kill me, but you yourself would live for only a split second longer. That is assuming you even have the gun."

"A girl should go nowhere without a gun, not even to a

posh restaurant. It's the American way." Irene shrugged her shoulders. "Well then. All things considered, it would seem we are already at stalemate."

"I would go further than that and say I have you in mate. There are limited moves available to you."

She favoured him with a quirky, lopsided smile. "If you insist. It certainly seems that this restaurant is a trap – a gilded one, but a trap nonetheless – and I have blundered into it and its jaws have closed on me and there is not a hope of escape. Bravo." She clapped her hands softly and ironically. "I suppose, therefore, that I have no choice but to tell all."

"We could spend the rest of the meal chatting inconsequentially, or failing that in awkward silence," said Holmes, "but yes, you telling all would be my preference."

Irene finished her consommé, then said, "It was two and a half years ago in Brattleboro, Vermont…"

*

It was two and a half years ago in Brattleboro, Vermont, and the Trenton Opera Company were nearing the end of a tour of New England. Based at the Taylor Opera House in New Jersey's capital city, the company had spent most of the winter and early spring zigzagging through Connecticut, New Hampshire and Massachusetts, with occasional forays northward into Maine, playing a selection of scenes, duets and arias in theatres and music halls before small but appreciative audiences. It was not what you might call profitable but it usefully occupied an otherwise fallow period and helped keep the performers' voices in trim, ready for the summer season.

Irene Adler was the star attraction. Her turn, towards the end of the show, was always hotly anticipated. When she sang, she held an auditorium spellbound from first note to last. Her rendition of *"Ah! fors'è lui che l'anima"* from *La Traviata* was invariably met with rapturous applause, and who better to express Violetta's longing for freedom and the right to lead her own life than a woman who espoused those very ideals herself?

Not every show put on by the Trenton Opera Company was a triumph. A night at the Essex County Playhouse in Arkham, Massachusetts was plagued by problems, from instruments in the orchestra spontaneously going out of tune and limelights refusing to work, to the curtain being rung down when it shouldn't and not rising when it should. None of these technical hitches could be ascribed to human error. It was almost as though some malignant power resented the pleasure the company gave and was doing its best to ruin the occasion. Meanwhile in a musty, mildewed town hall at the port of Innsmouth, also in Massachusetts, the audience were oddly muted. Throughout the performance they sat there barely moving, their eyes reflecting the stage lights in a strange, blankly pale fashion. When they clapped, the sound was feeble and muffled. "Damp" was the word that sprang to mind.

By the time the company reached Brattleboro, in the foothills of the Green Mountains, the performers had been travelling for several weeks and were starting to tire of one another. All that time spent cooped up together in railcars and average-at-best hotels was generating the kind of familiarity that bred contempt. Irene was becoming sick of one of her co-stars in particular, a tenor who had only just joined the group. He had set his cap at her and would not take no for an answer. He thought he was rakishly irresistible. She thought he was a pest.

They had a rest day at Brattleboro, and Irene wanted very much to spend some time on her own. So she arranged a little excursion for herself, hiring a buckboard wagon and heading out of town to sightsee. The countryside around those parts was pretty, all secluded valleys and rolling forest, interspersed with covered bridges crossing placid rivers and quaint villages where the nineteenth century had barely begun to make inroads.

She drove northward at a steady lick. The sun was warm

and the budding tree branches cast dappled shadows on the roadway. After a while she was pleasantly lost, and as it was nearing lunchtime she stopped at an inn a few miles outside Bellows Falls.

The place didn't look up to much but she was hungry and doubted she would find anything better nearby. As she entered, she spied a playbill posted on a message board by the door. It was for the Trenton Opera Company tour, and among the acts featured upon it, there, prominently, was herself. Her name was accompanied by a fairly accurate likeness of her face, above the legend "The Beauteous Singing Sensation! The Canary of New Jersey!" It would have been churlish to argue with the first of the two epithets, but she was not much fond of the second. Canaries did nothing but sit in cages and aimlessly tweet.

There were a dozen or so locals dining at the inn, and Irene took a table as far from everyone else as she could. She hoped nobody would recognise her, but that hope was dashed when the innkeeper's wife came to take her order.

"Why, it can't be!" the woman declared, bunching her hands beneath her chin. "Oh my, but it is. You *are* Irene Adler, ma'am, are you not?"

What could Irene do but give a gracious nod of assent. She could not pretend she was someone else, not with her own image displayed right outside the inn.

"My dear Lord!" said the innkeeper's wife. "We saw you sing but two nights ago, over in Londonderry. It was magical. Hank! Hank!" She was calling to her husband at the bar. "Hank, look who it is. Irene Adler. At our inn, no less."

The innkeeper came over, beaming from ear to ear. "Miss Adler. An honour. We heard you sing just the other evening, over at —"

"Yes, dear, I've already told her that," said his wife.

"I said to Betsy here afterwards, 'Betsy,' I said, 'I'm not the opera-going type, but that Irene Adler, I think she might have made a convert out of me.' Didn't I say that, Betsy?"

"You sure did, Hank."

"And you know what she said to me? She said, 'Are you sure it was her singing and not those bewitching eyes of hers?'" The innkeeper guffawed. "She's a pistol, my Betsy."

Irene ventured a polite laugh.

"Anyways, what'll you be having? It's on the house. Anything you fancy."

"I insist on paying."

"The Canary of New Jersey pay? No, sirree. Not at my inn."

The meal was mostly indifferent, although the gravy and biscuits were not bad. Finishing, Irene rose to go, only for the innkeeper to sidle over to her with a sheepish look, his wife just behind him.

"Would it be an imposition, Miss Adler, if I were to ask a favour?"

"You'd like an autograph?"

"Well now, that would be mighty kind, and no mistake. But actually I was wondering if you wouldn't mind… Only if it's not too much bother… But if you'd be agreeable to…"

His wife dug an elbow into his ribs. "Out with it, Hank."

"Would you sing for us? Don't have to be a lot. Just a couple of tunes. Thing is, we don't get much in the way of culture out here in the sticks, and I'm quite sure these folks" – he motioned at the other diners – "won't ever have heard a voice like yours. Of course, if I've overstepped the mark…"

Irene could hardly refuse his request. She had just had a free meal, after all. It wouldn't hurt to, as it were, sing for her supper.

At her nod, the innkeeper preened with delight and, in a loud voice, demanded hush from the room. Then, with all the hyperbole and swagger of a circus ringmaster, he introduced her. "Trust me, folks, you are in for a treat. You won't have heard the like in all your born days."

Irene bowed to her audience and launched into "*Voi che*

sapete" from *The Marriage of Figaro*. She thought the tune famous enough that even these boondock-dwellers would know it, but her performance drew blank looks and the applause at the end was polite rather than enthusiastic. Sensibly, she switched to traditional songs: "I Bought Me a Cat", "Hush, Little Baby", "Oh Shenandoah". These went down a storm, with everyone joining in. By the time she was done, Irene had won over the entire room. She left the inn to the accompaniment of whoops and cheers.

Outside, as she was unhitching the wagon, she was approached by two men who had followed her out. They were both of them lean, raw-boned backwoods types. One had a long, square-cut beard that went down to his collarbone, while the other sported a wispy moustache and a battered Unionist forage cap. Each had a rifle slung over his shoulder, a Winchester repeater.

The backwoodsman with the cap removed it and, clutching the brim with both hands, said, "Pardon me, ma'am. Tain't like me ter do this kinda thing, but I just wanted ter tell ya, that were some downright beautiful singin'."

"Thank you for saying so," Irene replied.

"I think I now know what the angels are gonna sound like when I get to them pearly gates."

The other backwoodsman butted in. "Sinner like you, Natty, you ain't ever gettin' to no pearly gates, that's fer damn sure. Hell no."

The one called Natty rounded on his companion. "You mind your mouth, Zeke," he snapped. "This here's a proper lady. She don't want to hear none of that 'damn' and 'hell' talk." He turned back to Irene. "I apologise for my friend. He lacks couth."

"It's fine," Irene said. "But I appreciate your good manners, sir, and your gratitude. Now, if you wouldn't mind, I'll be on my way."

"Of course, ma'am. Of course. I just wanted to tell ya

that it ain't only your voice that impressed me so. It's the way you were actin' out the songs while you were singing 'em. That first one especially. I don't know nothin' about that fancy opera stuff, but even so I could tell you were becomin' someone else as you sang. You got sorta all wide-eyed and youthful. Leastways, that's the impression I had."

"Well, Mr…"

"Natty. Just Natty'll do. Ain't no one calls me Nathaniel, not since my ma died."

"Well, Natty, you may not know opera but you are perceptive all the same. As it happens, that aria is sung onstage by a boy. Or rather, the role – Cherubino – is customarily played by an actress dressed as a boy. He's an amorous adolescent page who gets up to all sorts of high jinks."

"Then that makes sense," said Natty. "It's a heck of a gift you've got, miss, an' I'm mighty glad that you happened our way."

"Me too," said Zeke.

"You're both most kind." Irene made moves to climb back up onto the wagon.

"Sorta makes me feel bad 'bout doin' this."

Irene looked round in time to see Natty swinging his rifle at her, butt first. Light exploded across her vision, followed by darkness.

*

Some time later, Irene came to. She was bound hand and foot and draped belly-down over a horse's saddle. She felt sick and dizzy. The horse was plodding along an uneven forest trail, and with every jolt of movement, a spike of pain went through her head and her nausea worsened. She could not suppress a moan.

She heard Zeke's voice. "Think she's waking up, Natty."

"'Bout time," Natty replied. "I was beginnin' ter worry I mighta hit her too hard. Miss Adler? Miss Adler?"

Irene turned her head to see Natty's face – upside down, since she herself was inverted – leaning close to hers. He and Zeke were walking alongside the horse.

"Gotta tell ya, I sure do regret treatin' you like this," he said. "Tain't how a lady oughta be tret."

"Untie me," Irene said thickly. "Let me go, right now, and I swear there won't be any repercussions."

"Can't do that," Natty replied, with a rueful shake of the head. "We gotta get ya where we gotta get ya."

"And where is that?"

"You'll see."

The bumping, swaying journey continued for half an hour more. Irene focused on breathing steadily, trying to clear her head. She wanted to have her wits about her when they reached their destination, wherever that was. The moment she was off this horse, she would show Natty and Zeke what a serious mistake they had made. Even trussed up, she was far from helpless.

Finally the horse was halted. Natty and Zeke heaved her off its back and lowered her to the ground. Irene paused to get her bearings. They were in deep woods. There was nothing to be seen but verdure and nothing to be heard but birdsong and the breeze rustling the branches.

"Gonna free up your feet now," Natty said, "but your hands are gonna stay tied. We got us some walkin' ter do, see."

As he loosened the knots at her ankles, Irene raised both arms and whacked her elbows down hard onto the top of his forage cap. Natty yelped and tumbled backwards, clutching his head. Irene tugged the ropes from her feet, staggered upright and made a run for it.

A rifle shot rang out. Irene heard the bullet buzz past within inches of her head.

"If I were you, Miss Adler, I wouldn't go a step further," said Zeke.

Irene ran on. She heard the Winchester's action being worked.

"I'm warnin' ya. I'm a darned good shot. I can clip the whiskers off of a muskrat at fifty yards."

A second bullet came her way. This one went through the puffed sleeve of her jacket, practically grazing the skin of her arm.

Zeke had not been lying about his marksmanship.

"Care to try for a third? Mebbe in the leg? We need you alive, but nobody said nothin' about intact."

Irene slowed to a halt. Grudgingly, sullenly, she turned round.

"That's better," said Zeke, squinting down the rifle's sights. "Now, you just walk back this-a-way, nice an' easy."

Natty got up off the ground, rubbing the crown of his head. "You're a tricky minx fer sure, Miss Adler. Guess I shoulda seen that comin'. Good thing I got such a thick skull." He put his cap back on. "Zeke, keep that gun trained on her. I'm gonna put these ropes back on her feet, but this time I'm gonna hobble her."

He did as promised. Now Irene's ankles were attached to each other with enough slack in the rope for a stride length but no more. Her hands remained fastened in front of her.

"We're gonna leave the trail," Natty said, "and head off cross-country. I see you got some sorta pants on rather'n a skirt."

"They're called Turkish pantaloons," Irene said tartly. "As recommended by the suffragist Elizabeth Smith Miller. They're practical while at the same time preserving feminine modesty."

"Handy for walkin', that's fer sure. Same goes for them boots of yours." They were sturdy side-buttoning boots, calf-length, with low heels.

"I hadn't anticipated I would be going on a trail hike today," Irene said, "but now I'm glad I chose to dress as I did."

They left the horse tethered and set off in a line, with Natty at the vanguard and Zeke taking up the rear, his rifle aimed at Irene's back. The terrain was rugged and the journey was mostly uphill, through dense undergrowth. It would have been tough going even if Irene had had full, uninhibited use of her limbs. She stumbled more than once.

They waded across a shallow stream just above where it debouched into a gorge as a waterfall. They scrambled up a boulder-strewn slope. They skirted the occasional fallen tree. Now and then Natty would glance round and enquire whether Irene wanted to rest. She shook her head adamantly and continued onward, matching him and Zeke step for step.

If only her hands weren't fastened. Then she could have reached for the gun she kept tucked into the waistband of her pantaloons. She could feel it there, just above her tailbone and hidden by the flap of her jacket: her Remington Model 95 Derringer. The tiny nickel-plated, double-barrelled pistol was a pretty thing with an ivory-inlaid grip. It held only two bullets, but under the circumstances two would suffice. The .41 rimfire rounds were tiny but perfectly effective, not least at point blank range.

"Where are we?" Irene asked. "Where are you taking me?" She could only assume the backwoodsmen had abducted her for nefarious purposes. They were leading her to a remote location, somewhere where a person's screams would never be heard, and there they would attempt something unspeakable. But an attempt was all it would be, let there be no doubt about that.

"Place called Round Hill," said Natty.

"And what's at Round Hill?"

"We gonna tell her, Natty?" said Zeke.

"Don't see why not. It's this stone, see. This big black stone."

"You've dragged me miles out into the wilderness," Irene said, "against my will, all in order to show me a stone?"

"Yeah, but tain't just any stone," said Zeke. "Nuh-uh. It's a stone as came here from up there." He pointed skyward. "Way up there."

"From space? A meteorite?"

"Guess you could call it that. Came down this-a-way just last year. Me'n Natty was out huntin'. Came this sudden streak of light in the sky, blinding bright."

"A thunderclap, too," said Natty. "Fair split the earholes."

"We saw that streak comin' in at an angle, and it went down over the horizon, and I said to Natty, 'Whatever that is, it's gonna hit over by Round Hill,' 'cause I know the lay of the land round these parts. Then another loud thunderclap reached us, the sound of that thing smashing into the earth, and we spied this kinda plume of smoke rising up. Only, tweren't smoke, it was a bunch of dirt and such, all thrown up high into the air. I knew a bit about meteors and so forth, and I was all in favour of going over there to Round Hill and taking a look-see. Natty weren't so sold on the idea, but I talked him round, on account of I'd heard that scientists and museums and suchlike pay top dollar for rocks from space."

"That sure got me interested," said Natty.

"Took us a day or so to find the meteorite," Zeke said. "You can see for yourself how thick these woods are, but then we came across the mess it left behind as it came in to land. Trees with their tops torn off, some knocked over altogether, broken branches lying around – a whole trail of debris, like a small hurricane had been through. Then there was the meteorite itself. It had pounded into the earth and was lyin' there half buried in the middle of this crater, and it was all steamin' and such, an' givin' off heat. But what was strange about it was how it didn't look like just any old rock. It weren't rough or lumpy or nothin'. It had a shape, edges, like it had been sculpted. Stranger still, there were all these growths around it."

"Growths?" said Irene.

"Sure. In the crater. As though seeds or somethin' had

scattered off the rock when it came down, and already they'd taken root and were sproutin'. Natty and me, we went for a closer look, only we were cautious about it."

"Mighty cautious," said Natty.

"We saw that those growths were plants," said Zeke, "mushrooms an' lichens an' the kind. But none like either of us had ever seen before. They were plants you wouldn't find the match of anywhere else. Not here in Windham County, not in Vermont, mebbe not anywhere in the whole wide world."

"Plants from space," said Natty, "same as the rock."

"The meteorite itself, now that we were up close to it, had these markings. I couldn't make head nor tail of them, but I could only think they were in some language I didn't recognise. All in all, Natty and I realised we had something extraordinary on our hands. We made camp and spent awhiles discussin' what we were gonna do. How to dig the meteorite up. How to get it back to civilisation. How to convince some scientist types it was a genuine space rock and we weren't just some fraudsters tryin' ter make a fast buck. And all the time, the mushroomy growths kept growing, getting bigger and spreading, so fast you could almost see it happenin' in front of you. Wasn't long after that that we learned somethin' about what they could do."

"Do?" said Irene.

"You'll find out for yourself soon enough," Zeke said. "'Tain't much farther. Just up over yonder ridge. Ten minutes an' we'll be there."

*

Irene was confused but also, in spite of everything, intrigued. This was no mere fancy yarn Natty and Zeke were spinning – the meteorite, the markings on it, the strange growths around it. There was depth of detail to the story, more than she believed simple men like these could have dreamed up. It really was as though they had something they wanted to share with her, no matter that they had felt obliged to knock her unconscious and frogmarch her through lonely, trackless woods in order to get her to it.

Her head was still throbbing from the blow from Natty's rifle stock. The pain was centred around the contusion she could feel tightening the skin on her brow just above one eye. Meanwhile the Derringer dug into her lower spine, tantalisingly close yet for the moment unreachable. She was thirsty. She was angry. Meteorite notwithstanding, there would be a reckoning, she vowed. Natty and Zeke would not get away with this.

They forged onward. Irene became aware that the sky was darkening – or was it that the tree branches overhead were more densely clustered here than elsewhere, filtering the sunlight more effectively? She detected an unusual smell in the air, too. Overlaying the agreeable odour of woodland vegetation was something sharp and pungent, a little like bleach and a little like yeast.

Not long after, they crested the ridge, and there, as promised, a few yards below where they stood, lay a big black stone.

The meteorite sat at the centre of a circular depression, embedded in the soil. It was roughly pyramidal in shape and about twelve feet tall, the exposed part of it. On its sides were markings, as Natty had described – columns of weird hieroglyphs carved into the surface. They resembled no script, ancient or modern, that Irene knew of.

The two backwoodsmen had not been lying about the plants, either. The ground surrounding the meteorite was a riot of strange, fantastic growths. Some were tall and fronded, others squat and lobate. Some were mushroom-like, with intricately frilled caps, while others were shiny bulbous excrescences sprouting upward from filaments which threaded this way and that across the earth in veiny profusion. Their colouring ran the gamut of purples, yellows and greys, all the shades of a bruise, with here and there a splash of bright scarlet or tawny gold. Irene had never beheld the like. In a way, the plants were more fascinating, and puzzling, than the stone from space.

"This is where we part ways," said Natty. "You go on down, miss. Me an' Zeke are staying put here."

"Will you at least undo these ropes?" Irene said. "You've got your rifles, and we know Zeke's a dead shot. What can I possibly do as long as you're armed and I'm not?"

The two men conferred briefly.

"All right then," said Natty. He produced a bowie knife and severed all the ropes.

Irene rubbed her chafed wrists. "Thank you. And I'm to walk to the meteorite, is that right?"

"If you would."

"And then what?"

"Wait an' see."

Irene set off down into the depression. She picked a careful path through the assorted fungal flora, stopping when she reached the meteorite.

Closer to, the hieroglyphs looked even more bizarre and incomprehensible. Some of them might have been pictorial, but representing what? Nothing appreciably earthly, that was certain. Nothing animal or vegetable or human. Some of them seemed just chaotic scribbles, such as a child might make with crayon on paper. Some, by the same token, had the stark simplicity of Nordic runes. The carving throughout was neat and precise.

The meteorite itself was so black that it might have been pure anthracite, yet unlike anthracite it was not dusty or brittle-looking. Rather, it was smooth and hard, and its surface caught the light in a way that lent it an almost iridescent lustre.

In addition to the hieroglyphs there were indentations in the stone, set at regular intervals. Each was a couple of inches deep and four or five wide and had a fringe of jagged glass shards around the inside of its rim. Further fragments of glass lay around the base of the meteorite, and Irene assumed that the indentations had been sealed pockets whose glass covers had shattered when the rock hit the ground, releasing whatever lay within. It was not difficult to infer what their contents had been: the fungal spores that had seeded the ground around the meteorite.

Having examined the meteorite for a minute or so, Irene straightened up and turned to face Natty and Zeke. Her back was to the rock now, and with it her hidden Derringer. All she had to do was get a hand to the gun without either of the backwoodsmen noticing.

"Well?" she said.

"Hold on, Miss Adler," said Natty. "Shouldn't be long."

"Until what happens?"

"They been lookin' for somebody like you." Natty said this as though it explained, indeed excused, everything. "Charged us with findin' somebody like you."

"Somebody adaptable," said Zeke.

"Yeah, that's it. Adaptable. And when we saw you singing, performing like you did – well, you just fit the bill."

"They want you. They need you."

"'They'?" said Irene. Making it look like just some casual gesture, she slid both hands behind her back. "What are you talking about? Who are 'they'?"

"The Outer Ones," said Natty. "The Outside Things. They got lotsa names."

"We're just doin' as they've told us," said Zeke.

"You should feel honoured, Miss Adler," Natty added. "What's about ter happen, it's a great privilege."

"But you've brought me here to kill me," Irene said. "Am I wrong? That's why you're keeping those Winchesters pointed at me. Do you think this is some sort of holy place? Am I to be a human sacrifice?"

"No, that ain't it at all," said Zeke. "These here guns is just ter make sure you stay right where you are."

"Me an' Zeke," said Natty, "we been comin' up to this spot regular-like, ever since we found the stone. It's become our secret place. Our special place. Them plants down there, see, they ain't any ordinary plants. They got this dust as comes off of 'em."

"Sorta like a powder."

"Yeah. An' it puts these voices in your head when you breathe it in, and you can hold a conversation with beings from far, far away. Leastways, the dust from one kinda plant can. Another kind, well, it gives a fella dreams."

"Great dreams. Magical dreams."

"Better'n booze," said Natty wistfully. "Better'n opium."

Irene's mind raced. So this backwoods pair had found the meteorite and its attendant fungi, and discovered that one or more of the plants had hallucination-inducing properties. They had kept coming back to partake of the intoxicant, as though nature had furnished them with their own private moonshine still. This, to them, had seemed much more rewarding than selling the stone to a museum.

"You mean for me to breathe in that 'dream dust' too, don't you?" she said. "Whatever for?"

"Tain't for us to know," said Natty. "Like I told yer, we're just followin' orders."

"Whose? These Outer Ones you spoke of?"

Natty nodded.

"And what are they? Figments of your imagination? Because that's what any sensible person would assume."

With her left hand Irene covertly raised the flap of her jacket. Her right closed around the butt of the Derringer. The pistol's maximum effective range was twenty-five feet, which put Natty and Zeke just within hitting distance. It was no match for their rifles, so Irene would have to draw fast, aim true, and make both bullets count.

"They ain't no figments, Miss Adler," said Natty. "You'll see for yourself in but a moment. I think I speak for both Zeke an' me when I say I hope there's no hard feelin's. Weren't us as chose you, not azackly. Tain't your fault you're so… What's that word again, Zeke?"

"Adaptable."

Irene tensed, ready to whip out the pistol.

That was when she noticed that one of the fungi close by her feet had started to pulse. The plant was an almost perfect sphere, and its surface was glossy brown chased with streaks of gold. With each pulse, the fungus swelled a little bit larger and its skin – if that was the word for its outer integument – grew thinner, gradually becoming translucent. Within the fungus Irene could now see a cloud of fine particles frantically spinning and billowing, seemingly agitated by internal pressures. She knew that shooting Natty and Zeke was her priority. Somehow, though, she could not take her eyes off the pulsing, swelling fungus and the mesmerising miniature maelstrom contained within.

She heard Natty say, "Here we go. Looks just 'bout ready to blow."

Then, all at once, the fungus exploded.

Powder erupted into Irene's face. It went up her nose. It stung her eyes, temporarily blinding her. It was between her lips, in her mouth. She could taste it on her tongue, both mouldy and spicy.

Briefly, she thought of those puffball mushrooms which emit their spores by bursting. Mostly, however, she thought that she must not inhale. The backwoodsmen had talked about breathing in the dust from the fungi. That was what they wanted her to do. That was what was supposed to happen.

She rubbed at her eyes with her left hand. She spat the dust – was it spores? – from her mouth.

But it was there in her nostrils. It coated her tongue and the back of her mouth. She had a feeling she had already taken some of it into her lungs.

Her head began to swim. She brought the Derringer round

and up. Dimly she heard a shout of alarm from either Natty or Zeke. "Dammit, she got a gun!" She fired at random, loosing off both rounds in what she hoped was the right direction.

The world seesawed beneath her feet. It was too late. The dust *was* in her lungs. It must be.

She collapsed back against the black stone. Then she felt herself jumping, without actually having jumped. It was as though she were leaping out of her own body. Her soul was being wrenched free.

She flew.

*

She flew through the gulfs of space, in the emptiness between worlds. It was cold and dark, the stars just tiny white pinpricks amid the endless black.

She flew across an immeasurably vast distance, at an immeasurably vast speed. Planets whirled dizzyingly by, and clusters of asteroids, and a comet. The sun grew smaller and fainter at her back. She seemed to be zigzagging left and right, through a series of branching turns. It was as though she was being shuttled violently along a network of paths, following a predetermined course.

She flew to the outer reaches of the solar system, far beyond the gaze of any astronomical telescope. Ahead of her loomed a tiny planet that hung lonely and remote in the abyssal void. Around it a handful of moons orbited. They were not perfect globes like the Earth's satellite but, rather, were pitted grey blobs that put her in mind of decomposing potatoes.

Irene sensed that this world was her destination, and sure enough she soon had entered its atmosphere and was descending towards its rugged, gloomy surface. Still at some considerable altitude she passed above a city, and then another, each a dense cluster of teetering, angular buildings surrounded by barren land. Both were gone from her sight before she could gain more than a vague impression of them, but shortly a third city hove into view, this one larger than either of the others, a metropolis perhaps equal in size to Boston. Her hurtling, headlong flight took her straight towards it, until she was soaring above its streets.

She was now travelling so low and slowly that she could take in details. The buildings of the city were terraced towers that rose like crooked cyclopean needles, and their masonry was formed of a gleaming black mineral which was identical, she thought, to that of the meteorite on Round Hill near Bellows Falls in Vermont. She noted that the towers lacked windows of any kind, although they did have doors at their bases – tall trapezoidal portals whose lintels bore carvings akin to those on the black stone.

There were what appeared to be public gardens dotted around between these edifices, with various forms of fungus serving as lawn and hedge and shrub. There was a river too, winding sinuously through the city. Its waters were a black, pitch-like substance that oozed along like molasses between its rocky banks.

As Irene glided through this alien metropolis, she wondered at how empty it looked. With so many buildings, and all of them so tall, its streets ought to be teeming with inhabitants. Yet wherever her gaze alighted, she saw no living creature. Dust piled up in drifts on the roadways, and the gardens looked rank and bedraggled, their paths all but obliterated by fungal growth. The city appeared, if not deserted, then unfrequented, and forlorn, too, as though its best days were long past.

Her rate of progress slowed further, and then, with whipcrack suddenness, she descended to the ground.

She stood for a while, dazed and disorientated. Little by little she recovered her wits and took stock of her surroundings. Light came from clumps of luminous fungi that were suspended from poles in a web of gelatinous threads. By their dim blue effulgence she saw that she was in an open space – an arena, she first thought, or a concourse – encircled by obelisks that were etched with more of those unfathomable hieroglyphs.

More imposing than these monoliths, and more unfathomable still, was a statue, which rose before her a good hundred feet high. It was fashioned in the likeness of some entity which almost defied description. It had mouths aplenty, this figure, each yawning wide and full of fangs, and it had tentacles in even greater quantity. Its legs were similar to those of a goat, and from numerous slitted apertures in its body smaller creatures were depicted emerging. They looked like maggots or grubs squirming their way out of necrotic flesh, but Irene sensed that they were actually the larger entity's brood. The thing was a mother, and the sculptor had portrayed her in the throes of giving birth. Clearly she could issue forth dozens of progeny at once, and perhaps it was a continuous act. Perhaps she was never not spawning.

What else could this misbegotten monstrosity be but a goddess in effigy? The arena, by inference, must be a place of worship, a temple dedicated to the hideous goddess and held sacred by whatever beings called this far-flung planet home.

At that point, just as Irene entertained this thought, a handful of the world's indigenes appeared.

They filed out from a nearby doorway in a procession, borne aloft on transparent wings akin to a dragonfly's. They had curved, pinkish bodies, each around five feet long, with segmented carapaces and spindly limbs that hung in paired rows from their abdomens. Their heads were ovoid and eyeless, and glowed with an eerie lambency like that of a will-o'-the-wisp. In all, they numbered a score.

The frontmost among them halted before her, while the rest fanned out to either side. Hovering on blurs of wing, the creatures observed her silently. Every so often one of them would turn to its neighbour, and the glow of its head would change colour. Patterns of light would ripple across that egg-shaped appendage in every shade of the spectrum, and sometimes in shades Irene could not name or recognise. She quickly ascertained that this must be how these beings communicated with one another. The patterns and colours constituted speech.

The one at the front settled to the ground, coming to rest on its multiple legs and tucking its wings behind its back. The others followed suit. The frontmost bent its head towards Irene, and she perceived a set of small, beaklike mouth parts below that glowing mass. With them the creature now uttered words, in a faint, rasping voice that sounded like a wasp trapped under a glass.

"We welcome you, Irene Adler," it said. "We have transported you in spirit-form from Earth to our world, Yuggoth, and now, here in the temple of Shub-Niggurath, we greet you."

"Shub-Niggurath!" said the others, in similar buzzing voices. They bowed towards the statue. "*Iä! Iä!* Shub-Niggurath!"

Shub-Niggurath, Irene thought, must be the goddess memorialised as the statue. The creatures hailed her not only vocally but in ecstatic firework bursts of emerald light that spiralled across their heads.

The veneration petered out.

Irene, with some effort, found her own voice. "Who— *What* are you creatures?" she said to the one who had addressed her and whom she took to be their leader.

"The name we call ourselves is this." The lights of its head swirled crimson and yellow. "Your race know us as the Outer Ones and as the Outside Things. You also know us as Mi-Go. I myself have this name." Another complicated pattern of lights passed over its head. "In the spoken tongue, it is Glaw Za-Jooll. I am a high priest of Shub-Niggurath, blessed be her name."

Again, the other Mi-Go saluted their goddess. "*Iä! Iä!*"

"And why have you brought me here?" Irene asked High Priest Glaw Za-Jooll. "What do you want with me?"

"It is very simple. We wish you to work on our behalf, Irene Adler. You are to be our servant, and in return we shall bestow upon you abilities like no other of your kind has ever possessed."

"What if I don't want them? What if I am nobody's servant?"

"That is your choice," said Glaw Za-Jooll. "You were selected by certain associates of ours who deemed you a viable candidate, according to criteria we set. Whether you accept our gift and the terms that go with it is up to you."

Irene was torn between bewilderment and irritation. "Criteria?"

"We know what you are. You are one who performs for the entertainment of others. You excel at it. You inhabit the parts you play. You transform yourself. You are—"

"Adaptable," she said, echoing the adjective Natty and Zeke had used.

"Just so. We would take that adaptability and make of it a superior version. We would create an improved, exalted Irene Adler."

"At the price of serving you," said Irene.

"You would be beholden to us, yes."

"And what would that entail?"

"Errands. Favours. Nothing that is onerous, and nothing that would offend your sense of propriety."

"Sounds very vague. You'll forgive me if I don't leap at the opportunity."

"Would it influence your decision," said Glaw Za-Jooll, "if I told you that your spirit self cannot return to your body without our sanction? You are on Yuggoth for as long as we wish you to be. That means indefinitely, if we so choose."

"You're lying."

Glaw Za-Jooll wriggled his crustacean-like body in a manner that to Irene very much suggested a shrug. "Why need I lie? This temple is the terminus of a conduit between your world and ours. It serves not only to guide you thence to here but to bind you in place. You come and go at our bidding. If we decide not to let you leave, you are here for the duration. Your body on Earth will remain an empty shell, slowly withering until it expires. Your spirit self, of course, will then expire too."

"So this isn't a negotiation," Irene said. "I am a hostage."

"What you are being offered is a chance to become exceptional. You will be remade. You will be greater than you can ever imagine."

"I imagine I'm pretty great already." Irene felt she could allow herself a touch of flippancy. The whole situation was so incredible, so fantastical, that she was half convinced she was dreaming.

"You need to make up your mind, Irene Adler," Glaw Za-Jooll said. "Yuggoth orbits far from the sun, and time here passes more slowly than on your planet. A minute to us is an hour of Earth time. How much longer dare you leave your body untenanted? How much longer do you think it can last, starved of nutrition?"

"I don't believe you."

"Can you afford not to?" said Glaw Za-Jooll placidly.

The choice, then, appeared to be no choice at all. Accept the Mi-Go's proposition and the conditions that came with it, or die.

Did it even matter? Suppose none of this was actually happening. Suppose it was all just some fevered delirium brought on by exposure to the fungus. Then whatever answer she gave was irrelevant. A bargain struck with a phantasm of the brain was not binding.

Irene looked at Glaw Za-Jooll. The Mi-Go's head shimmered expectantly, like a glass bowl full of fireflies.

She said yes.

Glaw Za-Jooll signalled with one limb, and another Mi-Go approached her, carrying a fungus identical to the brown and gold one that had detonated in her face on Earth. The Mi-Go held it in front of her, and the fungus began to beat like a heart, swelling, swelling, until all at once it erupted. Dust billowed out around Irene in a cloud. And then…

*

"And then?" said Sherlock Holmes.

In front of him and Irene were dishes bearing the remains of their entrée – tournedos à la bordelaise with broccoli, leeks and new potatoes on the side, which they had been tucking into while Irene told her tale. The bottle of Sauternes had been finished and replaced by an 1858 Romanée-Conti.

"And then," Irene said, "I came round. I was back beside the meteorite, in that wretched fungus patch. Natty and Zeke were there too, up at the lip of the depression. It had gotten dark, and they had built themselves a campfire and were roasting a small animal on a spit.

"I tried to move, only to find that I was wedged in place somehow. I looked down to see that I was almost entirely encased by a fungus. It was a mass of grey frills and folds, somewhat like a honeycomb and also somewhat like a human brain, much the way a morel looks. Evidently it had grown over me while I was lying there, wreathing itself around my body, although leaving my face exposed. I struggled to free myself. The fungus's grip was none too tight, but I felt hopelessly weak and could not seem to get my muscles to work.

"Natty must have seen me stir, for he came over. 'Hey there, Miss Adler,' he said. 'Let me help.' He began prising the morel off me, tearing it away in chunks. Presently I was liberated from it, and Natty helped me up. I was chilly and light-headed, and famished, too. I could barely stand unaided.

"'Now, you don't you exert yourself none,' he said, putting an arm around my waist to support me. 'You've been out a long whiles.'

"'How long?' I asked, and his answer was it had been the best part of twelve hours. That surprised me, because I'd been on Yuggoth for barely minutes, or so it had felt. Glaw

Za-Jooll had not been lying about the difference in the rate at which time passed on his world and ours.

"Natty guided me over to the campfire, where I warmed my extremities and got my circulation going again. Zeke offered me a sliver of meat on the tip of his knife. I have no idea what it was. When asked, all he would say was that it was 'critter' and it was good eating. I think it may have been gopher, or maybe woodchuck. Anyhow, I took it and ate it."

"Not a patch on this beef, I should imagine," said Holmes.

"Believe me, hungry as I was at that moment, it tasted nearly as good. I gobbled it down and asked for more. I was still feeling as weak as a kitten, but the meat restored some of my strength.

"I saw by the firelight that Zeke had a wound in his biceps. It had been dressed, but blood was seeping through the bandage. I enquired about it, and he said, rather resentfully, that it was my fault. Turned out that one of my shots had found its mark.

"'I've had worse, mind,' Zeke said. 'Tain't hardly nothin', little peppercorn-size bullet like that there Derringer of yours fires. Stings a mite, is all. I'll live.'

"I was secretly gratified that I had at least meted out some retribution. I thought that perhaps, if I was lucky, the wound would become infected and Zeke would die of gangrene.

"Natty asked what I'd seen while I'd been unconscious. I said, 'Nothing,' but he didn't believe me.

"'Guess you don't have to share with me what happened, Miss Adler,' he said. 'That'll be between you and the Outer Ones. Tain't my business to pry. But that fungus that spread all over you while you was out cold – that's gonna have done somethin' to ya, you mark my words. Me an' Zeke watched it all swell up and cover you, and we both of us thought there's no way you were gonna be wrapped up in that stuff, snug as a caterpillar in a cocoon, and it not have some effect.'

"Truth be told, Mr Holmes, I had no idea what to make

of the whole incident. I knew I hadn't dreamt any of it – Yuggoth, the Mi-Go, High Priest Glaw Za-Jooll, the bargain we'd struck – even though it had all the hallmarks of a dream. I knew, too, that it had changed my life irrevocably, although how, I wasn't sure yet. I doubt you can understand."

"As a matter of fact, I can," said Holmes. "A few years ago I underwent a not dissimilar experience. But let us keep the focus on you for now, Miss Adler. I presume those sophisticates Natty and Zeke guided you back to civilisation."

"I had little alternative but to go with them. I could never have found my way out of those woods by myself. We set off at first light, and parted company at the inn. I cannot say I was sad to see the back of those two. Then again, they were nothing but courteous and respectful throughout the whole episode. If one is to be kidnapped and made to suffer a weird form of drugging, let it at least be done chivalrously.

"The Trenton Opera Company's tour continued to its end. I told none of the troupe what had occurred, although they must have noticed a difference in me. I became withdrawn, aloof. I sang as well as ever, but offstage happy-go-lucky Irene was gone. In her place was distant, moody Irene.

"That didn't deter my would-be suitor, the tenor. With only a week left of the tour, he became yet more persistent. I snapped at him constantly, but he appeared to take this as a token of affection.

"All the while I kept wondering when and how Glaw Za-Jooll's gift was going to show itself and what services I would be expected to perform for him and his fellow Mi-Go. That was during the times I believed I really had travelled to another planet and conversed with representatives of an alien race. Other times I was able to persuade myself it had all been just a hallucination and nothing about me had fundamentally changed.

"The very last night of the tour was at the Music Hall in Portsmouth, New Hampshire. We put on a great show, and afterwards there was a lot of celebratory drinking. I didn't feel like joining in, so I repaired to my dressing room. I was in there removing my makeup when someone knocked at the door. In came the tenor, without waiting to be invited. He was inebriated. You can well imagine what happened next."

"He tried to force himself upon you," said Holmes. "The poor fool. Most unwise."

"He seized hold of me, and I was puffed up with fury, all set to retaliate. My trusty Derringer was in my bag, which hung on a wall hook, out of reach. The nearest object to hand that could be pressed into service as a weapon was a hairbrush. I groped for it with every intent of stabbing the tenor somewhere sensitive with its pointed handle. That was when, all of a sudden, a look of sheer horror came over him. He let go of me and stumbled backwards. He was staring at me, his eyes bugging out.

"'My God,' he gasped. 'Oh my dear God.' And he wrenched open the door and fled, as though the Devil himself was at his heels.

"I could not for the life of me think what I had done to terrify him so. I had not even picked up the hairbrush yet. He had shied away from me, utterly repulsed, as though that which had been so very desirable had abruptly become abhorrent.

"I caught sight of myself in the dressing-room mirror. Mr Holmes... I *was* abhorrent. My face was not my own any more. I scarcely even recognised my reflection. You know how a funhouse mirror at a carnival distorts your image? I was looking at a funhouse-mirror Irene. Except, there was nothing comical about it. My features truly were malformed. I touched them with my fingers to check. The contours of my face felt lumpen and unfamiliar, exactly as the mirror showed.

"I lapsed into panic. What had happened to me? Was I ill? Did this disfigurement mark the onset of some loathsome disease? Would it spread to the rest of my body? Was *this* what that morel had done to me, some delayed effect of my contact with it?

"I urged myself to relax, to try and think clearly. As I did so, I observed that my face in the mirror grew less horrendous, more like its old self. Feeling a twinge of hope, I calmed myself further. In response, my features became yet more normal. Soon enough I was looking at good old Irene Adler again, as God made her."

"What became of the tenor?" said Holmes.

"Only a man would think it worthwhile asking that question," said Irene.

"Humour me. For the sake of completeness."

"If you must know, he resigned from the company that same night and we never saw him again. He didn't say why he quit. He left without explanation. Since he had been drunk, he doubtless was able to dismiss what he'd seen as an effect of the alcohol. Yet it obviously had a profound impact. I like to think that, ever since, he has been more circumspect in his dealings with women.

"As for me," Irene continued, "I now had an inkling with regard to the nature of Glaw Za-Jooll's gift. The morel that had cocooned me must have bestowed the ability to reshape my physique. In the privacy of my apartment, back in Trenton, I began experimenting. What had happened in the dressing room had been spontaneous. The rage that had overtaken me had manifested as that distended face. Now I needed to train myself to do consciously what I had done without thinking.

"Learning how to initiate and regulate the process was exhausting but exciting. I spent day after day sitting in front of a mirror, figuring out just what I could make my body do. There seemed no limit to it. I could change my complexion, my hair colour, the colour of my eyes. I could increase or decrease my bulk, redistributing my mass in various ways. I could alter my figure. I could become a man. I could be old, young, and anything in between. It required effort and concentration, and it wasn't always painless. Yet it was, as with any voyage of discovery, thrilling.

"Once I had mastered the technique, I knew that the life of an opera singer was no longer for me. I foresaw all the things I could do, the places I could go, the adventures I could have, now that I possessed the power to transform my appearance however I wished. I could pass myself off as somebody else and live as they did. I could make myself the duplicate of a millionaire, a captain of industry, even a president. I could walk into a jewellers pretending to be the manager and walk out with half the contents of the vault in my pockets. I could rob a bank in broad daylight, and the police would never find the person described by eyewitnesses. I could spy for the government or a foreign power, selling my skills to the highest bidder. The possibilities were endless."

"And for the next two and a half years, you proceeded to explore them all," said Holmes, "making quite a name for yourself in the process."

Irene nodded. "I roved across the States, and latterly Europe, using my newfound talent to line my pockets and, I may say, having a high old time. It's odd, Mr Holmes, that I am not detecting a hint of scepticism from you about any of this. Most people, when hearing about aliens and fungi and bizarre metamorphoses, would at least be raising an eyebrow, if not lapsing into outright mockery. Yet you, whose watchword is rationality, are taking it all in your stride."

"My reputation is one thing. I am another."

"So it would seem. Tell me, at what point did it occur to you that my own reputation – adventuress, mistress of disguise, troublemaker – was not all there was to me?"

"When you had the audacity to bid Watson and myself good morning outside Baker Street."

"You knew that was me?"

"I had a strong suspicion. It was in your personality to crow about a victory. Before then, I had heard you were something of a chameleon but had not seen it for myself. You overplayed your hand that day, and you overplayed it again when you waylaid Watson and myself on Romney Marsh, this time in the guise of a farmer."

Irene chuckled. "You knew that was me too?"

"Had you done it just the once, I might not have tumbled to it," said Holmes. "Twice running, and I could only infer that here was Irene Adler, up to her tricks. His singing voice was surprisingly good."

"Sometimes I just can't help it," Irene said with a self-deprecating sigh. "I am my own worst enemy."

"The farmer was a means of reconnaissance."

"Yes. Through him I was able to establish that you and Watson were shadowing Professor Mellingford on his route back from Rye and I could not therefore confront him the same way I had before. I needed to get him alone and unguarded if I was to terrify him as effectively as possible."

A waiter whisked their empty entrée plates away, and Georges appeared a moment later with their pudding course, îles flottantes.

"Monsieur's glass is empty," he said. "Let me refresh it."

"No," said Irene. "Let me."

Georges was about to object, but she shot him a look. "*Naturellement.* If madame insists."

She picked up Holmes's glass and tipped the last of the Romanée-Conti into it.

"Would madame care for a new bottle?" Georges asked. "Or some dessert wine, perhaps?"

"No thank you. A coffee would be nice, though."

"*Bien sûr.* Monsieur?"

"Not I," said Holmes.

Georges clicked his fingers to a junior waiter, then indicated Irene. "*Un café pour madame.*" The man scurried off.

Irene returned Holmes's glass to him, while Georges glided away to attend to another table.

"I don't dare drink that now," Holmes said, indicating his wine.

"Why not?"

"You could easily have adulterated it."

"You mean drugged it?"

"Or poisoned. I was looking for some sleight of hand while you poured the wine, a tablet or some powder being stealthily dropped in. I didn't see it, but that isn't to say it didn't happen."

"Oh pooh!" said Irene dismissively. "As if I would stoop to that."

"To get out of the bind I have put you in, I doubt there is anything you would not stoop to."

"I have been nothing but forthright all evening, Mr Holmes. I have dealt plainly with you. It has been pleasant, even, unburdening myself to you like this. I have enjoyed your company and this excellent meal. Why ruin all that with something as tawdry as drugging you?"

"Fair enough," said Holmes. "Then shall we conclude matters?"

"What else do you need to know?"

"Who you are working for. Who is behind the campaign of extortion you have been so instrumental in."

"You're not going to get that out of me," Irene said. "There are limits."

"One might reasonably infer that you are acting as thrall to the Outside Things. High Priest Glaw Za-Jooll has called upon you to discharge one of those 'favours' he mentioned. After almost three years spent gallivanting about, doing more or less as you please with the Mi-Go gift, now the time has come to pay your due."

"Again, my lips are sealed."

"You will at least admit, surely, that you have expanded your repertoire of impersonations to include monsters."

"Hardly worth denying."

"Drawn from the pages of Von Junzt's *Unaussprechlichen Tieren*."

"A bestiary as fascinating as it is repellent."

"And all this has been at Glaw Za-Jooll's instigation."

Irene just smiled prettily.

"Need I remind you of all my paid agents in this restaurant?" Holmes said. "You are not leaving here until you have told me every last thing."

"To do that would be more than my life is worth."

"Your life, Miss Adler, is currently in my hands. As I have said, with the merest gesture I can have guns pointed at you. I can have you arrested and imprisoned for sedition."

"But why would you? When I am so very fetching?" She batted her eyelashes at Holmes.

"You have no idea what I would do in order to get at the truth."

"I know this much: you would lie through your teeth."

"I'm not sure I understand your meaning," said Holmes.

"I'm sure you do," Irene said. "These paid agents of yours whom you insist the premises are littered with, your so-called Sherlockian Defence... A blatant bluff, sir."

"I promise you it is not."

"Tell me, then, how you were able to book so many tables at one of London's most exclusive restaurants at such short notice, and on a Saturday night, too. It's a wonder you managed even to get this one."

"I have my ways."

"An evasion, not an answer," said Irene. "But let's suppose you did somehow pull off the trick and your agents are indeed all around us. I shall now proceed to prove why each cannot be working for you, debunking them in the order in which you presented them... First, your Mrs Molly Upshaw, the East End angel of mercy posing as a wealthy dowager. I have been studying her throughout the meal, even though she is sitting behind me. Those pepper and salt cellars" – she pointed to the silver cruet set on the table – "are as good as having eyes in the back of one's head. The pearls Mrs Upshaw is wearing are the genuine article, not imitation, and therefore unaffordable to someone from the lower echelons."

"She has borrowed them for the occasion."

"And she ate her soup as only the well-bred do, tilting the bowl away from her and scooping the spoon outward rather than towards herself."

"I coached her beforehand in dining etiquette."

"And the Pinkerton pair? So mutually besotted are they that they have not glanced anywhere else so much as once. Surely a paid agent would have looked towards our table occasionally, keeping watch for your signal, but those two have had eyes only for each other all evening. Who are your next shammers? Ah yes, the old married couple. The husband is desperately near-sighted, Mr Holmes. I saw how he held the menu up to his face and squinted at it. He can barely see past his nose. I could leer at him right now like a gargoyle and he would not even notice. And you expect me to believe this half-blind mole is keeping watch on me, let alone trusted with a gun? As for the wife, she looks thoroughly miserable. They both do. I have seen marital indifference, and those two are perfect exemplars of it."

"Can you not accept that they might be excellent actors?"

"Take it from a professional, that level of shared loathing and ennui is hard to fake. You can acquire it only through bitter experience. Then there is the sandy-haired fellow with the four-in-hand necktie. You really blundered there, Mr Holmes. Unfortunately for you, you see, I happen to know him. He is a duke with whom I have had dealings, to his detriment and my profit. I know, too, his companion in the check suit. He is his secretary and acted as go-between when His Grace needed to recover, for a fee, certain compromising materials that came into my possession."

"Might it be that that is precisely why I employed the duo?"

said Holmes. "They know you and have good reason to want you behind bars."

"Unlikely, given that His Grace vowed he would shoot me if he ever saw me again. It's a good thing, as far as I'm concerned, that when his and my paths last crossed I looked very different. And finally, that curly-haired waiter. Now, he has not been able to take his eyes off me since I sat down, and to be fair, I have not minded at all. If you are truly acquainted with him, then I would very much like you to introduce us sometime. If, by the same token, you procured his services as a covert agent, expecting subtlety, you should ask for your money back. In short, Mr Holmes, pretending these strangers were in your employ was a neat piece of extemporisation but it has not held up to scrutiny."

"Believe what you wish, Miss Adler. We remain in stalemate."

"Do we?" said Irene.

"I have omitted to mention the two plainclothes policemen stationed outside the restaurant."

"You must be referring to the pair of tramps I saw as I arrived, squatting on the pavement across the road, begging."

The vexation Holmes felt must have shown on his face.

"Oh yes," Irene said with a merry laugh. "Their clothes may be rags and their faces dirtied, but otherwise those two make less than convincing vagrants. I dropped a shilling in their cup as I passed by. I have yet to meet tramps with such neat haircuts as theirs, or with fingernails so well trimmed."

"Even so," said Holmes, "they are under orders to detain you, should you happen to leave the premises unescorted."

"How will they know it's me, when I am capable of shifting into any shape I choose, as you are well aware?"

"Can you change the outfit you are wearing?"

"Not easily, I admit, but it isn't impossible. A tuck here, a little bit of rearranging there. I'm certain I can find some way of dodging them."

The waiter brought Irene her coffee. She thanked him, then levelled her gaze at Sherlock Holmes.

"The fact is, Mr Holmes, you are in mate, not I."

"How so?"

"You are not the only one who can claim to have a paid agent on the premises. And mine, unlike yours, is the genuine article. He is, as it happens, one of the waiters who has been serving us this evening. Not Georges, but one of his flunkeys. The old fellow with the receding chin and stupendously Gallic nose. Clovis is his name, and he used to have sizeable gambling debts. Now he does not. And in return for my generosity? Well, I can only assume you failed to detect a slight bitter tang to your îles flottantes. The sweetness will have covered it up."

Holmes looked down at his pudding. All that remained in the bowl was a scraping of custard and a few flecks of meringue. "Ah. I see. You lied about not drugging me."

"Don't worry," Irene said. "It's nothing fatal, just a powerful sleeping draught. Already it has begun to take effect. You may not have noticed but your speech is becoming slurred."

"It has done no such thing." Even as Holmes uttered the denial, he could hear how thick and clumsy the words sounded. His tongue was going numb. His lips felt like rubber.

Irene sipped her coffee. "You thought you were a move ahead, Sherlock. But I have been a move ahead of you."

Holmes registered that she had used his given name, and the familiarity this implied somehow did not strike him as inappropriate. He tried to raise an arm to seize hold of her. It would not budge.

"You…" he mumbled. "You have told me so much. Why not everything?"

"I have told you as much as I am willing to share." Irene's voice seemed to be coming from a long way away, deep in an echoing cave. "Rest assured that you have ruined my employers' extortion scheme and they see little point in pursuing it further.

Be content with that. But a word of advice. There is a wider plan in play. Plough your own furrow. Leave the rest of the field well alone."

She finished her coffee and rose from her seat. The room was now pitching and yawing around Holmes. He was a cockleshell boat in rough seas, tossed helplessly this way and that. Only by a supreme effort of will did he manage to remain upright in his chair. Apprehending Irene, even calling for assistance, was beyond him.

"All said and done," she said, "I have enjoyed myself tonight. There are few men I consider my equal, fewer still with whom I would be willing to engage in a battle of wits across a dinner table. It has been an invigorating duel. To bring the chess metaphor to a close: queen takes king. It was inevitable. Adieu, Sherlock Holmes."

The last thing my friend saw before passing out was Irene Adler blowing him a kiss.

*

"Good grief!" I said as Holmes concluded his narrative. "And she just left you there unconscious?"

"Slumped across the table," my friend replied. "I was lucky not to have ended up face down in what remained of my îles flottantes. Before exiting the restaurant, she did have the courtesy to slip Georges a pound note and ask him to take care of me. Something I'd eaten had disagreed with me, she told him. Georges could not have been more solicitous. I came round to find him bending over me, patting my cheek, brow furrowed in concern. All the other diners were staring and muttering. It was about a quarter of an hour before I fully regained my faculties. By then, of course, Miss Adler was long gone."

"Your two policemen failed to intercept her on her way out, I take it."

"She left by a tradesman's entrance at the rear," said

Holmes. "While everyone's attention was on me and my plight, her tame waiter – Clovis – smuggled her out through the kitchen, or so I gather. It was, I must admit, masterfully planned. If there is one consolation, it is that I did not have to pay for the meal. Georges would not hear of it. 'It is our fault if the food caused you upset, monsieur. We must compensate you somehow. The good name of Fontaine's must be upheld.'"

"And you didn't tell him you had been drugged? Oh, Holmes! For shame!"

"I didn't have the heart to. And my wallet was grateful for his offer. I am not made of money, Watson, and Fontaine's is far from cheap."

"You warned me that Miss Adler had outplayed you," I said. "I didn't realise quite how comprehensively."

"If one must lose, best lose to a worthy opponent."

"What now?" I said. "It seems there will be no more extortions. The Dagon Club will be pleased about that. But what about Irene Adler? She remains at large. Will you be pursuing her in the hope of bringing her to justice?"

"I'm not sure, Watson," Holmes said. "She is, if nothing else, elusive. Were she to go to ground, I don't think even I, with all my powers, would be able to unearth her."

"You know, it's funny. I have seen a photograph of the woman, but in the flesh I have encountered her only when masquerading as a man and a formless spawn. I wonder if I shall ever get to see with my own eyes what she actually looks like. I suspect not."

"And that would be your loss, Watson. Your great loss."

A thought occurred to me. "I wonder…"

"What do you wonder?" said Holmes. "Out with it."

"Well," I said, "it's the fungus connection. Miss Adler was granted her chameleonic abilities by a fungus."

"So?"

"Remember Dr Felder from earlier this year?"

"How could I forget him."

"He used fungus spores as a cancer treatment, and according to his notes he obtained them from an '*Amerikanische Frau*'. And is not Irene Adler an American woman?"

Holmes regarded me with a knowing look. "Well done, my friend."

"Ah. Of course, you had worked it out already."

"I have certainly entertained the idea that Felder's *Amerikanische Frau* might be Miss Adler. Given the role fungus played in her transformation from opera singer to mistress of metamorphosis, it is not difficult to draw a line from one to the other. Yet the supporting evidence is scant, and the reasoning scantier. If she gave Felder those spores, why? What does a potential cure for cancer have to do with a plot to weaken the foundations of the empire? The two things would seem to run counter to each other."

"Unless she already knew, as Felder did not, that those spores cause more harm than good. There are many ways to sabotage a nation. Killing ordinary citizens is one."

"Killing them and then bringing them back to life, or at least a semblance thereof? No. Nor could Felder's cancer treatment ever have been utilised in such quantities as to affect the population significantly."

"It might lower national morale to have the undead running riot," I pointed out.

"That I cannot gainsay," said Holmes. "So far, however, no other doctor has made an attempt to replicate Felder's work, at least to our knowledge. That suggests to me that the whole enterprise is a dead end. Something was tried and found not to succeed."

"So much for that theory," I said.

"On the contrary. I don't believe that the fungus connection, as you put it, is coincidental. I perceive fragments of some kind of grand conspiracy here. What I am unable to do, as yet, is piece those fragments together into anything meaningful. Miss Adler spoke of 'employers' with plans.

Who are they? The Mi-Go? Or beings of a more terrestrial persuasion? And what of the 'wider plan' she alluded to? Hum."

Holmes sank back into his chair and his eyes took on that defocused, faraway look that told me he was lost in thought. He might remain in this state for hours, perhaps availing himself of pipe or cigarette but otherwise not moving or communicating in any way. Were I to speak to him, at best I would receive a grunt in reply, and else a terse rebuke. I took my hat and coat and my leave.

Homeward bound, I wondered how soon it would be before my friend alighted upon the solution to the problem. Surely not long.

Nor would it be long, I thought, before Irene Adler – this woman whose continual besting of Holmes only seemed to increase his esteem for her – re-entered his life.

On both counts, I could not have been more wrong.

PART III

Summer 1895

THE EVENTS OF SPRING 1895, WHICH BEGAN AT Bethlem Royal Hospital and ended in Essex, and which I have recounted in another of these secret histories, *Sherlock Holmes and the Miskatonic Monstrosities*, took a severe toll on Holmes. In the wake of that grisly and taxing adventure my friend lapsed into a state of nervous prostration lasting well over three months. During this period I was almost reluctant to leave Baker Street to go to work – I had by then become a widower and Holmes and I had resumed our cohabitation – for I feared I might return to find his condition worsened, even to the point of mortality. When he was not bedridden, too weak to rise, he would lounge around our rooms all day long in dressing gown and carpet slippers, and seldom did he venture outdoors unless absolutely necessary. None of the tonics I supplied him with roused him from his listless torpor for long, and he resorted frequently to a self-prescribed form of medication, namely the needle and a seven per cent solution of cocaine. Several times our landlady, Mrs Hudson, voiced her concern for his welfare to me, and all I could offer her in return were platitudes. In practical terms, my only recourse was to look after Holmes to the best of my abilities and pray he would rally.

Eventually he showed improvement and I was able to relax my vigilance. He was even well enough to take on the occasional case that came his way, although he would discharge it in a perfunctory fashion, with perhaps half the usual attentiveness. Equally, he might turn the prospective client away with an admonition to try the police instead. By then I was supporting both of us through my income as a general practitioner and my literary labours, so our finances were sound, but it aggrieved me to see Holmes wasting his talents.

At least I could console myself that he was no longer just plain wasting away.

During the seven years that had elapsed since his dinner at Fontaine's with Irene Adler, Holmes had made enquiries into the conspiracy of which she was a part, and also attempted to trace her activities. In neither endeavour did he meet with much success. He kept an eye out for reports of strange fungi and any reference to the aliens known as Mi-Go, Outside Things, et cetera. None was forthcoming. As for Miss Adler herself, every once in a while he might divine her handiwork in some society scandal or other – a blackmailing, an adulterous affair, a spectacular fall from grace – but never could he be sure, beyond a reasonable doubt, that she bore responsibility for it. She impinged on his sphere of consciousness like a fish rising to the surface of a pond; no sooner had the ripples appeared than she was gone, receding back into the murk.

Meanwhile he conducted research into the Mi-Go, consulting all the usual esoteric tomes. Information, however, was thin on the ground. He learned that the name Mi-Go was not one they had chosen. Rather, it had arisen on Earth thanks to reported historical sightings by Nepalese hill tribesmen of creatures which bore a superficial similarity to those extraterrestrial beings. Certain scholars of the occult had conflated these with the Nepalese folklore surrounding the Mi-Go, or Abominable Snowman, even though there was nothing to indicate that the two were one and the same. They had then conferred the name onto the Outside Things, perhaps through laziness, or perhaps because scholars have a tendency to want all aspects of the world organised and codified and will find order where there isn't necessarily any.

Holmes had developed a theory regarding Yuggoth itself, and to that end he had purchased an orrery – or rather, had prevailed upon me to purchase it for him – which he then modified, adding a ninth planet to its eight. This planet lay some way outside the known worlds of our solar system. He had inferred its location from details in Irene Adler's description of her journey to Yuggoth and also from scientific speculation regarding perturbations in the orbit of Uranus. Astronomers ascribed these to the gravitational pull of Neptune, but there was a growing consensus that another, as yet undiscovered planet lay beyond Neptune, and it – although being relatively small, perhaps no bigger than our moon – was also exerting an influence on Uranus. Holmes was firmly of the opinion that that planet was Yuggoth.

Now and then he would take the orrery down from the shelf, set it on the table, and study it. He would turn the handle and watch the little ivory spheres spin atop their brass armatures as the mechanism hidden in the base gently clicked. While the inner planets of this model solar system rotated quite fast, the outer planets moved more slowly, and Holmes's additional ninth planet, a tiny thing right at the periphery, was the slowest of all. Its progress was almost imperceptible even when he turned the handle swiftly.

On more than one occasion I found him sitting with the orrery partly dismantled in front of him, making adjustments to the extra gearing that he had installed to drive Yuggoth. Then he would reassemble it and once again watch the nine planets describe their circuits around the brass sun that sat static at their hub. His gaze would be fixed on Yuggoth as it inched along its course. For a day or so he would tinker with the orrery obsessively like this, taking it apart, fine-tuning it and putting it back together. Then the model would be returned to its shelf, where it might stay for months on end until the mood took him and he retrieved it.

"Yuggoth must be a dismal place," he told me once. "I estimate it to lie some three billion miles from the sun. It will be dark and freezing cold there all the time. The sun itself will appear not much larger than any other star in the sky, and a day, if a period of slightly alleviated gloom can be called a day, lasts approximately six times as long as a day on Earth.

The only form of vegetation that can possibly grow in such an environment is fungal. Fungi, unlike other plants, do not require sunlight in order to thrive. As for the Mi-Go, they are well suited to survive in such conditions, their insectile bodies being less susceptible to extreme cold than those of mammals. One might reasonably assume that fungi are their primary, indeed only, food source. One might even go further and posit that they have evolved a kind of symbiotic relationship with fungi. I suggest this because Miss Adler depicted them communicating with one another by means of luminescence in their heads. Several species of fungus are luminescent, so perhaps Mi-Go have, over the millennia, absorbed the relevant light-producing enzymes into their bodies and can manipulate these to generate patterns and hues as required."

"They seem to fascinate you," I said, "they and their world both."

"Why would they not, Watson? There has long been conjecture about the possibility of life on other planets. Camille Flammarion, the French astronomer, has written on the subject, as has his fellow countryman J-H Rosny. They have proposed the existence of, respectively, sentient plants and sentient crystals elsewhere in our solar system. But then the notion that aliens are real should be fascinating to anyone, the more so because these Outer Ones of ours have gone to the trouble of making contact with members of our race. It presents, in its way, as much of a revolution in mankind's understanding of his place in the universe as does the existence of Cthulhu, Nyarlathotep, Azathoth and their ilk. That said, we might ask ourselves why the Mi-Go are interested in us. What do they want? Are their intentions benign or otherwise?"

"They wrought changes in Irene Adler against her will," I said. "That is hardly benign."

"Perhaps they need emissaries. Perhaps Miss Adler and others are to be their representatives on Earth, tasked with promoting mutual understanding between our two races. The

Mi-Go have begun making overtures to us and will follow this up with full-blown diplomatic relations when the time is right."

"Do you really think so?"

"As things stand, I have no idea what to think, Watson," Holmes said. "There simply aren't sufficient data to extrapolate from. In time there will, I have no doubt, be more evidence to go on."

Such evidence arrived that summer.

*

One of the cases Holmes tackled shortly after recovering from his collapse concerned Peter Carey, a fifty-year-old retired whaler captain murdered at his home near Forest Row. Carey was a violent character who met a violent end, run through with a harpoon. This implement was driven into him with such force that it transfixed his body to the wall of his "cabin", a wooden outhouse where he slept at night, separate from wife, adult daughter and servants. In light of his vicious temper, and also his swarthy complexion, he had come to be known among those in his industry as Black Peter, and I appropriated the name for the title of the account I published chronicling the case in 1904.

As ever with my "official" writings, I embellished certain details of the affair and omitted certain others. For current purposes it suffices to say that Carey was killed by former shipmate Patrick Cairns, as in the published tale. However, the cause of the fatal argument between the two men was not a cache of stolen stock exchange securities – my own invention – but a certain tin box.

"Carey swore he no longer had it," Cairns said to Holmes, me and Inspector Hopkins after we three had apprehended him at Baker Street. "Told me he'd got rid of it. He had no right to do that. What was in that box belonged to the both of us. Besides, I was sure he was lying. He was never the type to throw anything away. You've seen his cabin, yes? Crammed with mementoes, it is. So I challenged him. 'Tell me where that damned box is,' I said. He kept insisting it was long gone, and good riddance. Well, there I was, with a fair bit of grog in me – and a fair bit of animosity towards my former captain, which had been smouldering over the years – so I raised my fist and I went for him. Carey pulled a knife. I grabbed a harpoon off the wall. It sort of fell into my hand, and next thing I knew, I'd run him through with it."

"Very powerfully," said Holmes.

Cairns shrugged his shoulders. "I used to be a harpooner. When you've stabbed whales, the human body is nothing by comparison. Carey didn't die straight away, mind. He was stuck fast to the wall, and he raised his head and looked at me, and there was this ghastly expression on his face, this terrible gloat. And you know what he said? 'Knock and you shall find.' Those were his exact words. He said it twice more: 'Knock and you shall find.' And then he started to cackle, a vile, scornful sound. The laugh ended in a torrent of blood from his mouth, and his head sagged and his eyes closed, and that was it for Black Peter. At which point, the horror of what I had done caught up with me, and I turned tail and ran."

"And what is in this tin box?" Holmes enquired.

"Things of great value, or so we thought."

Holmes pressed him, but Cairns would not reveal more, other than to say, "You're better off not knowing. The contents of that box are not natural, that much I'll say. There is nothing in it that any sane human being should wish to own."

Little did he realise that such words were catnip to Sherlock Holmes.

Accordingly, the very next day my friend travelled back to Woodman's Lee, Peter Carey's house. Work obligations prevented me from accompanying him thither, but he supplied a full report afterwards. He told me he was able to convince Carey's widow and daughter that he needed to examine the cabin one more time, in order to affirm Cairns's guilt once and for all. Neither woman was much fussed what Holmes did with regard to Carey, or to Cairns for that matter, who in many ways had done them a favour. They were glad simply to have been relieved of the burden of living with Black Peter, who had treated them both abominably.

"My husband was never the same after he gave up the sea for the life of a landsman, Mr Holmes," Mrs Carey said. "He was a Puritan in many respects, but when he drank it brought out the anger in him, the brunt of which was borne by us twain. Often I urged him to return to the sea. I wanted him gone from home, if I am honest, but I thought, too, that it might be the saving of him. By returning to the place where he belonged, the oceans, he might quell whatever was raging in his breast. He refused. His last voyage, he said, had been enough, and perhaps one cannot blame him."

"Why not?"

"Well, it ended in disaster," replied she. "I don't know the long and short of it. Peter would never talk about it. All I know is that whatever could go wrong did go wrong and it put him off seafaring forever."

Holmes digested this information, assessing its pertinence. "I am grateful to you, madam," he said, "for your time and your patience. I shall be as quick as I can in your late husband's cabin."

"Oh, take as long as you like," Mrs Carey said. "Do what you will in there. Rip the place apart for all I care. That cabin has long been an eyesore, and I have little love for it. Now that Peter is gone, I plan to have it torn down, and then when it and all the junk that he filled it with is just a heap of debris, I am going to set it alight. And my daughter and I shall dance around that pyre, you can be assured. We shall dance and laugh."

Anyone who remembers 1895 will remember the drought that plagued England during the first half of that year. An arid spring was followed by a sere summer, and the day Holmes re-entered the cabin, the mercury was as high as it gets in this country. Consequently the cabin interior was oppressively hot and stuffy. Not only that, but its floor and walls still carried the dried black encrustations of Carey's blood. The heat, the stench of the rancid blood, and the flies which hummed about in their hundreds, all conspired to make it as uncongenial as a place can be.

Tying a handkerchief over his mouth and nose, Holmes set to examining. He ran an eye over the numerous keepsakes and trophies that Carey had accumulated over the course of his seagoing career: rolled-up maps and charts, a pair of compasses, a sextant, pieces of scrimshaw, a shark's tooth, a narwhal tusk, a weathered old cap and peacoat, and more. Amid this array of nautical memorabilia, no tin box of any kind could be seen.

Recalling Carey's dying words to Cairns – *knock and you shall find* – Holmes meticulously rapped the walls and the floorboards with his knuckles, in the hope of disclosing some false panel that hid a secret compartment. This too proved a bootless exercise.

Having gone outside for a breath of fresh air, he returned for a second assay. This time he fixed his attention on the coating of dust that covered practically everything in the cabin, and the new angle of approach yielded results. He noticed that in one corner, just next to Carey's writing desk, there was a rectangle of floor that was more or less dust-free. It measured roughly two feet by three. A box of some description must surely have lain there.

Next, he saw that the dust on one of the shelves had been disturbed. The shelf bore a row of maritime logbooks, a couple of dozen in all, organised in order of date. A narrow furrow in the dust indicated that the last logbook in line had lately been drawn out and reinserted.

Holmes flicked through several of the other logbooks first, establishing that each was a record of a voyage Carey had commanded. Their content was unremarkable.

However, the last in line, the one which had not long ago been perused, was a very different proposition.

Hailing from 1883, it provided an account of a journey into the northern latitudes made by the whaler *Sea Unicorn* under Carey's captaincy. Nothing in its opening pages led Holmes to believe that it differed from the rest. There were the usual entries relating ship's position, weather conditions, notable incidents among the crewmen, and other pro forma remarks, alongside the odd personal comment.

Soon, though, it became apparent that this was the disastrous last voyage that Carey's widow had spoken about, and Holmes found himself reading with a mounting sense of intrigue. He forgot the sweltering squalor of the cabin. He sat there amid the detritus of Black Peter's life but his mind was elsewhere, up in the frigid climes of the Arctic, on that whaler with Carey and crew as they encountered something awesome and awful, trespassed where they should not have gone, and paid the price for their imprudence.

*

I have the logbook in my possession still. It is a battered, board-backed thing, its pages brittle with age. Carey's handwriting is faded but legible, and is for the most part neat, although in later entries the penmanship becomes less certain, for reasons that will become apparent.

Over the next several pages I will reproduce its contents, edited to improve the narrative flow. Carey's spelling is erratic, and I have fixed that as necessary. I have also either deleted or ameliorated his saltier turns of phrase. As a document of misfortune and misery it is, I regret to say, unrivalled.

*

MONDAY 10TH SEPTEMBER

Departure from Dundee harbour at the slack of the tide. Weather set fair. Hit a slight chop out of the mouth of the Tay. Steaming northward at a steady 4 knots. Engine running smooth.

This is my first time aboard the *Sea Unicorn*. She is a 170-foot-long beauty, only a few years old, fitted with a 280-horsepower steam engine but bark-rigged too, for fuel conservation. I am confident of her seaworthiness and her range and capabilities.

Similarly, I believe I preside over as decent a crew as any captain might want, from First Mate Crabtree and Bosun Gillen down to the lowliest deckhand. They are thirty-six in number, and of them all, the one I am gladdest to have aboard is Harpooner Cairns. He and I have sailed together several times and I think him a likeminded individual, both tough and serious. I might even say he's a friend. His record speaks for itself. He is a dab hand with a harpoon and will have nothing to do with an Allen's Gun or any other such device. "A man doesn't need explosives to help him kill a whale," he says. "He just needs a strong right arm." I am counting on him to bring in a good harvest.

THURSDAY 13TH SEPTEMBER

The Shetland Isles are behind us, our last sight of land for the nonce. We have switched from steam to auxiliary sail and a following wind drives us nicely along. If all goes according to plan we will reach the whaling grounds just as the humpbacks begin their migration south with their newborn calves. So far the men's spirits are high, although complaints have been lodged about the cook. He is a Spaniard, Sanchez, new to me but he came highly recommended. But he insists on adding garlic to everything. I have taken him aside and warned him that the British stomach does not tolerate garlic easily.

FRIDAY 14TH SEPTEMBER

Tonight Sanchez served up something he called "paella". A sort of pottage made with fish and rice, it did not go down well with the men. Someone called it "the sweepings off a fishmonger's floor". Bosun Gillen reported the problem to me in my quarters. I went to the mess and made Sanchez go back to the galley and prepare some good old lobscouse instead. His sneer could have curdled milk. I shall have to watch him. A ship's crew, as Napoleon said about an army, runs on its stomach. Upset their digestion and you upset everything.

WEDNESDAY 19TH SEPTEMBER

We reached Victoriahavn at first light, and the men are making the most of a few hours' shore leave while Crabtree and I supervise the taking on of fresh water and provisions. We are still well stocked from Dundee but one should always top up whenever possible. After Victoriahavn there will be no more ports.

There is little to do for entertainment in this Norwegian town except drink the local liquor, aquavit, and find an accommodating woman, if that is one's fancy. It's wooden huts here mostly, with a few sturdier municipal buildings down by the wharves. These are the headquarters where Victoriahavn's principal trade, shipping out iron ore from Swedish mines, is overseen.

I fell into conversation with one of the dockhands helping load the *Sea Unicorn*. He had a word of warning for me. "Early winter coming," said he, a typically dour Nordic type. "You can feel it in the bite of the wind. And it'll be a hard one. Don't be long up there amid the ice, Captain. Turn home as soon as you can."

I replied that I would turn home when the *Sea Unicorn*'s holds were groaning with whale oil and baleen, and not a moment before. The dockhand just shrugged his shoulders at me, although I could not tell whether that meant he didn't care or it was my own lookout if I didn't heed his warning.

THURSDAY 20TH SEPTEMBER

While navigating out of the fjord from Victoriahavn to open sea, we spied a pod of killer whales off the starboard rail. Sleek and evil creatures. I once watched a dozen of them harry a young sperm whale until it was exhausted, whereupon they tore it to bits. They did not eat it. They massacred it purely for sport.

Still, we took the sighting as a good omen. A whaling ship wants to meet whales.

TUESDAY 25TH SEPTEMBER

The *Sea Unicorn* continues to make good headway. Bearing nor'-nor'-east under full sail. Her bow wave is impressive. She has, as the saying goes, a bone in her teeth.

We are now in the Barents Sea. Nothing but iron-grey water in all directions to the horizon. Conditions remain good. Moderate swell.

FRIDAY 28TH SEPTEMBER

Today the cry went up for the first time on this voyage: "There she blows!" Able Seaman Jones was on lookout and saw plumes to the west. We turned and searched the area but found nothing. The crew are now ribbing Jones mercilessly. Poor eyesight, visit to the optician is in order, that sort of thing. Jones takes it in good part.

MONDAY 1ST OCTOBER

Our first kill of this trip. Five humpbacks were seen breaching less than a mile off. The *Sea Unicorn* pursued under steam at flank speed, and when we were close enough we launched the whaleboats. Magnificent rowing by the men brought them swiftly within harpooning distance, and Cairns speared one right through the lung. The whale sounded and the harpoon rope paid out, but I know a fatal strike when I see one, and shortly the beast was back to the surface and wallowing in distress. The spume that jetted from its blowhole was bright pink.

When it had settled and was floating helplessly, Cairns's boat drew alongside and he stepped smartly across from the stern onto the whale's back. He had an untethered harpoon which he drove down into its brainpan with impressive force. Within minutes the thing was dead.

Its carcass now lies roped beside the ship and the men are working through the night stripping away hide and blubber and hauling it aboard. Sharks have gathered to tear at the dead whale's underside. We are in a race with them to see who gets the lion's share.

Meanwhile the other four humpbacks are circling us. Deep cries resonate through the *Sea Unicorn*'s timbers. If one didn't know they are mindless beasts, one might think the whales are mourning their dead comrade.

TUESDAY 2ND OCTOBER

A tragedy. It is my sad duty to relate that overnight we lost one of our complement. Able Seaman Hamish McGovern was working a shift atop the humpback when he lost his footing and slipped into the water. His fellow workers immediately downed their flensing tools and threw him a line. Alas, it was dark, and even by the light of the lanterns suspended from the ship's gunwales McGovern could not find the end of the rope. The men reeled it in and threw it to him again, several times, to no avail. Then came a pitiful cry from McGovern and he vanished beneath the water. He resurfaced seconds later, gibbering and screaming, saying that he had been bitten by a shark. Next moment he went under again, and this time he did not come back up.

At dawn I conducted a brief service of remembrance,

committing McGovern's soul to the Lord's keeping. Then I ordered the men back to work. Some grumbled, but they know not to rouse my ire. I gave them a look and they obeyed.

By day's end the humpback was little more than bones and guts, and the trypots are now bubbling away on deck, rendering chunks of blubber down to oil. The smell, as always, is atrocious. One never gets used to it.

I shall now undertake to compose a letter of condolence to McGovern's family, although when I am going to get the chance to post it, heaven alone knows.

WEDNESDAY 10TH OCTOBER

The Norwegian dockhand was not wrong. The weather is already turning wintry. We are due north of Bear Island, on course for Svalbard, and it has been sleeting for three days straight. The decks have become icy, treacherous underfoot, and every man who comes in from watch has frosted whiskers and a chapped nose. I have never known it to get so cold so early in the year.

FRIDAY 12TH OCTOBER

A small iceberg floated past us today. This is not a good sign. At least a vessel like the *Sea Unicorn* is designed to cope with the worst the polar regions can throw at her. Her wooden hull is both sturdy and flexible and can handle pack ice with no trouble. Even if she were to become icebound – God forbid! – she can withstand the pressures exerted on her in a way that her steel-hulled equivalent cannot.

Engineer Moorhouse reports that all is well down in the engine room. We have so far used up only a quarter of our coal stocks. Whales, however, have been thin on the ground. Since the kill eleven days ago there has been no sign of any, not even a distant breach. The crew are far from happy about this, for they are all on commission. The less produce we bring home, the less they earn. They are not, however, disheartened as yet. They know that whaling is not an exact science. We can go where we think the whales are, but the whales themselves don't always realise they're supposed to be there.

SUNDAY 14TH OCTOBER

Our fortunes changed today, for the better and then the worse. A large pod of humpbacks came into view. We steamed right into the heart of it, and out went the whaleboats. Things looked promising until one of those giant brutes came up right under one of the boats, capsizing it. Every man jack aboard went into the water and had to be rescued. They can all count themselves lucky they were pulled from the waves in time, before the cold stopped their hearts. Naturally they had to be brought back to the *Sea Unicorn* and got out of their wet clothes and warmed up with hot tea, and by the time their wellbeing was assured, the whales had moved on. The whaleboat itself was damaged beyond repair and had to be left behind.

A victory for the humpbacks. Damnably annoying, but at least there was no loss of life.

SUNDAY 21ST OCTOBER

A whole week and not a single whale. We have sailed west of Svalbard into the Greenland Sea. The waters here should be teeming with them. Could it be that they know a hard winter is coming and have migrated early, to escape the onset of the ice?

The crew are grousing all the time but I've got Bosun Gillen keeping them busy below decks, making them do odd jobs. If it wasn't so wretchedly cold I would have them up top exercising every day, to burn off some energy. I find myself having to bark at one or other of them over some infraction on an hourly basis. I am famed for having a bad temper, but I prefer to think that I am placid unless roused. Don't give me cause to be angry with you and we shall get along fine.

TUESDAY 23RD OCTOBER

I have had to discipline our ship's carpenter, Lusk, after he threatened Sanchez with a knife. According to those who were in the mess at the time, he threw his plate aside and leapt at the Spaniard, grabbing him and swearing at him foully. "I shan't eat another damned bite of this pigswill!" he declared, with his knife at Sanchez's throat. If the other men hadn't pulled him off, he might well have killed him.

I flogged Lusk personally. I know it's a bosun's job but I would never ask a subordinate to do something I wouldn't do myself. Lusk was hauled to the gangway, First Mate Crabtree read out his offence in front of all the men, and I delivered a dozen lashes with the cat to his bare back. I went easy on him and did not draw blood. The only blood there was came from Lusk's lip, which he gnawed to stop himself crying out in pain.

WEDNESDAY 31ST OCTOBER

Where the hell are all the damn whales?

FRIDAY 2ND NOVEMBER

We are forging through pack ice. Every time a chunk hits the prow, a loud boom shudders through the ship. The wind has dropped altogether and we are burning through our coal stocks fast. Engineer Moorhouse reckons that unless the wind picks up, we have enough coal to get home, but only if we turn now. In other words, we are reaching the point of no return.

If we limp back to Dundee with precisely one humpback's worth of oil and baleen in the holds, our financiers will be less than happy. I shall probably never captain a whaler again.

SUNDAY 4TH NOVEMBER

Met an American whaler today, the *Francis Dudley* out of New Bedford. We hove to alongside, and her captain and I had a cordial, if shouted, exchange across the gap between our ships. He, like us, has been having a dry time of it. He stated his intention to round the southern tip of Greenland into the Labrador Sea and try his luck there. I remain adamant that the Greenland Sea will yield results. We bade each other farewell and good fishing.

WEDNESDAY 7TH NOVEMBER

An extraordinary day. I can hardly put into words what I have seen.

It happened as I was taking a turn on deck, just after the forenoon-watch three bells tolled. The sun had risen and the air was clear. I turned my face west, to behold a wondrous sight. A shape was passing across the sky, directly above the thin white line that marked the coast of Greenland, a mile or so distant. I can only describe it as long, pale and fleshy-looking, with a sort of bulb at one end that expanded and contracted as though inflating and expelling air. I judged its size to be 1,000 feet from stem to stern and 400 or so in diameter, but this could only be the vaguest of estimates.

I called to Able Seaman Tomelty, who was on watch at the bow. "Do you see that?" I cried.

"I see it, Cap'n," came the reply, "but I'm blowed if I know what it is."

He and I watched the thing for a full minute. I sensed that it was both descending and slowing, sinking gracefully towards earth in a shallow arc. Down it went, to the very edge of the horizon.

"Mark its final position as best you can," I told Tomelty.

"Aye aye, sir."

I hastened aft to the helm and ordered Midshipman O'Neal to alter course. He, too, had spied the airborne object. "What in God's name is it, Captain?" he asked.

"You have as much idea as I do," said I. "But whatever it is, we must chase it and find it. If it comes down in the sea, that is one thing, but should it come down on land, it is ours for the asking."

In truth, I didn't much care what that flying behemoth actually was. All I knew was that it represented a change in our fortunes. Some dazzlingly rare phenomenon had chanced our way, and there was nothing to be lost by investigating it, and perhaps much to be gained.

FRIDAY 9TH NOVEMBER

We have searched along the Greenland coast for two days straight, and I am beginning to despair. There are countless islands, bays and inlets around here. That giant shape in the sky could be anywhere, and that's assuming it made landfall and is not now lying on the seabed in several fathoms of water.

The crew have taken some persuading that this pursuit is a worthwhile use of our time. Even though Tomelty and O'Neal can corroborate what I saw, I have heard mutterings. "The captain is mad. The captain is seeing things. The captain is chasing phantoms." Gillen reports that Lusk the carpenter is openly voicing displeasure, but then that is hardly surprising, given how he has cause to resent me. However, Gillen warns that Draycott, one of the boatsteerers, is the fellow I need to watch out for. Draycott is a sly sort, and were he not so exceptionally capable at the tiller of a whaleboat, I would not countenance his presence on any ship of mine.

I keep explaining to the men that, in the absence of whales, our best hope of making this voyage profitable is by locating that leviathan of the air. It offers the possibility of salvage, or else may yield materials for which the likes of the Royal Society or one of the universities might pay handsomely. Even just knowing where it is, so that a scientific expedition might be organised to study and recover it, could fetch us a pretty penny.

SATURDAY 10TH NOVEMBER

The search continues. The wind is a feeble breeze, barely capable of stirring a sail. Moorhouse is repeatedly expressing concern about the coal. I should not ignore his warnings but I feel compelled to press on regardless.

Today Draycott's malcontent talk turned insubordinate, and I made him run the gauntlet, a punishment that has fallen into disuse but, to my thinking, still has a place in maritime life. I flogged him, after which he was forced to walk backwards between the other crewmen, who were lined up in two rows. They were under orders to beat him as he passed, with the proviso that anyone who held back would receive the same treatment himself. Lessons must be set, and learned.

SUNDAY 11TH NOVEMBER

This afternoon I distinctly overheard someone whisper "Ahab" behind my back. It came from a group of half a dozen men gathered on the foredeck, and I had no way of telling which of them said it. I spun round and gave them all a piece of my mind. I was the Black Peter of my reputation, the fierce, roaring martinet. The fear in their eyes was good to see. Fear means respect.

We must find the leviathan of the air soon. It is out there somewhere on this desolate, uninhabited shoreline. It waits for me.

MONDAY 12TH NOVEMBER

Success! Just as daylight was waning, the *Sea Unicorn* rounded the horn of a wide rocky bay and there it was: the leviathan. The mainland sloped shallowly towards the sea here, and the thing was situated a short way inland, lying roughly parallel with the shoreline. It did not look like it had come to rest so much as crashed. It sagged in places, as though it were collapsing under its own weight. That bulb at its stern was now just a mass of loose, overlapping folds.

I could not resist a moment of exultation. "There! There!" I said to the men. "Didn't I tell you? Didn't I say?"

The men crowded at the rail to see. They nudged one another and gesticulated, setting up a hubbub of amazement and disbelief that was punctuated with the occasional oath. Even those dissidents Lusk and Draycott were overcome with wonderment.

Putting telescope to eye, I made out a circular aperture in the leviathan's flank. In front of this I spied several pinkish shapes on the ground. I was unable to determine what they were but something about them reminded me of lobsters or shrimp.

"What's the plan, sir?" asked First Mate Crabtree.

"It'll be dark soon," I replied. "Nothing we can do until tomorrow."

The *Sea Unicorn* now sits at anchor in the mouth of the bay. I suspect I shan't sleep much tonight.

TUESDAY 13TH NOVEMBER

We put out in a whaleboat as soon as dawn broke. The sky was overcast and threatening snow. I had handpicked the half-dozen crewmen who were to accompany me on this first exploratory sortie. I included both Gillen and Cairns in that number, since they are the most level-headed mariners aboard, apart from Crabtree, to whom I entrusted charge of the ship in my absence. I had the feeling that in this particular enterprise I would be needing companions who can keep their wits about them.

As we approached the shore, I was pleased to see that my initial estimate of the leviathan's size had been more or less accurate. What struck me most about it was that it clearly was not manufactured. No hand had built this thing. It was an organism. Nor was it any kind of animal, but rather it was composed of vegetable matter. It was, in short, a single plant, grown to vast proportions.

We put ashore, running the whaleboat up the rough shingle beach. The path to the leviathan was littered with boulders that were coated with ice and snow, and the going was so tricky that it took us a good twenty minutes to cover just a few hundred yards.

Then we were in the thing's shadow. It hulked over us like some toppled titan.

My eye went straight to the aperture I had seen yesterday, and to the shapes that lay scattered before it, which numbered around twenty. I could only assume the hole was some kind of hatchway to the leviathan's interior. The shapes would seem to confirm it, in as much as they were living creatures, or rather, the corpses of once-living creatures. They must have come from within the leviathan. It was, in other words, a ship, and they were its passengers, or else its crew, or a combination of both.

And they were, one and all, quite dead. No question about it. We moved circumspectly among them, eyeing up each in turn. A couple of the men had their knives drawn, just in case. The creatures were almost as large as humans and had carapaces and wings like those of insects. Their heads were smooth, glassy and egg-shaped, while their limbs were spindly appendages tipped with pincers. I could only reason that they had either crawled or flown out of the leviathan after it landed. Perhaps they were already dying as they did so. That or they perished swiftly, not long after emerging.

Gillen prodded one of them with the toe of his boot in a gingerly fashion, just to check that no life lingered. It did not stir. He kicked it to make doubly certain. There was a ripple of nervous laughter from the other men.

"What on earth can they be, Captain?" said Cairns.

I did not say what I was thinking, namely that they were not of this earth at all. Instead I gestured towards the hatchway. "Who's for going inside?"

"Are you asking for volunteers?" said one of the men.

"I would prefer not to enter that thing alone."

In the event, all of them agreed to come with me. We clambered up to the hatchway, whose edges were ragged, almost as though it had been cut open from inside. We entered a short tunnel which likewise appeared hewn. The creatures, it seemed, had had to burrow out of the leviathan, carving a passage through its shell. Prior to that they had been sealed within.

In short order we found ourselves in a chamber whose contours were irregular and multifaceted. Walls and floor felt spongy. The air smelled musty. Through a portal in one wall we could see a similar chamber, and another one beyond that. I was loath to venture any further just yet, however. There was no illumination save for the daylight coming in through the hatchway. We would need lanterns. I also felt that we had pushed our luck as far as we should for one day. Tomorrow we could return, better equipped.

Back on board the *Sea Unicorn*, I announced my intentions to the assembled crew. "This is the find of the century," I said, "and our task is to plumb its depths and learn what we can about it."

"What do you reckon it is, Cap'n?" someone enquired.

"I cannot tell you where that thing has come from or why it is here, not with any certainty. I have a theory – and mind you, it is just that, a theory – which is that it originates from nowhere on this planet."

"It's from another world, you mean?"

"It is a vessel that has travelled through the void to get here, from Mars, from Venus, who can say? A space-ship, you might call it. And those creatures who occupied it, and now lie dead beside it, are alien beings. Whether they came to Earth on purpose or by accident, our world's environment has not proved congenial to them. I repeat, this is the find of the century, and it has fallen to us to bring the news back to civilisation. To that end, I am proposing that we retrieve whatever portable items we can from the space-ship, along with at least one of the alien bodies, and take them to England as proof. I hasten to add that we shall all share in the renown which is going to come from this discovery, and likewise any financial reward that accrues from it, the latter in the same percentage shares as we would were it our normal cargo of whale product. Are we all in agreement about that?"

There came a loud, rousing cheer from the men.

Tonight, the mood on board is excited and festive, and why would it not be? Nothing I said to the crew was a lie. We will become famous as a result of this, and we will benefit financially too, I am sure. I am equally sure, though, that one of us stands to profit the most. Who now knows the names of Cook's crewmen, or Columbus's, or Drake's? Leaders are remembered by history, followers forgotten. Of everyone aboard the *Sea Unicorn*, it is Captain Peter Carey alone whose immortality is guaranteed.

FRIDAY 16TH NOVEMBER

Three days of delving deeper and deeper into the space-ship has garnered us an assortment of oddities. I hesitate to call these items treasures, for some of them are ugly, some of them downright sinister-looking, and all of them are of unknowable purpose.

The space-ship is a labyrinth of chambers connected

to one another not only horizontally but vertically, meaning that ladders as well as lanterns have been required in order to negotiate its interior. I have the impression that the craft was inhabited in, as it were, three dimensions. That is to say, its erstwhile occupants, being winged creatures, had no need of staircases, and the positioning of the portals between chambers – here in a ceiling, there in a floor – reflects that.

We have found small cells which I can only take to be individual bedchambers. We have found communal areas and storage areas. We have found what appear to be larders, stocked with fungus or lichen which must have been the creatures' food. There are some parts of the space-ship we have not been able to gain access to, simply because a ceiling has fallen in or a portal has become compressed flat. Now and then we have felt the vessel shift abruptly around us, sometimes quite alarmingly. Its structure does not appear to be able to support itself now that it is on the ground. The soft, fibrous tissue of which it is composed is buckling under its own weight.

This has put a time constraint on our labours. There is a sense that the space-ship's integrity may not last much longer and it will at some stage collapse in on itself altogether.

A further time constraint comes in the form of the weather. Snow has been falling heavily for the past three days, and the pack ice in the bay is solidifying. By my reckoning, we have two more days at most before the *Sea Unicorn* gets frozen in. That cannot be allowed to happen. I have no desire to spend the entire Arctic winter stuck here, and nor do any of the crew, I am quite certain. We must grab what we can from the space-ship while we can, then make haste for home.

SUNDAY 18TH NOVEMBER

We have not been able to put it off a moment longer. The *Sea Unicorn* is heaving her way out of the bay, under full steam. The floe has not yet quite joined up to become a single, unbreakable sheet. Ice cracks and shatters around the ship's bow as she butts her way through. If fortune favours us, we will be in clear seas soon.

Down in the holds there are numerous artefacts from the space-ship: lumpen things, globular things, gelatinous things, things that pulse with an eerie lambency, things that are fashioned from strange metals – not forgetting, of course, the bodies of two of the creatures. The men have lashed them all down tightly, and not just to keep them in place. It is as though they want to be assured the things will stay in the holds and not somehow stray into other parts of the ship of their own accord. I can understand that feeling.

THURSDAY 22ND NOVEMBER

We have escaped the clutches of the ice and now have a following wind propelling us along at a respectable 5 knots over open water. We are crossing the Norwegian Sea, Iceland to the south-west of us. In a fortnight or so we should reach British shores.

The triumphal mood that attended our departure from the space-ship has abated but the men remain cheerful. I have heard more than one of them discuss how he intends to spend the money that is coming his way. Every time, the sum mentioned increases.

Their expectations outstrip feasibility. My own do not. Any public body wishing to undertake an expedition to visit the space-ship will necessarily have to call on my expertise, and mine alone. I have taken careful bearings and know its exact position. No one else will be asked to captain the ship that transports the scientists thither, and for that reason I will be able to name my price. I would not be surprised if, beyond that, a knighthood beckons.

My future, both immediate and long-term, would appear to be plain sailing.

SATURDAY 24TH NOVEMBER

A fight broke out this afternoon below decks, with, I'm sorry to say, fatal consequences. A disagreement arose between two men, Yardley and Ingles, the former insisting that the latter had sneaked into a hold and purloined one of the items from the space-ship, an accusation roundly denied. As tempers rose, a belaying pin was produced, and Ingles was bludgeoned to death.

Yardley now languishes in the brig, and Ingles's body has been sewn inside a length of sailcloth by our sailmaker and consigned to the deep. Nothing is missing from the holds.

It was the kind of tawdry little spat that is a part of shipboard life and is, unfortunately, all too common.

To be on the safe side, I have posted men to guard the entrances to the holds round the clock.

SUNDAY 25TH NOVEMBER

One of the men on guard duty has been overcome with nausea and now lies prostrate in his hammock. He is an old hand and swears he has never known seasickness before. Besides, we are passing through relatively calm waters. It is very queer.

MONDAY 26TH NOVEMBER

Now another of the men on guard duty has come down with the same complaint.

Both men were stationed outside the same hold, and thus, spurred by curiosity and some inexplicable instinct, I went down into that hold to take a look around. There I found that one of the space-ship artefacts is no longer intact. When brought aboard it was an almost perfect sphere, the size of a football, with a blotchy purple colouration and an odd, resilient feel to it. Now it appears badly damaged, as though split open from within. It sits in two halves, conjoined at the base, and from its interior numerous fronds have emerged. Like vines, these have wreathed themselves in all directions along the ship's timbers. They branch and branch again, and as I stood there examining them I could almost have sworn that they were still growing, before my very eyes.

I can only assume that the thing – fruit, vegetable, whatever it is – has ripened and, as part of the natural order for this particular species of plant, burst open and bloomed. I have ordered that the vines, or sprouts, or shoots, whatever the term for them is, be cut away and that the whole lot, including the purple sphere that generated them, be jettisoned.

TUESDAY 27TH NOVEMBER

The pair on guard duty have recovered from their nausea. However, the men tasked with removing and disposing of the item from the hold, Boothe and Coleby, have taken ill. Purple swellings cover their skin, like buboes, and they are feverish and sweating. The *Sea Unicorn* does not have a physician aboard – it is not compulsory on merchant ships – but Crabtree has some knowledge of medicine, being the son of a dispensing chemist. He is treating them with purgatives and antipyretics from our stores. So far there has been no noticeable improvement in their condition.

WEDNESDAY 28TH NOVEMBER

Boothe and Coleby are both dead, and now poor Crabtree is exhibiting the same symptoms they did, down to those loathsome, disfiguring purple buboes. He has been quarantined in his cabin, where he lies tossing and turning in his bunk and moaning with distress. The hammocks in which Boothe and Coleby were lying when they died have been cut down and have joined the bodies of those who last occupied them, in the deeps. As an additional precaution, I have had the crew's sleeping quarters scrubbed from top to bottom with caustic soda.

Unsurprisingly, the crew have become restive. They are certain, as am I, that direct contact with the purple sphere and its outgrowths was the source of the deadly sickness and that the sickness is contagious. Even proximity to the sphere is injurious to the health, if the experience of the two men on guard duty is anything to go by. We can but hope that, with the sphere gone and Crabtree isolated, the danger is past.

THURSDAY 29TH NOVEMBER

I record, with no little personal sorrow, the untimely passing of First Mate Thomas Crabtree.

No captain likes to lose his first mate, the more so in this instance because Crabtree was of sound character and an exemplary second-in-command. He took orders well, without cavil or quibble, and served as a reliable conduit between me and the rest of the ship's complement.

I have forbidden the crew from entering his cabin, not that any of them is likely to want to. In fact, to make sure, I have had the door nailed shut. Crabtree's body will simply have to remain there until we reach port.

SATURDAY 1ST DECEMBER

Gillen tells me that both Lusk and Draycott are up to their old tricks. They have got together and are sowing discord among the men. They're arguing that the alien artefacts are too hazardous to be kept aboard. What if there is another of them that spreads a lethal contagion like the purple sphere? What if they harbour an even greater danger? Yes, there is money to be made from these things, but money is no good if you're not alive to spend it.

So far, Gillen tells me, the majority of the crew seem in favour of keeping the artefacts. The reward outweighs the risk, as far as they're concerned. But he warns me that if there is another incident and further deaths, the balance of opinion could tip the other way. Then I could have a full-blown insurrection on my hands.

SUNDAY 2ND DECEMBER

Today, several of the men have begun complaining of headaches. The pain is so severe, they are unable to carry out their duties.

MONDAY 3RD DECEMBER

The plague of headaches continues. Now well over a dozen men are laid up and useless. They are haggard-looking and pale of complexion. All of them speak of a low, pulsing sound that seems to be emanating from within their brains. Sometimes it is so loud, they can hardly bear it.

TUESDAY 4TH DECEMBER

Fully half of the crew have succumbed to these headaches. The *Sea Unicorn* is sorely undermanned. I have told the crewmen keeping watch over the alien artefacts to attend to their normal duties instead, in order to make up the shortfall. I suspect nobody is much interested, anyway, in entering the holds, not now.

Lusk and Draycott, who are among those who remain headache-free, are blaming the problem on the alien artefacts. I am not sure they're wrong.

WEDNESDAY 5TH DECEMBER

I can scarcely bring myself to relate what has happened. The men with headaches have become deranged. That is the only word for it: deranged. They have begun attacking their shipmates in the most vicious manner imaginable.

These outbreaks of violence are unprovoked, and I have seen for myself how ferocious they can be. All at once, a man will hurl himself at another, gnashing his teeth. He looks as though he wants to tear his victim apart with his bare hands. He is gripped by a wild frenzy, such that it can take three people or more to restrain him.

For a time, as these attacks proliferated, it looked as though anarchy would engulf the *Sea Unicorn*. However, I was able to marshal the rest of the crew and gain control of the situation, and one by one the deranged men have been subdued and corralled.

There are too many of them for the brig to hold, of course. Four reside in there now, its maximum occupancy, and I have released Yardley in order to make room for them. The rest are locked up in various cabins, and only I have the keys to the doors. They all have water to drink and some dry rations to eat, but not much of either. How they share it out between them, or if they even do, is none of my concern.

The madmen howl in their captivity. I can hear it even as I write this entry. The noise echoes through the ship, a massed ululation that mingles with the creak of her timbers and the crack of her sails. It is as though we have a score of wolves aboard.

We limp onward, doing the best we can to sail the ship with our severely depleted numbers. We cannot reach land soon enough.

THURSDAY 6TH DECEMBER

The howling never stops. Sometimes the confined men throw themselves at the doors of the cabins. They rage and rave.

In one cabin, they appear to have visited their savagery on one another. It is now silent in there, and I have no wish to open the door to see what has happened. A stream of blood has trickled out through the gap between door and threshold. That is evidence enough.

FRIDAY 7TH DECEMBER

The howls are now few and far between. The madmen seem to have exhausted themselves.

Lusk is insisting that I release them, saying they must be harmless now, but I cannot see any alternative other than to leave them where they are. Their welfare is less important than the safety of the rest of us.

SATURDAY 8TH DECEMBER

This morning I went down to the holds, in order to investigate whether Lusk and Draycott are right and the alien artefacts really are the source of the madness. Perhaps I should have done this sooner. All I can say is that I have been too preoccupied with tackling the problem itself to address its possible origins.

I first inspected the bodies of the two alien beings. They, packed in ice to preserve them, appear unchanged. I asked them out loud if they knew what was going on aboard the *Sea Unicorn*. "Your silence is deafening," I said. "Well, you keep the answer to yourselves then. See if I care." Then I laughed hollowly, wondering whether I, too, was succumbing to the madness.

In another of the holds my gaze was drawn to a peculiar metallic object, something with a disc-shaped base and a quantity of thin rods protruding from it like the spikes of a hedgehog. I well recalled coming across it aboard the space-ship and speculating as to its purpose. I selected it as one of the artefacts we should take with us simply because it was so unfathomably odd-looking.

As I approached it now, I sensed a vibration coming from it. When I touched it with a tentative hand, I felt it throb beneath my fingertips. Could this have been causing the headaches and the ensuing madness? I remembered how the headache sufferers had talked of a pulsing sound that seemed to come from their own brains. Had this object been beaming out some kind of invisible waves – magnetic in origin, perhaps, like the forces that act upon a compass – which had an adverse effect on some people, but not all, within its scope of influence? Was it a device whose purpose was to disorder minds, enflaming them into a state of feral insanity? A weapon designed to pit one's foes against one another and thus render them incapable of defending themselves? Perhaps it had activated itself by means of some timing mechanism, or the movement of the ship through the waves had jostled a switch within.

Whatever the truth, I knew it was not wise for me to remain in close proximity to it for long. I might have been immune to its influence thus far, but I had no wish to test that. I snatched up the device, went on deck and, leaning over the transom, dumped it into the sea. It vanished into the ship's wake.

The decision clearly was the right one, for since then there has been barely a peep out of any of the confined men. I have put an ear to the cabin doors and heard from within just soft mutterings in bewildered tones.

SUNDAY 9TH DECEMBER

Lusk and Draycott came to me today, heading up a delegation. They have demands.

The confined crewmen must be freed. They themselves have been calling to be let out. They say their headaches are gone and their supplies of food and water have run out, so that they are hungry and desperately thirsty. They appear to have no recollection of what they did to earn their incarceration.

"If you won't hand over the keys, Captain," Lusk said, "we will simply hack the cabin doors down."

"Give it another day," I said in response. "If those men are still calm tomorrow, then we will know for certain that the spate of madness is over."

Lusk and Draycott agreed to this, although I don't doubt for a moment that neither of them is wholly placated. As

Lusk said, "You are at fault here, Captain Carey. No one from the lower decks is under any illusion about that. If you hadn't been so keen to plunder that space-ship of yours…"

"I don't recall any of you objecting to the idea at the time," I said. "You seemed quite taken by the prospect of the income the artefacts would bring."

"We still are," Lusk growled. "That is the only thing preventing us from hanging you from the yardarm right now. You just watch yourself, Black Peter. One more calamity, and it is over for you."

The way he uttered my nickname – dripping with contempt and spite – confirms, as if I didn't already realise, that the prevailing mood among the crewmen is going from mutinous to murderous. Lusk knows he has the support of the preponderance of them and thus feels emboldened, else he wouldn't have dared speak to me like that. There is the real possibility that at some point, if the fates are unkind, I may have to flee for my life.

If so, I am not going to do it alone. One man in an open boat in northern seas in winter will be lucky to survive. In company of other sailors, however, he stands a better than average chance.

Therefore, later today, I privately summoned to my cabin the handful of crewmen I feel I can count on, to wit Gillen, Cairns, Moorhouse and Sanchez the cook. The last may not be as intimate with me as the others are but he is grateful that I punished Lusk after the carpenter threatened his life. That has earned me his loyalty. Also, he is in a position to be very useful to my plans.

"Unless matters improve between now and whenever we put in at Dundee," I said to them, "the five of us may have to consider abandoning ship."

"Why us?" said Gillen.

"If I am at risk, then so are all of you. You are regarded, in one way or other, as my allies. You are tarnished by association.

If the men turn on me, who's to say they won't turn on you as well? I am only thinking of your safety."

Of course I was really only thinking of my own, but the four of them were already anxious about the way things were going on the *Sea Unicorn*. They did not take much convincing.

"Now then," I said, once I was sure I had them on my side, "I want you, Sanchez, to set aside some provisions. Hardtack, pemmican, salted beef, a keg or two of drinking water – enough to last us a good two or three weeks. Be discreet about it, and keep it all somewhere safe, hidden away, but in a place from which you can retrieve it at a moment's notice."

"And what of the items from the space-ship?" said Cairns. "Are we to forget about those?"

"You leave that to me," I said. "Rest assured, if we have to jump ship, we shan't be doing it empty-handed."

*

The final series of logbook entries is written in pencil rather than pen. Here and there the text is difficult to interpret. Words are smudged or have been erased by drops of water, or else are so faint or so poorly inscribed as to be all but indecipherable. In every such instance I have done my best to infer from context what Carey actually wrote, and where that has been impossible I have left a blank.

*

WEDNESDAY 12TH DECEMBER

I resume making notes about our voyage, but under very changed and much more challenging circumstances.

The events of Monday 10th December remain painfully fresh in my memory, and yet it all seems to have happened an age ago, even if only forty-eight hours have since passed. I foresaw that further trouble was looming aboard the *Sea Unicorn*. What I did not foresee was how badly the situation would go awry, and how quickly.

As stated in my previous entry, I had begun making preparations to leave the ship. I had read the signs correctly. The discontent simmering among the crew was about to boil over into outright [BLANK]. Hence, following my clandestine meeting with Gillen, Cairns, Moorhouse and Sanchez, I spent much of the middle watch, the deadest hours of night, stealing back and forth between my cabin and the holds. On each journey I retrieved a single item from the collection of alien artefacts, secreting it in a canvas haversack. It was not a perfect method of concealment, and had I run into a crewman on the way from hold to cabin he might well have bearded me, demanding to know what was in the haversack, for some of the items were quite bulky. My only hope then would have been to brazen it out: "How dare you question your captain! The impertinence!" I was not sure whether this would have worked, my authority aboard the ship being much diminished by that point. It was a good thing, then, that I encountered no one during these furtive errands.

Once I had amassed a round dozen of the items, I transferred them to a large, watertight toleware box in which I normally keep spare clothing. It was a tight squeeze, but the pliability of certain of the artefacts made [BLANK] them all in that much easier. Would that I could have retrieved one of the alien beings to take with me, for their value might have been greater than that of all the artefacts combined. The corpses, however, were too big to make that practical.

I slept fitfully and was awoken in the early hours by a commotion from below. I stumbled out of my cabin and went down to the source of the disturbance, the mess. I found the place in uproar, with a terrified Sanchez surrounded by angry crewmen, all yelling and gesticulating. The Spaniard was bleeding from mouth and nose, and one eye had been blackened. Just as I arrived, I saw him struck in the belly by a fist. He doubled over, a wail of pain escaping him.

It came as no surprise to me that the man who delivered the blow was Lusk. "For the last time, answer!" the carpenter barked at Sanchez. "What were you setting aside those rations for?"

"Please," a cringing Sanchez begged. "Stop. I wasn't doing anything."

"I saw you with my own eyes, through the entrance to the galley," said Lusk. "Squirrelling away tins of pemmican in a sack. What for? Thinking of abandoning us, were you? You snivelling Spanish cur!"

At that moment Sanchez's gaze fell on me, and I saw hope and relief in his expression. I knew then that this was a pivotal moment. What Sanchez said next might very well prove my undoing.

And so it did.

"Captain Carey!" he cried. "You tell them. I was only doing as you asked."

All eyes in the mess turned on me.

"What's that, Captain?" snarled Lusk. "Ordered Sanchez to hoard food, did you? And whyever would you have done that?"

The other men growled and jeered. The answer was obvious. In some way or other, I had been meaning to betray them.

There seemed no point defending myself or trying to reason with them. My plan was unravelling before my very eyes. I was [BLANK].

I turned on my heel and ran. I don't think Lusk and the others were quite expecting this – they were used to Black Peter lowering his horns and charging at any opposition – and so, in their surprise, they did not give chase straight away. That was my first stroke of good fortune. My second was almost immediately bumping into Moorhouse.

"Captain?" said the engineer. "I heard shouting. What's going on?"

An idea formed in my head on the spot. Desperation is the mother of invention.

"Moorhouse, listen," I said. "Sanchez has been careless and now the whole crew know what we are up to. We have little time. I shall get a whaleboat ready for us. You, meanwhile, must provide a diversion."

"How?"

"I want you to start a fire in the engine room."

"Start a…? But sir, that's madness."

"Make it a big one. Make it something they have no choice but to attend to as a matter of urgency. Light an oily rag and toss it in the coal bunker, that should do the trick. That or something like it. Hop to it, man!"

Moorhouse hastened off, while I made for my cabin. I pocketed this logbook. It will serve as written testimony of the space-ship's existence and whereabouts. I then picked up the tin box by the handles.

As I emerged from the cabin with it, there was Cairns.

"The jig is up, isn't it?" said he.

"It is, Cairns. Hear that?" The sound of enraged crewmen rang through the ship. Clearly audible above the general baying was Lusk's voice, inciting riot. "They are out for blood. Our blood. Come with me."

We ascended the companionway to the forecastle. I slammed the hatch shut and dogged it tight. This would buy us some time. Then I ran to the nearest whaleboat, dumped the tin box into it, swung the boat on its davits so that it hung above the water, and began cranking the handle to lower it.

"What about the others?" said Cairns. "Gillen, Moorhouse, Sanchez…"

"If they make it, they make it. If not, that is their hard luck. Do you want to live or not, Cairns?"

Cairns was able to make the same calculation that I had. When you get down to it, saving your own skin always comes first.

As the whaleboat's keel touched the water, there came a hammering on the underside of the companionway hatch, followed by a bout of thwarted cursing. Next moment, a panicked cry emanated from below, one that was hoarse and full of dread.

"Fire! Fire!"

The cry was shared by others, spreading through the ship.

Cairns and I slid over the gunwales and dropped into the whaleboat. I untied the ropes from the cleats while Cairns slotted oars into the rowlocks. Bending our backs, we hauled away from the *Sea Unicorn*. It was still dark at this point, but a thin pale line on the eastern horizon showed the promise of dawn. By the time we had rowed thirty yards, I could just make out, amid the dimness, a thin skein of smoke rising from the ship. It came from one of the hatches just abaft the funnel.

"Good work, Moorhouse," I muttered under my breath.

I truly believed that the flames would soon be extinguished. Moorhouse would not have set a fire that could not be put out easily. I regretted that neither he nor Gillen were on the whaleboat with Cairns and myself. I did not, however, feel the same remorse about Sanchez. The cook, through his own [BLANK] and incaution, had forfeited my sympathies.

We were perhaps a hundred yards from the *Sea Unicorn* when she exploded.

There was a sudden, blinding blaze of light amidships, accompanied by a tremendous booming roar. The *Sea Unicorn* briefly surged upward, then subsided back down. Cairns and I stopped rowing and simply stared. One could tell, just by looking, that the ship was severely, indeed fatally, stricken. She sat crooked in the water, and even as flames billowed up from her, she started to wallow. I can only assume that Moorhouse's act of arson in the engine room had been more effective than he intended. That's the trouble with fire on a ship, and that's why it is one of the things sailors fear most. It can swiftly get out of hand, and even with water all around you, dousing it is no straightforward matter. If I were to hazard a guess, this one had perhaps ignited the coal dust that permeated the air in the engine room. That is the likeliest reason for so catastrophic an outcome.

Now we saw men on deck, silhouetted against the flames, rushing to and fro. Some of them attempted to lower the remaining whaleboats. The *Sea Unicorn*, however, had taken on such an [BLANK] list to starboard as to make this impossible. They then resorted to jumping into the water.

"We should go back," Cairns said. "We should pick up as many of them as we can."

"No," I said. "How many do you think we can fit in this boat with us? How do we decide who to take aboard and who to leave? They are mutineers," I added. "They made their choice. Now they must deal with the consequences."

"But what of Gillen? Moorhouse?"

"It is too late for them. It is too late for anyone aboard."

The ship continued to founder, until all at once her bow rose into the air while her stern went under. Standing almost vertical in the water, she slipped swiftly backwards. Down she sank amid a welter of bubbles, smoke and steam, down beneath the waves. The last Cairns and I saw of her was her bowsprit lofted to the skies vainly, like a drowning man's arm. Then she was gone.

Speaking of drowning men, the crew who had made it off her in time thrashed about in the waves. Their cries reached Cairns and me in our whaleboat, and were pitiful to hear. Many of these men had ascribed to the old sailor's maxim about never learning to swim, for why, if you should fall into the sea without hope of rescue, would you want to prolong the agony? They were lost within moments.

The ones who were able to stay afloat lasted only a little while longer in those wintry conditions. Their voices grew ever more plaintive, and faint, as they called forlornly for their mothers and pleaded for divine help that was never coming. At last they fell silent, and the only sounds were the wind sighing and the splashing of waves.

Cairns looked grimly at me, and I at him.

"Just you and me, Captain," said he.

"Aye. Let's take up our oars and start rowing again."

"Where to?"

"South," said I. "We are not far from the main shipping lanes. By the grace of God, a passing vessel will spot us and pick us up."

"By the grace of God," Cairns echoed. "I believe we may well have forfeited our right to that."

But he started rowing regardless, and so did I.

We have rowed all day, and now, by the fitful light of a candle from the whaleboat's meagre stores, I pen these words. I do not know whether Cairns and I will be rescued. It feels good, however, to keep a record of our situation, and I shall continue to do so for as long as I am able. It is like throwing a lifeline to the future.

THURSDAY 13TH DECEMBER

We take it in turns at the oars, so as to make the most efficient use of our energies. One of us toils while the other rests, in two-hour shifts, and thus the boat keeps constantly on the move. Our muscles ache. Our hands are rubbed raw.

Would that there was food aboard, and a supply of fresh water. Our throats are parched, and we are half faint from hunger.

FRIDAY 14TH DECEMBER

Not so much as a glimpse of a sail. Our efforts at the oars have become lacklustre. I can see that Cairns is already close to giving up hope. I am not far behind him. Sometimes we have no option but to lie upon the thwarts, exhausted beyond measure, and let the currents carry us where they will.

SATURDAY 15TH DECEMBER

Today, a small respite. It rained hard. We opened our mouths and let the rainwater pour in. We then collected as much of it as we could in the bailing piggin, using the cloth of the waif flag as a kind of funnel.

Feeling strengthened, Cairns took up one of the harpoons and stood at the prow in his customary [BLANK] position. Wondering if he might have gone a little mad, I asked him if he was hoping to bag a whale.

"No, Captain," replied he. "A large fish, perhaps."

I thought it a futile exercise but kept my counsel. He stood there for a full three hours, poised. Then all at once the harpoon lanced down into the water, and next thing I knew, Cairns was hauling aboard a large, handsome Atlantic cod. The fish flopped and [BLANK] on the burden-boards. He held it in place, skewered on the harpoon's barb, until its struggles subsided and it gasped its last. Then we skinned it and carved it up, eating strips of its flesh raw and tossing the guts overboard.

"Cairns, you are an excellent fellow," I told him. "A prince among men. A true champion."

Our rowing for the rest of today has shown renewed vigour. Though we are soaked to the skin and chilled to the bone, we both feel hope again.

TUESDAY 18TH DECEMBER *(I think)*

I can barely hold the pencil to write. I feel that [BLANK] and we are doomed.

Cairns has not caught another fish since that cod and has given up trying. He barely stirs, and when he speaks, it is a meaningless mumble. His lips are cracked. His eyes are glazed. He [BLANK]. He is a picture of despair.

Is this ordeal our punishment for leaving the crew of the *Sea Unicorn* to drown when we could have saved even a few of them? Is God condemning us to a slow, lingering death? If so, maybe we deserve it.

???DAY ???TH DECEMBER

I think of my wife and young daughter. I am surprised I have not thought of them sooner. They are not often on my mind, I must admit, even at the best of times. I am neither a good husband nor a good father, and I am well aware that neither of my next of kin holds me in any great affection. It is too late to remedy that. I shall die out here in these freezing watery wastes, and I shall die unloved, unmourned, uncommemorated.

TUESDAY 25TH DECEMBER

Even as I write these words, my hand trembles with disbelief. We were found! We have been rescued! Cairns and I sit by a stove in a warm cabin, our bellies full, our thirst slaked, and from time to time we look at each other and grin and shake our heads. If I were the sort to put stock in Christmas miracles, this is surely one.

Our whaleboat was spotted by a lookout aboard the *Francis Dudley*, the very same American ship the *Sea Unicorn* encountered over a month ago in the Greenland Sea. I have no recollection of the boat being hauled alongside her with gaff hooks or my limp body being hoisted onto her deck. Neither does Cairns. Both of us were unconscious, as close to death as a man can get. Twelve hours and a couple of meals later, and we are well on our way to recovery.

The *Francis Dudley*'s captain, one Enoch Thorne, has been as hospitable as one might hope for. He can perhaps afford to be magnanimous, since he has had a profitable few weeks. The Labrador Sea teemed with whales, he tells us. The pickings were rich, and his holds are full to bursting.

I am not as envious of him as I might otherwise have been. My toleware tin box was retrieved from the whaleboat along with me and Cairns, and I have it with me now. We have rich pickings of our own.

Captain Thorne wanted to know how we two ended up shipless and adrift. I concocted a tale about a storm and gigantic waves that swamped the *Sea Unicorn*. She started taking on water, I said, and I had no alternative but to give the order to abandon ship. We took to the boats, Cairns and I being the last men off. In the tumult of the storm, our boat was separated from the others. We have no idea what befell our fellow crewmen but we fear the worst.

Privately, Cairns and I agree that these are the facts of the matter. We are two shipwrecked mariners, survivors of the sinking of the *Sea Unicorn*. Whether we are the sole survivors, only time will tell. This is our story and we are sticking to it.

We also agree that whatever money accrues from the contents of the tin box will be divided equally between the two of us.

The *Francis Dudley* is putting in at Liverpool on her way home, and Cairns and I will disembark there.

From now on, it is dry land only for me. I have no wish ever to go to sea again.

*

The next entry in Carey's logbook is dated three years later.

*

TUESDAY 3RD AUGUST

I do not keep a diary or a journal, so I have nowhere else to vent my feelings except here.

I have spent the best part of three years attempting to interest certain august bodies in the space-ship up in Greenland. I have written letters, I have met with a variety of learned individuals, I have repeatedly explained how I and my crew explored the huge, strange craft and amassed a collection of items from inside it – all to no avail. I have patiently exhibited to these people the items I managed to retain, and also shown them the pages from this logbook relating to the space-ship's discovery, as authentication. Anticipating responses ranging from fascination to wonderment, I have received instead only laughter and ridicule. I have been informed, again and again, that my story is preposterous, that the logbook entries are purest fiction, and that the artefacts are "homemade gewgaws", "nonsensical rubbish" and "a bizarre, inexplicable assortment of trinkets and fripperies". I have been dismissed as a hoaxer, a deluded fool, and worse.

It does not help my case that I have no academic credentials. Nor do I come with a stainless reputation. It may have been accepted by all parties concerned that the *Sea Unicorn* went down in stormy seas, with the loss of all hands save two. From newspaper reporters to the ship's owners to Lloyd's of London, everyone is agreed that this is the truth. Nonetheless, doubts linger. How come only Patrick Cairns and I occupied a whaleboat that could have held up to a dozen men? How come there were no reports by other sea captains of storms in that area at that time? How come the other whaleboats have never been located? I have answered such queries plausibly and persuasively, yet a cloud of suspicion hangs over me still, and I cannot shake it off.

Cairns has been away at sea all this time, earning a living. I have been keeping him abreast of my efforts and my lack of progress, via mail. His answering letters, posted from various ports around the world, have grown increasingly weary and despondent. The last of them was a tersely worded missive saying, in effect, that I was on a hiding to nothing and should give it up. I wrote back, doing my best to sound encouraging and hopeful, but the sentiments rang hollow even to me. Cairns has not replied since.

Over the course of my career I have saved up just enough money to retire on, as long as I and my family live frugally. Therefore, unlike Cairns, I remain on land, as I vowed I would.

But that presents another problem for me. Even if I were able to convince someone to mount an expedition to rediscover the space-ship, I myself would not – cannot – participate. I will admit it: I am frightened of the sea now. I cannot bear even to be on the coast and gaze out over the waves from the safety of shore. The sea nearly killed me. I have chosen to live far inland, here in depths of the Sussex countryside, so that I will never have to look at it again. Captaining an expedition up to Greenland? Not a chance.

How Cairns dares to expose himself to the cruel, capricious embrace of the oceans, after all we endured, I don't know. He must have nerves of iron.

So much for the boundless riches I thought would be mine.

*

Another entry, some two years later, in 1888.

*

THURSDAY 24TH MAY

I have managed to sell several items from the tin box. The man who bought them is an odd fish – a foreigner, some kind of aristocrat, with a Germanic accent and a very silky way about him. He told me he heard about me through an acquaintance, one of the university professors whom I approached a couple of years ago. He was keen to purchase the entire contents of the box, but I could not bring myself to say yes. I still retain the faint hope that those artefacts may somehow guarantee my future prosperity. In the end, I let him cherry-pick what he wanted, and after some haggling we agreed on a price: £50. It is a tidy sum and no mistake, but hardly the king's ransom I once dreamed of.

I have had no communication with Cairns for some while now. None of my contacts in the maritime world know where he is. I will just have to keep the money for myself.

*

Following that, 1891.

*

WEDNESDAY 11TH NOVEMBER

The same Germanic fellow called again, asking if I had changed my mind and was willing to sell him the rest of what's in the box. His offer was generous, and I can't say I wasn't tempted. Nevertheless, I turned it down. My refusal drew from him a very dirty look and some words muttered in his own language which, even though foreign to me, I could tell were uncomplimentary. Obviously, like many a posh sort, he's not used to taking no for an answer, and the way he scowled at me, with thunder in his eyes, might have made another man quail and yield. Sadly for him, I'm hard to intimidate.

"Nothing you have here, my friend, is worth much to anyone but the likes of me," he growled.

His words sounded like bluster to me. "We'll see about that," I said.

Obstinacy is both my best friend and my worst enemy.

*

The next, and penultimate, entry is dated just a fortnight before Carey's death.

*

WEDNESDAY 12TH JUNE

A letter arrived this morning from Patrick Cairns, out of the blue, postmarked Southampton. "I'll wager you never expected to hear from me again," it begins. "You probably even thought I was dead." He is right on both counts.

"Well," the letter continues, "here I am, alive and well. I have spent the past few years in Newfoundland and Nova Scotia, working as a stevedore and casual labourer to earn a crust. I have had to give up harpooning. My arm is still strong, but my eyesight is not as sharp as it used to be."

Cairns goes on to say that he has decided to return to England. "Call it nostalgia, or just the fond whim of an ageing man," he writes, "but I'd like to see the motherland again and look up some old friends and acquaintances." He proposes to pay a call on me, a couple of weeks hence.

I can hardly refuse, but what then? Cairns comes, and inevitably he will ask about the tin box and its contents. It currently lies on the floor next to me as I sit here writing. He may well want to look inside it. I know I would, were our roles reversed. After a dozen years, who would not be curious to peek, once more, at the souvenirs of the strangest adventure of his life?

If that happens, Cairns will see that a number of the items are missing and he will know that I have sold them and he will want his cut. But the £50 I earned from them is long spent. These days I barely have two pennies to rub together.

My only recourse is to pretend to him that I have disposed of the box and everything in it. I will claim that, because it was proving worthless, I threw it out.

I should have done so anyway, years ago, but I continue to cling to the possibility that somehow I may yet be able to garner a handsome return from it, past experience notwithstanding.

I may not be able to bring myself to get rid of the box, but I can put it somewhere where Cairns will not find it, not easily.

*

The final entry comes just a day later.

*

THURSDAY 13TH JUNE

It is done. I feel like a pirate of yore. I have buried some treasure. Treasure which nobody wants but I want nobody else to have.

No "X" marks the spot. This does: 21° 15' 54" S, 44° 34' 33" E

*

I first read the logbook at Baker Street, after Holmes returned with it from Forest Row.

"So," he enquired as I finished, "what do you make of it?"

"Black Peter Carey's arrogance and selfishness not only cost the lives of almost an entire ship's complement," I said, "but eventually proved his own undoing. There is something of a Greek tragedy about it all. Even Carey's death – harpooned like one of the whales he used to hunt – has a certain dark Sophoclean irony."

"Yes, yes, try not to approach the thing with the eye of a literary critic, Watson. Think like a detective."

"Surely that is your job."

"I am hoping my skills are rubbing off on you," Holmes said, "and that way your dramatisations of my cases will become more analytical and less lurid."

"Well, if they are lurid, their luridity is what makes them so popular, and their popularity is what makes them so lucrative. Need I remind you that my income supports both of us?"

Holmes dismissed my retort with an unapologetic wave of the hand. "Let us concentrate on the matter at hand. Back in 'eighty-three, Carey and company happened upon a giant spacefaring craft up on the coast of Greenland. Clearly this space-ship was some kind of gigantic fungus, with that pulsing bulb at one end its method of propulsion. Clearly, too, it had transported a number of Outside Things to Earth from Yuggoth. What else can those pink, insect-like creatures he describes have been but members of the Mi-Go race? Are we agreed on that?"

"We are."

"The Mi-Go in the space-ship... What should we call them? There ought to be a word for it. Space pilots? Interplanetary sailors? No, something more specific. I have it! Fungonauts. The fungonauts in the space-ship died almost straight away upon reaching here. We can speculate on the reasons."

"The extreme Arctic cold?"

"No, Watson. Think! What do we know of Yuggoth from Irene Adler's testimony?" Holmes took his modified orrery down from its shelf and pointed to the ninth planet he had added. "Here is a world scarcely touched by the sun's warmth. Icy coldness is nothing to its denizens. It is their natural milieu." He moved his finger inward to the ivory sphere representing Earth, which was painted a mottled blue and green. "I would suggest, rather, that the blame lies with either our planet's atmosphere or the greater intensity of the sunlight here. As to the first proposition, insects do not have lungs. Instead they breathe by means of pore-like openings in their exoskeletons known as spiracles. An insect the size of a human, which is essentially what a Mi-Go is, would require an exponentially large intake of oxygen in order to survive. Yuggoth must have an oxygen-rich atmosphere that makes this possible, and the space-ship was likewise equipped with such an atmosphere to sustain the fungonauts. By contrast, Earth's atmosphere is comparatively oxygen-poor, so that the fungonauts, upon emerging from their sealed vessel and taking their first tentative steps upon our planet's surface, suffocated and perished."

"Seems reasonable."

"Alternatively, the level of sunlight to which we humans are accustomed is anathema to them. Animals that live in near-total darkness, such as are found in caves and in the soil, cannot abide the sun. Their hides do not protect them, and the sun's rays bake them from within. So it was with our Mi-Go visitors. Either of these hypotheses – lack of oxygen or susceptibility to sunlight – would explain why Earth is uncongenial to them to the point of lethality."

"Then they were foolish to come."

"What if they did not know beforehand how dangerous it might be?" said Holmes, setting the orrery back on its shelf. "What if the space-ship was a pioneering expedition which, much like the *Sea Unicorn*'s final voyage, ended in disaster?"

"I grant you the possibility."

"The space-ship landed in northern climes because the Mi-Go knew the temperatures there would suit them. They just did not know how inhospitable Earth is for them in other ways. The failure of the expedition would explain, too, why they have not made the attempt again in the decade or so since. Not to our knowledge, at any rate. Once bitten, twice shy."

"In which case," I said, "it makes sense that their next step would have been to recruit terrestrial ambassadors like Miss Adler. If they wish to reach out to mankind but have found that they themselves cannot survive on Earth, they need go-betweens."

Holmes nodded. "That is if their intentions are friendly," he said. "If not, then the fungonauts were an expeditionary force, here to establish a beachhead."

"Which would account for the items they brought with them that proved so injurious to the health of the *Sea Unicorn*'s crew: the purple spherical fungus with its lethal infection, and the metallic device whose invisible emanations spread madness through the ship. Both could have been designed specifically to harm human beings, by a race that has been

SHERLOCK HOLMES and the HIGHGATE HORRORS

observing us for some while and assessing our susceptibilities and vulnerabilities."

"Yet it is conceivable, Watson, that they were meant purely for self-defence. Let us compare the fungonauts to human explorers venturing into an unknown continent. They have no idea whether the natives are going to be friendly or not, so naturally they bring rifles, just in case. They may be there for the most benign of reasons — discovery, science, fostering relations with another race — but it does not hurt to take precautions, does it? Regardless, the foray to Earth did not succeed, and so the Mi-Go back on Yuggoth have resorted to subtler tactics."

"Infiltration? Making unwilling agents out of the likes of Irene Adler?"

"Perhaps. In any case, I think the contents of Captain Carey's toleware tin box may prove instructive. Therefore we must find where he buried it."

"He has provided us with a significant clue to its location, surely," I said, motioning to the logbook. "We have the exact co-ordinates, to the nearest minute of latitude and longitude."

"Do we? Fetch down the world atlas, would you? Thank you." Holmes opened up the weighty tome and started leafing through. At last he came to the double-page spread he sought. He ran a finger slowly down along a line of longitude, then across on a line of latitude. "Here we are. 21 degrees, 15 minutes, 54 seconds south, by 44 degrees, 34 minutes, 33 seconds east." The finger had come to rest on an island.

"Buried treasure on an island," I remarked. "Carey was right: very piratical. Like something out of Stevenson."

"Again, you and your literary-mindedness, Watson," Holmes said with a sigh. "The island in question is Madagascar, and the co-ordinates point to a spot about thirty miles inland from its west coast."

"Carey certainly went to some lengths to hide the box."

"Come, come! The logbook tells us that the letter from

Cairns alerting Carey to his imminent visit arrived on the twelfth of June, and Carey buried the box on the thirteenth. Are you honestly saying Carey travelled all the way from Sussex to the Indian Ocean in the space of a day?"

"Well, no, of course not. That would be absurd."

"So the box is not on Madagascar."

"I have the impression you knew that all along. This business with the atlas has been by way of a demonstration, to show up my ignorance."

"Am I so very transparent?" said Holmes with a smile. "Consider who we are dealing with: Black Peter Carey, an avaricious egotist who treated all around him with disdain and spite. He hid the tin box from Patrick Cairns and planted a false lead to its location in his logbook, on the off-chance that Cairns might think to look there for clues. Cairns, don't forget, would have seen him writing in it while they were in the whaleboat together. When Cairns killed him, Carey used his dying breath to provide the key to unlocking the truth, but being the vindictive scoundrel that he was, he did it in a cryptic way that would only confuse Cairns more."

"'Knock and you shall find,'" I said. "What can that mean in this respect?"

"Watson, have you ever heard of a knock code?"

"I have not."

"It's a system used by convicts to communicate between their cells without the guards realising. Sailors employ it too, as a means of passing information from cabin to cabin without having to shout. It's based on sequences of taps. Here, let me show you."

Holmes took a sheet of paper and a pencil and drew a grid consisting of five squares by five. He wrote a letter of the alphabet in every square apart from one, in which he wrote two.

When he was done, it looked like this:

	1	2	3	4	5
1	A	B	C/K	D	E
2	F	G	H	I	J
3	L	M	N	O	P
4	Q	R	S	T	U
5	V	W	X	Y	Z

"The system operates rather like co-ordinates for latitude and longitude," he said. "To represent a letter, one first taps out the number of the row it lies in, then the number of the column. So, for instance, to convey my initials one would tap four times then three times, for the S, followed by two times then three times, for the H." He illustrated the example by rapping on the tabletop. "Whether one tap followed by three signifies C or K can be inferred from context."

"I see," I said.

"So if we take Carey's co-ordinates…" Holmes wrote 21° 15' 54" S, 44° 34' 33" E on the sheet of paper. "Then erase the symbols for degrees, minutes and seconds thus…" He went to work with a rubber. What remained was 21 15 54 S 44 34 33 E. "We are left with a readily interpretable knock code. All we have to do is leave the S and E as they are and fill in the letters that correspond to the numbers."

He did just that, so that a word appeared below the string of mixed numbers and letters.

21	15	54	S	44	34	33	E
F	E	Y	S	T	O	N	E

"Feystone?" I said. "Sounds like a place name. Where is it?"

"Try 'What is it?'," said Holmes. "The Feystone is an ancient monument dating back to Neolithic times – a dolmen consisting of one flat stone supported by a quartet of upright stones. It lies in the Ashdown Forest, a couple of miles south of Forest Row."

"Did you know this already too, just as you knew the co-ordinates were not for Madagascar?"

"Again, yes. But I always enjoy elucidating my findings to you, Watson. It has become an indispensable step in my process."

"Then the tin box is buried at this dolmen," I said.

"I should say so."

"And we are to dig it up?"

Holmes patted me on the shoulder. "With the pair of us putting our backs into it, it should not take long. Now, where do you think we can get hold of a couple of shovels? I imagine Mrs Hudson can help on that front. Then it's off to Victoria to catch the East Grinstead train."

"You mean to go now?"

"Why not? No time like the present."

"But it's past five o'clock," I said. "We shall be lucky to get to Forest Row while it's still light."

"All the more reason to hurry."

*

Armed with shovels, Sherlock Holmes and I strode across the ragged heathland of the Ashdown Forest. Ahead of us, atop a low rise, lay the megalithic structure that was the Feystone. It stood silhouetted against the setting sun, dark and huge, like some rough-hewn table made for gods to sit at. I estimated its height at ten or eleven feet, and each of the stones from which it was composed must have weighed several tons. As much it was an impressive feat of primitive engineering, I found myself wondering what had prompted the people of prehistoric times to build it.

Holmes seemed to read my thoughts. "Nobody quite knows what the Feystone's purpose is," he said. "Dolmens may have been burial sites, reserved for important members of the tribe, such as the chieftain. It's equally possible they were used for druidical rituals. Archaeologists just aren't sure. This particular one has garnered a special reputation over the centuries. It is widely believed to be a gateway to fairyland – 'fey', of course, being a synonym for fairy. Tradition has it that on certain nights – equinoxes, solstices, Halloween, May Day eve, those times when the barrier between this world and other realms is said to be at its thinnest – the fairy folk emerge from their kingdom via the Feystone and run riot. According to local superstition, you keep yourselves indoors on such nights and make sure your livestock are safely barricaded inside their barns. Otherwise the pixies and pookas and sprites might sour the milk in your cows' udders, frighten your sheep to death, or, worse still, kidnap unwary children and spirit them off to the fairy realm. The summer solstice was on the twenty-first of June, by the way. We have missed it by two days. In case you were worried."

"I was not," I said. "I don't believe in fairies."

"Neither of us believed in demonic gods or human-reptile hybrids or slavering monsters, Watson, until we were forced to think otherwise. There are many reasons not to dismiss folklore, for it often has its roots in truth. Fairies may simply be a race of powerful, sophisticated magical beings who interacted with mankind in the past but now spend their days in self-imposed exile, in their otherworldly hinterland. Sometimes they might still venture forth to wreak mischief, but mostly they are content to have withdrawn from mankind's purview, their deeds remembered in songs and fables."

"Well, if I ever meet one, then I will credit their existence. Until that time, I feel we have a large enough roster of inhuman entities to contend with already."

"Well put, old friend. So, here we are." We had reached

the Feystone. "And there," Holmes said with a gesture, "unless I am much mistaken, is the spot where Carey's tin box lies." He was indicating a patch of bare soil among the grass that grew below the dolmen's capstone. "It is the right size, judging by the rectangle of dust-free floor in Carey's cabin, and the earth was turned, by the looks of it, approximately ten days ago, which accords with the date in his logbook."

"How can you tell that?"

"Shoots of new grass have just started to push through. That commonly takes ten to fourteen days."

"Fair enough. But why bury the box here? Why beneath a dolmen, when he had the whole of the Ashdown Forest to choose from?"

"You have answered your own question. The Ashdown Forest covers hundreds of acres. If you mean to bury something so that you can find it again without too much trouble, do it at a prominent landmark. Now, are you going to carry that shovel or are you going to use it?"

We set to digging, and the sun bade its final farewell to the day and a breeze began whispering through the bracken and heather. Twilight faded quickly from the sky and the moon rose, but it was in its slimmest phase, the merest shaving of silver, and shed little illumination. Fortunately Holmes had had the foresight to bring along a dark-lantern, and by its yellow glow we continued our endeavours.

We excavated a hole roughly two feet deep without any sign of the tin box.

"Carey was taking no chances," I said, pausing for a moment to rest my aching back. I glanced around. Beyond the light from the lantern lay utter darkness. The lantern itself shone brightly, its lambency reflecting off the Feystone's four uprights and capstone. Holmes and I were enclosed in a nimbus of brilliance, while everywhere else was shadow.

The breeze strengthened, its whisper becoming a hiss. I felt a sudden prickle of unease. By daylight the heathland had had a rough, undulating beauty. Now it was an unknowable black void, where anything might be lurking.

"Let's hurry it up, shall we?" I said, bending again to my task.

A few minutes later, Holmes's shovel struck something hard and metallic with a clang.

"A-ha," said he.

Some further digging and a little bit of scraping, and we had uncovered the top of a large box. The dark-lantern picked out the gilt markings on its black surface, and I was able to descry the name of a prominent London robemaker.

Holmes and I burrowed around it until we had exposed all four sides. Then we paused again and each took a nip of whisky from my hip flask.

"You seem on edge," my companion remarked.

"You'd think I would be used to this sort of thing by now," I said. "Antics, usually nocturnal, in strange, wild places. Yet I'm not. There's always something that gets the hackles rising, even if it is only one's imagination working overtime."

"We both possess powerful imaginations," Holmes averred. "The difference between us is that yours lacks discipline and errs towards the fanciful. Mine, on the other hand, is channelled exclusively into the art of detection. I do not give it the liberty to wander."

"Was that supposed to be reassuring?"

"It was supposed to divert your attention back to the job at hand. We are nearly done. We just need to pry the box out of the ground."

Squatting, we reached into the hole and rooted around with our fingers until we were able to slide them beneath the box.

"On my count," said Holmes. "One. Two. Three."

We heaved, we strained, and all at once the box came free. It was as though the earth had been unwilling to relinquish it. We hefted it up – it must have weighed around thirty pounds –

and laid it down beside the hole. Holmes brushed away the last remnants of dirt clinging to it, then tried the lid.

"Locked," he said. "I thought it might be. But that shouldn't be a problem. Bring the lantern over, Watson. Direct the beam on the keyhole. That's it. Good." He produced his penknife and slid the blade into the slot. "This sort of lock is not too difficult to jimmy. It's more for ornament than security." He jiggled and twisted the penknife.

The breeze had become a wind. Around us, fern fronds rustled and shivered. I envisaged the encircling undergrowth thronged with wildlife – animals and worse: things that were more than animals but less than human. These creatures were watching us from the dark, curious, excited, an audience in the round, drawn to our performance here on this well-lit stage. I tried to shake the mental image out of my head, but it stuck fast. Holmes was right about my imagination. It was ill disciplined, and when I most needed it under control, that was when it grew unruliest.

All at once there was a loud click, and the box lid sprang ajar. Holmes gave a grunt of satisfaction.

"Now then," said he. "Let us set eyes on these alien artefacts." He raised the lid. "Keep that light trained this way, Watson. And hold it steady, if you would. There we go."

Inside the box there was a lidded cylinder fashioned from some kind of metal and adorned with knurled knobs and other protrusions, along with a kind of small, circular window, akin to a porthole, inset into its side. There was something like a large, round polyp encased in a net-like substance. A third item was pear-shaped and palely translucent, with what appeared to be a wooden handle.

I ran the lantern beam over these and other oddities, noting that the ones fashioned from metal reflected the light in a manner I had never seen before. It was as though the material was nacreous, but some of the colours that chased across its surfaces did not belong to the standard spectrum.

I could not even name them. They were colours not of this world, alien colours.

"Quite a haul, eh?" said Holmes. "Do you doubt these originate from another planet?"

"Not for one second," I replied. "Every word in Carey's logbook is true."

"I cannot wait to get them home and study them. There is much to be learned here, Watson."

Holmes closed the lid of the box slowly, almost reluctantly, as if he couldn't bear to deprive himself of the sight of such marvels. He stood, then bent and gathered up the box with both hands.

"You take the lantern and lead the way," said he. "Don't forget the shovels."

"Aren't we going to fill in the hole?"

"Why not leave it as it is?" An impish smile tweaked the corners of Holmes's mouth. "The locals will assume the fairies did it. It will give them something to talk about for months."

"Now who's a mischief-maker?" I said. "Are you sure you're not part fairy yourself?"

With the dark-lantern held aloft before me, I set off across the tussocky terrain, Holmes following. About three quarters of a mile away lay the track where we had left our hired dog-cart, its horse tethered to a tree. We retraced our footsteps thither, without incident, and Holmes loaded the box into the back of the cart before unloosing the horse and climbing up to the driver's seat to take the reins. Meanwhile I lit the cart's lamps, and shortly we were making our way back to East Grinstead at a stately plod.

Overhead, the stars scintillated in their thousands. Perched beside Holmes, I gazed up at them and thought of Yuggoth. Perhaps the Mi-Go home world was one of those stars, like its planetary companions such as Saturn or Venus. Perhaps some of its inhabitants were presently looking towards the star that was Earth and thinking of this world, just as I was thinking of theirs. Objects from Yuggoth now lay in the back of our dog-cart. They had been transported across millions of miles of barren, airless void, then been brought from the Arctic to England before winding up in our possession. The very notion, the sheer enormity of what it implied, boggled the mind.

I retained the hope that the Outside Things meant us no harm; they were simply extending a cautious hand of friendship towards the people of Earth. Although we and they were physically quite unalike, and they could not survive on our world and perhaps we could not on theirs, they wished to strike up a relationship. Our two races were perhaps the only intelligent forms of life in the entire solar system. We might not be near neighbours, but that did not mean we should not talk. Both sides would surely benefit from the exchange.

And if the Mi-Go's objectives were not so benign?

I did not want to think about that.

Holmes, as he drove, began humming a tune – Schubert's "*Das Lied im Grünen*" – and I knew this to mean he was feeling pleased with himself. He had every right to be. He had solved another case and had collected some trophies that could prove revelatory. He was doing what he had been put on this Earth to do.

As for me, I wrestled with my misgivings, and my misgivings did not quite win.

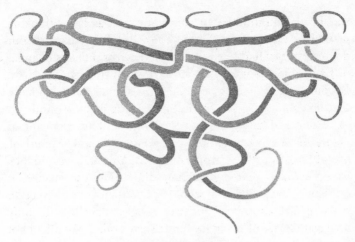

PART IV

Autumn 1898

THE TELEGRAM ARRIVED ON A BLUSTERY OCTOBER day not long after Sherlock Holmes and I had finished taking lunch.

"It's from MacKinnon of the Yard," said Holmes.

"Ah yes. Late of the Josiah Amberley case," I said.

"None other. Fine fellow. One of the Met's brighter luminaries, or at any rate one of their less dim ones. Now then, what does he have to say? Oh. Dear me."

"What is it?"

Holmes passed the telegram to me. It read:

AMBERLEY ESCAPED STOP MANHUNT LAUNCHED
STOP ADVICE WELCOME STOP

"That is not good news," I remarked. "He was in Broadmoor, wasn't he?"

"With all the other madmen. And now he is not."

"Do you think MacKinnon's manhunt will round him up?"

"The police have numbers in their favour," Holmes said. "What they lack in brains, they make up for in manpower. Amberley, however, is not your common-or-garden lawbreaker. He combines a degree of Machiavellian cunning with a complete absence of scruple, and this makes him formidable. It is not surprising, really, that he has slipped out of incarceration, and it will not be surprising if he manages to elude Her Majesty's constabulary."

"If only he had been hanged for his crimes, rather than imprisoned."

"Not for want of trying on my part. The judicial system had other ideas. Well, if it is advice young MacKinnon is after, I am happy to give it to him. Let us make haste for Broadmoor.

En route, we shall stop at the telegram office so that I can let the inspector know the matter is in hand and ask him to alert the authorities at Broadmoor to our imminent arrival."

An hour later we were aboard a Great Western Railway train and steaming out of Paddington towards Reading. As London receded behind us, Holmes said, "Perhaps it would help if we were to review the facts of the Amberley case, in order to see whether we can shed new light upon it."

"Very well."

We had the compartment to ourselves, and Holmes stretched out his long legs and got comfortable.

"The double murder committed by Josiah Amberley, retired colourman, just last summer," he began, "seemed to provide solid prima facie evidence of Mi-Go involvement in human affairs. For that reason alone I was excited by it."

"I know. It has been several years since your dinner with Irene Adler."

"Several? A whole decade."

"And three since we dug up Black Peter Carey's toleware box. All this time, we have turned up very little further activity relating to the Mi-Go and their plans."

"I have had my lines cast," Holmes said, "as have Mycroft and the Dagon Club, but there has been nary a nibble. On those rare occasions when I've felt there is something to reel in, I have done so only to find that the fish has wriggled off the hook. Sometimes I have asked myself whether the whole thing isn't just some blind alley. Could it be that the Outer Ones have changed their minds? That their efforts so far have come to naught and they have aborted their mission, whatever it was?"

"Or," I said, "they are playing a long game."

"A very long game, conducted with considerable patience. Then again, perhaps patience is not required. A day on Yuggoth is six times as long as a day on Earth. A year there lasts the equivalent of around two hundred and fifty of our years. That, at least, is if my calculations with my orrery are correct.

Perhaps, then, the Mi-Go perception of time differs wildly from ours. They operate at a tortoise's pace while, to them, we are hares rushing madly about. But back to Amberley. He came to me as a client, asking to engage my services regarding a crime he himself had in fact committed."

"The nerve of him. 'Pure swank', as you put it. He presented himself as devastated because his wife had made off with another man and also with a deed-box containing a goodly portion of Amberley's life's savings in cash and securities. He hired you to find them, when all along he himself had slain them."

"I certainly had my doubts about him when we met," said Holmes. "He told me about his younger wife and his equally young friend Dr Ray Ernest, with whom he played chess regularly, and how the pair of them had absconded together, taking a great deal of his money. He painted a portrait of a doting husband who had been sorely betrayed. Yet throughout it all he struck me as a touch too melodramatic, a touch too 'woe is me!' You can overdo the misery, you know. Then – more pertinently – there were the encrustations of paint beneath his fingernails. I instantly identified it as wall paint and could only infer that Amberley had been busy redecorating."

"And why would one repaint one's house when one's wife had just made off with another man and a fair bit of one's worldly wealth?" I said. "Who would have the equanimity under those circumstances?"

Holmes nodded. "As a first step to confirming, or disproving, my suspicions about him, I despatched you to The Haven, Amberley's house in Lewisham, to interview him. And what was the first thing that caught your eye when you got there? A two-foot-tall alabaster statuette that stood on a pedestal in an alcove in the hallway."

"I recall the moment well. I had to bite my lip to stop myself from exclaiming aloud."

"You recognised it on the spot."

"Tentacled, goat-legged, with multiple fanged maws and a host of maggot-like progeny crawling from openings in its body…"

"Shub-Niggurath."

"The goddess Shub-Niggurath," I said, "just as depicted in the *Necronomicon* and, moreover, as described by Miss Adler. No great beauty, she. I mean Shub-Niggurath, obviously. Amberley caught me staring at the statuette and asked what I thought of it. I havered, saying something like, 'It has a very striking look.' I enquired as to how he had come by it, and Amberley replied that he had picked it up at an antique shop. He too had found the statuette striking, he said, and although the shop owner was unsure of its provenance, Amberley himself reckoned it was some tribal totem brought back from one of the more benighted corners of the globe, the East Indies or thereabouts."

"My immediate thought, upon hearing you relay his words, was that he was spinning you a yarn," said Holmes. "One does not give something as hideous as a statuette of Shub-Niggurath pride of place in one's house, on a pedestal in one's hallway, where all comers will see it. Not unless one thinks it aesthetically appealing, which nobody in his right mind would. Rather, one sets it there to make a point. Just as a devout Christian hangs a crucifix on his wall, so a worshipper of Shub-Niggurath would display a token of his faith prominently. If my nostrils had not already been twitching, that would have set them off."

"My nostrils literally twitched," I said, "because the smell of fresh paint in the house was overpowering."

"Validating my supposition about the paint beneath Amberley's fingernails. But there had to be better evidence of foul play than a penchant for queer knickknacks and an incongruous desire to daub fresh paint on the walls of one's home. Hence I sent you and Amberley off on a wild goose chase to a remote corner of Essex, so that I could take a look around The Haven for myself, unimpeded."

"'Take a look around'. Quite the euphemism, Holmes. You broke in like a burglar."

"Needs must," said my companion. "Amberley had shown you, in passing, the door to his strong-room, where among other things he had kept the deed-box which his wife allegedly plundered. It was there that I concentrated my efforts. I picked the lock, and once the door was open, the first thing I noticed was a strong musty odour. I set to inspecting the room minutely. First I spied a few drops of dried black liquid on the floor. I scraped some up with a thumbnail. When wetted, the scrapings turned bright red."

"In other words, blood."

"The merest speckling of blood, but noteworthy nonetheless. Then, in a corner, I spotted a powdery residue. It was just a smattering of turquoise granules, but close scrutiny with my glass suggested to me that this was organic matter, spores or pollen of some kind. I put my nose to it and discerned that it gave off a more pungent version of the musty odour which permeated the room. In other words, here was the source of the smell – the same smell that the smell of fresh paint was intended to mask. Careful not to touch the stuff with my bare hands, I scooped some into an envelope, for later examination. It did not escape my notice that there were the marks of brush hairs in the residue."

"Someone had swept the floor but missed a bit."

"That's it. Next, I turned my attention to the strong-room's walls, where I perceived smeary traces of chalk in a great number of places. You know how a blackboard can never be wiped truly clean? Same with those walls. Someone had scrawled all over them in chalk, from skirting board to ceiling, then erased the inscriptions. But again, as with the sweeping, the attempt to eradicate evidence was inefficient. Here and there the ghostly remnants of words were visible. And they were words in R'lyehian."

At that moment, with a piercing screech of its whistle,

the train entered a tunnel. Our compartment was cast into darkness, and the sound of wheels on rails, amplified within the tunnel's confines, rose to a deafening roar.

"R'lyehian," I said, when we had emerged back into daylight. "The language of Cthulhu and his kin. An unspeakable tongue."

"Unspeakable in more ways than one," said Holmes. "On the strong-room's walls I was able to distinguish three words more or less clearly. They were '*vulgtagln*', '*uln*' and '*iä*' – respectively, 'pray to', 'summon' and 'hail to you'. Even more tellingly, I found the sigil for Shub-Niggurath. From all of this I could draw only one conclusion. To my experienced eye, a ceremony had been conducted in that room, and judging by the drops of blood, it had been a sacrifice of some sort."

"A human sacrifice," I said. "Amberley had invited Shub-Niggurath to accept his offering of an unfaithful wife and her paramour, as a mark of his devotion."

"Such was my thinking," Holmes said. "He wanted the pair dead anyway, out of pure jealous rage, but he elected to turn the killings into a tribute to the loathsome goddess whose statuette he displayed so proudly in his hallway."

"Convenient, to indulge one's basest impulses but dress it up as an act of religiosity."

"Be that as it may, I now had Josiah Amberley pegged as a double murderer, but also as an active acolyte of Shub-Niggurath, she who is also known as the Black Goat of the Woods With a Thousand Young. However, a few droplets of blood, some spores and a handful of faint chalk marks which would look like gibberish to the untrained eye – these did not constitute irrefutable proof of his crime. There had to be bodies. Where were they? I checked the rest of the house, without success, then headed out into the garden."

"Where you soon found a disused well."

"A dog kennel rested on top," Holmes said, "concealing the opening. Furrows in the lawn suggested the kennel had been recently dragged into position. I pulled it aside, and down below, in the well, there they were."

"Mrs Amberley and Dr Ray Ernest."

"A repugnant sight. The well had been partly filled in some time ago, so that it was now a narrow pit only eight or nine feet deep. Therein lay the two corpses, more or less upright, face to face with their limbs entangled."

"As though embracing. Lovers even in death."

"Yes, yes, very poetic, Watson, but these two were far from being Romeo and Juliet, picturesquely dead in the tomb," said Holmes. "Dried blood was caked around their noses and mouths. Beetles crawled all over them. Bloat had begun to set in, the sight of which, in tandem with the stench of decomposition, told me they had been dead at least three days. And that was not all. Down there with them were the remnants of some kind of large, spherical fungus. I leaned in to examine it. It was turquoise, like verdigris – the same colour as the powdery residue on the strong-room floor. It would have been the size of a lawn bowls ball in its intact form. Now, it was splayed open, its innards exposed. My thoughts went straight to Irene Adler and her experience in the Vermont woods."

"When that fungus erupted like a puffball mushroom," I said, "showering her with spores from within."

"Evidently the same principle applied here. This fungus too had exploded, but with somewhat different results. It wasn't a means of astral transportation but a tool of murder. Inhaling its spores had killed Mrs Amberley and Dr Ernest. Their lungs had ruptured and they had choked on their own blood. This I was able to confirm later when I tested the spore sample I had collected in the strong-room. I placed a mouse in a cage along with piece of cheese dusted with a few grains of the stuff. The creature took one bite of the adulterated cheese, and rapidly began bleeding from mouth and nose. It perished within seconds."

"A vile weapon."

"Deployed by a vile man. I could only assume that Amberley must have lured his wife and Ernest into the strongroom. Once they were inside, and at his mercy, he slammed the door on them and locked it. There they were, trapped, with those chalked, unintelligible inscriptions all around them and that strange turquoise fungus on the floor, ripe and ready to erupt. It must have been alarming, to say the least."

"And then agonising, when the fungus burst open and showered them with its deadly cargo. One can only hope it was over as quickly for them as it was for your mouse."

"Quite," said Holmes. "It was while I was peering at the fungus in the well that I heard noises from nearby. Someone was climbing over the wall from the street. I swiftly replaced the dog kennel and took refuge behind a tree. Who should I see walking across the garden but a certain other consulting detective. The moustache, the sunglasses, the military bearing…"

"One Mr Barker," I said. "Also known as your 'hated rival on the Surrey shore'."

Holmes acknowledged the epithet – which he himself had coined – with an ironical tilt of the head. "Barker has set up his own detective agency and his methods are very much modelled on mine. He styles himself the 'south bank Sherlock Holmes', and I will allow that he has had a few modest successes. And now here he was, intruding upon The Haven much as I had. I felt moved to emerge from hiding and confront him. He was both startled and pleased to see me. We compared notes, and it transpired that Barker had been hired by Dr Ernest's family to look into the fellow's disappearance. 'Apparently, Mr Holmes, we are pursuing the same case from different ends,' said he. 'Shall we join forces? Two great brains are better than one.' While I balked at the implication that Barker's intellect was on the same plane as mine, I felt I had no choice but to agree to his proposal. Had I brushed him off, it would only have compelled him to work harder, in an effort to outdo his exemplar and show himself to be my superior."

"In the pursuit of which goal, he would have got in your way."

"Very probably. But also, I saw an opportunity to make Barker useful to me. I already had it in mind that I would need to 'tidy up' the murder, as it were."

"You mean dispense with its esoteric elements."

"Exactly. Much as you do with your stories, and Mycroft with his Dagon Club, I felt I should 'cleanse' the case by stripping it of anything inexplicable to the general public. That way the law would have a far more straightforward job securing Amberley's conviction and he would be guaranteed the eight o'clock walk and the hempen rope. As things stood, the murders might be deemed an act of madness and he could end his days in an asylum, which would be better than he deserved. To that end, I sent Barker off to look round the house. While he was gone, I uncovered the well and retrieved the fungus using a spade from the garden shed. I dug a hole and buried the fungus."

"I know you have since disinterred the thing and burned it. Very wise."

"Of course. Having replaced the dog kennel over the well yet again, I then re-entered the house. Barker was upstairs, crashing around in a rather clumsy quest for clues. I stole into the strong-room and rubbed out the few remaining R'lyehian words. I then wrote 'We we—' in indelible pencil on the wall, a foot above the floor."

"In a deliberately wavering, unsteady scrawl."

"Just so," said Holmes. "I called Barker down and showed him the words. He said he had looked in the strong-room earlier and hadn't spotted them, and praised the acuteness of my eye. I pointed out a gas pipe that ran into the room from the corridor outside. I wondered aloud whether the repainting Amberley had been doing was in any way relevant. I let Barker slowly piece things together. Amberley, he concluded, could have shut his wife and Ernest in the strong-room, then turned on the gas tap outside and flooded that airtight chamber with gas, suffocating them. As for the 'We we—', he said it could have been an attempt by one of the victims to write 'We were murdered' as they lay dying. Perhaps, Barker mused, the strong smell of paint was intended to cover up another smell, the lingering odour of gas. I clapped hand to forehead as if amazed at the fellow's perspicacity. 'Why,' I exclaimed, 'you must be right! On every count! How brilliant of you.' You should have seen the look on his face then, Watson. Like a patted dog, he was."

"You allowed him to work through the chain of deduction, doing it in such a way that he thought he was making the inferences all by himself," I said. "You played him."

"Like the proverbial fiddle."

"Better, it would seem, than you play the actual fiddle."

Holmes harrumphed. "I knew then that if I could convince Barker this was the truth of the murders, I could similarly convince MacKinnon, and anyone else. It only remained to 'find' the bodies. Barker and I combed the garden. I became curious about the dog kennel, or affected to. I enlisted Barker's aid in moving it aside, and thus did he and I discover the well and its gruesome contents – he for the first time and I as though for the first time. We both recoiled in shock, although mine was feigned where his was not."

"Your thespian talents coming to the fore, as ever."

"It was a sustained, well-modulated performance, even if I say so myself," Holmes said. "All in all, through sham and cajolery, I had managed to secure Barker's full complicity. We parted company, with an agreement to reconvene at The Haven in the morning in order to effect Amberley's arrest. Then I went back to Baker Street."

"Whither I myself returned the next day, with Amberley, after our sojourn in Essex," I said.

"The two of you had spent a day and a night visiting a rural vicar who purportedly had information relating to the eloped couple."

"But who did not, because that was a complete fabrication, made up by you. You were out when Amberley and I got in, but you had left instructions with Mrs Hudson that we were to meet you at The Haven."

"It was a rather ill-humoured Watson and Amberley who greeted Barker and myself in Lewisham."

"One can hardly blame us for that," I said. "Our trip had been a complete waste of time."

"But necessary," said Holmes. "Amberley had had to be decoyed away from home somehow. And no sooner did he walk in than I accused him of the killings. He responded with aggression, and there was considerable strength in his body for a man his age."

"And considerable agility, what's more, for a man with an artificial leg."

"We restrained him nonetheless, and Barker hurried off to fetch MacKinnon. The inspector was satisfied with our account of how the murders had been committed – the gas pipe, the 'We we—', all of it – and I allowed Barker to take the lion's share of the credit for uncovering the truth."

"It was a highly plausible scenario."

"So I thought. But alas, the law was not satisfied with it, and thus, despite my best efforts, Josiah Amberley was not executed, but rather wound up being detained indefinitely at Her Majesty's pleasure. Until now, at least."

The train pulled in at Reading, where we changed for the North Downs line towards Guildford. Again, we found ourselves in an empty compartment and thus felt at liberty to carry on our conversation.

"I remember how Amberley reacted as you elucidated your falsified version of his crime to Inspector MacKinnon," I said. "He grew ever more amused and kept chuckling. I didn't know then that you were eliding the occult elements out of it. I just thought Amberley was posturing."

"He was, to a certain extent. You will recall how, as MacKinnon's men were taking him away, he pointed to the statuette of Shub-Niggurath. 'And what do you make of *that*, oh-so-brainy Mr Sherlock Holmes?' he said. 'How does that fit in to this pretty little scheme of yours?'"

"And you replied, nonchalant as anything, 'I have no idea what that even is, Amberley. Some tribal totem from the East Indies or thereabouts, perchance?' It rather tickled me, you echoing back at him what he himself had said to me."

"I spotted you trying to mask a smile."

"But here's the thing," I said. "Amberley could not have been unaware that you had tampered with the crime scene. Weren't you worried? We didn't discuss it at the time, but you had faked evidence. Amberley could have levelled just that accusation at you, a mistrial might have been declared, and things would then have got very awkward. You could have even wound up in court yourself on charges of perverting the course of justice. In hindsight, you took quite a risk."

"A calculated risk," my friend said. "I told you, I needed to simplify the situation. MacKinnon didn't have to know that the murders were a human sacrifice to an eldritch god. Neither did Barker. Neither, more importantly, did the judge, the barristers and the jury. Bringing Amberley to trial and successfully securing the death penalty for him would be much easier if it was merely a case of 'cuckolded husband kills his wife and her lover by mundane means'."

"And Amberley has kept mum, so your gamble paid off."

"Not a gamble, a calculated risk," Holmes insisted. "I imagine that, had the judge put on the black cap and pronounced the death sentence, Amberley might have kicked up a fuss. But without any proof of what I had done, it would have been Amberley's word against mine, and who is more apt to be believed, a convicted murderer or a detective with connections to the police? More likely, any such protest on his part would have been dismissed as the desperate ravings of a guilty man. As it was, Amberley knew he had got off lightly and therefore saw no need to rock the boat. Credit to him, he had played it skilfully in court. He remained composed throughout the trial, but at opportune moments he essayed a symptom of mental instability, a little tic or fidget, a distant stare, a mutter, nothing ostentatious but enough to suggest currents of madness beneath that calm surface. It worked, and while the verdict was never in doubt, the judge took the view that this man was plainly not of sound mind and commuted his sentence to life imprisonment."

"Except he is imprisoned no longer," I observed. "Somehow Josiah Amberley is a free man."

"Something I rather feared might happen. Hence I would prefer that he had been hanged. He is a dangerous fellow to have at large."

I gave a grunt of assent. "So then," I said, "are you any wiser for this recapitulation of ours?"

"Not particularly, but the details of the case are fresh in our minds again, if nothing else."

"What of its Mi-Go connotations? Shub-Niggurath, an unusual and deadly fungus…"

"They remain tantalisingly unsubstantiated. Nothing Amberley did suggests he is part of some larger scheme, and he refused to tell me how he came by the fungus, which may, of course, be a thing of merely terrestrial origin. Yet he might nevertheless be an agent of the Outer Ones, which makes it all the more imperative that he is recaptured."

With that, Holmes fell into a frowning contemplation of the passing countryside, which lasted until the train began to slow. Thereupon he leapt to his feet.

"We are approaching Crowthorne Station," said he. "Our stop, Watson. Up you get!"

*

Broadmoor Criminal Lunatic Asylum, to give it its full name, had sat for more than thirty years atop a ridge of hill overlooking the village of Crowthorne to the west, and the town of Sandhurst to the south. Around its cluster of three-storey buildings spread several dozen acres of rolling grounds, bounded by a high wall. The architecture, all narrow, arched windows and dark red brickwork, gave off an aura that was both imposing and austere.

The clock above the gatehouse was striking five as Holmes knocked on Broadmoor's huge main door. An orderly appeared, and Holmes presented his card. "We are expected," said he.

The orderly went away and came back a couple of minutes later accompanied by a tall, somewhat anxious-looking man in a slate-grey three-piece suit and high-collared shirt.

"Richard Brayn, Superintendent of Broadmoor, at your service," said this fellow by way of self-introduction. "Come, gentlemen. My office lies this way."

In a plushly furnished room, Brayn invited us to take a seat and offered us sherry.

"So, Mr Holmes, Dr Watson, you are here in connection with the abscondment of Josiah Amberley," he said.

"That we are," said Holmes.

"Inspector MacKinnon has assured me of your bona fides. He is currently out with his men, combing the area. I trust they will find Amberley soon."

"I share that hope. In the meantime, I should like to know how Amberley managed to get out. Broadmoor is reputed to be one of the securest establishments of its kind."

"It has become so under my watch," said Brayn. "Unlike my predecessor, Dr Nicolson, I am not of the view that psychiatric patients can be rehabilitated, nor that they should be coddled. I come from a prison background, and the regime I preside over here is tough. Safety both for my staff and for the wider public is my abiding concern. Hence I feel more than a touch of chagrin that Amberley, an incurable maniac if ever I saw one, has slipped through my grasp."

"Take us through the events surrounding his escape," Holmes said. "Be sure to omit nothing."

Brayn folded his hands across his stomach. "Yesterday evening, Amberley was in his cell at lights out. Come the morning, he was not."

"The cell door was locked overnight?"

"Of course. It was unlocked at breakfast time by the orderly in charge of the wing where Amberley was held. Ellis is the man's name. He opened the door to find Amberley gone and another orderly in his stead."

Holmes cocked his head. "Another orderly?"

"Yes," said Brayn. "The fellow was sitting on the floor, in his underclothes. Vance, his name is. He looked dazed and perplexed. Ellis helped him to his feet and sat him on the bed. Vance had a black eye and a sizeable lump on his forehead and was scarce able to string a sentence together. Nonetheless, Ellis was able to ascertain that Vance had entered the cell the previous evening at bedtime. It is customary here to look in on the inmates last thing. Most suicides happen at night, and this is a way of insuring ourselves against that possibility. If there seems grounds for concern, the inmate will be put on a suicide watch and checked at regular intervals until dawn."

"But on this occasion, Amberley must have pounced on Vance as he came in and battered him unconscious."

"So it would seem."

"He then stole Vance's clothes, took his keys, left the cell, locked the door after him, and walked out of the premises unhindered. Am I right?"

"As he was wearing an orderly's uniform, it's unlikely he would have been stopped at the gate."

"Simple yet fiendish," I said.

"I suspect not all inmates could have pulled off the deception," Holmes said.

"With the majority," Brayn said, "even if they were dressed as an orderly, some instance of erratic behaviour would have given the game away."

"But not Amberley. He is an enthusiastic dissembler and can easily pass for sane."

"I should like to speak to both the orderlies concerned," said Holmes, "Ellis and Vance. They may be able to shed further light on what happened."

"The former is here today. As for the latter, I believe he is at home, recuperating from the attack. I will call for Ellis." As Brayn rose from his chair, a thought struck him. "Oh. You said be sure to omit nothing. There is one piece of information that may or may not be of relevance. Yesterday Amberley had a visitor."

"Interesting. Who?"

"The name currently escapes me," Brayn said, "but his appearance was distinctive, for which reason I have no trouble describing him to you even though I saw him only in passing. He was tall, dark of complexion, with a burly, martial look about him. He wore a moustache and also a pair of grey-tinted sunglasses."

Holmes leaned forward in his seat. "Tell me, did he also have a Masonic tie-pin?"

"He certainly had a tie-pin, but I wasn't close enough to make out its nature."

My friend turned to me, a look of eager fascination on his face. "Who does that sound like to you, Watson?"

"It sounds to me," said I, "very much like Barker."

"Barker?" said Brayn. "Now that you mention it, that may well have been what he was called. Evidently he is known to you."

"And to Amberley," said Holmes. "Barker and I were both instrumental in bringing Amberley's crime to light."

"Why would Barker want to visit Josiah Amberley?" I said.

"To gloat? To clear up some nagging question? Who can say?"

Brayn was rifling through a desk drawer. "He would have had to fill in the requisite forms. I have the paperwork somewhere... Ah yes. Here it is. 'Barker.' No forename or even initial, just 'Barker'. 'Relation to inmate: known associate. Stated reason for visit: personal.' All correct and above board."

"And yet an unexpected development," said Holmes. "I shall have to ask Barker myself why he came. In the meantime, Mr Brayn, if you would kindly summon this Ellis fellow for us...?"

*

Ellis the orderly confirmed Brayn's account in every respect and was able to supply a few further details.

"Since he came here, Josiah Amberley has been as good as gold," said he, standing before us in Brayn's office. He was a giant of a man, but with a humble, unassuming way about him. His hands looked as though they could have crushed pebbles to gravel, yet he was wringing them anxiously, like a child keen to ingratiate himself. "A chatty sort. Takes an interest in us orderlies. Knows all our names. I'm not saying I like him. You can't be friends with the inmates. It's the rules. But he's never given us a moment's trouble. Not till now."

"It's your job to open the cell doors in your wing, yes?" said Holmes.

"Every morning, six a.m., regular as clockwork."

"But not to lock them at night."

"No, sir. I go off-duty at six in the evening. The night shift does the locking up."

"So you went into Amberley's cell this morning, to find a colleague where Amberley should have been..."

"Fair boggled my mind, it did. There was old Arthur Vance, stripped to his longjohns, just coming to, all writhing and groaning, and with a big black eye swelling up half his face and another bruise on his forehead. Wasn't hard to work out what had happened. We've all of us been jumped on by an inmate when we're not looking. It's a hazard of the job. But Amberley was supposed to be one of the peaceful ones, so no wonder Vance's guard was down. Soon as I'd made sure he was all right, I told him to find himself a spare uniform and head home. Then I raised the alarm. Funny thing was, Vance was supposed to be off sick last night."

"Is that so?" said Holmes.

"Yes. He clocked off yesterday morning as I was clocking on, and he mentioned to me in passing that he was feeling a bit under the weather and probably wouldn't be coming in that evening. He asked if I'd arrange for someone to cover his shift if need be, and I told him I would. I just assumed he'd got better after a good night's sleep. A good *day's* sleep, I should say."

"Is it possible that it wasn't Vance in Amberley's cell?"

"Oh no," said Ellis. "It was him all right."

"And why was it not noted by other members of staff that he wasn't around from bedtime onwards?"

"Each orderly on the night shift is in sole charge of a wing," said Brayn.

"So there would be no interaction between Vance and the orderlies in other wings?"

"Not unless necessary."

"Interesting. Might I prevail upon you, Mr Brayn, to give me Arthur Vance's home address? I should like to have a word with him."

Brayn consulted his files and wrote the address down on a piece of paper. "He lives in the village, at a cottage down near Chaucer Woods. Shouldn't be hard to find. Are you telling us it might not have been Vance at all last night but some impostor?"

"I advance it as a possibility only," said Holmes. "While the real Vance was indisposed, an accomplice of Amberley's took his place, disguised as him in such a way that even a colleague like Ellis could not tell the difference, not least with his face partly distended by two major contusions. The assault on the bogus Vance was staged, since Amberley might not have successfully overwhelmed a real employee. The impostor would have first visited all the cells in the wing but Amberley's. That way the other inmates would be safely locked up and not on the loose, which might have aroused attention."

"Those bruises didn't look staged," Ellis commented.

"The pair went out of their way to make it look convincing. Amberley is wealthy. I am sure he will have made his accomplice's discomfort worth the while."

Brayn looked crestfallen. "My goodness. Right under our noses. The effrontery of it."

"Josiah Amberley is not to be underestimated," Holmes said. "This thing was planned by him, probably well before he was sent to Broadmoor. He worked out how he would escape and recruited an assistant to facilitate it."

Ellis cursed. "If only I'd been more cautious, maybe I would have noticed it wasn't Vance, especially as I knew he might not even be turning up for work that night. But he looked so sorry for himself."

"Your concern for him overrode all other considerations," I said.

"I echo the sentiment," said Brayn. "You have nothing to be ashamed of, Ellis."

The giant looked on the verge of tears. "You are too kind, sirs."

Sherlock Holmes got to his feet. "I thank you for your time and trouble, gentlemen."

"Mr Holmes," said Brayn, rising to shake my friend's hand, "I hope you won't think too poorly of us at Broadmoor. Our record has, until today, been exemplary."

"Not a bit of it, sir," replied Holmes. "Your regime appears fit to cope with anything. Anything, that is, except Josiah Amberley."

*

On our way out of Broadmoor, Holmes paused to interrogate the orderly on duty at the entrance. The man was seated on a chair just inside the main door.

"It is gone six," Holmes said to him. "You have just come on shift, I take it?"

"I have, sir."

"And you were here at your post yesterday evening?"

"I was."

"Did one of your night-shift colleagues depart earlier than scheduled, not long after lights out?"

"One of them did, as it happens."

"Did you recognise him?"

The orderly frowned. "Now that I think about it, I didn't. We have a fair number of staff here, though. I can't say as I keep track of them all."

"Was there anything unusual about him? His manner? His gait?"

"Well, he was walking rather heavily, sir. Plodding, you might say. I asked him what the matter was, and he told me that he'd just received word of a death in the family. The sad news had been telephoned to Mr Brayn, who had then summoned him to his office and relayed it. That, to me, explained why the fellow looked so downcast and walked in such a way, and also why he was leaving before shift's end."

"Thank you," said Holmes. "That will be all."

As my companion and I made our way back downhill to Crowthorne, I said, "Amberley just breezed out of the place. The sheer neck of the fellow!"

"I wouldn't say 'breezed', Watson, but that excuse about a death in the family was a clever subterfuge. Amberley's gait is distinctive, after all, and might have attracted suspicion."

"Ah yes. His artificial limb."

"How could he disguise his impedance? Simple: he

pretended he was a man in shock. We can always check with Brayn about the telephone call, but I don't see the need. It was clearly a lie."

We found our way to the cottage where Vance the orderly lived, a cosy little woodside residence with creeper-covered walls. A twist of smoke spiralled up from its crooked chimney.

Our knock at the door was answered by a woman who admitted to being Mrs Vance. Holmes enquired about her husband, to be told that he had come down with "a bad dose of the bellyaches". He was presently asleep, she said, and she asked if we might come back later.

At that moment, a man emerged from a back room, dressed in pyjamas. "Who is it, Dora?" he asked. "I heard voices."

"Two gentlemen, Arthur, wanting a word."

"We have just come from your place of work, Mr Vance," Holmes said. "How are you faring?"

"Not so well," the man said, and no question, he looked ill. His face had a greasy greenish sheen and he was clasping his stomach. "I don't know what's come over me. Normally I have innards of iron, but yesterday morning I started to feel a bit queasy and it's only got worse since then. In fact, gents, if you don't mind, I need to go back and lie down again, lest I pass out."

"Before you do that," said Holmes, "might I prevail upon you to let my friend take a look at you? He is a general practitioner."

Vance consented, and I performed an examination, gently palpating his abdomen and putting an ear to it to listen to the bowel sounds. I found tenderness and distension, but no indication of obstruction or abnormal masses.

"All the signs of simple gastric disorder," I opined. "Nothing sinister. Drink plenty of fluids, Mr Vance, and use paregoric to help ease any discomfort, if you haven't done so already."

"You certainly don't seem well enough to have gone to work yesterday evening," Holmes said.

"Good God, no," said Vance. "Spent the whole night here, in agony."

"I can vouch for that," said his wife.

Holmes tendered his apologies to the couple for having troubled them, and we left.

"Tell me, Watson," Holmes said as we headed towards the train station, "in your professional opinion, is Arthur Vance faking his complaint?"

"Not a chance," I said. "Aside from the other symptoms, he exuded the *smell* of sickliness. I've encountered it many a time, and it is distinctive and cannot be feigned."

"How about poisoning?"

"That I cannot affirm, not without conducting further tests. I can, with some definitiveness, rule out certain contaminants. If Vance had ingested mercury, for example, he would have exhibited breathing difficulties. Likewise, with arsenic or antimony, he would have complained of a burning sensation in the mouth and throat."

"But it is not impossible that he was poisoned?"

"Not impossible, no. You think that's the case?"

"I am willing to entertain the notion," said Holmes. "Vance being laid low, his absence enabled Amberley's accomplice, masquerading as him, to enter Broadmoor last night in his stead. An awfully convenient illness, don't you agree?"

"Unless he was incapacitated deliberately."

"Exactly."

"And all of this was orchestrated by Amberley. Oh, he is a thoroughgoing scoundrel, that man," I said, with feeling.

"You'll have no argument from me on that front," said Holmes, adding, "But he will be behind bars again soon. I swear it."

*

Every day for the next week and a half, Holmes sent a telegram to Barker, inviting him to drop by at Baker Street for a chat.

There was never any reply. He even went to Barker's office in Camberwell, only to find the premises untenanted. "Where is he?" he said to me when he returned from that fruitless trip. "What is he up to? What is his game?" Meanwhile he pursued various other lines of enquiry relating to Josiah Amberley, but for all that he approached the matter with his customary persistence and thoroughness, he repeatedly came up against a dead end.

As was Holmes's practice when stymied, he threw himself into research as a means of keeping himself distracted, so that the great engine of his brain had some fuel to consume even if it was not the fuel he desired. Sometimes this meant poring over arcane literature, be it the dread *Necronomicon* or another tome from his extensive library of the occult. At other times he indulged in scientific study, and in recent years he had taken to casting an eye over the contents of Peter Carey's tin box. He would draw out the Mi-Go artefacts one by one and subject each to lengthy scrutiny. The strange cylinder, in particular, fascinated him. Roughly the size of a hatbox, its purpose proved unfathomable to him, no matter how often he examined it. He reckoned it was built to contain something, and certain mechanical elements in its construction suggested it had some sort of preservative faculty, but he could not think what precisely was meant to go inside it. With the organic items, meanwhile, he might shave off a sample and place it under his microscope or else try various reagents on it. He had determined that all of these fungal things were in a dormant, inert state and therefore presented no danger. Nonetheless he was at pains not to touch any with his bare hands, and habitually, when dealing with them, he would wear goggles and keep his mouth and nose covered.

Holmes was just embarking on one of these periodic surveys of the items, not long after Sunday breakfast, when the doorbell chimed. He quickly closed the tin box and stowed it in a wooden chest which was stencilled, misleadingly, BRIC-

A-BRAC. Then, with a glance at the mantel clock, he said, "Eight is rather early for business hours."

"Especially at the weekend," I added, looking up from the newspaper. I had just been reading an article about Josiah Amberley, as it happened. The report had little to say other than that the escapee from Broadmoor was still on the run and the police were widening their search to include all ports.

"And that tread upon the stairs carries a distinct rhythmic heaviness," said Holmes. "It's almost a march. It seems I have not spent all that money on telegrams in vain."

"You think it might be…?"

Sure enough, before I could utter the name Barker, the man himself entered. He stood for a moment with his chest puffed out and his fists by his hips, thumbs pointing down his trouser seams, as though on parade. "Gents. Apologies for the intrusion. The Lord's Day and all."

"Not a bit of it, Barker," said Holmes. "Come in, sit down. You look, if I may say, rather weary and careworn."

"That I am, Holmes. Do I smell coffee?"

"Some remains in the pot. Watson? Would you do the honours?"

"Much obliged, Doctor." Barker drained the cup, then wiped droplets of coffee from his moustache with the back of his hand. "What a week I've had," he declared.

"You have been busy," said Holmes. "Too busy, it would appear, to respond to the dozen wires I sent you."

"Yes. About that. Doubtless you are aware of Josiah Amberley's disappearance."

"Well aware."

"Doubtless, too, you know that I paid him a visit the day before he was reported missing."

"You would be correct in that supposition."

"I didn't think for a moment that Sherlock Holmes would not be on top of the matter," Barker said with a wry smile. "Startled me somewhat, Amberley going on the run like that, all of a sudden. When I saw him, he seemed resigned to his lot. Content, even. He must have realised he was lucky to be in Broadmoor and not buried in a prison grave. Still, he was always a wily one. Probably he was making it seem like he was the last person who'd try to escape. Fooled me for certain."

I could see Holmes biting his lip, as though to prevent himself from saying something along the lines of "Fooling you, Barker, is not so hard."

"But why did I go and see him?" Barker continued. "That's the question you want answering."

"And?" Holmes prompted.

"There remained one or two aspects to his crimes that I found puzzling. I wanted my curiosity satisfied."

"Aspects such as?"

"The blood filling the victims' noses and mouths, for one. That is not a common symptom of gas poisoning."

"The coroner stated that exposure to domestic gas, in sufficient concentration, can cause pulmonary oedema," Holmes said. "Would you query his verdict?"

"Not at all," said Barker. "It just struck me as unusual. Another question was what became of the deed-box Mrs Amberley and Dr Ernest were alleged to have stolen."

"There never was any deed-box. That was an invention of Amberley's."

"I know that now. Amberley himself confirmed it."

"You could simply have come to me for this information, Barker," Holmes said, a touch exasperatedly. "You didn't have to travel all the way up to Crowthorne."

"I rather felt I had done the bulk of the work of solving the crime, Holmes. Why would I think you might know more than me? Besides, you're much in demand. Your time is precious. I didn't want to bother you. Especially not with trivia."

"But there's something else the matter, isn't there?" Holmes narrowed his flinty grey eyes. "Your failure to respond to any of my telegrams, unless it is rudeness, denotes an undue level of preoccupation. I am of the view that you have been pursuing some new case, one that is arduous and time-consuming. Furthermore, you have made no progress, hence you have come to Baker Street in order to canvass my opinion. The consulting detective is consulting the consulting detective."

Barker bowed his head in rueful acknowledgement. "You have me there, Holmes. Would that there were a little less triumph in your tone."

"No triumph," said Holmes. "Merely professional satisfaction. By all means, tell me what is flummoxing you so, Barker. If I can help, I shall."

*

"It started a couple of days after my visit to Broadmoor," Barker said. "I received an anonymous letter, with a ten-pound note slipped inside the envelope."

"How fortunate for you," said Holmes. "If only we could all receive such missives."

"The letter requested that I look into an act of vandalism in Hammersmith. I could only assume my professional services were being engaged, owing to the presence of that tenner."

"Are you in the habit of regarding unsigned letters as though they constitute a commission?"

"When they have money in them, yes," said Barker. "We're not all rich and famous, you know. We don't all get page after page in *The Strand* devoted to our exploits and have the Peelers eating out of our hand."

I refrained from correcting him on the "rich" part. Famous Holmes undoubtedly was, but his earnings were minimal and would not have amounted to a living wage were I not supplementing them from my own income. As for the police, he had done enough to merit their toleration, but he was not as feted in their ranks as my chronicles would imply.

"I just took it," Barker continued, "that some philanthropic soul wished me to investigate what he considered a crime, but did not wish his identity known."

"Do you still have the letter?"

"I do not. I threw it away."

"Oh, Barker!" Holmes said reprovingly. "You have adopted my methods, and yet you neglect one of my basic principles, which is that anything and everything may hold a clue. This letter of yours could have yielded reams of data, and you 'threw it away'." He sighed. "Describe it to me anyway."

"Plain vellum. Handwritten, using capitals only."

"Postmark?"

"I don't remember."

"And what did it say?"

"Something along the lines of 'The shopfront of Parrish and Sons Vintners on King Street in Hammersmith has been defaced. Why?'"

"That's all?"

"That's all," said Barker. "At any rate, I headed west, and lo and behold, Parrish and Sons Vintners had indeed had its windows splashed with paint."

"Paint?" said Holmes.

"Paint. In liberal quantities. The proprietor was scrubbing the last of it off when I got there. He was perplexed indeed. 'Who would do such a thing?' he wailed to me. 'I'm an honest wine merchant. I am well respected in the area. I have good relations with all my customers. If I have offended somebody, I'm damned if I know whom.'"

"Did you attempt to verify his assertions?" Holmes enquired.

"Of course I did," replied Barker. "I asked around. Nobody I spoke to had a bad word to say about Parrish or his two sons, or for that matter his wife and daughter. By all accounts he is a loving paterfamilias, a churchgoer, he donates to charitable causes, he is on the square like me…"

"A paragon."

"Wholly undeserving of such ill-treatment. So I changed tack and sought eyewitnesses. The vandalism had occurred during the small hours, however, and I could find no one who saw anything suspicious. I spent that entire day in Hammersmith, and the next. I did enough work to give the sender of the letter his full ten quid's worth, but came up empty-handed. And that would have been it, except what should arrive the very next morning but a second letter."

"Which," said Holmes dryly, "you have also disposed of."

"All right, you've made your point," said Barker. "Don't rub it in. This one, like the first, came with a ten-pound note inside."

"Suggesting it came from the same sender as the previous one."

"That and it had the same handwriting and was on the same notepaper."

"What did it say?"

"It mentioned an Egyptian mummy at the Victoria and Albert Museum which had been damaged the day before."

"Oh yes," I said. "I remember reading about that. Someone slashed the thing quite badly with a knife. They haven't found out who."

"It happened late in the afternoon, when the museum was almost empty," Barker said. "Whoever did it must have been very subtle. Sidled up to the mummy as it lay there in its open sarcophagus, hacked it about, then left without a single soul noticing. None of the curators or guards realised anything was amiss until doing their rounds at closing time. I made a few enquiries but got nowhere. I could only come to the conclusion that there are some mad folk about. What can the mummified remains of some long-dead pharaoh have done to deserve being mutilated? At any rate, there I was, twenty pounds to the better but with two mystifying cases on my hands."

"Neither of which you had settled," Holmes said. "Did it

not occur to you that the sender of the letters might himself have some connection with the acts of vandalism?"

"As in might even be responsible for them? It crossed my mind. But why, then, would he want them investigated by London's foremost consulting detective?"

My friend gave a hollow laugh. "*South* London's, possibly."

"I'm just teasing, Holmes. Everyone knows which of the two of us is the more celebrated, if not necessarily the more accomplished." Barker's eyes twinkled behind the grey-tinted lenses of his glasses. "What I need is a companion like Dr Watson here, a master wordsmith who can raise my profile in print. My door is always open, Doctor, should you wish to take me up on the offer."

I snorted.

"Fair enough," said Barker. "But to resume…"

"There's more?" said Holmes.

"A third letter. And a fourth, for that matter. But one thing at a time. The third came hot on the heels of the second, and read, 'Cockerel beetles smashed outside Sherman's on Pinchin Lane.'"

"I'm sorry, *cockerel* beetles?"

"I think that was the word," said Barker with a frown.

"Not, perchance, cochineal beetles?"

"Come to think of it, it might have been that."

"I rather suspect it was. I have not heard of a cockerel beetle, whereas the cochineal beetle is a well-known species, native to the Americas."

"And Mr Sherman, the Lambeth birdstuffer and animal merchant, is no stranger to us," I interposed. "We hired a sleuth hound from him once: Toby, the half spaniel, half lurcher."

"It was Sherman who sold the beetles in the first place," Barker said. "He told me they'd been bought by a customer who placed his order by post, under the name John Smith. Smith sent him cash and told him to deliver the beetles to a numbered post box, from which they'd be picked up. Sherman did as requested. Three dozen cochineal beetles" – he pronounced the unfamiliar word slowly and carefully – "in a cardboard container with holes punched in it for air. Smith, he confided in me, had paid well over the odds for them, something in the region of thirty pounds, so he wasn't going to ask too many questions."

"Sounds like Sherman all right," I remarked.

"Next morning, when he opened up his shop, those same beetles were on the pavement outside. They had been crushed flat, every last one of them, as though stamped on. 'It was them children round here,' Sherman told me. 'Must've been. Wretched brats. They guy me good and proper, they do, knocking me up at all hours and running away. This is just their latest lark.'"

"Local tearaways," said Holmes, "purchased the beetles under a blatant pseudonym, only then to leave them outside Sherman's shop, squashed? It hardly stands to reason. To go from playing knock down ginger to such an elaborately organised prank is some leap."

"More to the point," I said, "thirty pounds. Where would ragamuffins like that have got the money from?"

"That's what I thought," said Barker. "Sherman was adamant it was them, however, and nothing would change his mind."

"And the fourth letter?" Holmes prompted.

"It told me about windows getting broken at a wallpaper factory in Deptford, near Greenwich Park. Messrs Harper, Whitman and Company. I went down there, and the glaziers were already in, making repairs. Stones had been thrown during the night. Neither Mr Harper nor Mr Whitman had any idea who could have done it. I asked if they'd had a disgruntled ex-employee, someone they had had to fire."

"A commendable avenue of enquiry."

Barker greeted the praise with a shrug, as if it were no more than his due. "They replied in the negative," he said.

"They told me they pride themselves on their business ethics. They pay their workforce well and strike fair deals with their suppliers. They have no enemies that they know of. They surmised it was probably just some drunk passing by, who'd had a skinful and thought it'd be fun to smash some windows."

"And that was the final act of vandalism in the series?" said Holmes.

"So far," Barker replied. "The fourth letter came just yesterday morning. Today being Sunday, I'm not expecting a new one. Tomorrow, possibly."

"Well now…" Holmes offered both me and Barker a cigarette, then lit one himself. "What do we have? A chain of random-seeming incidents, each with no apparent connection to the others, yet linked by these mysterious – and regrettably disposed-of – letters sent to you, Barker, with a financial inducement enclosed. It looks to me as though somebody is playing a game with you."

"That is the conclusion I am beginning to draw. But who? Who would go to all that trouble, sending me hither and yon across London to chase up these destructive events?"

"And paying you ten pounds each time, into the bargain."

"Not that the money's not welcome… but yes."

"The why of it is unclear," Holmes said, "but I should have thought the who of it was fairly obvious."

"I beg your pardon?"

Holmes blew smoke out of his nostrils. "Josiah Amberley, of course," said he.

Barker looked bewildered.

"Come, come," Holmes said. "Think it through. A retired colourman who made his fortune in the artistic materials trade. A seller of paintboxes, among other things."

"So?"

"Colours, Barker. Colours. That is the connection between the four acts of vandalism, and it points us ineluctably to the culprit, namely Amberley."

Barker scratched the back of his scalp. "I don't see. I mean, yes, paint was used at Parrish and Sons. I think it was white."

"The paint was a calling card. Its hue is immaterial. It announced Amberley's intentions in a roundabout way. Paint, paintboxes, colours... A pert little thematic trick."

"A wine merchants, a slashed mummy, squashed beetles, broken windowpanes – what relevance do colours have to any of those?"

Holmes said, "Why was a vintners attacked, of all the trade outlets on Hammersmith Broadway that could have been chosen? Why not a butcher's shop, say, or a bakery? Simply because there is a colour known as glaucous."

"There is?" said Barker.

"A greyish-blue shade. It has another definition, too. It is a botanical adjective pertaining to the whitish waxy bloom found on certain fruits, principally plums but also..."

Holmes looked at me, then at Barker, then at me again.

"But also..." he repeated.

Barker and I looked at each other.

"But also..." Holmes said a third time. He shook his head sadly. "Must I spell it out?"

The answer came to me. "Grapes."

"Grapes!" Holmes wagged an approving finger at me, as one might at a child who has successfully added two and two. "*Vitis vinifera*, the common vine grape, carries a glaucous coating, and if I need to tell either of you gentlemen what fruiting body wine is made from, then truly I am in the company of philistines."

"All right," said Barker, "so we have one colour there, glaucous. What about the mummy?"

"I think I can answer that one," I said. "Mummy brown."

"Thank you, Watson. Give yourself another pat on the back. Mummy brown. Also known as Egyptian brown. A paint pigment made from ground-up mummified remains. It has been manufactured since the seventeen-hundreds and was a special favourite of the Pre-Raphaelite Brotherhood of recent memory – Millais, Rossetti and their ilk."

"Well I never," said Barker. "And I suppose you're going to tell me that someone makes a paint out of those beetles too."

"I am going to tell you exactly that," said Holmes. "Cochineal beetles, when dried, crushed and soaked in an acidic alcohol solution, produce the bright red colour known as carmine, which is used in textile dyeing, food colouring and oil paints."

"And the wallpaper factory?"

"There," Holmes said, "the theme becomes somewhat tenuous, but I believe if you look through the paper, Watson, you will find an advert placed by Messrs Harper, Whitman and Company. Around about page five. Yes? Tell me, does it say they produce a wallpaper pattern that is picked out in Scheele's Green?"

"It does," I said. "'A fleur-de-lys flock motif in brown and Scheele's Green, three farthings a yard.'"

"The colour is not as much in vogue as it used be, but some society matrons still line their walls with Scheele's Green paper, drape their windows with Scheele's Green curtains, and illuminate their salons with Scheele's Green candles."

"How ingenious," said Barker. "This does all sound like the sort of thing Amberley might set up."

"There's more," said Holmes. "The theme is not merely colours but colours which in some way or other are unpleasant. The glaucous coating on fruit acts as a deterrent to insects, preventing them from climbing on it and feeding on it. Mummy brown has become unpopular among artists these days. They have more or less renounced its use, in part because its source material is becoming scarce, but also because nobody much cares for daubing their canvases with what is effectively human corpse matter. As for carmine…"

"Crushed beetles," I said, pulling down the corners of my mouth.

"Indeed. And Scheele's Green is produced by mixing a copper sulphate solution with a sodium arsenite solution. Arsenic, I need hardly tell you, is extremely poisonous, even in compound form, and there have been reports of women fainting due to the smoke from Scheele's Green candles, and similarly of children wasting away in rooms liberally decorated in Scheele's Green, most likely due to fumes being given off by the wallpaper if it becomes damp. Perhaps not surprisingly, the toxicity of Scheele's Green has led to a decline in its popularity, and it has largely been supplanted by zinc oxide and cobalt green, both much safer substances."

"So Amberley himself is performing each act of vandalism," said Barker, "and then he sends me a letter inviting me to investigate it. Why? What earthly purpose does that serve?"

"As I said, the why of it is unclear," Holmes replied.

"Could it be some elaborate revenge? I helped get him convicted of murder. Might he derive some perverse pleasure from watching me run around futilely, following up all these petty crimes of his?"

"Thanks in part to you, he ended up imprisoned for life. All he is doing to you, since his escape, is causing you inconvenience. As vengeances go, it does not seem proportionate."

"The forty pounds you have made," I added, "can hardly be deemed a nuisance, either."

"All very true," said Barker. "Then there must be some deeper layer to it, one we can't yet fathom."

"I wouldn't say that," said Holmes. "There *is* a deeper layer and I have fathomed it. Moreover, it enables me to predict where Amberley will strike next. Watson, would you be so kind as to fetch the map of London. It's over there, in the cubbyhole with… the other maps."

He actually meant arcane scrolls, but Barker was not to know.

I located and extricated the map.

"Excellent," said Holmes. "Now unroll it and spread it out on the table, while I find a pencil."

Barker and I looked on as Holmes bent over the map, pencil in hand.

"King Street, Hammersmith," said he, "is here." He marked the spot with an X. "Next, the Victoria and Albert in Kensington. There we are." He drew a second X. "Thirdly, Pinchin Lane in Lambeth. There. Lastly, to Deptford, near Greenwich Park." He pointed to the map. "Would the wallpaper factory be about here, Barker?"

"Indeed."

"Good. That fits." Holmes straightened up. "Now, gentlemen, observe the four X's. Tell me what you see."

"Bless me!" Barker exclaimed. "They're practically in a row."

"So they are." Holmes took a ruler and joined up the four X's with a straight line. "Amberley chose the sites for his vandalism with the utmost cunning and precision, not only so that they supported his colour theme but so that they aligned geographically. There is an eastward progression here from first to last. It stands to reason, then, that were a fifth act of vandalism to occur, it would lie somewhere on a line extrapolated from the existing line."

With the ruler, he extended the line by a few inches, through Woolwich, terminating in Dartford.

"I'm not sure how much that helps," I said. "The line covers a fair amount of ground. Along it lie houses, shops, factories, parks, all sorts. Amberley's colour theme is broad enough that almost anything can fit into it."

"But if we are to anticipate his next move," said Holmes, "we must work out where it is likely to happen. Then we can ambush him."

"We must also work out when," said Barker.

"Oh, that isn't a problem. It will happen today."

"Today?"

"He has been operating on alternate days, Barker. One day, vandalise. The next, a letter to you arrives. The fourth letter came yesterday. Therefore, today is the day of the fifth vandalism."

Holmes's "hated rival" shook his head wonderingly. "How did I not see that?"

"You have been too caught up in it all," my friend replied. "Amberley has been leading you a merry dance, and you have been so busy following the steps that you have not perceived the tempo. What I suggest to you is this. Go home now, get some rest, regroup. I will apply myself to the problem, and as soon as I have the answer, I will contact you."

"No, I shall stay and help. I'm loath to burden you with sole responsibility for this, Holmes. I am the one Amberley has targeted. Perhaps my visiting him at Broadmoor acted as a catalyst. Seeing me reminded him how I played a role in his capture. I provoked his escape, albeit inadvertently."

"We don't know that. His escape plan appears to have been set in train well before your visit."

"Regardless, I demand that I should be involved in bringing him in."

"I'm not saying you won't be. You have earned the right, and we would certainly benefit from your strong right arm when we catch up with him. However, I do my thinking better alone. Watson will vouch for that."

"Really, Barker," I said, "you can contribute best by not being present. I know this from experience."

Barker seemed to weigh it up. "Very well. But, Holmes, you will get in touch the minute you have the solution."

"You have my word on it," Holmes said.

"The *minute*."

"Absolutely."

Barker made his exit. Even before he was out of the room, Holmes was bending over the map again, peering closely at the section of south-east London traversed by the extrapolated

SHERLOCK HOLMES *and the* HIGHGATE HORRORS

line. I resigned myself to a lonely morning watching my friend ponder, smoke, scowl and pace the carpet in circles, so I was somewhat taken aback when, as Barker shut the front door behind him downstairs, Holmes began to laugh.

"What?" I said. "Have you cracked it already?"

"Oh, Watson." Holmes put hand to mouth several times, attempting to stifle his mirth. "What a dunce Barker is."

"He is not in your intellectual league, that's for certain – who is? – and he thinks rather too highly of himself. I'm not sure, however, that I would call him a dunce."

"A complete dunce! And Amberley knows it. He hasn't just been leading Barker a dance, he has been pulling his strings like a marionettist. All these manipulations – the vandalism, the letters – haven't been merely to get Barker questing around like a blind bat. They have been designed to bring him to my door. I am Amberley's real target, not my paltry imitator."

"How can that be?"

"Elementary," said Holmes. "Amberley has presented Barker with a series of mysteries which he knows the 'south bank Sherlock Holmes' lacks the wit to solve. Who else would a stumped Barker turn to in his hour of need? Only his model and inspiration."

"In which case," I said, "we must assume that you are the true object of Amberley's revenge and he means to ensnare you. Barker has unwittingly brought you the bait, and Amberley is waiting for you to walk into the trap."

"Quite. And I know the trap's whereabouts." Holmes placed the tip of his forefinger on the map, at a point a couple of inches along the line from the X at Deptford. "It is here."

"Shooter's Hill," I said. "I am not even going to try to guess what relevance that place has to Amberley's colour theme. Just save me the trouble and tell me."

"It has no relevance whatsoever."

"What?"

"The colour theme has run its course," said Holmes. "It

has done its job of confounding Barker and enabling us to identify its originator. The next stage in Amberley's plan is altogether more sinister."

"I don't like the sound of that."

"Nor should you. On Shooter's Hill may be found a group of Bronze Age barrows. We know that ancient ceremonial sites have a mystical resonance and have been used over the centuries for occult rituals. Think of the burial mounds on Box Hill where I underwent my dream-quest, or more recently the Feystone. We know, too, that Amberley is an acolyte of Shub-Niggurath and has made a human sacrifice to her. I believe he wishes to repeat the exercise, at these barrows, and this time his victim is to be the man responsible for his downfall."

"And that does not mean Barker, does it?"

"Of course not. It means the fellow who *actually* put him in prison, not the bungler who only thinks he did."

"You," I said.

"Me," said Holmes, with a nod. "Josiah Amberley intends to murder me, in the name of Black Goat of the Woods With a Thousand Young."

"And you plan on going to Shooter's Hill and giving him every chance to do so?"

"When the man you are seeking waves a hand and says, 'Here I am,' it seems churlish to waste the opportunity."

"Why not wait? You'll be able to catch up with Amberley some other way, surely, and in circumstances more propitious to you than him."

"After he has gone to such lengths setting me this elaborate little puzzle of his?" Holmes chuckled. "Why, Watson, it would be an insult to both him and me if I did not rise to the occasion."

*

"Shrewsbury pink?" said Barker as our cab clattered through the streets of Peckham at dusk. "That's a new one on me."

"It is a form of hunting pink," said Holmes, "devised almost a century ago by the fifteenth Earl of Shrewsbury. Standard hunting pink is scarlet. Shrewsbury pink is a few shades lighter – close, in fact, to actual pink. The earl was an avid huntsman, and during his lifetime, livery in that colour was worn by all the local hunts around his family seat in Staffordshire. It has since fallen out of favour and been supplanted by the traditional pink."

My friend was feeding Barker arrant nonsense, and Barker, by the looks of him, was swallowing it whole.

"And how does it relate to these burials mounds we're heading to at Shooter's Hill?" Barker said.

"The barrows lie on the estate of Shrewsbury House, another of the family's properties."

"But the other colours Amberley has referenced all have connotations that are unpleasant. That was your word for it. Can the same be said for Shrewsbury pink?"

"In so far as hunting with hounds is classified as a blood sport," said Holmes, "then yes."

"Oh, he's a devious so-and-so, is Josiah Amberley," Barker growled. "Very devious. It's a good thing that we are more devious still. And," he added, "that some of us have come ready for trouble."

From a pocket of his overcoat he produced a revolver.

"An Enfield Mark I," I said. "Self-extracting, so that when reloading you eject only the spent cartridges and keep the live rounds in the cylinder, all in a single action. Lovely piece of design."

"You know your guns, Doctor. I've read that you favour a Webley Pryse top-break, do you not?"

I produced my own revolver for show. "It hasn't let me down yet."

"Neither has this beauty me." Barker waggled the weapon in the air. "How about you, Holmes? Are you armed too?"

"I tend to leave the gunplay to Watson," said Holmes.

"I must say, I'm looking forward to a rematch with Amberley," Barker remarked. "Perhaps, God willing, there'll be reason to use this on him." He stroked the Enfield lovingly, then stowed it away.

It was fully dark by the time our cab deposited us at the bottom of Plum Lane, near Shooter's Hill. By moonlight we ventured up that road towards Shrewsbury House, and presently reached the borders of the property. The estate boundary was demarcated by a low wall which we had no difficulty surmounting. We entered woodland and walked through a carpet of fallen leaves that were damp and mouldy enough not to crackle too loudly underfoot. A barn owl screeched from the treetops, a fox answered with a wail, and I felt a chill which wrapping my ulster more tightly around myself could not dispel. I was undeniably apprehensive about the coming confrontation with Josiah Amberley, and during the afternoon I had tried to dissuade Holmes from seeking it.

"It seems the height of foolhardiness," I had said to him. "Amberley cannot think that Sherlock Holmes, having rumbled his scheme, will be oblivious to the fact that it is a trap. He will therefore be at pains to ensure that there is no evading it."

"Will he?" Holmes had said. "Or will his arrogance again prove his undoing? Once a swanker, always a swanker, Watson. Let our retired colourman, in his overconfidence, do his worst. It won't be enough."

I had wondered whether it was Holmes who was displaying overconfidence, but had not voiced the thought. Instead, I had left him to his own devices and gone to my room to clean my Webley. A sidearm in good working order was always a useful bulwark against bullishness.

At least we had Barker with us. For all the apparent antagonism between him and Holmes, I felt that the pair had an understanding, one based upon mutual respect. They might not be friends but they were allies, and Barker, with his military background and his Enfield, would be a good man to have on one's side in a scrape.

The woods thinned, and ahead, on the brow of the hill, I spied a half-dozen barrows. They stood silhouetted against the moon-bright sky, a series of grassy prominences ranging from thirty to seventy feet in diameter and rising to five feet high at the apex. As earthworks went, they were unspectacular, and yet there was a certain ineffable desolateness to them. Beneath these mounds lay the mouldering remains of chieftains whose names were long forgotten. Great though they may have been in life, and mourned as their deaths surely had been, now their memory was lost to history and all that was left of them were these anonymous tumuli. *Sic transit gloria mundi.*

Abruptly Holmes halted and held up a hand, indicating that Barker and I should halt too.

"See there?" he said, pointing. "Someone has been digging."

I peered through the darkness and saw that one of the barrows indeed sported a large hole in its side. Excavated earth was scattered all around the opening, and a couple of spades lay on the ground, as though abandoned in haste.

"More vandalism," said Barker. "Or could this be called desecration? I don't know if pagan burial places are considered sacred or not. It fits Amberley's pattern nonetheless."

All at once I was conscious of movement ahead. A shape emerged from the far side of the barrows, a robed and hooded figure, gliding into view.

My breath caught in my throat. The figure was not alone. Another appeared behind it, also robed and hooded, and another, and yet more. With their faces hidden, they were like the ghosts of monks, silent and sinister.

Holmes tensed beside me, and I heard a sharp intake of breath from Barker, who was just to my rear. There were eight figures in all, and they moved towards us with eerie, sedate slowness.

"Cultists," I whispered to Holmes.

"Indubitably," came the reply.

"They have superior numbers, but I doubt they are armed. We can take them."

So saying, I delved into my pocket for my revolver.

From behind me came the click of a hammer being cocked. Barker had evidently had the same idea.

Then I felt the barrel of a gun being pressed to the back of my head.

"Ah-ah, Doctor," said Barker, his voice right in my ear. "Stay your hand."

I gasped. "Barker. What – what is the meaning of this?"

"The meaning," Barker replied, "is very simple. Draw your weapon, Dr Watson, and I shoot you stone dead."

*

I could scarcely believe it. Barker was holding me at gunpoint!

"What are you doing?" I asked him.

"He is doing," said Holmes calmly, "what his paymaster has engaged him to do. You had better oblige him, Watson."

"Listen to your friend, Doctor," Barker said, "else a 265-grain bullet will enter your skull and leave the other side, taking half your brain with it. Now, thumb and forefinger only, take out your Webley by the grip and pass it to me."

I hesitated. Could I turn, deflect Barker's gun aside, and lay him out with a punch?

The barrel of the Enfield ground harder into my head.

"I know what you're thinking," Barker said. "Just be a good boy and do as I say. I've killed before, in my soldiering days. I've no qualms about killing again."

"Listen to him, Watson," Holmes said. "Whatever happens here, it's not worth you losing your life over."

Outrage and vexation churned within me, but Barker had the upper hand. I had no choice but to comply.

I drew out my revolver with thumb and forefinger, as instructed.

"Gently does it," said Barker. His tone was damnably silky and insinuating. "Nice and slow. Hold it up so I can see it. That's it. I'll be having that, thank you."

The revolver was plucked from my grasp.

"Disarmed, are they, Barker?" said a familiar voice. It emanated from the nearest of the robed figures, who drew back his hood to reveal the haughty, wizened features of Josiah Amberley.

"Watson is, Mr Amberley," Barker replied.

"What about Holmes?"

"He told me he isn't carrying a gun."

"Check his pockets anyway," said Amberley. "He's a slippery one."

Keeping the Enfield to my head, Barker leaned round to rummage through Holmes's pockets. I aimed a glance at my friend, indicating that this might be a moment to make a play for Barker. Holmes subtly shook his head. His eyes said he didn't deem it worth the risk.

"Not a sausage," Barker announced.

"Excellent," said Amberley. "The whole thing has been nicely done, Barker. You have more than earned your wage."

"Thank you, sir."

"Now then, Mr Holmes," Amberley said. "Step forward, if you would. Bear in mind that any false move, the slightest attempt at trickery, and your precious companion dies. If I even think that you are up to something, I shall give Barker the order to shoot."

"And I shan't hesitate," Barker said.

"There you have it. Straight from the horse's mouth. Do you understand, Mr Holmes?"

"I understand perfectly," said Holmes. "Don't worry, Amberley, you have nothing to fear. I shall be as meek as a lamb."

"That's what I like to hear."

Holmes gave me a look which I think was meant to be

reassuring, then walked towards Amberley and the other robed figures. At a gesture from Amberley, two of the cultists took hold of my friend by the arms. The remainder produced torches and lit them. All at once the scene became markedly more bizarre and ominous, as the flames crackling up from the torches cast everything into a chiaroscuro of flickering orange light and deep shadow. The cultists mustered around Amberley, and he led them uphill in a procession towards the opened-up barrow, with Holmes being frog-marched along in their midst.

Barker and I remained where we were.

"You are a filthy mercenary, Barker," I said through gritted teeth. "You won't get away with this."

"Your opinion matters little, Dr Watson, and your threats still less. Just don't go getting any funny notions in your head. That's a guaranteed way of getting a *bullet* in your head."

"You sold us out, you traitor."

"That would imply I was on your side to begin with. I never was. Not since Amberley approached me via an intermediary while he was in Broadmoor. He made me a very generous offer. An opportunity to help do away with Sherlock Holmes *and* get paid for it – how could I refuse?"

"All that stuff about the anonymous letters and the acts of vandalism, it was just nonsense, wasn't it?"

"Oh, the vandalism happened," Barker said. "You know it did. You read about the mummy being slashed, after all. And the other instances were genuine, too. They had to be."

I understood why. "Because otherwise, if Holmes had looked into them and found out they didn't happen, the whole charade would have swiftly unravelled."

"But as for the unknown perpetrator... Well, that was me."

"You?" I said.

"Who else? I committed the crimes, then pretended to investigate the crimes. How's that for irony?"

"For felony, more like. I suppose your visit to Amberley in Broadmoor was you getting your final orders."

"Firming up a few last details, yes."

"And the letters, the ones you said you threw away? I'll wager they never existed."

"Never existed, and even if they had I would never have 'thrown them away'. As if I would be so negligent! It was all an elegant confection, and I can't believe Holmes fell for it, but he did, hook, line and sinker. Chalk one up to Barker."

"To Amberley, don't you mean? He came up with the plan. The colours, the locations in a line, all pointing to here. Don't tell me you did. You don't have the brains."

"Don't try and insult me, Watson. It won't work. The vandalism scheme was indeed all Amberley's invention. But I was the one who sold it to you and your friend, and for that I deserve some credit."

"You really loathe Holmes, don't you?" I said.

"Loathe is too strong a word for it," Barker said. "Resent him. Find him an irritant. Feel I would be better off without him."

"So then it's professional jealousy? That's what has driven you to throw in your lot with Amberley?"

"Professional *pragmatism*," Barker said. "Why does the world need two consulting detectives when it can manage with one? And why should that one not be me?"

"You're despicable."

"And you're standing here with my gun to your head, Doctor, so I would advise you to keep civil and not irk me."

"You realise that these people are about to sacrifice my friend to some heathen god?" I said.

"I don't much care what they do to him," Barker replied. "It's none of my business. All that matters to me is Amberley's coin and a London without my hated rival on the Middlesex shore."

He chuckled throatily, and I was seized by an urge to hurt

him. Revolver or not, I wanted to wrestle him to the ground and pound him until he was a bloody, insensible mess. It was all I could do to keep myself from acting upon the impulse.

By now, the torchlit procession had reached its destination. The cultists were gathered around the hole in the barrow, and Amberley addressed them.

"My brothers," said he, "my fellow worshippers of Shub-Niggurath, we stand here tonight to render unto our goddess an offering like no other. A great man is about to meet his doom, for the sake of the Black Goat of the Woods With a Thousand Young. To you, Shub-Niggurath, queen of fertility, we show due reverence. To you, wife of Yog-Sothoth, mother of the twins Nug and Yeb, we send the soul of this defender of justice, as a token of our veneration. To you, as you sit on your obsidian throne in the howling gulfs beyond, we give one who brings light to the world, in the knowledge that you will embrace him with your darkness. Accept our gift, oh terrible, miasmic one. *Iä, Shub-Niggurath! Iä! Iä!*"

The other cultists took up the cry. "*Iä, Shub-Niggurath! Iä! Iä!*"

Amberley motioned to the pair holding Holmes, and they bent him double and thrust him head first into the hole in the barrow. Stumbling, my friend disappeared from my sight.

Another cultist picked up a wooden pallet and stood with it, poised to place it over the opening. I could see that it would fit tightly in place. The cultists must, I thought, be intending to entomb Holmes. Doubtless they would heap earth into the hole first before setting the pallet on top to plug it.

Horrible as this prospect was, my supposition was to prove incorrect. The truth was far worse.

Amberley donned a pair of leather gloves and opened a cardboard box. Then, with a pair of tongs, he carefully drew out a spherical object that shone a bright turquoise in the torchlight. He held it aloft for all to see.

"Behold, the instrument of our offering's demise," said he. "A fruit of sublime noxiousness, ripe and ready to deliver instant death. *Iä, Shub-Niggurath!* The soul of Sherlock Holmes is coming to you, so that you may feast upon it. Open wide your many maws and imbibe his essence to the last drop."

The turquoise sphere could only be the same species of deadly puffball mushroom with which Amberley had killed his wife and her lover, and as I watched, appalled, he leaned down and tossed it into the hole. Immediately the cultist with the pallet slammed that square of wooden planks into position, shutting Holmes in with the puffball mushroom. All of the cultists now stepped back, putting a goodly distance between them and the barrow.

For several long, slow seconds, nothing happened.

Then, from within the barrow, there was the sound of a dusty, muffled detonation.

The puffball had exploded.

"Holmes!" The cry sprang to my lips, and futile though I knew it to be, I could not withhold it. "Holmes!" I heard my voice growing hoarse with despair and horror. "*Holmes!*"

*

The minutes that followed must rate among the worst of my life.

An expectant hush fell over Amberley and his fellow cultists, while from the barrow there was a ghastly silence. Then came sounds of gasping and choking. These rose to a horrible crescendo, growing ever wetter and more guttural. At last they subsided, and silence returned.

My heart felt as cold and heavy as a cannonball.

Sherlock Holmes was dead.

Josiah Amberley had succeeded where so many others had tried and failed. He had slain the best and wisest man whom I had ever known, and the hell of it was that Holmes had gone meekly to his doom, not daring to resist because I was being held hostage. To protect my life, my friend had surrendered his own. I knew I would carry the guilt for that to my grave.

Amberley told the other cultists that they needed to wait. "The spores must disperse and settle first before we open up the barrow. Let us allow ten minutes. Then we may gaze upon our victim's body and know for certain that we have earned ourselves the blessing of Shub-Niggurath."

For a time I was dumbstruck with grief and shock, but eventually my voice came back to me.

"Barker," I said, "you had better kill me. If you do not, I will dedicate myself to hunting you down and ruining you. The same goes for Amberley and his cronies. That will be my life's work from now on. I vow it."

"Oh, you're going to die, Doctor," Barker said. "You need have no worries on that score. We can't leave you alive after what you've just witnessed."

"Then do it quickly, you fiend."

"I shall, once we're assured that Sherlock Holmes is well and truly dead."

Time crawled, but at last Amberley was satisfied that it was safe to reopen the hole in the barrow. The pallet was removed. Amberley peered in, holding a torch before him.

"He looks dead," he opined. He gestured at a pair of cultists. "You two, haul him out. Be careful not to touch the fungus itself or any of its spores. Should you get some on your hands and then touch your mouth or nose, you too will perish."

The limp form of my friend was dragged out of the barrow and dumped unceremoniously at Amberley's feet.

"So this is how it ends for you, Mr Holmes," Amberley jeered at the corpse. "You beat me once. Now I have exacted my revenge. This is the fate of all who oppose Josiah Amberley. I have a goddess who empowers me. My faith in her makes me unstoppable."

Every word of this speech made my blood boil. My hands bunched into fists. Now was my moment to fight back. I was going to wrest the Enfield out of Barker's grasp, kill him, and then, with both his gun and my own, kill Amberley and as many of the other cultists as I could manage. If I failed in the attempt and Barker shot me first, so be it. I no longer cared whether I lived or died.

Then I heard one of the cultists say, "Begging your pardon, Josiah, but I see no blood on Holmes's face. Isn't there meant to be blood? You said there was when you used the fungus last. Significant amounts of it."

"There should be," Amberley replied. His usual confidence remained in evidence – but was there just the tiniest trace of doubt in his voice? "Let me look."

At that moment, a miracle happened.

Sherlock Holmes sprang up from the ground and seized Amberley.

I was startled by this turn of events, but not as startled as Barker. He cursed in disbelief, and all at once the barrel of the gun was no longer pressing so firmly against my head.

I knew I would never get a better chance. I drove my elbow into Barker's midriff. This elicited a very gratifying yelp of pain, but I did not pause to relish it, for I was already pivoting to face him. Barker was stronger than me, younger, and had had proper military training. In straight hand-to-hand combat with him, I did not have a hope of winning. I just had to be more ruthless and brutal.

I grabbed his gun hand. I wrenched the Enfield round and up so that the barrel was pointed beneath his chin. I slid my forefinger inside the trigger guard, over his.

Behind those grey-tinted lenses, Barker's eyes widened in fright. I don't know what look was on my face, but I assume it to have been one of sheer, blazing determination, and Barker, seeing it, understood that all was lost.

I squashed his finger down on the trigger. The muzzle flash was blinding, the report deafening.

As my vision and hearing cleared, Barker slumped to the ground. The top of his head was missing.

"A 265-grain bullet has entered your skull and left the

other side, taking half your brain with it," I snarled at him. "Farewell, Barker. You weren't Holmes's rival. You weren't fit to shine his shoes."

I snatched up the Enfield and fished in Barker's pockets for my Webley. Then, with a revolver in each hand, I spun round to look towards the barrows.

Sherlock Holmes was holding Amberley in a complicated *baritsu* grip. The retired colourman writhed, attempting to free himself. The other cultists milled around in consternation. Not only had their sacrificial victim somehow survived, he had apprehended their leader. There had also been a gunshot, and now Barker, Amberley's accomplice, lay dead. This was not the plan. Everything was falling to pieces.

One of them, overcoming his bewilderment, made a move to aid Amberley in his struggle with Holmes. I put the fellow straight on that idea, with a warning shot over his head. He gave a start and cringed back in alarm. The others, learning their lesson from his example, stayed put.

Then Amberley gave an almighty heave and almost succeeded in disentangling himself from Holmes's clutches. He might have been old and spindly but he was far from feeble. Holmes responded by kicking Amberley's right leg from behind, hard. The straps holding the limb in place came loose and the leg went flying out from under Amberley's robes. Off-balance, the colourman toppled.

Next instant, Holmes inserted thumb and forefinger into his mouth and blew a loud, shrill whistle.

From the woods behind me there came the thudding of footfalls. A dozen – no, two dozen – uniformed policemen poured out from the cover of the trees. They homed in on the cultists. Some of the latter fled in panic but were swiftly intercepted and detained. The remainder just stood in place and succumbed sheepishly to the handcuffs.

Amberley crawled on his belly towards his false leg. Just as he was within reach of it, Holmes interposed himself between him and his objective. He picked up the limb. Amberley raised a hand, as though beseeching my friend to return the prosthesis. It was almost pathetic, the act of a man who had lost everything but still wished to retain some dignity.

Holmes shook his head slowly, and then hefted the artificial limb in one hand and swung it at Amberley, foot end first. It was a precise, vicious strike, straight to the temple, and the colourman was instantly rendered unconscious.

*

Following that, events unfurled swiftly.

In charge of the policemen was Inspector MacKinnon. The smart, youthful official made sure every one of the cultists, the insensible Amberley included, was rounded up and secured. Only then did he come over to consult with Holmes.

"Sir," said he, "you have again handled a case in masterly fashion. I feared we would never get that villain Amberley back under lock and key."

"Just promise me that this time he remains so," said Holmes.

"Oh, he will, you can be sure of it. At least for as long as is required before we hang him. With your attempted murder to add to his crimes, I suspect that shan't be long. And this time, he won't be whiling the hours in Broadmoor, either."

I myself was simply relieved that Holmes was alive and unscathed. I watched him converse with MacKinnon and then, with the inspector's blessing, conduct a short, private interview with each of the cultists in turn, and my heart was filled with gladness and admiration.

Once Holmes was done and I had him to myself, I wrung his hand and told him how delighted I was that he had survived his ordeal in the barrow. There may even have been a tear in my eye.

"Thank you, Watson," said he, "but there is no need to be quite so effusive. I was perfectly safe. I anticipated that

Amberley might use the same method of murder twice and made provision for that eventuality."

"But how could *I* have known you did?" I said. "As far as I was concerned, Amberley killed you."

"Oh ye of little faith. In turn, I will say I had every confidence that you would get the better of Barker. I even predicted that the surprise of my 'resurrection' would give you the opening you needed to deal with him – and deal with him you did, with characteristic forthrightness, for which you are to be congratulated."

"You took a lot on trust there, Holmes. Had my reflexes been a fraction slower, or Barker's a fraction faster…"

"But they were not," replied my friend. "Besides, if all else failed, there was always MacKinnon. I contacted him this afternoon, while you were off in your room polishing your revolver, and made arrangements that he and his men would lie in wait near the barrows until I gave them the signal to move. He stood poised to leap to your assistance, should it have been required. Not only that, he had a constable, a noted marksman, with a rifle trained on Barker. You were in far less danger than you thought. Now, come. Let us find a cab and get home. I am feeling chilled after my brief sojourn in the underworld and would like to get warm again. Also, I imagine you have some questions."

"A few."

"Then I shall answer them in the comfort of our sitting room, beside a roaring fire. I rather fancy a cup of Mrs Hudson's excellent cocoa, as well."

*

An hour later, that was exactly our situation. The hearth at Baker Street blazed and we each of us nursed a cup of steaming cocoa.

"In a nutshell," said Holmes, "I knew from the outset that Barker was putting us on. His purported motive for visiting

Amberley at Broadmoor was clearly a sham. The timing of it was suspicious, too, occurring as it did on the same day Amberley made good his escape. He must have gone there to let Amberley know that everything was set for him to start laying the trail of vandalism across London. Amberley, in return, would have confirmed that his breakout was impending. It was a last meeting between conspirators to go over their plans a final time."

"So you weren't fooled by Barker at all?" I said.

"Not a bit of it. The scheme teetered on absurdity from start to finish, but for me the deciding factor was his inability to produce the anonymous letters. He knew he could never have presented anything that would have stood up to my scrutiny. He decided it was better simply to pretend the letters had been discarded. On the whole, I thought it preferable to play along and let Barker think he had duped me. Then we could keep him close until such time as he revealed his true colours."

"Did you know that Amberley led a cult?" I asked.

"Not as such," Holmes replied, "but I had a strong intimation that his worship of Shub-Niggurath was something shared with others. Why keep that statuette on display, if not to show off to likeminded individuals where his allegiance lay?"

"What about the puffball mushroom?"

"What about it?"

"Don't be coy," I chided. "How come you were immune to its effects? Did you hold your breath?"

"I was inside the barrow for ten minutes," Holmes said. "No one can hold his breath for that long. Anyway, did you not hear me as I spluttered and choked?"

"Yes, I did. I realise, now, that that was not genuine."

"Purest playacting."

"But you cannot have avoided breathing in the spores."

"Doubtless I inhaled plenty of them. The fact is, Watson, I have spent weeks preparing for just such a moment. This was in a spirit of experimentation more than anything, although I did wonder how long Amberley would be content to remain in Broadmoor and I felt that, should he escape, seeking revenge on me would be among his priorities. What I did was inure myself against the turquoise fungus."

"How?"

"By virtue of introducing a single spore into my body, once a day, over the period since Amberley's arrest and incarceration."

I struggled to conceal my dismay. "You did what?"

"I still had the residue from the fungus in his strong-room," Holmes said equably. "Every morning, on my own in my bedroom, I would take out one spore from the envelope with a pair of tweezers and swallow it."

"Madness. You took an unconscionable risk with your life."

"I thought it safe enough. I was following the principle of variolation, as espoused by Buddhist monks who ingest trace amounts of snake venom to protect themselves against snake bite, and similarly the longstanding practice among the Chinese of smearing a tiny wound in the skin with cowpox to confer immunity to smallpox, the very technique which Jenner refined and popularised at the turn of the century. My body thus gradually built up a resistance to the spores' inherent deadliness."

"That was the theory, but you could not have known that this homespun vaccine of yours would work in practice."

"The balance of probabilities favoured a successful outcome."

"That isn't an unqualified yes."

"It is as close enough to a yes as I am willing to give," said Holmes, taking a sip of his cocoa. "I thought the game, as the saying goes, was worth the candle."

"Did you have to go through with it?" I said. "Letting Amberley and friends inter you? Becoming their sacrifice?"

"To preserve your life, of course I did."

"But you had MacKinnon and his men lying in wait

throughout. You could surely have given the signal and summoned them at any time, even before you were shoved underground."

"And what would they have arrested the cultists for then? Digging a hole? Wearing robes after dark? Brandishing lit torches within the Greater London area? Even worship of an Outer God is not a criminal offence, although perhaps it ought to be. Whereas now MacKinnon can have the lot of them arraigned on a collective charge of attempted murder."

"Murder by lethal fungus."

"Stranger methods have been used."

I pondered briefly. "Can it be," I said, "that Amberley and his cult are the grand conspiracy of sedition we have been looking for all this time? The same one Irene Adler has worked for? There is the Shub-Niggurath link, after all, and Amberley may well have obtained his puffball mushrooms through the auspices of the Mi-Go. It stands to reason."

Holmes wagged a finger at me. "Now there, Watson, you are using your brain. Indeed, this entire enterprise has been, in part, an attempt by me to ascertain once and for all whether Josiah Amberley has been acting on behalf of the Mi-Go in some capacity. Does he provide the connective tissue going back all these years to the attempts to hobble Professor Mellingford and the other British notables, and further still to Dr Felder and his fungal reanimates?"

"The answer, I trust, is yes," I said. "Which means that, in defeating him and his cult, you have brought an end to the conspiracy, at long last."

"No." Holmes looked sombre. "No, I have not."

I heaved a sigh. "No?"

"You saw me interviewing Amberley's associates. He and they, it transpires, are merely a group of bored urbanites in search of thrills, something to add spice to their otherwise humdrum existences. They found it through their shared devotion to a foul heathen goddess. They will now have plenty of time to rue that choice – that is, when they are not too busy with hard labour."

"Except for Amberley himself, who is due to pay the ultimate price."

"He took it too far, and dragged the rest of them along in his wake."

"Then as far as the ongoing Mi-Go mystery is concerned," I said, "this whole affair has been of little relevance."

"Not so," said Holmes. "There is still the matter of Amberley's accomplice, who aided his escape from Broadmoor."

"I assumed he was one of Amberley's fellow cultists."

"I asked each of them if he had been the accomplice. To a man, they denied it. They were too unsettled to be lying."

"Who was it, then?"

"I don't know for sure," Holmes admitted, "but I wonder whether it might have been a certain mistress of disguise whom you mentioned but a moment ago. It would be well within Miss Adler's chameleonic capabilities to have posed as Arthur Vance, the asylum orderly. First she would have ensured that he would fall ill on the night in question."

"How?"

"Not a problem for one as resourceful as her," said Holmes. "She could have slipped some drug into his food, or else brushed past him in the street and surreptitiously transferred a poison onto his skin. Then she entered Broadmoor disguised as him. Possibly Amberley did not even need to hit her, for she could easily have faked the bruises which she, as Vance, sported. Likewise, Miss Adler could have supplied Amberley with the puffball mushrooms, to enable him to kill his wife and her lover and then attempt the same on me."

"To what end?" I said.

Holmes half smiled. "If I am not flattering myself too much, her goal was to misdirect me. She hoped I would infer, as you did, that Amberley and company were the conspiracy. Knowing that I would uncover their activities sooner or later, she helped them, while at the same time, without their realising, she was setting them up as a decoy."

"But you could well have perished in the process. I know you and Miss Adler are antagonists, but not to the degree where she might seek your demise. She did not murder you at Fontaine's, after all, when she could have."

My friend shrugged his shoulders. "She is well aware of my capabilities. She could be safe in the assumption that I would outsmart Amberley."

"Well, you have scuppered her plans, if nothing else," I said. "Now all you have to do, in order to ascertain whether or not Irene Adler was involved, is get Amberley to admit it."

"I'm sure I can prevail upon MacKinnon to give me access to Amberley in his cell. It shouldn't be too hard to make him confess. His type love to crow. They can't help themselves."

*

I'm afraid I must report that Holmes had no luck in that regard. Josiah Amberley, for all his overweening arrogance, could not be persuaded to reveal how he had come by the puffball mushrooms or whom his accomplice was. Holmes tried and tried but got nowhere.

"You were duped," Holmes told him. "You and your associates were pawns in someone else's game. Does that not make you feel exploited? Manipulated? Emasculated? Does that not anger you?"

"To a degree, it does," Amberley replied. "But my discomfiture is mitigated by the knowledge that I know something you do not, Mr Holmes, and that no amount of inveigling or wheedling on your part is going to make me share it with you. If I can incommode you by taking the information you want to my grave, then take it to my grave I shall. This shall be my final victory over you."

And so he did, and so it was.

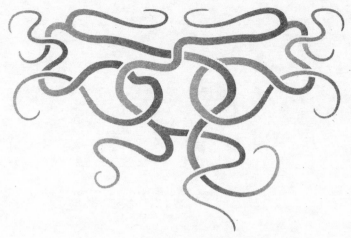

PART V

Autumn 1902

I WALKED HOME WITH A SPRING IN MY STEP, FOR ALL that it was a cold, drizzly September evening. The rain might have dampened my clothing but not my mood.

Letting myself in to Baker Street, I offered a warm greeting to Billy, our page, who was at his usual station on a chair just inside the front door. The lad had been with us for almost three years and was as fresh-faced still as when he first entered our employ.

"Doctor," said he, looking up from the book in his lap. "How was your day?"

"Most pleasant. What's that you're reading?"

Somewhat shyly, Billy showed me the cover.

"*Villette*," I said. "I wouldn't have had you as the Brontë type. Tales of piracy and derring-do, that's more the thing for a boy your age. Still, reading is reading. Good for you." I tousled his hair.

"Thank you, sir," Billy said, smoothing his ruffled locks back into place. There had been a brief wince of displeasure on his face when I touched him, and I made a mental note not to repeat the action. I still thought of him as a child, but he must have been sixteen or seventeen now, nearly a man. My affectionate gesture would have seemed patronising rather than paternal.

No sooner had I entered our rooms than Sherlock Holmes braced me with an enquiry that contained more than a hint of rebuke. "And what, pray, have you been up to, Watson? You went out straight after breakfast, without a word about where you were destined."

"A difficult confinement," I replied. "The summons was urgent."

"Really?" said Holmes. "And how fares the new mother?"

"Well," I said. "Very well. She and baby both."

"And is it customary for mothers to kiss their doctors after the successful delivery of a child?"

"I don't understand."

"I see a tiny smear of face powder on your cheek, as might have been transferred thereto from a feminine cheek. I see, too, a single long blonde hair adhering to your shirt collar. I can only assume you came by both courtesy of your patient."

"Yes," I said quickly. "Yes, that is exactly it. After the birth, the woman gave me a quick peck on the cheek. Out of gratitude."

"What's queer," Holmes went on, "is that I spied a strand of the same length and hue on your jacket sleeve four days ago. It was present when you came home after attending the United Hospitals Challenge Cup Final at Kennington. Tell me, do many men in the stands at The Oval wear their hair down to their shoulders?"

"There were a few women in the crowd," I offered. "I may have brushed up against one."

Holmes gave an impatient tut. "Oh, come along, Watson. You forget whom you are talking to. It is quite clear to me that you were neither at the rugby then, nor at a birth today. Indeed, I can list three other absences in recent weeks for which you have not given me an honest account. Correct me if I'm wrong, but you, Watson, have been squiring a lady."

I decided to come clean. "You have me there, Holmes. Yes, I have lately been enjoying the company of a certain woman. A very charming and pleasant one, might I add. I met her last month. In fact, I may say that I saved her life. She was about to step off the kerb into the path of a heavily laden pantechnicon which she had failed to see. I grabbed her by the elbow and pulled her back to safety. Once she had overcome her shock, we got to talking. I learned that she was a widow, recently returned to London from Singapore, where her husband had worked for the colonial legislative council until his sudden death from typhoid. She had few acquaintances in the capital and was evidently not accustomed to the traffic. In short, she was lonely and dislocated. We went for tea, where we talked some more. Since then we have met several times, as you are aware, and during the course of those encounters she and I have become... companionable."

"You have developed an understanding."

"I would not go that far, but undoubtedly an intimacy is forming."

"But why lie about it?"

I hemmed and hawed. "I suppose I thought you might not approve."

"Not approve?" said Holmes. "Of my great friend finding the love of a woman after so many years without?"

"You don't consider it... well, a betrayal?"

"If, Watson, you desert me for a wife again, I shall take it hard, I'm sure." Holmes's tone was ironical, albeit not wholly unserious. "I shall, however, get over it, and you and I shall continue our adventures together just as we've always done, and indeed, just as we did while you were with your Mary. If I am upset in any degree, it is simply because you did not see fit to take me into your confidence about this matter sooner."

I felt a wave of relief. Keeping the blossoming relationship a secret from Holmes had been preying on my mind. I had planned to tell him about it once I was surer of it. Now that the thing was out in the open, and his response had proved so sanguine, I could relax.

"I presume, then," I said, "that should the lady and I enter into wedlock in the future, I will have your blessing."

Holmes wafted a hand. "It is not mine to give, but I shall certainly raise no objection. Now then, with all of that settled, sit yourself down. A client is imminent."

"Excellent," I said, taking a seat and helping myself to one of Holmes's cigarettes. "Something juicy and lucrative, I hope. And, moreover, conventional."

In the past few years Holmes had been taking on more and more cases that carried not the slightest whiff of the supernatural or the occult. As a result his reputation had been considerably enhanced and his fame had spread even further among the respectable echelons of society. The prosperous came to his door, and he in turn had prospered, so that he was now in real life almost the Sherlock Holmes he was in my fictions, the world-renowned avatar of all that is rational and empirical. I would not say he had grown comfortable – his temperament was too restless and mercurial for that ever to happen – but he was a sleeker, better-balanced and altogether healthier individual than before. The eldritch fever, if I may call it that, had abated in him, although it lingered yet.

"Whether it is conventional or not remains to be seen," came the reply. "The client is Sir Hartley Winter, the noted tea importer, and he is due any minute— Ah! The doorbell."

Shortly, Billy showed our visitor in. This was an affluent-looking individual with grey-flecked hair and a brisk, no-nonsense air about him.

"It's Kitty, my daughter, Mr Holmes," said Sir Hartley, getting down to business straight away. "Or rather, it's the fellow she is consorting with, an Austrian aristocrat. Baron Adelbert Gruner is his name. I see from your face that you know the scoundrel."

"By reputation only," said Holmes, "and nothing I've heard inclines me in his favour. In polite continental circles he is renowned as an idler and philanderer, with a penchant for collecting curios, but that is only the half of it. In truth, Gruner has a vicious streak, and his attitude towards the fairer sex is callous bordering on malicious. He has left many an innocent girl ruined. One is on record as having taken her own life following her association with him. He also stands accused of killing his first wife and was saved from the gallows only by the timely and suspicious death of a witness. It is generally believed that he moved to England because he was hounded out of Europe."

"Then, if I tell you that my dear young Kitty has fallen under his spell, you will understand my concern."

"Very much so."

"I have remonstrated with her at great length," Sir Hartley said, "begging her to break it off with him. I have even confronted Gruner himself. All in vain. Both insist they are in love, and Gruner went so far as to imply that marriage is on the cards. I am at my wits' end." He gnawed an anxious knuckle. "Nothing good can come of their relationship, and I hate to see my beloved child, my only offspring, throwing away her future like this."

"That might not be all she is throwing away."

"What do you mean, Mr Holmes?"

"Evidently you are unaware that, since Gruner's arrival on these shores, he has made two female conquests prior to your daughter, and both young women have subsequently disappeared."

Sir Hartley blanched. "Disappeared?"

"Cornelia Waunchope and Abigail Roxbury-Trent," said Holmes. "Their respective next of kin have searched for them, to no avail. The police have been notified, but there is no clear indication of foul play. Gruner, for his part, maintains he had nothing to do with the disappearances. He says each relationship ran its course and ended, after which the girls, he presumes, must have either travelled abroad or taken refuge with friends."

"Rather than go back to their families?" I said.

"In the case of Miss Waunchope, her nearest and dearest had more or less disowned her, such was the friction caused by her taking up with Gruner. As for Miss Roxbury-Trent, she was orphaned when young and has spent her adult life in a rather irresponsible fashion, gadding about town supported by a sizeable inheritance and mixing with some very unsavoury company. Various disreputable behaviours have resulted in estrangement between her and her relatives."

"How long have you known about the situation with Gruner and these two girls?" I asked.

"It has developed over a few months."

"And all this time you have done nothing about it?"

"What am I to have done, my friend?" Holmes retorted. "If I were to investigate every missing person case that happens, I should be doing little else. Had Scotland Yard or the girls' families come to me, that would have been a different matter."

"Nonetheless, there is likely a pattern there, and a sinister-seeming one."

"And it is quite possible," said Sir Hartley, growing yet more agitated, "that my Kitty might be next in line. My God! Mr Holmes, it is imperative that you act on my behalf."

"What function can I conceivably discharge, Sir Hartley?" replied Holmes. "It is not within my remit to step in between two lovers and divide them."

"Not even if one of them could be endangered by her closeness with the other?"

"Would you have me play the heavy with Gruner? But there are many more intimidating-looking specimens in London than I."

"No, I would prefer the matter to be resolved with subtlety and discretion," said Sir Hartley, "both of which qualities you are famed for. How about this? You convey to Gruner, in person, a handsome cash offer from myself. Phrase it howsoever you wish, but make it plain that providing he agrees to have nothing further to do with Kitty, he will find himself generously rewarded, to the tune of..." The tea importer named an impressively large figure. "And of course, your fee for this service would be commensurate."

Holmes mulled it over for a few moments, and I caught his gaze and gave him a look strongly urging him to consent to Sir Hartley's request.

In the end he said, "Very well. I shall undertake the task."

"Capital!" exclaimed Sir Hartley. "You have brought a measure of calm to a father's troubled heart."

"I cannot guarantee your Kitty will be disentangled from Gruner's clutches, but I will do my best."

*

No sooner had Sir Hartley Winter departed than Holmes shook his head ruefully. "Watson," said he, "it comes to something when Sherlock Holmes is reduced to running errands for the rich. Where is the mystery here? Where is the great thorny problem to tax my brain?"

"A meeting with Gruner may turn up clues as to the two absent girls' whereabouts," I pointed out.

"Indeed, there is that. Ah well. Gruner resides, I believe, in Kingston. It is too late to call on him this evening. I shall head down there on the morrow. Not that I hold out much hope of it being a propitious exercise."

*

But the Holmes who returned from Kingston was a very different Holmes from the one who had left Baker Street earlier in the day with foot-dragging reluctance. He seemed excited and invigorated, his grey eyes a-sparkle.

"How did it go with Baron Gruner?" I enquired.

"Captain Peter Carey, Watson," replied Holmes. "Remember him?"

"Black Peter? It's a while since I've thought about the man. Indeed, I try not to think about him. There was never any good in that perfidious old seadog, and the world is a better place without him in it. What about him?"

"You will recall, I'm sure, how he claimed in his logbook that he had sold a number of Mi-Go artefacts to a foreign buyer?"

"Now that you mention it, yes. What has any of this to do with your visit to Gruner?"

"He described said foreign buyer as 'some kind of aristocrat, with a Germanic accent and a very silky way about him'."

"But the person's identity has remained unknown to us."

"Indeed," Holmes said. "Until now."

"So who is he, this fellow?"

"Who do you think?

"Can it be… Gruner?"

"It certainly can."

"Good heavens! How did you find that out?"

"Pass me my tobacco slipper," said Holmes, grabbing his briarwood pipe, "and I shall tell all."

*

The Kingston mansion which Gruner called home was, in Holmes's words, "a rambling pile of quite surpassing ugliness". Gruner greeted his visitor courteously enough in his study, and after a few pleasantries were exchanged, Holmes broached the topic he had come to discuss.

At first, Gruner was amused. He maintained that he and Kitty Winter were very much in love and that an engagement was in the offing. However, when Holmes brought up the matter of Sir Hartley Winter's cash offer, the baron became affronted.

"Money?" he snarled. "I have been considering going to him to ask for his daughter's hand in marriage, and now he throws this at me? A bribe to leave Kitty alone? *Tchah!*"

He uttered the outraged interjection so energetically, spittle landed on Holmes's cheek. Holmes was not convinced that this was accidental.

An insistence that Gruner might be wise to take Sir Hartley up on his proposal was met with even greater vituperation, at which point Holmes resorted to veiled threats. He mentioned

Gruner's misdeeds in Europe and brought up the names of Cornelia Waunchope and Abigail Roxbury-Trent.

Thereupon the other man became downright aggressive. "What do those two have to do with anything, Mr Holmes?" he growled.

"Would you wish me to look into their disappearances? I have a certain reputation when it comes to the uncovering of crimes."

"Crimes! What crimes? Two silly girls drop from view, not wanting to be found. Where is the crime in that?"

"That is precisely what I could determine."

"Enough, Mr Holmes," Gruner barked. "I will not be spoken to like this. If you do not leave my presence by the count of five, *mein Herr*, I will bloody your nose."

Holmes was unconcerned by the threat. Although Gruner was his junior by some fifteen years and well muscled, my friend's proficiency at *baritsu* and boxing remained undimmed. When voices and fists were raised against him, he was never intimidated.

He chose not to engage Gruner at that level, however. What would fighting the baron accomplish, other than to inflict pain and humiliation upon the fellow? It certainly would not change his mind regarding Kitty Winter. Indeed, it might entrench him more firmly in his position.

Instead, Holmes bade Gruner a curt farewell and took his leave.

That was when he had a rare stroke of luck. Upon exiting Gruner's study, with the man himself following aggressively behind, Holmes passed a doorway. The door stood ajar, and in the room beyond a maid was polishing the glass front of a display cabinet. The cabinet was one of several, and although Holmes caught only the briefest glimpse of its contents, he saw that they were all items of esoterica – effigies, fetishes and suchlike. The room, he realised, must house the baron's collection of curios. But what really caught his eye was a hatbox-sized metal cylinder which had a prominent position in the cabinet. It was the twin of the cylinder in Carey's tin box, down to the little porthole and various knurled mechanical protrusions. It was, in short, a Mi-Go artefact.

As soon as Holmes clapped eyes on the cylinder, he intuited a possible connection between Carey's buyer and the Austrian lothario who at that moment was raging behind him and calling him a slanderer and a coward and worse.

After beating a somewhat hasty retreat from Gruner's house, Holmes's first port of call was the library in Kingston. The baron had been resident in England for a little over a year. What Holmes wanted to know was if he had ever ventured onto these shores prior to that.

In the library's reading room he leafed through back issues of the London newspapers, paying particular interest to the society columns. Sure enough, Baron Adelbert Gruner had graced England with his presence on two occasions before moving here permanently. His notorious reputation on the continent had garnered him several inches of excitable press coverage during those visits. The first was in the spring of 'eighty-eight, the second in late autumn, 'ninety-one.

*

"You hardly need me to tell you, Watson," said Holmes, "that those dates correspond with the two occasions Carey had dealings with his aristocratic Germanic customer, as recorded in his logbook."

"That and the presence of the cylinder in Gruner's house would seem to put it beyond doubt," I said. "Gruner bought from Carey."

"Indeed," said Holmes. "Therefore I am now taking a professional interest in our Austrian baron on two counts. First and foremost, there is the question of Miss Winter and her unwise affiliation with him, not to mention those two previous conquests of his whose current whereabouts are unknown.

Then there is Gruner's penchant for Mi-Go artefacts. What does that signify? Does he have some direct connection with the Outside Things, or with our maddeningly elusive cabal of Mi-Go allies?"

"It could be that he is unaware of the artefacts' true provenance. He may understand that they are exotic, even unnatural, but not realise whence they originate."

"That is what I feel moved to discover: why Gruner purchased them and how much he knows about them. I am hoping that that avenue of enquiry will dovetail nicely with resolving the Kitty Winter situation and establishing the fate of her two predecessors."

I stubbed out my cigarette. "What is your approach going to be now?" I asked. "You have challenged Gruner directly, to no avail. What next?"

"For the moment, I myself am going to do nothing. You, Watson, on the other hand…"

I allowed myself an inward groan. "I'm being recruited, am I?"

"I'd rather think you might volunteer," said Holmes. "A young woman's honour is at stake, and perhaps her safety as well, while two other young women are missing. The gallant John Watson is never found wanting when there are females in peril. His putative second wife would surely agree about that."

I sighed. "What would you have me do?"

*

Two days later I turned up at Gruner's mansion. It was as Holmes had described it: memorably unprepossessing, a long, low, turreted edifice whose lack of symmetry and overall architectural inelegance was somewhat mitigated by the extensive, lushly planted grounds that surrounded it. I handed the butler my card, which Holmes had had printed specially the previous day and which read "Dr Hill Barton, Dealer in Oddities".

"I have telephoned ahead and the baron is expecting me," I told the butler, then added, with a nod at the leather briefcase I was carrying, "I am bringing something that might be of great interest to him."

"Very good, sir. Step this way."

A footman ushered me into Gruner's presence, and my first impressions of the man, in spite of what I knew about him, were not altogether unfavourable. He was devilishly handsome, with slicked-down, raven-black hair and a moustache waxed into two little tips that stood to attention beneath his nose. When he rose from his chair to greet me, he stood several inches shorter than me but displayed a lean, sinewy physique that suggested both strength and athleticism, which his firm handshake substantiated. His eyes were dark and languorous, with a knowing glint in them, and his mouth seemed fixed in a perpetual smile. In short, I could easily understand why women might find him irresistible. He exuded charm and sophistication and made one feel quite at one's ease. If I hadn't known him to be an out-and-out villain, I could well have found him agreeable company.

"Dr Barton," said he, in a voice like the purr of a satisfied lion. "A pleasure to make your acquaintance. I must confess I have not heard of you before, even though you work in a field, the collecting of curios, with which I am more than familiar."

Holmes had coached me rigorously in my cover story. "I have not long been in this neck of the woods, sir. Until now, Bath – the Avon area more generally – has been my stamping ground. But the pickings there have grown slim, so I have decided to try my hand in the capital. Your name has come up in many a conversation. Baron Adelbert Gruner, they say, has a discerning eye and a taste for the exotic and the arcane. They say, too, that he can be very generous."

Gruner chuckled. "They say that, do they? *Ach*, it is true that I have been known to pay over the odds, but then I am not a poor man, and we love what we love, don't we? Often we love it to our own detriment." He clapped his hands together. "Enough preamble. Come. Show me what you have got for me."

I placed the briefcase on the table and opened the lid. "This came to me via the widow of a man called Peter Carey."

"Carey? I know the man. A widow, you say?" Gruner's accent sharpened the first W of the word to a V. "Carey is dead?"

"He died some seven years ago. His widow and daughter, finding themselves in financial straits, chose to sell off his personal effects. Certain items which he kept in a tin box were proving difficult to dispose of. I made a low but, I feel, reasonable offer for the lot. The widow and daughter, you see, did not perceive the true value of the items. They did not realise how unusual and rare they are. To the layman such artefacts look unsightly and incomprehensible, but to those in the know they have an uncommon appeal."

Gruner beckoned eagerly. "Let me see. Let me see." His eyes were agleam, and I recalled Holmes assuring me that mention of Carey's name would get Gruner salivating. The Austrian had wanted everything in Carey's box and would jump at the chance to purchase now what he hadn't been able to before.

From the briefcase I took out an object wrapped in a velvet cloth. As I unfurled the cloth to reveal what lay within, Gruner let out a little gasp.

It was a fungus not much bigger across than the palm of my hand, plump, milky-white, and roughly mushroom-shaped, with fine, delicate filaments that hung from the underside of its cap like the fronds of a willow tree. The cap itself sported dark blue freckles all over its surface, tiny dots which, catching the sunlight from the windows, seemed to sparkle with a gemlike lustre.

"Yes," said Gruner. "Oh yes. I recognise this one. I saw it before, at Captain Carey's house. I wonder if it still reacts as it did then. Watch."

He placed a hand over the filaments, and all at once, as though roused by its proximity, they stirred. They reached up towards his fingers, questingly, like iron filings gravitating towards a magnet. He drew his hand away before they made contact, and the filaments sank back down, resuming their former inert state, in a manner I could not help but think of as disappointed.

Yesterday Holmes had demonstrated to me this same bizarre activity in the fungus, so witnessing it now at Gruner's house did not come as a surprise. All the same, I found it disconcerting to watch the limp filaments suddenly come to life and seek to touch Gruner's hand, as though desirous of some kind of union.

"Neither alive nor dead, this fungus," said the baron. "It exists in a state of torpor, and perhaps may do so indefinitely, unless stimulated into motion by the nearby presence of a living being. Carey claimed that it came from another planet. He said he harvested it, along with the other items in his box, out of a huge crashed vessel which he reckoned had flown to Earth from the far reaches of space. Did you know that?"

"I did not. I never met Carey himself."

"Do you yourself think it is a thing from space?"

"Not my place to speculate, sir," I replied.

"Might it be parasitic, perhaps? Or carnivorous? Could that be why it seems to crave contact with my flesh?"

I shook my head. Holmes had advised me not to get drawn into in-depth conversation with Gruner. Dr Hill Barton, the persona I was adopting, was a plain speaker, a man of few words, interested in money but not much more. "I deal in oddities, sir, as my card says. That's all. Odd this fungus certainly is, but wherever it originated and whatever its properties may be, my appreciation of it begins and ends with its price. Speaking of which…"

"Yes. Yes, of course, Doctor. I propose twenty pounds."

Without another word, I began rewrapping the fungus in the velvet cloth.

"No, wait," said Gruner with an earnest gesture. "That was only my little joke." *Joke*, coming from his Germanic lips, sounded like *choke*. "We are both men of the world. Fifty pounds."

"I had a yet larger figure in mind."

"Then you suggest the price, Dr Barton, and I shall tell you whether it is agreeable or not."

"Seventy."

A sharp intake of breath from Gruner was followed by a low whistle. "Some would call that outrageous. Some might even say it was – what is the English phrase? – daylight robbery."

"If you want the fungus," I said, "that is what it costs."

I had no qualms about extorting so huge a sum of money from Gruner. If he was half as iniquitous as I believed him to be, then I didn't mind screwing every last penny out of him that I could. He deserved it, and more.

"Very well, then," the Austrian said with a sigh of resignation. "You see before you a man in the grip of an obsession. Will a cheque suffice?"

At my nod, he began making out a cheque to Dr Hill Barton.

"Payable to the bearer, if you don't mind," I said.

With a cluck of the tongue, Gruner tore up the first cheque and scribbled another.

"A pleasure doing business with you, sir," I said, slipping the cheque into my breast pocket.

"The pleasure is mostly yours, Doctor," Gruner said. "Yet I cannot deny there is a large amount of it on my part. Ownership of such curios is my private vice, and I enjoy indulging it. Do you, by any chance, still have in your possession the rest of the contents of Carey's box?" He added this last in an airy fashion, as though it were an afterthought.

"And if I did?"

"I would be in the market for any of those other artefacts."

"Would you now. Well, we shall see."

As he showed me to the door of his study, Gruner said, "I do not suppose you would like to view my collection?"

"I'm quite busy, as it happens," I replied. "I have two further appointments today."

"That is fine, that is fine. I perceive that you do not share my mania. To you, it is the buying and selling that matters, nothing else."

"Perhaps another time."

Then a thought occurred to me. Holmes had told me simply to secure a deal for the fungus and leave, but I wanted to return to Baker Street with more than just money. A little additional information about Gruner and his interest in Mi-Go artefacts, if I could extract it, would surely not go amiss.

"But I suppose I do have a few minutes to spare…" I said.

Gruner showed me to what must have been the room Holmes had caught a glimpse of. Within it lay a dozen glass-fronted display cabinets, and within those lay a panoply of strangeness and perversion. There were idols and icons, relics and rarities. There were preserving jars that contained malformed human foetuses, animals of a kind rarely if ever found in zoos, and diseased bodily organs, each floating in its own little bath of formaldehyde. There were primitively fashioned effigies and totems, the kind of ritual objects used in unspeakable rites. There was a pair of hollow iron dodecahedrons that could have been part of a weapon or else dice for some unknowable game. There was a crumbling book spread open at a page which carried a detailed illustration, a map of countries and oceans that did not correspond with any on Earth.

Gruner pointed out a golden dagger. "That is Mesoamerican, Aztec or Mixtec, I am not sure which. The runes inscribed into the blade are in one of the pre-Columbian languages, perhaps a prayer to a sun god. And that bronze coin is from Atlantis, so I am told. The face moulded into it is that of an amphibious man, most likely an Atlantean king. Oh, and that piece of rock is a chunk of meteorite. See the scorch marks? See, also, how it seems to glow faintly."

I must confess I could have easily spent an hour or two in that museum of his, peering at the artefacts. Gruner had assembled an eclectic, broad-ranging collection that would have fascinated even the layman, let alone someone like myself who had had more than his fair share of experience with the uncommoner aspects of the world.

That was until my eye fell on a petroglyph, hewn out of some rockface. It wasn't much larger in diameter than a dinner plate and its surface was etched with an image of a hunching, bat-winged entity with a large bulbous head and a mouth bristling with tentacles.

I thought immediately of the carved figure I had come across in a remote quarter of Afghanistan, perched atop a hundred-foot granite pillar at the entrance to the lost city of Ta'aa. A chill came over me as I recalled the carnage that had ensued not long after our expedition passed that forbidding monument. More than two decades on, and still the horrors of that episode haunted me.

"Ah, you like that one, do you?" said Gruner. "He is a god, a very, very ancient one. His name is hard to pronounce. It goes something like 'Catharsis'."

I refrained from correcting him. "Well, really, I think I've seen enough. Very interesting, Baron Gruner. Very interesting. You are to be commended. But now I really must be going."

As Gruner escorted me to the front door, he said, "Do you wonder, Doctor, what compels me to collect these things?"

"I presume it's their rarity. Possibly they have some worth as investments, too. Some men collect artworks, after all, as an appreciating capital asset."

"Oh, the financial side of it has little appeal for me. I do not treat them as commodities. No, it is subtler and deeper than that." Gruner's expression turned sly and self-deprecatory. "As you may or may not know, I am something of a womaniser. I cannot pretend otherwise. I love the pursuit, the attainment, the conquest. I love to hold a woman in my thrall. I love her submission and her utter compliance. But then, when that is accomplished, I grow bored. Once a woman is mine, I no longer desire her, and so I move on to the next one." He shrugged his shoulders. "Some would call that a failing. I prefer to think of it as a symptom of a restless heart and a lively mind. The curios I collect, by contrast, never pall on me. I find them endlessly captivating. The more anomalous they are, the less likely I am to tire of them. Women come easily to me, and I understand them and their ways, and so I do not value them. The curios are the opposite. Does that explain it to you?"

I kept my face impassive. "You have made yourself very clear," I said. "Thank you for your business. Good day to you."

"And good day to you, Dr Barton."

On the train up to London, I thought back over the whole encounter. I realised that I had just met, in Baron Gruner, a truly despicable human being. I felt unclean. Even the cheque in my pocket felt unclean. I resolved to donate the money to an almshouse for women, or else one of the charities for distressed gentleladies. It seemed the least I could do, turning something tainted into something good.

*

I was keen to report the success of my mission to Holmes, but found him in a distrait mood when I got back to Baker Street. He held up a hand as soon as I entered our rooms, palm out, indicating that I should hush. Then for the next several minutes he sat with his head on one side, his eyes half closed in concentration.

None of this was particularly unusual behaviour for Sherlock Holmes, and normally I would have shrugged it off, but what was strange on this occasion was that he was wearing his checked tweed travelling cap, the kind sometimes known as a deerstalker. He had the earflaps tied down, and the presence of this garment, incongruous enough in context, was made all the more so by the fact that it was paired with dressing gown and slippers. He looked as though he could not decide whether he was indoors or out.

I helped myself to a whisky and soda, and waited patiently for Holmes to be finished with his musings, or whatever it was he was busy doing.

Eventually he turned to me. "Well done with Gruner," he said. "You acquitted yourself with aplomb."

"You are aware that it went according to plan, then? How could you tell? Was it my expression? No, with you it is always something more tangible than demeanour. You must have ascertained somehow that the briefcase is empty, perhaps by the way I was carrying it. Or else you have discerned the outline of Gruner's folded cheque in my breast pocket."

"Or none of the above," said Holmes. "I do not doubt you have noticed what is on my head."

"I was debating whether to mention it or not," I said. "The day is cold, admittedly, but the fire in the hearth is giving out a goodly warmth and I should not have thought headgear necessary. I presume it is not simply because Paget keeps drawing you wearing such a hat in his illustrations for *The Strand*; you are always rather scornful about that. I'm left thinking either that you're following some new sartorial trend of which I'm unaware – 'This season, the well-dressed gent is not to be seen at any fashionable salon or dinner party without his domestic chapeau' – or that you have taken leave of your senses."

Holmes smiled. "There is another option, Watson. Concealment."

My companion reached beneath his chin and undid the cap's ties, then bared his head.

His left ear was subsumed beneath a milky-white

hemispherical mass which I swiftly identified as a fungus of the same type I had just sold to Baron Gruner. It bulged outward from the side of his head, those tiny dark blue speckles that adorned its surface glinting in the firelight.

I could not mask my surprise. "The stem of that thing," I said, "is it lodged inside your ear?"

"More than that," said Holmes. "The hyphae – the filaments which depend from the fungus – are currently rooted deep in my auditory canal, bonded with the inner workings of my ear. It is not the pleasantest of sensations, I can assure you. It both stings and throbs, like the worst sort of earache. The urge to tear the thing free is almost overwhelming."

"But in God's name, why? What on earth is this in aid of?"

Holmes tied the earflaps back down. "The why of the hat is simple. I should not wish Mrs Hudson, or Billy, or the maid, to come in and find me with a fungus protruding from my ear. I would rather they saw me in the hat and thought it 'just another of Mr Holmes's eccentric habits'. As to the fungus, the explanation is also simple."

"Somehow I suspect it is not."

"Communication," said Holmes. "This fungus here is propagated from the fungus you succeeded in selling to Baron Gruner – and, by the way, you are to be congratulated on securing seventy pounds for it. Quite the extortionist." Before I could enquire how he knew the exact sum, he continued, "I cultivated the offshoot fungus not long ago, having studied the original intermittently over the years. My experiments on it suggested that its desire to form a bond with a sentient host, as evidenced by the predisposition of the hyphae to reach out to any nearby living creature, arises from the need for symbiosis. You, of course, know what that is."

"A mutual relationship between different organisms," I said. "The term was coined by the German mycologist Albert Frank and derives from his study of lichens. A lichen, it seems, is not a single organism but two, an alga and a fungus, living codependently."

"Similarly," said Holmes, "one can regard the affiliation between bees and flowers as symbiosis: the bee gets nectar, the flower is pollinated. There are numerous other examples, and this fungus is one. It wants to merge with a host. I have not yet managed to ascertain what it gains from the relationship, other than that perhaps the host, being capable of locomotion, is able to transport it around and the fungus thus has the opportunity to spread its spores further afield than otherwise. As for the host, in this instance me, the benefit is that whatever the parent fungus experiences, the offspring fungus does too, and by being intimately attached to the offspring fungus as I am, I may participate in that link. The pair of fungi, you see, are conjoined in some indefinable, non-physical manner. I cannot even begin to speculate how it works; I know only that it does."

"In other words, anything the parent fungus knows, the offspring fungus also knows, and so do you." I said this perfectly aware of the absurdity of it, yet at the same time accepting it as fact. My and Holmes's lot in life was to treat the incredible as commonplace.

"Just so, Watson. Now, were I to have installed the offspring fungus upon my eye, it is conceivable that I would somehow be able to 'see' whatever is happening around the parent fungus. The trouble with this is that, while I am intrepid, I am not *that* intrepid. I have no idea what the effect of fungal hyphae latching on to my cornea might be, and I am loath to jeopardise the sight in one eye."

"Whereas the hearing in one ear is expendable?"

"If necessary. Besides, vision is of limited use when it comes to covertly monitoring an individual's activities, especially if one is receiving information from a static source. One would behold only whatever happens to fall within the parent fungus's field of view. Hearing, on the other hand, affords far greater scope for gathering intelligence."

"You mean to say you are eavesdropping on Baron Gruner by means of these related fungi?"

"I mean to say exactly that," Holmes replied. "I installed the offspring fungus in my ear not long after you left Baker Street, and have been listening in on everything that has gone on around the parent fungus since then."

"That is…" I groped for the words. "…extraordinary. And disturbing. And slightly repulsive."

"It is all those things, and more," said Holmes.

"Could you not have warned me? It would have been polite, at least, to tell me that you were going to be privy to everything I was doing. I feel impinged upon."

"Oh, you needn't worry on that account. All I have heard today is my friend Watson being his unfailingly virtuous self. Chivalrously helping an elderly lady get her luggage onto the train. Chatting with the ticket inspector. Giving his carriage driver a handsome tip. Not to mention, while conducting his ruse as Dr Hill Barton, showing himself to be a canny negotiator. I admit I did hear you let out the occasional lovesick sigh in idle moments during your travels, and can only deduce that you were thinking about your new inamorata. I believe at one point you may even have hummed a few bars of 'Jeanie with the Light Brown Hair', like the shameless romantic you are."

I felt my cheeks growing hot with embarrassment. "Really, Holmes…!"

"But right now," he went on, "I am party to the goings-on at Gruner's household. I can hear practically everything that is being said within the vicinity of the parent fungus, which at present sits, if I am not mistaken, in Gruner's study, where you left it. The sound is not always clear, like a poor line on a telephone, but I can follow the majority of the conversations. Earlier, for instance, just as you came in, Gruner was berating his valet for not pressing his trousers properly. The poor servant grovelled and apologised, although he uttered a few disparaging words about his employer soon after, presumably once he was out of Gruner's earshot. The fungus could pick up his grumblings well enough, even if Gruner could not."

"One might call it a form of wireless telegraphy," I said, "an organic version of Preece and Heaviside's experiments with radio induction."

"Do you think I should give it a name? A 'mycophone' perhaps. Oh, excuse me. Gruner is speaking again."

Holmes's attention drifted away from me, reaching across the dozen miles to Kingston, and I marvelled both at this cunning method he had devised for spying on Gruner remotely and at his readiness to endanger his own bodily welfare in the pursuit of an investigation. For he had not vouchsafed how he intended to remove the fungus from his ear after he was done with it. If the fungus's hyphae were firmly attached to the delicate bones and membranes of his auditory meatus, would separating it from them not inflict damage, perhaps the lasting kind? My medical hackles were up. I wanted to tell Holmes how rash and reckless he was, but I knew that he would not listen. In more ways than one, he would turn a deaf ear to my concerns.

*

Holmes kept the fungus *in situ* for the next few days. He remained confined to our rooms, usually with the deerstalker on, and went about his normal business, poring over the newspapers, conducting some experiment at his chemistry bench, or performing a regime of exercises he had developed which combined calisthenics with *baritsu* movements. He had made the last a part of his daily routine since 1897, the year I was finally able to persuade him to abandon his detestable habit of taking regular injections of cocaine. At first the balletic exercises had served as a diversion from the discomforts of withdrawal, but in time they had become an effective substitute for the drug, in that they helped keep his mind clear and working at peak efficiency, a natural rather than artificial stimulant.

I noted that occasionally, when walking or exercising, he might make a misstep and lose his balance. Likewise, when standing, he would sometimes have to support himself with a hand on the furniture. This phenomenon became ever more pronounced until in the end I could not withhold from remarking upon it.

"It looks to me as though the fungus is interfering with the functioning of your inner ear and thus upsetting your equilibrium," I said. "How much longer do you intend keeping it in place?"

"As long as I have to, Watson," came the reply.

"You realise, don't you, that parasitism is another form of symbiosis."

"You think the fungus is feeding off me, like some sort of leech?"

"I don't know. All I know is you cannot go on with it attached to you indefinitely. That would not be wise."

"I am not done with it yet," Holmes said adamantly. "It has not outlived its usefulness."

The fungus's usefulness showed itself on an irregular, unpredictable basis. All at once, Holmes would give a start and desist from whatever he was doing, his body stiffening and his eyes taking on a distracted look. I quickly apprehended that this meant something was happening at Baron Gruner's house and that Holmes was not to be spoken to or interrupted until the event he was eavesdropping on had run its course. I started thinking of these episodes as lacunae, little hiatuses during which my friend was physically present but mentally elsewhere.

One evening, during supper, Holmes halted mid-mouthful and stayed that way, stock-still, food sitting on his tongue half chewed, for a full thirty minutes. It was as though a spell had been cast on him, temporarily freezing him in time.

As the minutes ticked by I grew concerned, fearing that he had fallen victim to a seizure. Even by the standards of his lacunae, this was a long one and seemed to absorb him entirely. Had the fungus perhaps eaten through the walls of his eardrum and penetrated a blood vessel in his brain, triggering a cerebrovascular incident?

At last he roused himself, swallowed his food, took a drink, and said, "Most illuminating."

"What has happened? What did you overhear?"

"Kitty Winter has dropped by to see Gruner, alone, unchaperoned."

"That is bold of her. I doubt her father would approve."

"From what I can gather, she has had a serious falling-out with Sir Hartley. He forbade her from seeing Gruner again, to which she said she would call on him whenever she felt inclined, accompanied or otherwise, whether her father permitted it or not. 'Damn propriety,' said she to him, 'and damn you.'"

"Harsh words for a daughter to utter."

"Harsher still for a father to hear. She and Gruner are now out of range of the parent fungus, but the rest of their talk showed how she is profoundly in love with the fellow. He, in turn, is playing the moonstruck paramour to the hilt. I shall spare you the worst of their dialogue, other than to say it was so glutinously sentimental it would not have been out of place in a Marie Corelli novel."

"Ugh. I thank you for small mercies, Holmes."

"What is of note is that Miss Winter spoke of eloping, and Gruner did not appear averse to the idea, although when she tried to get him to commit to a date, he prevaricated. 'My sweet little Kitty,' said he." Holmes's impersonation of Gruner's accent and oleaginous tone was spot-on. "'*Mein süßes kleines Kätzchen.* Must we rush into things pell-mell? Marriage, yes, in time, but can we just not enjoy being in love as we are for now?' At that, Miss Winter became aggrieved and raised the topic of Gruner's former lovers. 'Papa says you are something of a brute when it comes to women. He even says that you murdered your first wife and that two other girls with whom you have been romantically linked are missing and feared dead.' Oh, Watson, the wounded note in Gruner's voice when he replied to that! As if he had been stabbed through the heart!"

"What did he say?"

"He denied it vociferously. He called the accusations baseless rumours and claimed that certain persons, envious of his wealth and status, would stop at nothing to undermine his reputation. Miss Winter, I'm afraid, lapped this all up. Gruner added that, to his mind, Sir Hartley Winter was an overbearing tyrant who would not let his daughter be free to make her own choices and find her own path in life, to which Miss Winter said, 'Papa loves me and is only trying to protect me, but I am an intelligent person and better versed in the ways of the world than he thinks. He still regards me as the babe he dandled on his lap all those years ago, and since Mama died he has tried to preserve me in his mind as that innocent little creature, despite all evidence to the contrary.' Gruner remarked – and I did not have to see him to know he was leering as he said it – that she was certainly not little and anything but innocent. A coy giggle was Miss Winter's response to that, and there followed a long bout of lascivious kissing."

Holmes paused to take a swig of wine. Then, absently scratching an itch beneath his deerstalker, he resumed his account.

"After that, Miss Winter returned to the theme of Gruner's past conquests. She wanted assurance that she was not to become the next in a line of rejects, and dropped broad hints that she was expecting a ring on her finger within the coming days, if not right there and then."

"There can be little question that the girl is a willing participant in the relationship. I am not sensing much coercion on Gruner's part."

"He is too adept and subtle a seducer for that. Kitty Winter may think she is working her womanly wiles on him, but he remains the true manipulator. The last thing I heard him say to her, before they moved out of range of the parent fungus, concerned catching the ferry to France at the weekend. 'I know of a beautiful little chapel in Auvers-sur-Oise, just outside Paris. The priest there can, I'm sure, be persuaded to officiate, given the right financial incentive. How does that sound?' To Miss Winter, it sounded 'perfect'. 'Then I shall make the arrangements,' said Gruner, which elicited ecstatic cries of 'darling Adelbert' and 'my sweet Austrian strudel' from his intended."

"You have made that last part up."

"I wish I had, Watson. Perhaps we are just too old and fossilised to remember how syrupy the talk between lovers can get. I doubt you are anywhere near as mawkish with your new lady. At any rate, the couple are now elsewhere in the house and I suspect that is the last I shall hear from them for the night."

"Do you think they really are going to elope to France?"

"I think Gruner is the type who would say anything in order to satisfy his immediate needs. If, however, he does mean to follow through with the elopement plan, we have a time and a destination. I'll convey the information to Sir Hartley in the morning and leave it to him to decide the next move. He can detain his daughter, making sure she is unable to leave the house. Failing that, he can intercept her and Gruner before they ever get to Auvers-sur-Oise."

The matter seemed settled, and Holmes picked at the now cold and congealed main course in front of him for a moment before shoving it aside and ringing the bell to summon Mrs Hudson.

"Nothing wrong with your saddle of mutton, I trust, Mr Holmes?" said our landlady, clearing away the plates.

"Not at all, madam. My appetite is not good today, that is all."

Mrs Hudson cast a brief glance at Holmes's deerstalker. By then she must have been well accustomed to seeing him wearing it around the house, but something in her expression suggested she divined a connection between it and Holmes's unfinished meal. The problem could not be with her cooking, so perhaps the hat was cutting off the circulation to his brain.

"Having said which," Holmes went on, "I do smell the delicious aroma of plum duff coming from downstairs. I would not say no to a helping of that, with plenty of custard. The same goes for Watson, I am sure."

The rest of the evening passed uneventfully, although Holmes seemed on tenterhooks, as though anticipating – indeed, hoping for – a fresh instalment of the goings-on *chez* Gruner.

It came later that night, and it came devastatingly.

*

I was sound asleep when Holmes burst into my bedroom.

"Watson! Watson!"

I blinked blearily up at him. His face, by the light of the candle he carried, was fraught with dismay.

"What is it?" I said.

"The worst thing," Holmes replied. "Oh, the very worst. I did not see it coming and I have been powerless to prevent it. All I have been able to do is listen – listen helplessly as a heinous crime unfolds elsewhere."

I sat up. "Explain."

"I shall," said he. "But first, let us dress, and then pray we find a cab. We must get ourselves down to Kingston as soon as possible."

It was a raw night, with a hard wind blowing and rain coming down in sheets, but fortune favoured us and we were soon snug in a hansom, wending our way south-west through the tempestuous dark. It was then that Holmes regaled me with an account of the events he had overheard earlier.

He had stayed up late, keen to keep monitoring events at Gruner's house via his mycophone. Just as the clock struck three and he was thinking of turning in, voices came in his ear. One was Gruner's. The other was coarse, bullish and not unfamiliar, for it belonged to a man with whom Holmes was reasonably well acquainted: Shinwell "Porky" Johnson, a fixture of London's criminal underworld.

"He is an all-purpose rogue," Holmes told me. "Fence, bodyguard, enforcer, provider of false alibis, and willing to engage in whatever other low occupation might earn him a crust. He has served two sentences in Parkhurst and claims to be reformed, but he is not. Oh, he may 'nark' on his comrades now and then, and he has even performed the occasional small service for me, but Johnson thinks only of Johnson first, and as long as the job pays, he will do it, regardless of legality."

Shinwell Johnson, it transpired, had been summoned urgently by Gruner.

"Came as soon as you called," he said as he arrived in Gruner's study, where the parent fungus still sat. "Although, on a night like this, I'd much rather be tucked up in my cot. Another girl, is it?"

"Yes. Yes."

"And what is the lass's, as it were, current condition?"

"She is upstairs, out of it."

"Sleeping?"

"Deeply."

"You ain't chloroformed 'er yet?"

"Not yet. Leave it to the last moment, those were your instructions, Mr Johnson. So that you have more time to conduct your business unimpeded."

"Glad to see you've been paying attention, your baronship," said Johnson. "Don't want 'em waking up too soon. Cause me no end of nuisance, that can. Well, the brougham's outside. Lead me to her."

Gruner, it seemed, was not yet ready to proceed. "Why, Johnson?" he said morosely.

"Why what?"

"Why do they become so attached, these women? Why can they not just fall away of their own accord once their usefulness is done? Why must I have to scrape them off like barnacles? Cornelia, for instance."

"First one I took off your hands, right?"

"She had nowhere else to go," said Gruner, "no one she could turn to after I ended it between us. She became distraught, snivelling all the time, and she would not leave, no matter how hard I tried to make her. She stayed here for days on end. It was unbearable."

"Until I offered to remove her for you," said Johnson. "Just like I did with that next lass, Abigail something-or-other."

"*Ach*, she turned quite poisonous, did Abigail. In retaliation for what she perceived as mistreatment at my hands, she said she was going to call some fellows of her acquaintance and have them, as she put it, 'deal with' me. For a well-born girl, she has spent her life consorting with some very undesirable types."

"Types like me, you mean?"

"Oh no, Mr Johnson. The utter dregs of society. Veritable *Untermenschen*. But I will not give in to threats, least of all from a female."

"So again you contacted me," said Johnson, "your personal dustman, the bloke what collects up your castoffs and disposes of 'em for you, all tidy and discreet-like."

"Indeed. You know, I would ask where you take the girls, what you do with them…"

"But we agreed you weren't going to," said Johnson. "It's better that way. What you don't know won't hurt you."

"But they live?" said Gruner.

"Do you care? They're alive when they leave my supervision, that much I can assure you. Just don't worry yourself about it, your baronship. You carry on with your happy little silver-spoon life like you always have. I'm the one doing the dirty work, not you. Granted, it costs, but then money's no object for a nob such as yourself."

Gruner sighed. "You are right, Mr Johnson. Please understand that I do, in my way, love these women. If only they did not love me back so strongly, so smotheringly."

"Must be awful, being rich and handsome and having the ladies crawling all over you," said Johnson. "I'd happily have your problems. I mean to say, look at me. I'm no oil painting. Red face like this, and big round belly. No wonder they call me Porky. I'm not even loaded, like you. Any appeal I have for the opposite sex is limited."

"This present girl is pleasant enough," said Gruner, "but complications have arisen. Her father is behaving most aggressively and I must get rid of her."

"Easier to wash your hands of her through me, yes?"

"Yes. I have rather come to rely on your services as my 'personal dustman', Mr Johnson."

"For your sake, I don't know how much longer I oughter keep providing these services," Johnson said, sounding a warning note. "All these former lovers of yours vanishing – people are bound to talk."

"Let them. No one has convicted me of anything yet, and no one ever will. But anyway, enough maundering. You have a job to do."

"Right-ho," said Johnson. "Better hop to it, then, bettern't I?"

This was as much as Holmes had heard, and he concluded his account by saying, "It's a bad business, Watson. Very bad. Gruner alone is ruthless enough, but with Shinwell Johnson at his beck and call, there are no bounds to his villainy."

"Will we get there in time to save Miss Winter?"

My companion shook his head sombrely. "I fear not. But still, we must try."

*

At long last, after an anxious drive of an hour and a half, we pulled up at the gates to Gruner's mansion and stepped out into the rain. Holmes stumbled as he alighted from the cab, and would have fallen if I had not caught his arm.

"Holmes," I said, "that fungus is coming off you tonight, and that is my final word on the matter. Look at you. You are so dizzy, you can hardly stay upright."

He shrugged away my hand. "Don't mollycoddle, Watson."

"I mean it. As soon as our business here is done, you are to rid yourself of the thing."

I told the cabman to wait, saying there was an extra half-crown in it for him, at which the poor, sodden, shivering fellow just nodded. Holmes, in the interim, had passed through the gates and was making his way up the drive. I caught up with him easily, for his steps were slow and faltering. His balance was, it seemed, now so off-kilter that simply placing one foot in front of the other was a challenge. He looked like a man wading through a swamp.

The house loomed ahead, dark and unlit. There was no sign of a brougham outside. Holmes pounded on the front door, and in due course the butler appeared, clad in nightwear, lamp in hand. His face betrayed perplexity and not a little irritation. Holmes thrust past him and entered the hallway, where he stood and yelled Gruner's name at the top of his lungs. Presently, the Austrian aristocrat came out onto the galleried landing, fastening the cord of his dressing gown. His hair was tousled and his expression bleary and bemused. To look at him you would have thought he had been abed all night, sleeping the sleep of the just.

"You," said he, coming down the stairs. "Sherlock Holmes. Why are you here at this ungodly hour? And is that Dr Hill Barton with you? I had no idea the two of you were associates."

"It's Dr Watson, actually," I said.

"Ah yes. Of course it is. Well, that explains much."

"Where is she?" said Holmes through gritted teeth.

"Where is who, my dear chap?"

"You know damned well who. Kitty Winter. What have you done with her? Where has Shinwell Johnson taken her?"

Gruner blinked in surprise. "Kitty? I presume the girl is at home with her father."

"She was here earlier."

"That I cannot deny. Kitty and I passed a very pleasant evening together, and then she left. I have no reason to believe she is not now where I said. As for this… did you say 'Shinwell Johnson'? I do not know anyone by that name."

Holmes took a few quick paces towards Gruner, hands outstretched as though to grab him by the lapels and give him a good shake, but then his sense of balance betrayed him and he reeled. Only by some huge effort of self-control did he not collapse to the floor.

"Are you well, sir?" Gruner said, in tones of the utmost solicitude. "You look pale. Perhaps you are worsening for something. In weather such as this, one must be careful. One might catch a chill."

Holmes tossed his head from side to side, in hopes the action might somehow restore his equilibrium. Water droplets flew from the brim of his deerstalker. "Tell me where she is, you blackguard," he growled.

Gruner shrugged his shoulders. "If Kitty is not at home, then I cannot help you. Perhaps she has been waylaid on her journey back to London. The travelling conditions are atrocious, after all. She may, even now, be snug in the parlour of some hotel between here and the capital, waiting until morning when it is safe to carry on."

"You are lying. You know it. I know it."

The Austrian's expression hardened. "Are you insinuating that I have done something to that dear girl? That I have harmed her in some way?"

"No need for insinuation. I am stating it as fact."

"Then, sir, you are both discourteous and deluded. I love

my *Kätzchen*. Why, just this evening she and I talked of marriage! To suggest that I would mistreat her in any way – that I should even want to – is preposterous. Moreover, it is the height of impertinence."

By then, not only the butler was there with us in the hallway but a half-dozen other servants too, drawn from their sleeping quarters by the commotion downstairs. Their presence emboldened Gruner further.

"And moreover, saying such things in front of witnesses is rash indeed. I should call the police on you. I have every right to. You come barging into my house in the middle of the night, you defame me, you act in a threatening manner… Mr Holmes, I was under the impression you were an upholder of law and order, but you are behaving now like a common criminal."

I saw Holmes's hands clench into fists and feared what might ensue. Assaulting Gruner would only worsen the situation.

"We should leave, Holmes," I said. "There is nothing to be gained by antagonising Gruner. It will only play into his hands."

"Heed Dr Watson, Mr Holmes," Gruner said. "He gives wise counsel."

Holmes looked at me, then at Gruner, and gave a sullen nod. "This is not over, Gruner," said he. "Not by a long chalk. No other woman is going to suffer at your hands. I swear it."

"Be on your way, Mr Holmes, and do not darken my door again. I have been lenient with you this time. Next time, I shall perhaps not be so kind."

Holmes and I strode away from the house in morose silence, the rain pounding on our heads. Once we were back in the cab and driving towards London, I asked Holmes what he intended to do next.

"Find Miss Winter, if I can," he said. "Shinwell Johnson could surely help with that, but he is an elusive fellow and himself not easy to find. There are any number of night-clubs, doss houses and gambling dens where he might be holed up.

My foremost priority, however, is to get this fungus out of my ear. It has gone from aid to encumbrance."

"I am glad to hear that. The sooner you are shot of the wretched thing, the better."

"I must also speak to Billy."

"Billy? Whatever for?"

"I mean to ensnare Gruner, and Billy may prove instrumental in that."

"How can a page help?" I said. "Granted, he is personable and nimble-footed, but I don't see how those qualities will benefit us here."

"That, Watson, is because you do not know Billy quite as well as you think you do. You have heard me many times tell you there is a difference between seeing and observing. You have seen Billy practically every day for the past three years, but have you truly observed him?"

Holmes could not be persuaded to expand on this gnomic pronouncement, and I was left to wonder what it was about our page that I was missing. What particular aspect of the lad was so obvious to Holmes and yet so opaque to me?

*

As soon as we were back at Baker Street and had dried ourselves off, Holmes set about removing the fungus from his ear. He accomplished this by lighting a candle and then, with the aid of a shaving mirror, holding the flame to the fungus.

I looked on as the fungus began to sizzle and char. Acrid smoke drifted up from it, filling the air with a stench both earthy and bitter. As more of the fungus burned, so it gradually shrank and its attachment to Holmes's ear grew less tight-fitting. Then, all at once, it fell free, dragging those intrusive filaments out of his ear as it went. They were laced with blood.

The fungus landed on the floor with a soft plop and lay on the rug with its blood-slick hyphae writhing and coiling, as though in agony. Holmes fetched a pair of tongs, picked it up, and dropped it in the hearth. The fire which he had kindled there earlier consumed it. The hyphae shrivelled to nothingness, and the main body of the fungus was soon no more than a blackened, lifeless lump, scarcely distinguishable from the crackling firewood around it.

In the bathroom, Holmes rinsed out his ear thoroughly. His ear kept leaking blood, so I applied disinfectant, cotton wool and a bandage. After that, we both helped ourselves to a much-needed snifter of brandy.

"I feel better already," Holmes remarked. "The dizziness is all but gone."

"I just hope any damage that has been done to your eardrum isn't permanent."

"It's now nearly eight. Let us breakfast while we wait for Billy to show up for work."

"Billy again. I still don't understand what use you intend to put him to."

"Then I shall endeavour to enlighten you. How often have you commented to me, Watson, on how little Billy seems to change?"

"More than once, I'm sure, and it's true. He came to us when he was thirteen years old, or thereabouts. Since then he has hardly grown. I don't think he shaves yet, and his voice is no deeper than it was. Most lads his age would not only have facial hair and be speaking in a tenor register by now, they would have gained several inches in height. They would be broader sideways, too. Billy seems stuck in time, perpetually preadolescent."

"Does that not strike you as unusual?"

"Development is slower in some youths than in others. Billy's ascent to manhood has been delayed but will arrive in due course."

"Or perhaps it won't. Billy is a more complicated individual than you suspect."

"You certainly are hinting as much, but beyond the fact

that he is lively-witted and enjoys working here, what else is there to him?"

"You have all the information you need," said Holmes, "and still you cannot make the deductive leap. Ah well. The truth will be revealed soon enough."

Food and coffee restored some vigour to our sleep-deprived selves, and shortly we heard Mrs Hudson admitting Billy in downstairs. Holmes straight away summoned the lad with a shout, and Billy presented himself in our rooms, standing erect with his hands behind his back. His livery was neat and tidy, trousers pressed, brass buttons polished to a gleam.

"Good morning, sirs," he said. "What'll it be? Message need delivering? Gun need cleaning? Something need fetching from the menders?"

"Sit down, Billy," said Holmes.

It was not a usual instruction for Billy, and he hesitated before complying.

"Don't worry," Holmes continued. "You've done nothing wrong. I have a special request, but before I outline it to you, I must first impress upon you that you are welcome to refuse. I would think no less of you if you did, and whatever happens, your job with us remains secure."

"I see," said Billy warily.

"For Watson's benefit, Billy, state how old you are."

"Sixteen, Mr Holmes. Seventeen next February."

"No, Billy. How old you really are."

The lad looked sheepish. "Must I?"

"I think it's time we brought Watson in on the secret. He has remained oblivious this long, but at some point even he was bound to tumble to it. We may as well get it over with, and you know as surely as I that he is a man of discretion. If we cannot trust him, who can we trust?"

I was puzzled. What could Holmes be talking about? What secret was this?

"I'm twenty-one," Billy said.

"Surely not," I declared. "It isn't possible. Not unless you have some kind of medical condition that retards the onset of puberty. Is that it? Do you, by chance, suffer from hypogonadism? The late Spanish anatomist Aureliano Maestre de San Juan first identified the syndrome, and it's believed to be related to poor function of the pituitary gland."

I expected Billy to acknowledge this diagnosis, or else frown and ask me to explain further. I did not expect him to burst out laughing, nor Holmes the same.

"Watson, Watson, Watson," my friend said. "You are wise in the ways of medicine, and in any other set of circumstances your conclusion would make perfect sense. You are, however, seeking an elaborate solution while overlooking the simpler and more obvious one."

"Well, what is it?" I said hotly. "What is wrong with Billy?"

"Nothing at all," said Holmes. "Billy is a perfectly normal, healthy twenty-one-year-old. Billy is just not Billy."

"Now I am more confused than ever."

Holmes gestured at the page. "The name given to Billy at birth was Wilhelmina Taylor."

"Wilhelmina…"

"Which shortens to Billy."

"You mean…?"

"I was born a girl, Dr Watson," said Billy, "but I choose to be a boy."

*

Just over a fortnight later, an incident occurred in one of the little lanes to the north of Piccadilly and east of Berkeley Square. A young woman was set upon by two ruffians as she walked home on a dark, foggy evening, around ten o'clock. What the dastardly pair intended with the girl, one may only speculate, but it surely cannot have been good.

In the event, she was spared a terrible fate by the timely intervention of a passing foreign nobleman, an Austrian by the name of Baron Adelbert Gruner, who was heading towards his flat in Mayfair after dinner at his club.

Through the swirling yellow vapour Baron Gruner spied the damsel in distress, and his immediate instinct was to go to her rescue. He cried out to her assailants, even as he broke into a run, "Unhand that woman! Leave her be!"

They paused from their endeavours and looked on in startlement as Gruner came charging at them, brandishing the cane he carried. It was a Penang lawyer with a solid silver cap, the kind of walking stick that handily doubles as a weapon.

Gruner belaboured the ruffians with it, fetching them a few good blows around the back and arms and eliciting yelps of pain. In no time, the pair turned tail, volunteering a few gruff oaths over their shoulders as they fled.

The baron responded with a few oaths of his own. Then, composing himself, he bent over the young woman, who lay on the flagstones in a semi-recumbent posture, one hand to her forehead. Her cheeks were tear-streaked and her eyes bulged with fear, but for all that, Gruner could see that she was an exceptionally pretty creature. This pleased him, for Baron Gruner had a liking for the fairer sex – the fairer, the better.

"My dear thing," said he to the girl, "are you all right?"

"I… I do not know, sir," she replied in faltering tones. "I think so. Those men… they came out of nowhere. They spoke roughly to me, making dreadful insinuations. I tried to get away from them, but they seized me and manhandled me. I was so frightened."

"Think no more of them. They are gone, and they will not be back. Please, allow me to help you to your feet."

The girl took Gruner's outstretched hand. Graciously and solicitously, he brought her upright. Then, with that same hand, and no less gently, he grasped her chin and tilted her head to the left then the right, inspecting her face.

"No bruises," he said. "None that I can see, at least."

He let go of her chin in such a way that it seemed a caress.

"I believe I am unharmed," the girl said. "But oh, I am trembling all over." She held up a fluttering hand to prove it.

"But of course you are, you poor creature," said Gruner. "You have had a very trying ordeal."

"It was brave of you, sir, to intervene as you did. I cannot thank you enough. Whom do I have the honour of calling my saviour?"

"Baron Adelbert Gruner, at your service." Gruner executed a low bow. "And whom do I have the honour of having saved?"

"I am Violet de Merville."

"A lovely name to go with a lovely face."

Miss de Merville's blush was clearly visible, even in that fog-shrouded gloom.

"If I may say," added Gruner, "someone as entrancing as yourself ought not to go down narrow, dim-lit thoroughfares like this on her own."

"I was taking a shortcut home after an evening with friends. I have done it numerous times by day, and this *is* Mayfair."

"But rogues lurk in all corners of London after dark."

"I realise how foolish I have been," said Miss de Merville.

"Not foolish. Unwary, perhaps."

"My father is forever telling me I am too trusting, too apt to think the best of everyone. My father is General Ambrose de Merville, by the way."

"I regret to say I have not heard of him, but any military man automatically commands my respect."

"He is no longer serving, but he fought in the Transvaal and also saw action under Kitchener at Omdurman."

"A true servant of queen and country. Forgive me, *king* and country. It has not been long since the death of your monarch."

"Well, at any rate," said Miss de Merville, "I feel I am now recovered and can continue on my way."

"My dear thing, I cannot allow you to walk through this

wretched pea-souper alone," said Gruner suavely. "I offer myself as your escort. My principal residence is in Kingston but I have lodgings here, a *pied-à-terre* apartment for when I am staying in town. It is not far, a couple of streets away. I propose that you accompany me there, where I can arrange for you to have some hot tea, or something stronger if you prefer. Only when I am satisfied that you are fully well again will I permit you to leave, and even then I shall see you safely from my front door to yours."

He said all this with a note of friendly, cajoling insistence, but there was something about his manner that implied he would not take no for an answer.

To Violet de Merville, at any rate, his offer seemed too good to refuse. She was not concerned that the two of them might be alone in the apartment together. The wording "arrange for you to have some hot tea" implied the presence of a housekeeper or other such domestic retainer on the premises. Besides, the fellow was very handsome. Dashing good looks, courtesy, courage, and a European accent, too – it all made for a very beguiling package.

"You are kind, Baron Gruner, and I accept. My legs, I confess, do still feel somewhat unsteady."

"I am delighted to hear it. Your acceptance, I mean, not about your legs – although I may be of assistance there…"

He tendered her his arm. Miss de Merville took it, slotting her hand through the crook of his elbow, and like this, he supporting her, the pair strode off through the fog.

"I shall tell my father about you," Miss de Merville could be heard saying as they turned the corner at the end of the lane. "He is not home at present, but when he learns what you did, he will be very grateful. I would not be surprised if he sought you out, keen to thank personally the man who preserved his daughter's honour and perhaps life."

"I look forward to meeting him," was Gruner's reply. "I, in turn, shall thank him for siring such an alluring creature as you."

Miss de Merville's giggle rippled through the air, a sound so effervescent with merriment and enchantment that even the fog could not deaden its sparkle.

That was the incident, and exciting as it was, there was more to it than there might seem.

*

Sherlock Holmes and I, from our hiding place in a nearby basement area, listened as Violet de Merville's laughter dwindled away. We stood hunched in the hollow beneath a stone staircase, next to the entrance to the property's coal cellar. We had hastened thither straight after the attack on Miss de Merville, in which we, it perhaps goes without saying, were participants. For indeed, the two ruffians who had ambushed and ill-used her were none other than Holmes and myself. We were in heavy disguise, our clothes ragged and old, he with a long shaggy wig and various fake scabs and psoriatic blotches all over his face, I sporting plentiful artificial scars and an extravagant set of muttonchop whiskers made of horsehair.

As for Violet de Merville, she was our page Billy Taylor, likewise in disguise. A long chestnut-coloured wig covered that short-cropped mouse-brown mop of his, and this, allied with an expensive dress and gabardine from Liberty's and some touches of cosmetic, had transformed him into the wholesome-looking, vulnerable young woman who had proved so irresistible to Baron Gruner.

In short, the entire thing had been staged from start to finish, in order to bring Billy, as the fictitious Miss de Merville, into Gruner's orbit. It was no coincidence that the lane where the altercation took place happened to be a cut-through Gruner habitually used when returning to his apartment from his club. Holmes had learned that Gruner dined at the club – The Singletons' on St James's Street – every Thursday, and had shadowed him back and forth between it and his apartment on the previous Thursday and the one before, establishing that he always used the same route. Then it had been merely a case of Holmes, Billy and myself lying in wait, poised to commence our charade as Gruner approached. The fog had been a fortuitous bonus, further obscuring Holmes's and my identities and making our escape to concealment that much simpler.

"Well, Billy played that to perfection," Holmes said, after Billy and Gruner were long out of earshot.

"Yes, she did," I said. "I mean *he* did. Dash it all, I'm still finding this very confusing. I mean, I know there are men who dress as women, and vice versa, and not only on the stage. Krafft-Ebing talks about the phenomenon in his *Psychopathia Sexualis*, rather damningly."

"If you know anything about Krafft-Ebing, you'll know that he should have written a treatise on hypocrisy rather than on deviancy," Holmes observed with a wry grin. "As far as Billy goes, the matter is really quite simple. Billy is a boy. That is how he has chosen to present himself to the world, so that is who he is. His parents may have christened him Wilhelmina, but to himself, from the time he was old enough to realise who he should be, he has always been Billy. Billy was inherent in Wilhelmina, just as the butterfly is inherent in the caterpillar. Since achieving the age of majority, he now does as a male what he could not as a female, living and working independently of his family. They, I regret to say, have disavowed him. When Billy first sheared off his hair and swapped skirt for trousers, his father, he told me, beat him and practically threw him out of the house."

"Then in that case it cannot be easy for him to don dress and wig and masquerade as a young woman. It must raise complicated emotions."

"He only agreed to my plan out of the goodness of his heart and from a sense of righteousness. You were there when I recounted Gruner's activities to him. His anger was palpable."

"'I shall do it for you, Mr Holmes, and for the sake of all the women whom that rat has wronged.' Those were his words, and hearing them, I nearly cheered." I scratched at my whiskers. The spirit gum that fastened them to my face made my skin itch terribly. "And now, the trap has been sprung. Billy has Gruner hoodwinked. All he needs to do is keep him on the hook."

"That should not be too difficult," said Holmes. "Gruner is already smitten by Violet de Merville, the more so because he sees himself as her knight in shining armour and that appeals to his vanity. He will pay court to her at his apartment, then escort her home to the de Merville residence."

This was actually Lord Cantlemere's place in Belgravia, which His Lordship had been so kind as to lend us the use of, for that purpose.

"Thereafter," Holmes continued, "Miss de Merville and Gruner must meet again, and soon. I daresay Gruner will ensure that happens. Otherwise Billy will engineer it. That meeting will be followed by a third, perhaps a fourth. Then, inevitably, will come the invitation to Kingston, at which point Billy will be bait again but in a much more dangerous trap, one which will draw Shinwell Johnson into its toils. And it's Johnson we really want. Baron Gruner is a loathsome specimen, but Johnson is the one taking the girls away and doing Lord knows what to them, and has therefore assumed primacy."

"And since you have been unable to locate his whereabouts..." Over the past fortnight Holmes had dedicated himself to that task, in the hope that wherever Shinwell Johnson was, there Kitty Winter might also be discovered, or else some clue leading to her location. In spite of his best efforts, however, he had drawn a blank, and he had been forced to admit to Sir Hartley Winter that he was beginning to fear the worst.

"Since I have been unable to locate Johnson's whereabouts," Holmes echoed, "then the fox must be lured out of his den. Once we have apprehended Johnson, we will surely be able to learn where he took Miss Winter and the other two young women. After that, we may concentrate fully on Gruner and see to it that he gets his due comeuppance."

"And also establish what, if any, connection he has to the Mi-Go and their human supporters," I said.

"Oh, I am convinced there is none."

"You're sure?"

"Have I not mentioned this?"

"No, but then you have been somewhat preoccupied with the search for Johnson and setting a trap for Gruner."

"Gruner is shrewd in many ways," Holmes said, "but when it comes to his collection of curios, he is a blithering idiot. He has money but no discernment or expertise. Did you not hear him talk about his Mesoamerican blade with runes on it? Mesoamerican civilisations used pictograms, not runes. And his so-called bronze coin from Atlantis! Why would it have the image of an amphibious man on it? Atlantis, if the legends are to be believed, was an island city that was destroyed by the gods and sank beneath the waves. Its denizens were as human as you or I. I would suggest, rather, that that coin is currency used by the marine race known as the Deep Ones."

"Now that I think about it," I said, "it's surprising Gruner mispronounced the name Cthulhu."

"Not surprising at all when you realise how amateurish our Austrian friend is. He's a magpie for oddities and, just like a magpie, cannot tell the difference between gemstone and paste." Holmes motioned with his hand. "We have left it long enough. Gruner and Billy will have reached Gruner's apartment."

We climbed the steps from the area to street level. The fog was thickening, I thought, and its tarry, sulphurous haze stung the nostrils ever more acridly.

From a pocket, Holmes produced a small cardboard box. "You know what comes next, Watson."

"I wish you wouldn't."

"I am none too happy about it myself, but I need to

monitor Billy. I promised him I would not leave him wholly at Gruner's mercy. He made it clear he is quite capable of defending himself, and I do not doubt it, but Adelbert Gruner is an animal in guise of a man. Should he attempt anything untoward while Billy is in his apartment, we will know about it and be able to step in before things go too far."

I watched Holmes extract a blue-speckled fungus from the box. It was the offspring of another fungus which he had grown from a spore and which in turn came from the fungus he had previously used as a mycophone. The parent fungus of the one in his hand was currently lodged in a secret pocket inside Billy's dress. Holmes had had it sewn there, as a precaution, without Billy's knowledge. The reason for this subterfuge wasn't that he thought Billy incapable of understanding how the mycophone worked, or indeed of accepting that it did work. He just felt that posing as Violet de Merville was enough of a challenge for the lad without the additional onus of carrying an organic listening device on his person. Billy might also inadvertently betray the fungus's presence to Gruner if he knew it was there, and then Gruner might realise something was up.

Drawing aside his wig, Holmes put the fungus up to his ear. He had decided to insert it into the left one as before, on the grounds that if his hearing was to be put at risk again, he would rather the same ear be endangered than the ear that hitherto had had no interaction with the fungus. As to whether using the mycophone again would adversely affect his balance, we both agreed that last time it had taken several days for the problem to develop. The process had been cumulative. This time he intended to keep the fungus in place for a couple of hours at most.

The fungus's hyphae stirred and reached for the orifice like a cluster of fine, inquisitive fingers. Swiftly the mycophone was installed in position, my friend wincing slightly as the hyphae probed deep within his auditory canal and rooted themselves there. Then he let the wig fall back down to hide it.

"Now," he said, and his eyes adopted a faraway look as he began eavesdropping on Billy and Gruner. At the same time, he beckoned to me, and we began walking in the direction of Gruner's apartment. I took a moment to pat my overcoat pocket. There lay the reassuring bulk of my service revolver. As ever, I had brought it with me on an adventure with Holmes not in the hope of using it, but in the expectation that I might have to.

We halted within sight of the house, one of those grand, double-fronted Georgian terraced mansions with a columned porch, an imposingly large front door, and an ashlar façade whose pale sandstone masonry had been grimed by decades of London soot. Chinks of light, made blurry by the fog, glimmered around the curtains in several of its windows, including those on the second floor, which belonged to the Austrian's lodgings. Up there, Billy was now ensconced with Gruner, and as Holmes and I stood sentinel, some twenty yards away on the opposite side of the road, my friend relayed snippets of their conversation to me.

"Gruner is being ever so attentive to Billy. 'Are you comfortable there, my girl?'... 'How is the tea?'... 'No need to be afraid, Violet. You are quite safe with me. I may call you Violet, may I not? I feel we already know each other well enough for that. And you may call me Adelbert.' Billy, for his part, is striking a nice balance between cordial and coquettish. 'Really, Adelbert, your kindness is overwhelming. There aren't many men who would do so much for a woman they have only just met.'"

"It would be like something out of a Shakespearean comedy," I said, "if it weren't so serious. The rake exercising his charms on a girl, little knowing she is a boy in a girl's guise."

Holmes scarcely acknowledged the remark. His focus was elsewhere, up in that apartment.

Suddenly, he stiffened.

"Oh," he said.

"What is it?" I asked.

"Oh no."

"Holmes, tell me what you're hearing."

"My name, Watson," he said through tight lips. "Gruner just spoke my name. 'Tell me, Violet, how is it that you know Sherlock Holmes?'"

"What!" I exclaimed.

"We have been found out. 'No, don't play the innocent with me, *fräulein*. You think I did not recognise those two men? You think I do not realise this whole thing is a sham?' He is telling Billy he knows he has been sent by me to spy on him. Billy is denying it, of course, but Gruner is not having any truck with that."

"We have to get Billy out of there."

I made to move, but Holmes placed a restraining hand on my arm.

"Just a moment. Billy is getting up to leave. Violet de Merville is becoming quite terse. She's telling Gruner she has had enough of this nonsense. She has no idea what he is talking about and has never heard of any Sherlock Holmes. 'Spy on you? How absurd!' Billy may yet be able to extricate himself without our involvement."

"But involving ourselves is exactly what we must do," I said. "We can't leave him in Gruner's clutches."

"There's still a chance he can convince Gruner that he is mistaken. And it's working, I think. He is continuing to protest innocence and Gruner is being won over. Gruner is saying, 'So you really do not know Sherlock Holmes? But your attackers, for all that they looked and acted like common street thugs, bore a more-than-passing resemblance to him and his companion Dr Watson, and this is precisely the kind of chicanery that Holmes indulges in. Well, I could be wrong…' To which Billy is saying, 'Your abrupt change in mood has me quite shaken, Adelbert. I thought you and I were getting along famously, and now, out of the blue, you are accusing me of being not what I appear to be. A strange form of flirtation indeed.'"

Holmes fell silent, head cocked to the left, listening hard. I waited on tenterhooks for the next bulletin.

"Billy has swooned," he said eventually. "'I am feeling unwell. I cannot seem to stay on my feet.' An interesting tactic. Not what I would have recommended, but then Gruner is the kind of fellow for whom feminine frailty is attractive. By the sound of it, he is helping Billy to a chair. Now I'm not hearing anything at all. Gruner appears to have left the room. His footsteps are returning now. There is a swish of dress fabric. A lot of rustling. A door. Footsteps again, and if I am correct, they are descending…"

Holmes struck the heel of his hand against his forehead.

"Watson!" he ejaculated. "I have blundered. Descending! Gruner has picked up Billy's unconscious body and is carrying it downstairs. Quick. We haven't a moment to lose."

So saying, he sprang into action, sprinting pell-mell across the road. I followed hot on his heels.

Holmes hammered the brass door knocker hard.

"Open up!" he cried. "Someone, anyone, open up! It is a matter of life and death."

When there was no immediate response to his importuning, he turned to me. "Let us put our shoulders to the door. We may be able to force it. On my count. One, two, three…"

We threw ourselves bodily at the portal, but it was as sturdy as it was large. Under our combined assault it scarcely budged.

"Again. We must try again."

The door, however, remained steadfastly unmoved, whereas my shoulder was badly jarred. My Afghanistan wound, on the other shoulder, set up a painful protest of its own, as if in sympathy.

"One more go, Watson. Put all you've got into it."

I obliged, but the door stayed fixed firmly in its frame.

"It's hopeless," I said.

Holmes snatched up the door knocker again and started slamming it against its striker plate. I heard stirrings within the house. Various residents in their apartments were very vocally demanding to know who was making that infernal racket, and at so late an hour, too.

"There is devilry afoot," Holmes called out. "One of you must come to the door this instant."

Presently we heard the latch turning. The door opened a crack, and in the aperture there appeared a nervous face. It belonged to a thin, sallow gentleman in a velvet smoking jacket.

"Who are you?" the fellow enquired timorously, blinking through a pair of pince-nez spectacles. "What is the meaning of—?"

Holmes shoved the door fully open with a forthright thrust of the hand. The gentleman stepped back in surprise.

We entered a communal hallway where, in addition to the thin gentleman, we found a handful of residents assembled, some in nightwear. An elderly couple were perched on the staircase, halfway up and seemingly ready to retreat at any second, while the rest stood huddled in a corner. One man had had the forethought to bring with him a poker, which he held half raised, although he looked as though he had no idea what he might do with it. I realised that Holmes and I, in our disguises, made anything but a good impression. To these respectable folk we looked the very worst sort.

"Is there a back entrance?" Holmes said. "There must be."

The man with the poker tried to sound aggressive. "Now see here, you can't just come barging in like this."

"Never mind," said Holmes. "I'll find it myself."

He made for a corridor that led off from the far end of the hallway. I trailed in his wake, offering the residents a smile that I hoped conveyed sincere apology. "We are on very important business," I said to them. "A life is at stake. Please forgive the intrusion."

At the end of the corridor we came to an open back door. A short flight of steps afforded access to a long, narrow garden, beyond which stood a rear wall. The gate in the wall was also open, and hastening through it, we emerged into the alley behind, in time to see a two-horse brougham clattering away. Gruner was there, with an expression of profound satisfaction on his face. He seemed to have been anticipating our arrival.

"Keep an eye on him, Watson," Holmes ordered. "If he tries to run, grab him and don't let go."

"I shall go one better than that," I said, drawing my revolver, cocking it, and levelling it at Gruner.

The Austrian eyed the gun carefully. The smug smile did not leave his lips, but its crescent shape did flatten somewhat.

Holmes, meanwhile, set off at full tilt in pursuit of the brougham. The carriage, however, had got up speed and was already turning the corner onto the main road, the coachman whipping the horses hard. By the time Holmes himself reached the corner, the brougham was fifty yards down the road and disappearing into the fog. It was travelling at such a pace that not even the swiftest athlete could have caught up with it.

Holmes loped back, disconsolate.

"Got away, did he?" said Gruner. "What a pity."

The gloating insincerity in his voice was irksome, and my finger twitched on the trigger.

"That ridiculous getup you are both wearing," the Austrian went on. "Not as impenetrable as you might think. And anyway, I was prepared for something like this. I had a notion you might kidnap me and perhaps bully me into making some sort of confession. Sending a woman to worm her way into my confidence instead… much cleverer. Bravo. But I had my suspicions about Miss de Merville from the start, and after I got her home, I left her for a moment and went to check my copy of *Debrett's*. There is no General Ambrose de Merville. That was when I knew for sure that I must take action. I have a certain trusted employee who has proved helpful to me in the past. You know his name."

"Shinwell Johnson," said Holmes.

"Indeed. Ever since you threatened me at my Kingston house, vowing that no other woman was going to suffer at my hands, I have kept him on a retainer, in case of emergency. He has been staying with me, which no doubt has stymied any efforts you have made to locate him in his usual haunts. As soon as I had confirmed my suspicions about the so-called Violet de Merville, I sent him out to get the brougham ready."

Clearly all of this had happened before Holmes had installed the mycophone in his ear, and without Billy's knowledge either. Gruner had slipped off to another room and given Shinwell Johnson his instructions in private.

"And then," Holmes said, "all you had to do was add a sleeping draught to a drink you were preparing for Miss de Merville and wait for it to take effect."

"Yes. That is it."

"And now Johnson has spirited her away. I would ask you where to, but I am sure you don't know."

Gruner shrugged his shoulders. "Genuinely I do not, and I have never felt inclined to ask."

"You just let him take troublesome women off you," I said, "allowing you to wash your hands of them."

"That which I am ignorant of cannot be used against me, Doctor."

"Maybe not, but *this* can." I raised my revolver until it was aimed straight at his face.

"Not now, Watson," Holmes advised. "Gruner will keep. We have more pressing concerns, foremost of which is finding transportation. Come with me. This has been a night of failures, but still, all is not lost, not yet."

"Yes, go, the pair of you," said Gruner. "Chase after her. I very much doubt you will catch up, but go anyway, you big, brave, bold heroes." He started laughing. "Go follow your lost cause."

We headed off along the alley, with Baron Gruner's crowing laughter ringing in our ears. I was sorely tempted to turn back and give the Austrian what-for. I doubted I could actually shoot him in cold blood, but I would happily have given him a good drubbing. We had, though, delayed long enough, and so I refrained.

*

The first hansom that came by was occupied, as was the second. Holmes's frustration mounted, so that by the time a third cab happened along he was in no mood to scruple. He stepped off the kerb directly in front of it.

"Stop!" he demanded, hand held up.

The cabman spotted him in the nick of time, reining in his horse so that Holmes just managed to avoid being trampled.

"What d'you think you're up to, you lunatic?" the cabman barked. "A bloke can hardly see ten feet in this fog. Are you looking to get yourself killed?"

"I need to hire you," said Holmes.

"I already have a fare."

The fare in question leaned out over the half-doors in front of him. He was an imperious-looking gent in opera hat and fur coat. "Yes," said this fellow sternly. "He's taking me home, and you, you impertinent jackanapes, are standing in the way. Move yourself at once."

"I crave your pardon, sir," said Holmes, "but I must commandeer your cab. A life hangs in the balance, and every second lost is a second closer to calamity."

"How come you speak as you do," said the man in the cab, "but look like *that?*"

"It is complicated and I don't have time to explain. I will say just this." Holmes made an odd, stiff arm gesture. "Will no one help the widow's son?"

The man in the cab gave a start, then straight away stood and climbed out. He shook my friend's hand in an unusual manner, his fingers not quite fully engaged with Holmes's, then tipped his hat to him. "I don't profess to know what is going on here, but the very best of luck to you nonetheless."

"I am in your debt, sir."

Turning to the cabman, the former fare handed him a pound note. "Take this fellow and his companion wherever they wish to go."

Presently Holmes and I were settling down in our seats, while the cab's previous occupant carried on homeward on foot. Holmes banged on the roof. "Cabbie, drive."

"Where to?" came the reply.

"Head west. I will give you specific directions as and when. And go as fast as you can."

"In these conditions?"

"Then as fast as you are willing."

The cabman goaded his horse into motion, and we set off at a fair lick.

"Pretending to be a Freemason, Holmes," I said. "Have you no shame?"

"Needs must, Watson. I spied the compass-and-set-square ornament on that old fellow's watch chain, and inspiration struck. Judging by the pass grip he used and the pressure he applied to the knuckle of my ring finger with his thumb, he is a third-degree Master Mason. I one-upped him with the handshake of a Most Excellent Master."

"But isn't there some dire penalty for claiming to be a Freemason when you are not? Something to do with being killed and buried below the high-tide mark of the Thames with your tongue cut out?"

"We can discuss the dos and don'ts of feigning membership of a secret society another time. Now, I have to concentrate on catching up with Shinwell Johnson."

"But how? A hansom may be swifter than a brougham,

but he has a head start of at least half a mile. He could be anywhere."

"Elementary," my companion said, tapping his left ear. "I can listen. At present, the parent fungus in Billy's dress is picking up the clopping of horses' hooves, the rattle of wheels on road, and all the other sounds in proximity, and from these I can tell a great deal. For example, I know that Johnson has just driven through Hyde Park. The noise of hooves and wheels was deadened for a while, suggesting that he swapped cobbled road for one of the park's earthen tracks, either South Carriage Drive or North Carriage Drive. I think it must have been the north one because now I am hearing the distant chug of a steam locomotive and, yes, a train whistle. There is no other station near Hyde Park except, of course, Paddington. Driver! Aim for Paddington station, if you will."

We sped onward through the fogbound city, passing from the diffuse glow of one streetlamp to the next. In the patches of dimness between, the hansom's lanterns afforded scant illumination, most of it swallowed up by the fog's restless billows and coils. As London particulars went, that night's was unusually heavy. We were travelling practically blind, with nothing to guide us save whatever clues Holmes could glean via the mycophone, which he tallied with an encyclopaedic knowledge of the capital's geography.

"A church bell tolling the hour. That will be All Saints, Notting Hill, if I don't miss my guess. It's the only major church in the area. The clanking of train couplings. The railyards north of Wormwood Scrubs? Must be. Yes, there is the far-off clamour of male voices from the Scrubs itself. A prison is seldom anything but rowdy, even at night. The sounds of the carriage have become hollow and reverberant. A bridge. That must be where Scrubs Lane crosses over the Paddington Arm of the Grand Union Canal. If I am right, then Johnson will shortly be going under a rail bridge. Yes. Yes. Echoes."

Holmes conveyed information piecemeal to the cabman – which turns he must take, which streets to follow – and thus did we manage to stay in the wake of the brougham, albeit at long range. That said, the intervals between the other carriage passing a landmark and ours passing the same landmark grew incrementally shorter, meaning that we were gaining ground. Our quarry would soon be within sight, I thought, and I peered ahead, straining my eyes to catch a glimpse of it.

"What's this now?" said Holmes, half to himself. "A soft moan. A rustle of silk. I do believe Billy is coming round."

"That is good news," I said. "He may be able to effect an escape."

"Come on, Billy," Holmes said, as though the lad could hear the encouragement. "Wake up. It's only a sleeping draught, and you are young, with the resilience of youth. Fight, my boy. Fight for consciousness."

Moments later I let out a small, involuntary cry of triumph. Distantly amid the yellow gloom I had seen a faint flicker of light. It was bobbing around and could only be carriage lamps.

"There," I said to Holmes, pointing. "That's them, isn't it?"

"It is," Holmes replied. "I can hear a fainter version of our hansom's progress, through the mycophone. And Billy is trying to push himself upright, I believe. Seat springs are creaking."

"We've done it," I said. "We've got him."

Holmes sounded a note of caution. "Not yet. Johnson could still shake us off his tail in this fog." To the cabman he said, "You see that brougham ahead? Whatever you do, do not lose sight of it."

"Very well, sir. Any particular reason?"

"How about a gold sovereign, on top of the pound you already have? Reason enough?"

"Plenty, sir," said the cabman, and urged his horse on.

Soon we were no more than twenty yards behind the brougham. Just past the end of its roof I could see the head and torso of the driver, silhouetted against the nimbus of light from the lamps. In cloth cap and ulster, he cut a burly figure. This was the infamous Shinwell Johnson, then, disposer of cast-off women. I looked forward, when we met, to giving him a piece of my mind.

By that point we were on the Harrow Road, travelling north-west through Harlesden. On either side lay smart, detached houses interspersed with patches of scrubland and the occasional construction site, as befit a burgeoning middle-class suburb. The brougham was now tantalisingly close – so close that within a minute or so our hansom should be drawing alongside it.

Then Johnson glanced round. He must have heard a carriage coming up behind. Something evidently alarmed him – perhaps it was the hansom's pace, or the alert, intent posture of its passengers – for he faced forward again and lashed his horses furiously. The brougham pulled away, but our cabman, to his credit, refused to cede the race. Giving his horse a few smart licks of the whip, he quickly made up the lost distance.

We were just approaching a bridge over a railway line when one of the brougham's doors was flung open. Next moment, out flew Billy. He hit the roadway, rolling over and over in a flurry of silk and crinoline and fetching up in a heap beside the kerb.

Johnson realised instantly that his captive had made a bid for freedom. He hauled back on the reins, bringing the brougham to a halt. Applying the handbrake, he leapt down and hastened back towards where Billy lay.

Holmes ordered our cabman to halt too, and as the hansom slowed he thrust open the half-door on his side and jumped out while the vehicle was still moving. He hit the ground running. I, attempting a similar exit, was somewhat less agile. I mistimed my dismount, my feet slipped out from under me, and I went hurtling face first onto the road.

As I picked myself up, I saw Johnson closing in on Billy,

and Holmes closing in on Johnson. Johnson was nearer his target by a margin of several yards. Above the muffler he wore around the lower portion of his face, I made out a pair of dark eyes that glittered meanly.

As for Billy, he had recovered his senses and was getting to his feet, looking resolute if shaken. I saw him draw up his skirt with one hand and reach towards his foot with the other. He slid something from the top of his boot. Steel glinted in the gloom – the blade of a knife.

Then Johnson was upon him. He seized Billy by the hair and yanked hard. To his great surprise, the entire head of hair came away. He peered at the wig in his hand, dumbstruck. Billy seized the opportunity to lash out with the knife. He scored Johnson's chest with the tip of it, slicing through layers of clothing into flesh. Johnson, with a roar of pain and rage, tossed the wig aside and grabbed Billy by the wrist. He twisted Billy's forearm violently, forcing him to relinquish his weapon. As the knife fell from Billy's grasp, Johnson caught it with his free hand.

"Cut me, will you?" he growled. The muffler had fallen from his face, revealing hefty jowls and a ruddy, scorbutic complexion. "You little hussy! I'll show you. I'm not allowed to kill you, but that doesn't mean I can't scratch you up a little."

As he raised the knife to deliver his retaliation, Holmes covered the last few feet of ground between him and the two combatants. He lunged headlong into Johnson, seizing hold of his knife hand and propelling him bodily backwards. Johnson, helpless before the sheer impetus of Holmes's attack, was driven hard against the parapet of the railway bridge.

There, the pair of them grappled. Each was fighting for control of the knife while at the same time delivering punches and kicks. Billy joined the fray, prying Johnson's fingers off the weapon. The knife tumbled over the parapet onto the tracks below. Johnson responded with a swift, nasty backhand clout to Billy's temple, which sent the lad reeling and stunned.

Seeing as Johnson had been disarmed, I believed the contest between him and Holmes would now be completely even, if not slightly in my friend's favour. I was wrong, for Johnson was a brute of a man, and a desperate one at that. He fought with the snarling viciousness of a wounded, cornered animal. Blood seeped from the gash in his chest, dripping from the ragged ends of his torn clothing, but even this injury did not seem to hinder him. If anything, it made him angrier and more determined.

Holmes kept his end up, deflecting Johnson's punches and landing the occasional punch of his own, but he was on the defensive. The delicate art of *baritsu* was proving no match for Johnson's bullish onslaught.

"Watson," he called out. "Now might be a good time to produce your revolver again."

I had not even thought about the gun, so confident had I been that Holmes would be the victor in the struggle. I wrested it from my pocket and strode towards them. Johnson was in a state of frenzy, pummelling Holmes's ribs and belly like a bareknuckle heavyweight. I took careful aim.

"Shoot to wound," Holmes said, displaying great presence of mind even as he fended Johnson off. "He's no good to us dead."

I sighted along the barrel at Johnson's meaty shoulder. The man was moving around but the range was practically point blank. He noticed me, and spun away from Holmes in order to tackle me instead. Perhaps he thought he might reach me before I could loose off a shot. Perhaps, in that moment of crazed fury, he wasn't thinking clearly at all.

I squeezed the trigger, the revolver bucked in my hand, and Shinwell Johnson went staggering backwards, bellowing in pain. He collided with the bridge parapet with such force that he tumbled over.

"No!" cried Holmes in dismay. Like me, he was convinced Johnson had fallen. The drop to the tracks below was roughly twenty feet. That might not be sufficient to kill him, but there again it might.

We ran to the parapet, only to find that Johnson had not, in fact, fallen. How he had managed to catch the rim of the parapet with one hand, I do not know, but he had. Now he was hanging there, clinging on by the fingertips. His other arm hung limp and useless by his side. My bullet had hit him in that shoulder, and blood poured from the wound, adding to the crimson slick already coating his breast.

"Hold on, Johnson," Holmes said. "We will pull you up."

"You don't think I'm going to let you take me, do you?" Johnson gasped.

"You have no choice. Should you fall, you will break a leg at least, and perhaps your neck. Without our assistance, you are not getting out of this unscathed. I can promise you justice and a fair trial. Just tell me who you are working for. I don't mean Baron Gruner. I mean the people you were taking Violet de Merville to, the ones who need her alive. Who are they?"

Johnson's fingers began to lose their purchase on the parapet rim. Holmes leaned over and grasped the sleeve of his ulster with both hands, taking some of his weight.

"Answer me," he said. "Who are they? What do they want with these young women?"

"You think I'll just sing, Mr Holmes? That's not Shinwell Johnson's way." He let go of the parapet, so that Holmes was now supporting his entire weight. He began writhing, trying to slither out of the ulster.

"Watson, help me," Holmes said. "He's deucedly heavy."

I grabbed the sleeve too, and both of us braced ourselves against the parapet and began to haul. Johnson writhed harder, determined to resist us and take his chances falling.

That was when I heard it: at first a low, insidious rumble like distant thunder, then a hissing. Through the fog, some way down the tracks, a light glimmered like a jaundiced cyclopean eye.

"A train," I breathed. "A train is coming." At that hour it was likely to be a mail train, laden with freight.

Johnson's legs were dangling below the arch of the tunnel. The clearance between the train's smokestack and the tunnel ceiling could be no more than twelve inches.

"It's coming fast," I said to Johnson. "It's going to hit you."

A glance over his shoulder told him I was right. Even if he dropped to the tracks, he would not be able to scramble to safety in time.

His change of heart was as sudden as it was total. "All right, all right!" he said. "Pull me up! Quick about it!"

"And you'll answer my questions if we do?" Holmes said.

"Yes. Yes!"

Holmes and I heaved, but Johnson weighed a good sixteen stone. In addition, his ulster was starting to feel the strain, not least because its front had been carved up by Billy's knife. I felt seams in the coat begin to give.

The oncoming train hurtled ever closer, the growl of its engine and the steely churn of its wheels on the rails rapidly mounting in volume. Even if the engineer could see what was going on ahead of him, which I doubted, he would never be able to brake in time.

Johnson was becoming frantic. "For God's sake, hurry!"

By dint of great effort we managed to raise him so that only his feet were below the tunnel arch. I was sure the train would now not make contact with him.

Then, just as the train was about to plunge into the tunnel, the ulster tore and Johnson fell.

One moment he was there, suspended in space, his body limned by the beam of the train's lamp. The next he was gone from sight, carried forth by the front of the locomotive, which barrelled onward oblivious to the impact, its retinue of freight wagons snaking swiftly along behind it. Johnson did not even have time to scream.

Holmes and I were left holding the ripped, empty remains

of the ulster, which flapped like a wind-tormented flag in the vortex of the train's passing.

*

Police recovered Shinwell Johnson's body, such as it was, the next morning. Parts of him had been flung up the embankment on the far side of the tunnel. The rest was smeared along the rails. One constable, exhibiting the kind of gallows humour that was a prerequisite in his line of work, was overheard to remark that it was less a corpse, more a jigsaw puzzle.

Sherlock Holmes was bitterly disappointed that Johnson had evaded his clutches, and indeed, the full force of the law. He scoured Johnson's brougham for clues as to where the man had been intending to take Billy – doubtless the same destination to which he had ferried Kitty Winter and the two women Gruner had spurned before her, Cornelia Waunchope and Abigail Roxbury-Trent – but, to his great displeasure, there were none to be found.

"Truly, I needed the man himself," he said to me when we were back at Baker Street that same night, sometime during the small hours. "I would have prised the truth out of him in no time, I am sure."

By then both of us had shed our disguises and Holmes was sitting stripped to the waist while I tended to the various contusions he had received during the fight with Johnson. His upper body was almost entirely black and blue, and I gently dabbed tincture of arnica on the worst affected patches. The fungus had been removed from his ear and consigned to the fireplace, where it smouldered among the embers. I later established that use of the mycophone had indeed had a lasting deleterious effect on Holmes's ear but, happily, the loss in hearing quality was slight.

"Are you not glad that Billy is safe and well?" I said. "Isn't that some consolation?"

"I am, and it is," replied Holmes, "but Billy would never

have been placed in such grave peril had I been a touch sharper. I feel, too, that his salvation comes at the cost of the resolution to a larger mystery. Who, for instance, were these people Johnson was taking the girls to? And for what purpose?"

"Enjoy your victories, my dear fellow, however slender you may think them to be. And don't forget, Gruner awaits. We have something solid to pin on him now. He is guilty of kidnap, at the very least."

"I fear it may be hard to make the charge stick," Holmes said. "Nobody saw him carry Billy out to the brougham. Billy himself was unconscious at the time. It comes down to your word and mine against Gruner's, and absent any hard evidence of wrongdoing, such as an independent eyewitness account, I seriously doubt the Crown will be able to bring a prosecution against him. Even if it does, he can afford the very best lawyers, and they will keep him out of jail."

"It will be another blow to his reputation, though, surely – the mere suggestion that he has been involved in such an offence."

"His reputation has survived its fair share of scandal already. In a perverse way, he thrives on his status as a cad and a knave. He feels it lends him a dark mystique."

"Is it really hopeless?" I said. "Gruner gets away with his crimes?"

My companion shrugged, then winced at the pain the shrug caused his battered physique.

"Perhaps natural justice will catch up with Adelbert Gruner eventually," said he. "We can but hope."

In the event, natural justice arrived for Gruner sooner rather than later. The following day, the nobleman was attacked outside his Kingston mansion. Acid was thrown at him just as he was leaving to go for a walk, and the damage it wrought was extensive and horrific. The newspapers reported, with a certain ghoulish relish, that his handsome face was rendered a burned, twisted mess, he was blinded in one eye, and some of the acid even got into his mouth, so that the function of his lips and tongue was severely impaired. In short, Gruner's good looks and honeyed, seductive speech, the things upon which he took such pride and with which he so fascinated women, were ruined. I understand that not long after he came out of hospital he sold off both his properties in England and returned to his homeland, where, in a rambling mountain estate outside Innsbruck, he lived out his years as a lonely, embittered recluse.

The individual responsible was never caught. Members of Gruner's domestic staff, drawn outdoors by their master's screams of anguish, glimpsed a young woman running away across the grounds. A couple of them gave chase but she eluded them. None could furnish any details about her other than that she was quick on her feet and boasted a head of long, chestnut-coloured hair.

Holmes had his theories regarding the identity of the culprit, as did I, but the only time the subject arose, which happened the day after the attack, all my companion did was point at his chemistry bench.

"I have had to replace a bottle of oil of vitriol that has gone missing," he said. "I cannot for the life of me think that someone would have taken it, so I can only assume that I myself must have mislaid it. Clearly I am getting absentminded in my old age."

Billy, our perennially fresh-faced page, continued to serve at Baker Street for another year, until Holmes closed up shop and moved to the countryside. Billy himself moved overseas to a remote quarter of Saskatchewan, where he lives to this day, tending a ranch with a female companion. I gather he is very happy there, and he has every right to be.

PART VI

Spring 1903

WE WERE WAITING FOR A CLIENT TO SHOW UP AT Baker Street when Sherlock Holmes said, "You are wondering, Watson, how a 'V' might be changed to an 'E'."

It was no great intellectual feat working out how my friend had arrived at this observation.

"You saw me looking at that," I said, indicating the letters V.R., which Holmes, in a sudden patriotic fit several years earlier, had picked out in bullet-pocks on one wall of our sitting room.

"You are thinking," said he, "that it is now two years since our queen died and that my little piece of impromptu redecoration ought to be amended to reflect the King's accession."

"Or perhaps that the holes should be filled in and new wallpaper applied."

"You would so soon erase the memory of Victoria?"

"She is unforgettable. I just think that, two years on from her death, should we not acknowledge she is gone?"

"I am not still in mourning for her, if that is what you are implying," said Holmes. "I am not like those overzealous royalist types who continue to go around with black armbands on even now, wallowing in the whole maudlin excess of it. Is one not allowed to keep a symbol of one's admiration for the greatest ruler this nation has ever known, even after she has left us? She was the mother of our country, Watson. She held great significance for us all. Remember Professor Avery Mellingford?"

"Professor…? Good Lord, yes. That was, what, a decade ago?"

"A decade and a half. If you want an example of the influence Her Majesty had over any self-respecting Englishman, look no further than the way Irene Adler was able to beguile

Mellingford in the guise of a woman closely resembling the Queen. So, to answer your unexpressed query: no, I shall not be changing the 'V' to an 'E', even if it were possible to accomplish that with bullets. Nor shall I be covering up my little tribute. Now, where is she?"

For an absurd moment I thought Holmes was enquiring after the Queen's whereabouts. Then I realised he meant his client.

"She is only ten minutes late," I said.

"I specifically asked her to be here for eleven."

"Woman's prerogative and all that."

"Thus speaks a man who has been married and is shortly to place himself at the mercies of feminine timekeeping again."

"Oh, Holmes! Really!"

"I jest, Watson. Matrimony may not be for me, but I envy those who attain that state and are happy in it."

"I must say, late or not, this particular client is somewhat unusual for you."

"In what way?"

"You invited her," I said. "I can't think of another occasion when you have sought an audience with a client rather than simply expecting one to wash up at your door."

Holmes gave an enigmatic smile. "You will discover why, once Mrs Maberley gets here." He shot a forlorn glance in the direction of the mantel clock. "Assuming she ever does."

The name Maberley will ring a bell for those who have read my tale "The Adventure of the Three Gables". That was a story about the theft and destruction of a compromising manuscript. The truth, as the ensuing pages will show, was a whole lot stranger and more complicated.

A further ten minutes elapsed before, finally, the lady in question arrived.

Mary Maberley was a woman of a certain vintage who carried herself with an air of refinement and decorum. She was handsome now, and one could see that she would have been very comely indeed in her youth. Yet there was a haggardness to her looks – pallid skin, grey circles under the eyes, a redness to the eyes themselves – that suggested a recent encounter with tragedy. Confirmation of this supposition could be found in the fact that she was dressed head to toe in black. I did not assume for one moment that Mrs Maberley was one of the "overzealous royalist types" Holmes had spoken about earlier. She was a woman in the grip of a deep and very personal grief.

"Madam," Holmes said as she installed herself in the chair reserved for clients, "thank you for coming. I am sorry to impose on you at this very difficult time, and please accept my condolences on your loss."

"You are kind, sir," replied Mrs Maberley. "The death of a loved one is hard enough, but the death of one's own son…" She appeared on the verge of tears, but with some effort composed herself. I fetched a glass of water, from which she took a sip. Then she continued. "When your note arrived, I must confess I nearly threw it in the fire. Since that article about Douglas and me appeared in the *Illustrated London News*, a number of suspect individuals have got in touch. Mainly they have been psychic mediums, offering their services to contact my son's spirit and convey messages from him from beyond the veil. I have no time for such charlatans. There have also been a couple of unscrupulous rogues trying to inveigle their way into my good graces. They see a bereaved woman in very comfortable circumstances – one who has long been a widow and now finds herself without issue – and fancy becoming beneficiaries of my legacy."

"I assure you, my good woman, I am neither of those things."

"On the contrary," I chimed in, "much of Holmes's career has been devoted to foiling the schemes of just that sort of mountebank."

"Well, your name does carry an undeniable cachet, Mr Holmes," said Mrs Maberley, "and that is what saved your note from the flames. You told me you are interested in Douglas's death."

"Put like that, it sounds prurient," Holmes said. "I believe I wrote that the circumstances which led to your son taking his own life, and in particular his last words to you, had elements that intrigued me. With your permission, I would be keen to know more about both."

Mrs Maberley gave a rather severe sniff. "I don't really see what I will gain from talking to you. It won't bring Douglas back, will it?"

"But I may be able to make his death more explicable," Holmes replied. "You must be wondering what drove a young man – intelligent, from a stable background, with good prospects – into such depths of despair that he could see no alternative but to end his life."

"I confess it does bewilder me how precipitously Douglas went into decline and how distraught he was in those last days of his life. He was always such a level-headed fellow and I honestly believed nothing could derail him. And then those things he said when he was *in extremis*, those awful, incomprehensible things…"

"Which were quoted verbatim in the *London News*," said Holmes. "One can only assume you yourself were the source."

"I wish I'd never spoken to that wretched reporter," said Mrs Maberley. "He caught me at my most vulnerable. He promised me a sympathetic article, but what appeared was intrusive and sensational. No salacious detail was spared."

"Watson here has not read the piece. For his benefit, would you care to rehearse both the circumstances of your son's demise and the last words he uttered? In your own time. There's no hurry."

"Douglas came home one evening after a night out," said our guest, "and took himself straight to his room without even offering me a greeting. I heard him there, striding up and down, raving to himself. I went to the door and listened. It was babble mostly, tearful and frantic. I could make out perhaps one word in ten. I knocked and asked if everything was all right. After a pause, he answered that all was well and I should leave him be. I was not convinced, but Douglas was a grown man and I was loath to mollycoddle him. I entered his room the next morning after he failed to come down for breakfast, and that was when I… I found him." She took out a handkerchief trimmed with black ribbon and clutched it to her mouth. "He had hanged himself."

She broke into sobs. Holmes and I left a respectful interval while her fit of anguish ran its course, whereafter my friend gently prompted her. "And the words your son said, the ones that *were* intelligible to you…?"

"He said something about a room," Mrs Maberley told us. "'I have seen what's in that room… That room!' Then he said, 'No future. There is no future for us.' And the final thing I heard was 'me go'. He said it two or three times. 'Me go. Me go.' Like that. As though he meant to say 'I go' but had reverted to that stage of childhood when one has not yet grasped the proper use of pronouns."

I glanced at Holmes, who gave me a surreptitious nod in return. Could Douglas Maberley actually have said "Mi-Go"? It was questionable whether that part of his fevered ramblings – those two reiterated syllables – constituted a clear reference to the Outside Things. Holmes, however, had evidently decided the possibility was strong enough to merit investigation.

"With hindsight," Mrs Maberley said, "I can only infer that Douglas was trying to express a desire to leave the world. He wanted to *go*. Would that I had interpreted it correctly at the time. Then perhaps I might have ignored his request not to enter his bedroom and would have been able to offer him support and succour, to the point where he would have chosen living over dying. I will carry the regret to my grave."

"You have nothing to reproach yourself for, Mrs Maberley," I said. "You could not have foreseen what your son was going to do."

"Are you a father, Doctor?"

"I am not."

"Then you cannot hope to understand how I am feeling. No amount of consolation will help. I will never forgive myself for what happened."

"Perhaps, Mrs Maberley," said Holmes, "you could tell us a little more about poor Douglas's end."

"Very well, Mr Holmes. Dr Watson? This water is all very well, but might you have something a little more fortifying?"

A glass of Amontillado in hand, Mary Maberley resumed her account. "Douglas had not long returned from a posting overseas. He was an attaché, well regarded within the Foreign Office and destined, so everyone agreed, for great things."

"He was stationed in Italy, was he not?" said Holmes.

"Did it say that in the article? I think it did."

"It did, but regardless, I would have deduced it from your heart-shaped pendant. The pendant is the sole bright spot in your ensemble, and I can only assume you are wearing it because it has particular meaning. Furthermore, your hand has gone to it several times, an unconscious gesture that has corresponded with mentions of your son. From both these things I infer that the pendant has some connection with Douglas and that in all likelihood he gave it to you as a gift. It is Murano glass, from Venice. Nowhere else is glass that intricate and colourful made." Holmes spread out his hands. "Thus, Italy."

"He came back to England," Mrs Maberley said, "and was waiting for his next posting. There was talk of the West Indies, or even a consulship in India, but for some while nobody at the Foreign Office could quite come to a decision. Douglas was left with time on his hands and so he got into the London social scene, going to clubs and dances and meeting old friends. It was then that he fell under the spell of Isadora Klein."

Her features formed into a moue of distaste as she spoke the name.

"Mrs Klein is an American widow, hailing from Providence, Rhode Island, but of Brazilian extraction," she continued. "She was married to a German sugar king, and since his death has become the merriest of widows. All of London society falls at her feet, and by universal assent she is very beautiful, with the sort of dark Latin looks which no man, it seems, can help but be bewitched by. Douglas, I'm afraid, was one such, and she in her turn took a shine to him. And why ever not? My Douglas was debonair, witty, personable, ambitious. But he was also very much her junior and nowhere near as experienced as she."

The way Mrs Maberley said it, "experienced" was a synonym for "contaminated".

"She latched on to him the way a cat latches on to a mouse. She toyed with him and batted him about, and the more she abused his affections, the greater they grew. At times the poor boy would speak of her as though she were a goddess and proclaim her as the woman he would make his wife. At other times, he cursed her and vowed he would have nothing to do with her any more. Yet he kept going back to her. All she had to do was beckon and Douglas would run to her side.

"It was not my place to interfere, yet I devoutly wished he would give her up. I introduced him to several far more suitable young ladies, none of whom met with his approval, and all the while I prayed that the Foreign Office would make up its mind and send him abroad, somewhere far from that woman and her manipulative ways.

"Well, the Foreign Office did finally make up its mind, and Douglas was offered a very favourable position at the embassy in Cairo. I urged him to take it. It was a significant step up the career ladder. But do you know what he did? He turned it down. He said he preferred to stay in London. He could not bear to abandon Mrs Klein. He could not even think of life without her.

"It was around then that I learned that Isadora Klein ran a… I'm not sure what to call it. A social gathering? A salon? It is called The Cultured and it counts among its membership some of the country's elite. Douglas told me about it, saying she had invited him to join. He was terribly excited by the prospect. When I enquired just what The Cultured did, what its purpose was, he could not enlighten me. He did not know. He insisted, however, that it was an honour to belong to the group and there was no question of him refusing the invitation.

"'I have arrived, Mama,' he said. 'I am on my way into the very uppermost echelons. Can you not be happy for me? Are you not proud? I am sure Father is looking down on me right now and smiling. This is all he ever wanted for his son.'

"It was a calculatedly cruel thing for him to do, invoke the shade of his father, whom I had loved dearly and to whose opinion I had always deferred. I rebuked him for it, saying that his father would not have liked seeing him throw his life away over some woman of questionable morals and dubious integrity. At that, Douglas flew into a rage and stormed out of the house. I did not see him again for the best part of a fortnight. Where he stayed during that period, I do not know, but I would not be surprised if it was at Mrs Klein's house in Harrow Weald."

Holmes straightened up in his seat. "Harrow Weald, did you say?"

"Yes. A mansion called The Three Gables. It's there that The Cultured hold their soirées, or meetings, or whatever they are, with Isadora Klein playing the bountiful hostess."

"And you honestly have no clear notion of The Cultured's philosophy or the nature of their get-togethers?"

"None, Mr Holmes," said Mrs Maberley. "The name would suggest something to do with the arts, I suppose. Or perhaps the pursuit of physical culture. That's quite popular nowadays, isn't it? Exercise, developing the body. Or it could merely denote a certain selectness and exclusivity. Douglas never went into the specifics, however. He remained tight-lipped, as if sworn to secrecy. What I do know is that when he returned from his fortnight's absence, he had been inducted into The Cultured's ranks. He admitted that much to me and said how thrilled he had been to meet and mingle with some of the nation's top men and women, as an equal.

"He looked happy, and I was just glad that he had come home again, so I refrained from delving any more deeply into the matter. I had no wish to spark another row. I crossed my fingers and hoped he knew what he was doing and all would be well.

"It was following Douglas's second attendance at a gathering of The Cultured that he began to change."

"In what way change?" said Sherlock Holmes.

"He grew withdrawn," said Mrs Maberley. "His mood became morose. Where previously he had been light, now he seemed heavy. You know how cartoons in *Punch* depict someone walking around with a raincloud over his head? That was my Douglas. He would mope around the house, scarcely talking to me or even acknowledging my presence. Only a fool would fail to see that something was preying on his mind.

"I tried to find out what was bothering him so. I broached the subject a number of times, tentatively, without success. Douglas simply told me, in no uncertain terms, to leave him be. I was, he said, better off not knowing.

"It got worse. He stopped eating, and he could not sit still. He would forever be jiggling a leg up and down or tapping his fingers."

"The signs of deep-seated anxiety," I said. "Perhaps depression too."

"He was markedly less enamoured with Isadora Klein, what's more," Mrs Maberley said. "That was the one blessing about the whole wretched situation. He no longer spoke of her in glowing, rapturous terms. Rather, if he mentioned the woman at all, it would be in a muted tone, a lament rather than an encomium. From that, I could only infer that he and she were on the outs, once and for all.

"I assumed that Douglas would get over it in time. His broken heart would mend, and he would take up the Cairo appointment, which remained open. The future would be bright.

"Then a letter came from Mrs Klein. I do not know its contents, but it was evidently a summons. No sooner had Douglas read it than he went to her, like a dog when its master whistles. He may not wholly have wanted to go, judging by the gloominess of his expression as he left the house, but while relations between him and Mrs Klein might have soured, her hooks were still in him, sunk deep.

"That was the night he returned home in a state of the utmost agitation. The night he…"

"Yes," said Holmes softly. "I shall not require you to relate that experience yet again."

"He used a scarf she had given him," Mrs Maberley said. "Another detail I shared with the *London News* reporter and he took great delight in dwelling on. A beautiful long cashmere scarf. A love token. I can only think Douglas chose it as the method of his self-termination in order to show how much he despised Mrs Klein in that moment."

"Or, alternatively, how much he loved her."

"Yes. I suppose that is possible. If I had to choose between the two interpretations, however, I would prefer mine."

"Understandably," Holmes said. "And just to make it quite clear, you are sure you overheard Douglas, amid his ravings that night, talk about a room?"

"Yes."

"And 'no future'."

"Yes."

"You do not know what he might have meant by that?"

"Not for the life of me."

"Very well. But he definitely said 'me go'?"

"Ungrammatical as it was, that was the phrase," said Mrs Maberley, with certitude.

Holmes placed his hands on his knees, a gesture of finality. "Then you have given me all I need for now. I am grateful for your time, madam."

Mrs Maberley rose to depart. "Do you think there is more to this than there seems, Mr Holmes?" she asked.

"I cannot give a categorical answer to that just yet. There are one or two singular aspects to the affair which would appear to warrant further enquiry, but on the face of it, I am inclined to believe that your son was the victim of a cold-hearted woman's callousness; nothing more, nothing less. She ensnared him in a game of emotions which he simply did not have the wherewithal to play, and it destroyed him."

The mourning mother heaved a heartfelt sigh. "I feared you would say that. I would dearly love to see Isadora Klein punished for what she did to my Douglas, but no laws were broken. Only *he* was."

*

I showed Mrs Maberley out, and upon my return to our rooms found Holmes looking ebullient. His grey eyes glinted, and he was sitting with his legs drawn up and his arms wrapped around them, literally hugging himself.

"What do you make of it, Watson?" said he.

"Not as much as you make of it, if your jubilant tone is any indication."

"You have adopted your habitual mystified air, but really, you must be intrigued by the possible Mi-Go allusion."

"The word 'possible' is carrying a lot of weight in that sentence," I said. "I would substitute 'tenuous'."

"And Harrow Weald?"

"What about Harrow Weald?"

"Cast your mind back just a few short months," said Holmes. "Where was Shinwell Johnson's brougham when we finally caught up with it?"

"Harlesden."

"Where specifically in Harlesden?"

"On the Harrow Road."

"Heading northward. And what lies at the northern end of the Harrow Road?"

"Well, a fair number of places," I said, "Harrow Weald among them."

"Exactly. Now, this could, of course, be mere coincidence, but it is a noteworthy correlation all the same."

"Oh, come off it, Holmes!" I chided. "Are you seriously suggesting that Johnson was taking Billy, and likewise took those three girls before him, to this Three Gables place? That he deposited them with Isadora Klein for some reason?"

"With Isadora Klein and her so-called The Cultured, whoever they may be. Yes, I am suggesting just that. Now cast your mind back further – much further – to a certain Dr Felder."

"Dr Ulrich Felder? The fellow who brought those corpses back from the dead at Highgate?"

"Remember him?"

"Even after all these years, how could I forget?"

"From whom did Felder state, in his journal, that he had received the fungus he used to create his 'fungal reanimates'?" Holmes asked.

I racked my brains. "A woman," I said. "Definitely a woman."

"Well done. You have ruled out half the human race. See if you can narrow it down further."

"I have it!" I declared. "It was an *'Amerikanische Frau'*."

Holmes delivered a slow, ironic handclap. "Excellent. Now tell me, who fits that description?"

"You were always of the view that it referred to Irene Adler."

"But could it not refer just as easily to Isadora Klein? She is indisputably both a woman and from America."

"Well, I suppose so. This all seems like a bit of a stretch."

"Perchance it is," said Holmes. "Consider, however, that Mrs Klein was formerly married to a German and that Felder himself was German. The Teutonic link could be another coincidence but could equally be another noteworthy correlation. I would need to do some homework and check the dates, but it is not beyond the realms of feasibility that Isadora Klein was living in Germany at the same time Dr Felder was, and that the twain met."

"Yes, because Germany is a tiny nation made up of a handful of people, and everyone there knows everyone else."

"Sarcasm ill befits you, Watson."

"Fanciful speculation ill befits *you*, Holmes."

My friend dismissed my comment with a sniff. "There is a third noteworthy correlation."

"Or coincidence, as we sensible folk call it."

"The name 'The Cultured'," said Holmes. "What does one do when propagating tiny organisms such as fungal spores in a growth medium? What is the term for the process? As a clinician, you should know."

"Culturing."

"*Voilà*. The Cultured. Nothing to do with highbrow pursuits or building up muscle, as Mrs Maberley posited. Rather, a sly, sidelong reference to fungus, with which class of organisms the Outside Things have such a close relationship."

I could not suppress a scornful laugh. "This is preposterous stuff, Holmes."

"Is it?"

"You cannot surely be asking me to accept that these disparate facts are all linked."

"I am asking you to entertain it as a possibility."

"You are seeing things that are not there."

"What I am seeing, Watson, is an assemblage of gossamer

threads that seem to run in different directions but actually converge to form an intricate web. Here, at last, may lie the culmination of those various cases, all of which have carried associations with the Mi-Go but each of which has resolved nothing save its own individual mystery. Over the years, from Dr Felder to Black Peter Carey to Josiah Amberley, we have received glimpses of a conspiracy, yet when we have chased it, it has proved as elusive as any mirage. Now, courtesy of Mrs Maberley, and to a lesser degree Baron Gruner and Shinwell Johnson, we have a strong lead to pursue, one that may take us right into the heart of the thing. What if The Cultured are the cabal of Mi-Go allies whom we presume, with some justification, to exist? The group Irene Adler works for? The people who stymied the work of Professor Mellingford and his ilk? The people who set up Amberley's Shub-Niggurath cult as a decoy, to dupe me?"

"If that were so," I said, "it would be remarkable."

"It would," said Holmes. "It would point to fifteen years' worth of machinations, across which you and I have flown like a skimmed stone across a lake, touching down repeatedly but only disturbing the surface."

"And now, after so long, you have the opportunity of making a splash."

"At the very least, Watson, if there is the remotest chance that investigating The Cultured leads to uncovering the fates of Kitty Winter and the other two girls whom Gruner entrusted to Shinwell Johnson's tender care, it would be remiss of me not to take it."

He knew I could not gainsay that argument, and I conceded defeat with a bow and a shrug of the shoulders.

"To that end," said Holmes, "I propose to resurrect one of my alter egos."

"Which? The asthmatic master mariner? Captain Basil? Escott the plumber? One of your multidenominational array of priests?"

"No, it will be a fellow I use sparingly. I am fairly certain you haven't met him, or even heard of him."

Holmes fell into a contemplative reverie.

"Hum. Yes," said he to himself. "I do believe he is just the man for the job."

*

A month later, a new patient showed up at my practice complaining of lumbago and a touch of arthritis.

"Please, sit down," I said as he walked into my consulting room. He was a slope-shouldered, pot-bellied fellow with longish hair, a drooping, pendulous nose and, if his pink eyes and florid, broken-veined complexion were anything to go by, a clear penchant for strong drink. I had treated many a bon viveur in my time and knew almost any of his ailments could be ameliorated by an improvement in diet and a less sedentary lifestyle. I felt safe in predicting, too, that in addition to his other complaints he would have incipient, undiagnosed gout and was at high risk of developing kidney stones.

"It's Mr Pike, isn't it?" I said, checking the notes on my register which my receptionist had prepared for me.

"Langdale Pike, that's me," said the patient. The voice was as louche and languid as the rest of him, as though clear enunciation demanded altogether too much effort. "You come highly recommended, Doctor, and the fact that you can afford a general practice on Queen Anne Street, just a stone's throw from Harley Street, proves it. I have every reason to think that, with you, I am in good hands."

"Now then, according to my receptionist's notes, you suffer from lumbago."

"Terrible twinges in the lower back, Doctor, every time I sit down or stand up. Like being stabbed with a knitting needle."

"And arthritis."

"The fingers of my right hand, Doctor." Pike wafted them in the air like a particularly nonchalant orchestra conductor.

"Sometimes they ache so much I can hardly hold my brandy balloon."

"Tell me, Mr Pike," I said, "what is your profession?"

"Oh, I do a little of this, a little of that. I am, you might say, a purveyor of delicacies. I haunt the gentlemen's clubs and pick up the latest hearsay and society tittle-tattle, which I feed to certain columnists. It earns me a living. A very decent one. Four figures."

I jotted down the information in my casebook. "And do you take any form of regular exercise?"

"If you call gentle perambulations around the Pall Mall area exercise, then yes."

"Very good. Now, before I give you a physical examination, I have one more question. Would you mind telling me how long you have experienced the symptoms of being a consulting detective in disguise?"

Langdale Pike looked aghast. "I beg your pardon?"

I stuck to my guns. "I am asking how long you intend to maintain the pretence that you are not Sherlock Holmes, before you relent and admit the truth."

Pike studied me with the air of someone rueing his decision to commit his health to the care of a man who was plainly quite mad.

Then he burst out laughing, and it was laughter I knew very well indeed.

"Watson, Watson, Watson!" Langdale Pike declared, in Sherlock Holmes's voice. "Well done! I thought it would take you much longer."

I felt a mixture of satisfaction and relief. "You underestimated me."

"Clearly. What gave it away? Is it my eyes? I have reddened them with drops of salt water in hopes that that would draw attention away from the distinctive grey of the irises."

"I shall be honest with you," I said. "I have been playing the odds."

"How do you mean?"

"I knew you might pull a stunt like this. You have form for it. You present yourself to me as an alter ego and wait for me to catch on. That time you masqueraded as Mycroft, to name but one."

"My yardstick for a disguise is that if it can fool Watson, who knows me intimately, it can fool anyone."

"Langdale Pike is the third new male patient to have come to my door in the past month," I said. "With both of the others, either of whom could conceivably have been you, I made an offhand allusion to Sherlock Holmes in order to see how they reacted. One had not heard the name and displayed not a flicker of interest. The other confessed to being a fan of both you and my writing, and indeed added, somewhat shamefacedly, that this was in large part why he had chosen me to be his physician."

"You were a lot more confident in your approach to Langdale Pike."

"Holmes, you have named the fellow after the Langdale Pikes, a set of mountains in the Lake District. As aliases go, it practically screams 'invented'."

"In my view," said Holmes, "it appears so contrived that it could only be real. Pater and Mater Pike were such lovers of the Lake District, they named their darling boy after one of its most scenic assets."

"The clincher for me is the fact that Langdale Pike is so patently modelled on your brother. His mannerisms, his drawl, his status as a perennial clubman – all characteristics of the mighty Mycroft."

Holmes nodded. "True, but then the best impersonations are drawn from life. I salute you, old friend. Where others' perceptiveness dulls with age, yours grows ever more acute."

"It's your half-hour," I said, tapping the register with my pen. "The appointment is bought and paid for. Tell me what

Langdale Pike has been up to and what facts he has gleaned about Isadora Klein and The Cultured."

"Give me a cigarette," said Holmes, "and I shall."

Blowing out a cloud of smoke towards the ceiling, Holmes explained that he had looked into Mrs Klein's background, first by trawling the newspaper archives and then by roving clubland, as Langdale Pike, and artfully bringing her name into discussions with people he met there. He had learned whom she was known to consort with and then made overtures to various of those persons.

"Her immediate circle constitutes a veritable *Who's Who* of British society," he said. "Politicians, lawmakers, captains of industry, landed gentry, the cream of the artistic fraternity – you name them, she knows them. Nobody has a bad word to say about her. She hosts parties of extraordinary magnitude and lavishness, throwing the late Mr Klein's millions around like confetti. She is by all accounts an accomplished pianist and singer, she paints a very decent watercolour, and her beauty is remarked upon by all and sundry. Half the husbands she is acquainted with are in love with her, and half the wives insanely jealous of her."

Holmes had cultivated a friendship with someone who was especially close to Mrs Klein, a man called Morley Babington.

"The theatre impresario," I said. "He puts on everything from Shakespeare to 'Adelphi screamers'. I saw his *Lear* a few years ago. It was hugely popular, but a little too *grand guignol* for my tastes."

"Mr Babington deems Langdale Pike great company," said Holmes. "Pike is a fund of outrageous anecdotes, is as much of a trencherman and imbiber as Babington himself is, and revels in his bachelordom. The pair have gone to an exhibition of Greek sculpture together, and have attended the ballet and – ballet's antithesis – a boxing match. Babington even invited Pike to join him at the Turkish bathhouse. Much as I enjoy a Turkish bath, obviously I could not go as Pike, not when I have this padding on." Holmes patted his protuberant stomach. "Were I to emerge from the changing room wearing just a towel, revealing my usual lean physique…"

"You would have a hard time explaining where all the weight had vanished to."

"Precisely. Not to mention the problem of keeping all this face makeup intact in a bathhouse's humid atmosphere. I excused myself from that obligation, to Babington's disappointment, but in every other respect relations between him and Pike have gone swimmingly. Furthermore, I have managed to work hints about the Outside Things and Yuggoth into our conversations, and this has yielded results. Babington was moved to observe that I seemed well versed in some rather recondite subject matter, to which I responded that I was merely a dabbler, someone who devotes a few hours of his spare time to studying other planets and the denizens thereof. It was an interest, I told him, that was piqued by H.G. Wells's *War of the Worlds*, which I had read when it was serialised a few years ago in *Pearson's*. 'If there is life on Mars,' I said to him, 'why not on other planets of the solar system? And in those I include the putative ninth planet that is said to orbit beyond Neptune.' By returning to this topic intermittently, without appearing too insistent, I have convinced Babington that I would be worthy of introduction to The Cultured."

"Good Lord!"

"Oh, he has not stated as much, not explicitly," Holmes said. "He has not even mentioned The Cultured by name. He has, however, mentioned Isadora Klein, telling me I must meet her. 'You and she would have much in common,' he said, 'much to talk about.' And so, to cut a long story short, this very weekend I am to travel with Babington to The Three Gables in Harrow Weald, there to be ushered into the presence of the great lady. Or rather, Pike is."

"I shall be curious to learn how it all pans out," I said.

"You will be the first to know, Watson," said Holmes. "This

may lead to nothing. Equally, it may be that I have taken the first steps to infiltrating a secret society of Mi-Go sympathisers. A risky gambit, perhaps, but then what worthwhile undertaking is not?"

*

According to Holmes, the party at The Three Gables was a glittering occasion. The guest list would not have shamed a function at Buckingham Palace, and the copiousness with which the wine flowed was rivalled only by the abundance of the accompanying canapés, ferried among the partygoers by a horde of scurrying, livery-clad servants. Hugh Enes Blackmore, the noted Scottish tenor, was prevailed upon to sing a selection of comic songs from Gilbert and Sullivan operettas, and further entertainment was provided by a juggler whose act climaxed with him keeping five carving knives in the air while balancing on a unicycle.

Morley Babington was pleased to show off his friend Langdale Pike, like a child with a new bauble. He squired him around the room, making introductions. Pike, for his part, proved excellent company, eliciting scandalised gasps and gales of laughter from his interlocutors with some rather risqué snippets of gossip. "I cannot help myself," he was heard to remark more than once. "I am the very Devil when it comes to rumourmongering."

Isadora Klein herself did not put in an appearance until well after an hour into the proceedings. She arrived escorted by a fellow who could not have seemed more out of place in such surroundings. He was tall and brawny, wearing a bowler hat and a loud-checked suit, and amid a sea of white faces his coal-dark skin stood out in marked contrast.

Holmes recognised him in an instant. It was Steve Dixie, one-time prizefighter, with the flattened nose and cauliflower ear to prove it. In recent years Dixie had moved out of the boxing ring and into the criminal underworld, where he earned his keep as a ruffian-for-hire, ever ready to collect overdue debts, deliver blackmail messages in person, and intimidate witnesses into silence. What his menacing, heavy-browed features and bulky physique alone couldn't achieve, his massive, knotty fists could. He was also the prime suspect in the killing of a young ne'er-do-well called Perkins during an altercation outside the Holborn Bar the previous year, and while he had an alibi for the crime, it was hardly cast-iron. Holmes had taken only a passing interest in the case, however, since anything that thinned the ranks of London's felons didn't, in his view, require his services.

The presence of this hulking brute of a man at a high-class drinks party was made all the more incongruous by virtue of the fact that throughout the evening Steve Dixie scarcely left Mrs Klein's side. While she did the rounds, greeting all and sundry, clasping hands, kissing cheeks, Dixie loitered nearby, never more than half a dozen yards from her. His eyes were watchful and wary, constantly roving. Holmes knew a bodyguard when he saw one.

Why Isadora Klein felt she needed such protection – and at a party in her own home, no less – he could not fathom. Who among these carousing sophisticates might wish her harm? On the contrary, they fawned over her, the women curtseying before her as low as they might before a monarch, the men grinning like apes when she turned her gaze on them. She glided through their midst, a stately, glorious galleon to their little bobbing tugboats.

When it came Langdale Pike's turn to be graced by Mrs Klein's attention, he kowtowed just like the rest.

"This is Mr Pike," said Morley Babington. "You know, the one I told you about."

"Oh yes!" declared Mrs Klein in a sharp New England accent with just a hint of South America softening its edges. "Mr Pike. A pleasure."

"The pleasure, Mrs Klein, is all mine."

"Call me Isadora."

"If you insist. And you must call me Langdale."

Her hand rested softly for a moment in Holmes's. It was smooth and cool and felt feather-light. Steve Dixie, meanwhile, hovered in the background. Holmes was careful to keep the prizefighter in the periphery of his vision.

"Morley tells me you and he are very sympathetic, Langdale," said Mrs Klein. "He is glad to have met a man who shares his interests."

"It was kind of him to bring me," said Holmes.

"You are more than welcome here. Any friend of Morley's is a friend of mine."

"He has told me several times how wonderful your parties are, and now that I've seen one with my own eyes, I have to agree."

"This? This is nothing, Langdale. We have smaller yet far more exciting occasions than this, don't we, Morley?"

"We do, Isadora dear."

She fixed Holmes with a pair of dazzling dark eyes. Their scrutiny was intense, and in that moment he felt wholly unmanned, as though he were being mesmerised and his will was being sapped from him. When he told me this, I remarked that for a man as impervious to feminine charms as Sherlock Holmes, it was quite an admission.

"I understand," said Mrs Klein, lowering her voice somewhat, "that you have turned your gaze outward, beyond the confines of the Earth."

"Morley mentioned that, did he?"

"Do you think, perhaps, that gazes from other worlds are turned on *ours*?"

"It is not beyond the realms of possibility. Only human arrogance would deny the likelihood of races other than our own existing somewhere in the solar system, or in the wider universe for that matter."

"Do you wonder if they wish to be our friends or our enemies?"

"That, I would say, depends on many factors," Holmes replied. "One is whether we wish to be *their* friends. It would be a case for diplomacy, I reckon. As in all encounters between civilisations, if both are willing to be accommodating towards each other, then marvellous things may be accomplished. On the other hand, if there is resistance on either side, there will be friction and possibly conflict."

"A fascinating answer, Langdale." She turned to Babington again. "I like him, Morley. I like him a lot."

"I hoped you might," said Babington.

She rested her hand in Holmes's once more. "It was nice to make your acquaintance, sir. Perhaps we shall meet another time."

"I look forward to it," said Holmes.

Mrs Klein threw a knowing glance at Babington, then moved on to another guest, with Dixie in tow. The boxer scowled at Holmes as he passed him, and Holmes made sure that Langdale Pike reacted in a sufficiently daunted manner, grimacing and shrinking away.

"You've made a good impression on her," Babington said, patting Holmes's shoulder.

"If not so much on her shadow," Holmes said, gesturing at Dixie. "That look he just gave me… I'm fairly quaking."

"Steve? Oh, you mustn't worry yourself about him. He's like that with everyone. He growls and bares his teeth, but never bites."

"Why does she keep someone like that around?"

"He makes her feel safe," said Babington. "When you are a very rich woman, you never know who you can trust. With Steve at her side, Isadora can be sure that nobody is going to try and take advantage of her."

"But he's so…"

"So thuggish? But that's just it. Sometimes you need riff-raff in order to keep the riff-raff at bay."

Holmes chuckled, and the remainder of the party passed without incident. Carriages arrived promptly at midnight, and he was back at Baker Street by one thirty.

He did not hear from Morley Babington for several days, and then a note arrived, lavender scented, on mauve stationery, written in immaculate copperplate.

"Isadora has requested your presence at another gathering, the weekend after next," it read. "This one is a dinner party, for a select few. She tells me she thinks you will find the company congenial and your temperament will align nicely with theirs. Do say you'll go."

"And will you go?" I asked Holmes, after he had shown me the note.

"Naturally," said he. "What have I got to lose? If I am barking up the wrong tree, so be it. At least the catering will undoubtedly be first-rate, the wine likewise."

I left him in order to meet my fiancée for lunch, where our wedding plans were due to be the main topic of discussion. On my way out I passed Mrs Hudson in the hallway. She was standing on a chair, dusting the chandelier.

I hailed her. "How are you today, madam?"

Our landlady pivoted round, dropping her feather duster and almost falling off the chair herself.

"My goodness," I said. "I am sorry. I did not mean to startle you."

I held out a hand and helped her down to the floor.

"It's my fault," she said, bending to retrieve the duster. "I was miles away. When doing housework, I sometimes fall into a reverie, you see."

"Are you sure you're all right?"

"Quite sure."

"I have never known you to be nervous, that's all."

"Everything is fine, Doctor," the woman said sternly, sounding more like her usual self.

"I am glad to hear it."

"Perhaps… Perhaps it's because I'm concerned about Mr Holmes."

"About Holmes? Why?"

"He is working so very hard at present. I see him heading out time and time again, all got up in that fancy disguise of his. When he comes back, he often smells of alcohol, and at mealtimes he's barely touching the food I put in front of him. I suppose I should be used to his behaviour by now, but this seems excessive even for him."

"I can't reveal much about his current case," I said, "but I can tell you it happens to entail plenty of dining out and hobnobbing with the smart set."

"Nice for some."

"Which rather flies in the face of his image as a solitary, ascetic creature of intellect, don't you think?"

Mrs Hudson grimaced. "If you ever write one of your stories about it, you'd better leave out the socialising part. Your readers will not believe you."

"You would be surprised, my dear woman," I said, "just how much I do leave out of my stories."

And with that, I bade her farewell and hurried to the restaurant where my soon-to-be-wife awaited.

*

Langdale Pike shared a cab to Harrow Weald with Morley Babington, and they arrived at The Three Gables just as dusk was falling. Last time, the great, sprawling house had been fully lit, every window aglow, as though the building itself had put on its finery and wished to impress. This time only a few ground-floor rooms were illuminated, so that the upper bulk of the house loomed in empty silhouette against the purpling sky. It seemed to signal that tonight's event was going to be a more low-key affair.

In the hallway, the guests' outer garments were taken from them by a gaunt, pinch-faced housemaid. Babington addressed her as Susan and made a point of bantering with her, even though she was plainly a woman who lacked quick-wittedness and a sense of humour.

"You are looking especially lovely this evening, Susan," said he. "Have you done something different with your hair?"

"It is pinned down under a cap as always, Mr Babington. Nothing about it has changed."

"And that perfume you have on – is it rosewater?"

"I use carbolic soap in my daily toilet, nothing else."

"Would that we could all be as naturally decorous as you."

"I really don't know what you mean, Mr Babington."

When it came Holmes's turn to hand her his overcoat, Babington said, "Susan, this is Mr Langdale Pike. If all goes well, you will be seeing a lot more of him."

"Charmed I'm sure, sir," the housemaid said to Holmes. Then she added, "Langdale Pike. I swear I know that name from somewhere. Yes. I remember. I went on a walking holiday once, in the Lake District."

"And encountered the Langdale Pikes," said Holmes.

"That's it, sir."

"My parents named me after them. Their surname happening to be Pike, they thought it a fond tribute to the range of crags that so enchanted them on their honeymoon."

Susan's puckered mouth did an odd little something which, in hindsight, Holmes realised was its version of a smile.

"Lofty but not insurmountable, those mountains are," she said. "They look like they're hard to penetrate, but really there's less to them than meets the eye."

"An interesting observation."

"But no less true for that. I hope you have an enjoyable time, sir."

A large conservatory appended to the east wing of the house was the venue for the dinner. Brilliantly candlelit, it accommodated a long table with place settings for twenty. The cutlery was solid gold, the crockery Limoges porcelain, the glassware thumb-cut lead crystal. Most of the dinner guests were already present, and the last few filed in behind Holmes and Babington. There was mingling and some subdued chitchat, during which Holmes took stock of the complement. They were an odd mix, consisting of lesser-known society figures, here a matron fond of charitable causes, there a wayward member of the nobility, with a couple of academics thrown in, plus a goateed philosopher, a controversial pamphleteer, and a playwright whose productions, long on polemic but short on drama, were never well attended. If anything characterised them all, it was earnestness. They belonged to the class of well-meaning do-gooders, the type who talked a lot about social change and sometimes even effected it.

The moment Isadora Klein swept in, the mood in the room became animated and attentive.

"So good to see you all," said Mrs Klein. "Let us be seated and commence, without further ado."

Accompanying her, as ever, was Steve Dixie, who took up a position in one corner where he had a clear view of the entire conservatory. He would remain there throughout the meal, glowering around, the proverbial spectre at the feast.

There were place cards at every setting, and Holmes, somewhat to his surprise, found that Langdale Pike was seated at their hostess's right hand. Babington was down at the far end of the table but evinced no jealousy of Pike, only pride and delight that the man he had introduced into their company should be accorded such a privileged position.

In no time Holmes and Isadora Klein were deep in conversation, the hostess wanting to learn everything she could about him. Holmes had devised an in-depth history for Langdale Pike, starting with the aforementioned tale of his parents' honeymoon in the Lake District and proceeding from there, through a difficult schooling and failed stints at the Inns of Court and the Home Office, to his current self-administered vocation, which was, as he put it, being "the receiving-station as well as the transmitter for all the gossip of the metropolis". In that respect, Pike's life paralleled Mycroft Holmes's almost exactly, albeit in negative. Where Holmes senior had been an academic high achiever and had ascended effortlessly through the law and politics to carve out an indispensable niche for himself at the heart of government, Pike had accomplished little save for lining his own pockets through the airing of others' dirty laundry.

Holmes managed to steer the talk around to Mrs Klein's own life, and while she was a great deal less forthcoming than Pike, he ascertained that she had left New England in the mid-eighties after meeting Herr Manfred Klein there. The German sugar magnate had been looking to extend his business interests into the United States and made a fair few lucrative deals during his trip, but the real prize he brought home with him to Europe was the hand in marriage of Miss Isadora Maria Pereira Dos Santos.

The couple took up residence in Heidelberg, where Klein's main factory lay, and for a time they were perfectly happy, until Klein was diagnosed with cancer of the bowel. Surgery was performed and seemed successful, but the cancer recurred, this time inoperable. Mrs Klein nursed her husband through his final, terrible months and was at his bedside, holding his hand, when he breathed his last.

Her eyes moistened as she related this sad memory, and Langdale Pike was the epitome of concern, canting his head and making soothing, solicitous noises.

However, Holmes's ears had pricked up at the mention of Heidelberg, and more so at the mention of cancer.

"I trust," said he, "that you had a good doctor to see you through those dark days."

"Oh, the best, Langdale. One of Germany's foremost oncologists."

"His name?"

"Felder. Ulrich Felder. He was the one who carried out the

bowel resection on Manfred, and then attended to him when the cancer came back."

Willpower was a quality Sherlock Holmes possessed in abundance, but it took every ounce he had to keep a look of triumph from his face. Here was indisputable confirmation that Mrs Klein had known Dr Felder. It was a near certainty that she was Felder's *Amerikanische Frau*.

He pressed further, in order to confirm it. "You must surely have been grateful to him for the help he gave you and your poor husband."

"How could I not be?" came the reply. "I demonstrated it by supporting him in his research."

"Financially?"

"How else? I have no medical knowledge. It is not as if I could have volunteered as his laboratory assistant."

"It just strikes me that one could have helped him out in other ways," said Holmes, "perhaps by recommending patients to him or alerting him to potential new cures one might come across."

"I suppose one could have," said Mrs Klein.

"What has become of the fellow anyway? Has he made progress eradicating the disease?"

"Dr Felder is no longer with us, alas. He moved to London not long after my husband passed away, and died tragically in a house fire. Any oncological advances he made died with him."

"That seems a shame."

Mrs Klein laughed lightly. "This conversation has gone off at rather a tangent, don't you think, Langdale?"

"Forgive me, Isadora. I have an enquiring mind."

She narrowed her eyes at him. "Don't think I'm not wise to your game." Her tone was teasing but with a hint of steel to it.

"Game?"

"You are frank about your role as a purveyor of gossip. I'm minded to think you are trying to extract some out of me."

"Heaven forfend!"

"I should warn you, anything you see or hear within these walls is sacrosanct. It goes no further than here. Do I make myself clear?"

"I would never dream of being so indiscreet."

"You may even have asked yourself why I've allowed a fellow as loose-lipped as you to cross my threshold. And," she said, indicating their fellow diners, "let him be surrounded by such a rich seam of potential gossip-column fodder. Do you think I am foolish?"

"I think you are anything but."

"Then perhaps you're wondering what I see in you. Why are you, of all people, part of an assemblage like this?"

"You mean to say I don't belong in the company of intellectuals and philanthropists and idealists?" Holmes said with genial mock-offence.

"On the face of it, no," said Mrs Klein. "But Morley senses there is more to you than a cynical clubman, and I have faith in his judgement."

"My fascination with hypothetical alien races must stand me in good stead too, surely. I recall our conversation on that topic meeting with your approval."

"So it did. And you are affable company and seem to have a good heart. For all that, I reckon it's a good idea to have you right here at my side, where I can keep my beady eye on you and, if need be, use my considerable influence to curb you."

"The old adage: keep your friends close and your enemies closer."

"That only applies if you choose to be my enemy, Langdale. I would much rather have you as a friend. A trusted one."

Now she was all warmth and amicability again. She stroked Holmes's forearm, and her eyes were enthrallingly limpid.

"You can definitely count on me, Isadora," said he.

"I know I can." She uttered a high, musical laugh. "And you will see how much, after the meal's end."

Holmes had the distinct sense that he had just been tested and had passed. The answers given by Langdale Pike had been satisfactory and had earned him Mrs Klein's seal of approval.

Now, as course after course was served to the table, each a culinary masterpiece, and the wineglasses were constantly replenished, Holmes permitted himself to feel that he was making headway and that it was only a matter of time before the identities of The Cultured stood revealed. He was fairly confident, in fact, that they comprised the men and women in this very conservatory. There was just one tiny worm of disquiet gnawing at him. What exactly had Mrs Klein meant, "after the meal's end"? What would be happening then?

*

Postprandial cigars and coffee did the rounds. Then the serving staff withdrew. There was no mention of the women decamping to another room and leaving the men at the table to discuss masculine things, as was traditional. For several minutes, the dinner continued as before, but Holmes detected an atmosphere of anticipation that hadn't been there earlier.

At last Mrs Klein gestured to Steve Dixie, who disappeared into the house and returned bearing a small rosewood casket with a lock and other fittings made of brass.

Mrs Klein tapped her port glass with a fork, and a hush fell over the gathering.

"We have a newcomer among us, my friends," said she, with the tiniest of nods towards Holmes. "For those that don't know him, he is Langdale Pike, and although this is his first time in our company, I have vetted him to my satisfaction and feel it is safe to welcome him into our number. Any objections?"

Heads all around the table were shaken. Either everyone had implicit faith in Mrs Klein's discernment or no one dared contradict her.

"Langdale is a prime candidate for membership," Morley

Babington opined. "His interests are broadly aligned with ours. He would make a valuable addition to our group."

"I think so too," said Mrs Klein. "Therefore, *nem. con.*, it is agreed. Langdale Pike shall be brought into the fold. If, that is, you are willing, Langdale?"

"I don't see how I cannot be," Holmes replied. "This is all very exciting. I really have no idea what is happening. I only know that something extraordinary is unfolding, and I am curious to see what it is."

"That is just the attitude we like," said Mrs Klein. "Open-mindedness. Enthusiasm. A willingness to venture into the unknown."

Holmes rubbed his hands together in a show of eagerness. "What larks!" he declared.

Isadora Klein rose to her feet, and her manner became serious and authoritative. "Ladies. Gentlemen," she said. "Stand ready to reveal yourselves. We are The Cultured. We have sworn loyalty to a cause. Now, in the presence of this uninitiated man, let us display the mark of that loyalty."

Solemnly, with great ceremony, she unbuttoned one cuff of her long-sleeved dress and rolled the sleeve up to the elbow. Upon the underside of her forearm there was a circular patch of redness roughly the size of a tuppence piece. It looked like a very localised skin rash, a blemish on an otherwise flawless limb.

Other diners likewise exposed parts of their bodies. Predominantly it was the arm, but one man undid his dickey and bared his chest, while a woman adjusted her neckline to reveal her clavicle. Each bore a patch of redness akin to their hostess's.

"Give one another the sign of acknowledgement," Mrs Klein said.

Everyone at the table leaned towards his or her neighbour. Mrs Klein herself turned to the dinner guest on her left, extending her arm to him. He bent over so that his rash was directly adjacent to hers. As Holmes watched, the pair of red circles began to shift, as though awakened by mutual proximity. Each dispersed itself swirlingly across its owner's skin like wind-blown dust, settling to form a pattern, an asymmetrical tangle of straight lines and curlicues that Holmes had no trouble recognising. It was the sigil of the goddess Shub-Niggurath. He had seen it several times over the course of his life, perhaps most notably when it had been scrawled on the wall of Josiah Amberley's strong-room.

Every dinner guest performed this little ritual with the neighbour on either side, except Mrs Klein and the woman on Holmes's right, for the obvious reason that the man between them lacked their queer adornment. Then all the guests resumed their normal seated positions. Similarly, the sigils returned to their former state as circular red rashes, and clothing was rearranged to cover up the marks.

"I am not sure what I have just witnessed," said Holmes in a marvelling tone. "Did those things just move? Or have I perhaps drunk a little too much?"

"Your eyes did not deceive you, Langdale," said Mrs Klein. "Each of us has been granted this special mark. It tingles when another of our kind is close by, like an alarm bell, and we can then secretly confirm our shared fealty by holding the marks next to each other."

"But what is it?"

"A fungal infection, deliberately introduced beneath the skin."

Holmes blinked rapidly as though in perplexity. "No. I mean, yes. I can see how it might be that. But actually I am asking you what is the – the shape it becomes?"

"That," said Mrs Klein, "is a special, magical symbol. It represents a deity known as Shub-Niggurath."

"I beg your pardon?"

"The name is quite a mouthful, I admit. It is unlikely you have heard of Shub-Niggurath. Not many have. Suffice it to say she is an ancient, powerful entity, worshipped by certain friends of ours."

"Friends?"

Mrs Klein bestowed a forgiving look upon him. "You are being initiated into a number of mysteries at once, Langdale. It is a lot to take in."

"It is, Isadora, and I am trying my best. You call yourselves The Cultured, did you say?"

"That is us," said Mrs Klein. "These present here, and a few others besides."

"Are you some sort of secret society?"

"In a sense. We have banded together to pursue a simple but essential goal: securing the future of mankind."

"That all sounds extraordinarily noble, not to say idealistic." Holmes felt that Langdale Pike ought to exhibit at least a modicum of incredulity at this point. It would be suspicious otherwise. The man was supposed to be an incorrigible cynic, after all, who profited from people's capacity for hypocrisy and self-delusion. "And you think you have the means of achieving your aims?"

"Very much so," said Mrs Klein. "Remember when we spoke the other day, you and I, and our discussion strayed to races from other worlds?"

"I do."

"Those friends I just mentioned are from another world, and we are in regular communication with them."

"Bless me!" Holmes exclaimed, clutching hand to heart. "It is possible? Can it be? But how?"

"I am about to show you," Mrs Klein said. "They are wise, benevolent creatures who wish not only to forge an alliance with the people of Earth but to live here among us, guiding us to a better, brighter tomorrow. They hope to end our warlike ways and engender worldwide harmony."

"They sound positively angelic."

"Nothing so ethereal as that. They are living beings, just

like you or me. As different from us biologically as can be imagined, but flesh-and-blood entities nonetheless. In terms of philosophy and ethics they are more evolved than us, but that is only to our advantage. We can learn from them and, in tandem with them, accomplish great things."

"Do they have a name, this race of paragons?" Holmes enquired.

"Mi-Go," said Mrs Klein. "Their planet is called Yuggoth. And now I intend to converse with them and reaffirm the bond that has been established between them and us Cultured."

She clicked her fingers, and Steve Dixie stepped forward with his rosewood casket. By that stage of the evening, the candles were burning low. Several had gone out altogether, and the flames of the remainder guttered in their lumpen beds of melted wax. Their fitful light scarcely held back the dark outside the windows, while making everything within the conservatory dance and jump erratically.

Dixie laid the casket on the table in front of his mistress, who took out a small key and inserted it into the lock. Inside the casket lay a spherical fungus whose glossy brown surface was shot through with lightning-like zigzags of gold.

Holmes's alert, retentive mind recalled Irene Adler describing just such a fungus when she was taken to that large black stone at Round Hill in Vermont. It had exploded in her face like a puffball mushroom, and breathing in its spores had sent her on a psychic journey to Yuggoth.

"My, my," he said in wonderment. "Whatever can that be?"

"It is the means by which I am going to speak with the Mi-Go," replied Mrs Klein.

"Like a kind of telephone?"

"You might call it that. Now, pray silence, all. No distractions. And bear in mind that time on Yuggoth moves more slowly than time on Earth, so there is always a delay when it comes to relaying the responses I receive."

The other Cultured grew hushed and attentive. They

reminded Holmes of attendees at a séance, and indeed there
was much about the situation that resembled the average
parlour table-rapping session: the low, uncertain candlelight, the
expectation of something occult and otherworldly, and above
all Mrs Klein's demeanour, not dissimilar to that of a medium.
She was preparing to communicate with another realm and
bring back important messages, and this necessitated, it seemed,
a certain melodrama. She waited until the room was entirely
quiet, whereupon, with solemnity replacing the usual vivacity
on her face, she bent over the fungus. Holmes half expected
her to start chanting and imploring her spirit guide to manifest
from the Great Beyond.

The fungus began to pulse and swell, just as the one
encountered by Irene had. Holmes saw tiny particles whirling
around within its translucent shell, their activity becoming ever
more agitated and intense.

Then the thing burst, spurting a puff of dust into Mrs
Klein's face. She inhaled sharply at the same time, after which
she reeled back in her chair, clutching the table's edge. Her eyes
flew wide. She wheezed and gasped.

Holmes pretended to give a start, and he made a move to
lay a hand on her, just as someone unfamiliar with events like
these might do. The woman on the other side of him gripped
his arm and shook her head.

"She is fine," she whispered in Holmes's ear. "This is simply
what happens. Leave her be."

A couple of minutes passed, and then Mrs Klein cried,
"I am there! I have reached Yuggoth!" Her eyes were glazed
and distant. Whatever she was looking at, it was not in that
conservatory.

Two minutes more, and she said, "Here they come. Our
Mi-Go friends, gathering at the temple of Shub-Niggurath.
There is Glaw Za-Jooll. Hail to you, Glaw Za-Jooll! I have
journeyed to you across the gulfs of space, bringing greetings
from The Cultured."

Another long pause. Holmes had the opportunity to reflect that Irene's meeting with the Outside Things – including their high priest, Glaw Za-Jooll – had taken place while she was wholly insensible. Mrs Klein, by contrast, was in a kind of trance state, and he could only infer that through repeated usage of the fungus she had become expert at conducting this form of communication, to the point that she could retain a degree of consciousness throughout.

"Glaw Za-Jooll," she said eventually, "wishes me to convey his respects to you all. He restates his hope that through amity and cooperation we may bring about a fruitful union between our two races."

Another long pause.

"Yes, Glaw Za-Jooll. Preparations are well under way. It will not be long before you and your brethren walk among us. We look forward to welcoming you into the heart of the greatest empire on Earth, whereby you will be able to propagate your influence across the globe. You have waited long and toiled hard for this, as have we, and things are reaching their culmination."

Pause.

"There is one among us who is not yet a fully inaugurated member of our group. Therefore I must be circumspect in my answers. All I can tell you is that the work is going well. I am assured that the procedure will soon be so honed and refined that there will be no possibility of failure."

Pause.

"Thank you. Salutations to you and your people, and I shall renew contact with you again soon."

With that, Mrs Klein sank down in her chair, seemingly exhausted, like a balloon with some of the air let out. The Cultured waited patiently, and at last she gathered herself, straightened up, and braved a smile.

Throughout the foregoing, Steve Dixie had not stirred from her side, standing there with his arms folded and a clear determination to ensure that no harm befell her body while her mind was elsewhere. Now, without a word, he closed the rosewood casket with the depleted fungus inside and poured his mistress a drink, which she accepted gratefully.

"Thank you, Steve." She wiped spore dust off her face with a napkin, then locked the casket. "Take that away, will you. There's a good fellow."

As the former prizefighter exited the conservatory, Mrs Klein turned to Holmes. "So, Langdale, you may now have a clearer idea of the purpose behind the formation of The Cultured."

"I am… awestruck," said Holmes, giving every indication of being just that. "Would I be right in thinking that what I have just beheld was some sort of interplanetary communication? Good Lord! I am quite overcome. I think I need a drink too." He helped himself from the port decanter.

"I have engaged in colloquy with the Mi-Go for several years now," said Mrs Klein. "You could say I am their deputy on Earth. Having established an accord between our two worlds, I have expended a great deal of time and effort, and indeed, money, with a view to enabling Mi-Go to visit us in person."

"By building some sort of machine that can travel between their planet and ours?"

"No. Oh no. A far subtler and more ingenious method than that. But I'm afraid I cannot reveal more to you, not yet. You have taken your first steps to joining us, but until we are quite assured of your bona fides, certain details of our plans will have to remain known solely to initiates. You understand?"

"Quite, my dear lady," said Holmes. "I feel honoured to have got this far, and I shall strive to prove worthy of further trust."

"A good answer," said Isadora Klein. "You always seem to know just what to say, Langdale Pike."

*

A month later, the glibly plausible Langdale Pike attended a second dinner at The Three Gables, and a couple of weeks after that, a third. The roster of guests at each meal varied slightly. Some were regulars, others made just a single appearance. Holmes made a mental note of the attendees, and by his estimate The Cultured numbered at least forty in total. Not one of them could be described as anything but *bien pensant*. Their collective high-mindedness was such, Holmes said, that it dwarfed the Himalayas.

It was around this time that my fiancée and I got married. This second wedding of mine was a modest occasion but no less delightful for it. The attendees numbered no more than a dozen, and Holmes, as before, served as my best man. Our honeymoon took us to Deauville, where beautiful late-spring weather and a hotel boasting both a first-rate restaurant and incomparable views over the Channel helped make our stay on the northern French coast utterly delightful. We strolled along the promenade and relaxed at the hydrotherapeutic baths, and I gambled on the horses at the Hippodrome Deauville–La Touques and won handsomely.

When we returned to England, I paid Baker Street a visit at the first opportunity. By then Holmes had been to a fourth gathering of The Cultured, and he caught me up on events.

"Langdale Pike is fully embedded with them now," said he. "The infiltration is complete. See for yourself."

He rolled up his shirtsleeve. There on his forearm, just above the wrist, lay a raised, circular patch of redness the size of a tuppenny bit.

"Why, it could be pityriasis rosea, intertrigo, psoriasis, even eczema," I opined. "Any commonplace rash."

"It was introduced into my skin subcutaneously, using a needle dipped in a solution containing fungal spores," Holmes said. "Rather like a tattoo, but with ink made of diluted living plant matter."

"That must have hurt."

"Not to a man who used to inject himself with a hypodermic syringe on a regular basis. I barely felt a thing. Langdale Pike, however, whimpered throughout the procedure."

"Does it itch? It looks as though it does."

"No. The appearance of infection is just that, an appearance. I am told that the 'tattooing' must be repeated every few weeks. The mark will fade as the body seeks to heal it, and will eventually disappear altogether if not renewed. The way it tingles when it encounters a fellow mark is, I can tell you, somewhat unnerving."

"The Cultured have bestowed their seal of membership on you," I said. "Or rather, on Pike. Have you been able to parlay that trust into learning more about their plans?"

"Very much so," Holmes said. "Much progress was made while you were off gallivanting in Normandy. Congratulations on your wins at the races, by the way."

"I never mentioned that."

"You haven't had to. Deauville is famed for its racecourse among other attractions, and your penchant for gambling is well known. That tie you are wearing is brand new and made of Gauffre silk. Very expensive, and just the sort of thing a man buys himself when he has had a windfall. Ergo, you had a flutter on the nags, did well, and treated yourself to an item of French-made neckwear to celebrate. The inference is—"

"Yes, yes. I know. Elementary."

"But back to business," said Holmes. "I have intermingled with The Cultured not only at The Three Gables but elsewhere. I have contrived for Langdale Pike to bump into members in other social situations around town. To a man, and indeed, a woman, they sincerely believe they are engaged in an enterprise that will bring about world peace and a bright future for mankind thanks to the Mi-Go. Isadora Klein believes it most strongly of all, to the point where I might call her an ideologue."

"Is it possible they are right? Do the Mi-Go have our best interests at heart?"

"Every comment relayed by Mrs Klein from Glaw Za-Jooll points to it."

"Yet you sound doubtful."

Holmes reached for his pipe. "Let me lay the evidence before you, Watson, and you tell me what you think. Now that The Cultured have taken Langdale Pike to their bosom, I have learned various pieces of new data, and these have enabled me to draw together disparate threads that have cropped up in various of our investigations over the past few years and weave them into a tapestry. I shall start with Dr Ulrich Felder, back in 'eighty-eight. If, as I strongly suspect, Mrs Klein gave him the fungus with which he attempted his failed cancer cure, was it merely the action of a grief-stricken widow hoping to spare others the misery she herself endured? Perhaps. If, however, the fungus came originally from the Mi-Go, as it surely must have, would the Outside Things not have known how it would affect the human physiology? Would they not have been well aware that it would both hasten the growth of cancerous tumours and bring back to life those whose deaths it accelerated?"

"In which case, giving her the fungus to pass on to Felder and pretending to her that it would cure cancer is a strange act for such supposedly benevolent beings. Unless, that is, they were under the impression it might be genuinely advantageous to cancer sufferers."

"Hence we must ask ourselves whether they had an ulterior motive. Were the fungus's effects precisely the ones the Mi-Go wished to achieve? And if so, why?"

"Do you know the answer?"

"I have an idea," said Holmes, blowing out tobacco smoke, "but it is, as yet, a half-formed one, if that. Now let us turn to the next occasion when something related to the Mi-Go intruded upon our lives, which occurred later that same year."

"Your second brush with Irene Adler, following on from the King of Bohemia affair."

"Miss Adler's natural gift for impersonation was enhanced to the nth degree by exposure to that morel-like fungus in rural Vermont. She used it to coerce Professor Mellingford and others into acting against Britain's best interests. She did this in service to certain employers whom she refused to identify but whom we can be fairly sure were The Cultured, themselves working on the Mi-Go's behalf. Again, we must question how altruistic the Outside Things really are if subverting Britain's progress is on their agenda."

"If, however, peace on Earth is their goal, then their chosen targets for extortion make sense."

"Really, Watson?"

"Look at it this way. The First Naval Lord wanting to reduce the size of our forces at sea, a potential Viceroy of India publicly espousing the dismantling of the Raj, a munitions manufacturer curtailing output from his factories, Professor Mellingford abandoning his research into poison gas for the battlefield... This country, as the foremost world power, would be seen very visibly beating its swords into ploughshares, and where Britain leads, other nations might follow."

"There is some validity in that argument," Holmes allowed.

"But what about Josiah Amberley and his Shub-Niggurath cultists? How do they fit into this?"

"They were, as I suggested at the time, just a distraction. It was an attempt by Irene Adler to throw me off The Cultured's scent."

"No direct Mi-Go connection, therefore."

"Unless Miss Adler was acting under their instruction, which is not impossible. I think we should now spread our net wider and consider what else we know of Mi-Go activity on our world."

"Which isn't much," I said. "There is, I suppose, Captain Carey and the space-ship he found in the Arctic."

Holmes refilled and relit his pipe. "That is just what I am

referring to, Watson. The space-ship crashed on Earth back in 1883. At the time of reading Carey's logbook, we speculated as to why the Mi-Go aboard the vessel, those 'fungonauts' of ours, came to this planet. We wondered if they were perhaps a diplomatic mission, or else a military expedition."

"I err on the side of the former."

"Do you? Even allowing for those items they brought with them which caused so much harm to the *Sea Unicorn*'s crew and which could only have been anti-human weapons?"

"You said they might have brought them for self-defence."

"Self-defence is still offensive."

"But what about the fungus that you put to use as your mycophone? In the right hands it could be a revolutionary new method of interpersonal communication."

"But in the wrong hands a spying device," Holmes said, "as I amply proved by using it to eavesdrop on Baron Gruner."

"The wrong use for it, but for the right reasons," I said.

"Mrs Klein, at any rate, affirmed that the space-ship was a first attempt by the Mi-Go to make contact with the people of Earth. She and Langdale Pike were discussing Mi-Go biology, after Pike had expressed a desire to know what the Outside Things looked like. She went on about them at some length: their insect-like bodies, their glowing heads, and so forth. Glaw Za-Jooll, she then said, had once spoken of a valiant crew of volunteers who embarked on the lengthy voyage from Yuggoth to Earth. Their last report to him was transmitted just as they entered our planet's atmosphere."

"Transmitted fungally, I presume."

"Yes. The crew communicated with their home planet via the same method used by Mrs Klein and indeed Miss Adler. They told Glaw Za-Jooll they were having difficulty moving and breathing. They felt pinned to the floor, as though beneath an immense weight. Thus they were unable to maintain control of their vessel. Instead of making a smooth descent, the space-ship plummeted. The last Glaw Za-Jooll heard from the crew, they were crawling from the wreckage but evidently in the throes of dying."

"You surmised that they might have been killed by the richness of oxygen in our atmosphere, which suffocated them," I said. "That or exposure to our much stronger sunlight baked them to death. Neither of those things, however, would explain why the fungonauts started suffering ill effects *before* they landed."

"I did indeed postulate two differences between Earth's environment and Yuggoth's that would have accounted for the demise of the fungonauts," Holmes said. "Oxygen. Sunlight. I neglected to consider a third possibility."

"Namely?"

"Gravity. Prevailing astronomical thought has it that the putative planet beyond Neptune, which you and I know as Yuggoth, is far smaller than our own. There are suggestions that its mass is five hundred times less than that of Earth, and its gravity is therefore proportionately lighter. If so, there lies our explanation. The moment the fungonauts encountered our much heavier gravity, it crushed them. Within their exoskeletons, their organs were flattened. Their breathing spiracles collapsed. It would have been a dismal death, and the upshot of this ill-fated endeavour, whether it was diplomatic delegation or embryonic invasion, is that the Mi-Go learned they cannot survive on Earth. That would account for what the Outside Things did next, which was to send a very different kind of emissary here."

"What do you mean?"

"The meteorite, Watson. The carved black stone that landed in the Vermont woods and sowed a garden of fungi all around it. Those two backwoodsmen, Natty and Zeke, told Miss Adler the meteorite fell to earth in 1884, a year after the events in Carey's logbook. We may reasonably posit that the Mi-Go propelled it somehow to Earth, having first implanted it with fungal spores, which scattered themselves immediately upon landing, took root and grew."

"With the aim of opening a channel of communication between Earth and Yuggoth."

Holmes nodded through the blue haze of smoke that now surrounded him. "And recruiting certain humans to their cause, so as to achieve by proxy that which they could not in person."

"Why send the meteorite to such a remote region if they wanted it to be found? Why not a populated area?"

"I suspect that pinpoint accuracy over a distance of millions of miles is not easy," Holmes said. "But also, if your goal is to introduce yourselves quietly and with the minimum of fuss, firing a large rock at a major conurbation is not the way to go about it. Can you imagine the effect it would have were a meteorite like that to come down in central London? The impact alone would lead to devastation, panic and numerous casualties. The military would become involved, reporters would descend on the scene in their droves, crowds would gather to gawp... I mean, you too have read Wells. He has it about right, I think. But our Mi-Go, unlike Wells's Martians, aren't interested in making a bold statement. They seem to prefer the sidelong, stealthy approach, which betokens a certain underhandedness and reinforces the notion that they are not on the level."

"Or is it merely judicious caution?" I said.

"I wish, Watson, I were as inclined towards optimism as you," Holmes said. "I now know, at least, that the Vermont meteorite is not the only one they have sent our way. There has been another. That's to say, another for which there is reliable eyewitness testimony. There could well be more which we don't know about. Meteorites hit the planet at the rate of a dozen a day, so it is reckoned. Most are tiny and burn up to nothing in the upper atmosphere, but a fair few make it to the ground. Amid those numbers, a couple extra here or there would hardly make a difference."

"When you say 'eyewitness testimony', are you referring to Isadora Klein again?"

"Very good, old friend."

"I did wonder where she might have obtained her various fungi." I counted them off on my fingers. "Felder's supposed cancer cure. The one she uses to communicate with Yuggoth. The one that creates the mark of The Cultured. She must have got them from *somewhere*."

"And that somewhere is the Black Forest," said Holmes. "It lies just south of Heidelberg and comprises roughly two thousand square miles of dense, mountainous woodland. It is not dissimilar, in many ways, to Vermont's Green Mountains, so there is some consistency there in the Mi-Go's choice of targets. Mrs Klein told me she happened upon her meteorite while hiking in the Black Forest in 'eighty-six, not long after her husband's death, and was rewarded with a psychic trip to Yuggoth that paralleled Irene Adler's. I say 'happened upon', but she was led to the spot by the guide she had hired for the hike. A guide who, in the event, turned out to be not all he seemed."

"Doubtless a Mi-Go agent."

"Not just any Mi-Go agent. You may recall that it was around then that the very same Irene Adler was cutting a swathe through Europe as an adventuress and all-round mischief-maker."

"So Miss Adler was assigned by the Mi-Go to pose as a guide," I said, "and bring Mrs Klein to the meteorite."

"Not Mrs Klein specifically, but a suitable candidate of her choosing," said Holmes. "She opted for Isadora Klein because really there could not have been a better fit for the job of Mi-Go envoy. Wealthy, well connected, charismatic. Mrs Klein admitted that she was reluctant at first to accept the role, but then Glaw Za-Jooll made an offer too tempting to refuse. He knew how her husband had died, and he said he had a means whereby others might not have to go through the same ordeal."

"The so-called cancer cure."

"That sealed the deal for her," said Holmes. "But the cure did not work. It seems Mrs Klein has no idea that Felder's experiments went awry. She only knows that he died in a house fire while pursuing the research which she instigated and sponsored."

"At least it is now beyond dispute that Irene Adler is in cahoots with The Cultured."

"Mrs Klein did not actually identify Miss Adler by name. Yet the latter being her hiking guide seems so likely as to be incontrovertible, and we may assume the two women have been working together since on the Mi-Go's behalf."

I paused a moment to chew over the glut of information my friend had served up. "We still have yet to establish whether The Cultured are collaborators with the Outside Things or their unwitting dupes."

"I have had thoughts in that direction," said he. "Their contention that they wish to build a better world is certainly at odds with Douglas Maberley's despairing cries about 'no future'."

"The lad was not in his right mind, remember."

"Doesn't that make it more, not less, likely that he was speaking the truth? Often it is the mad who have insight. The sane are prone to deluding themselves."

"A neat little apothegm, Holmes," I said. "Neat, but dashed misanthropic."

"I don't deny that I have a tendency towards misanthropy," Holmes said. "It helps a criminalist to think the worst of people."

"And of aliens as well?"

"Them too. As it happens, Douglas Maberley may have furnished us with a clue to proving The Cultured's status either way."

"How so?" I asked.

"Let me answer your question with a question, Watson. What are your views on breaking and entering?"

*

Exactly nine days after Sherlock Holmes posed that rather freighted query, I found myself skulking amid shrubbery in the grounds of The Three Gables. It was a warm, moonless night, and I was wearing dark clothing, leather gloves and a woollen watch cap, with a scarf fastened around the lower half of my face, so that the only part of me that stood exposed was my eyes. My pockets held various implements, among them a small hammer, a dark-lantern and a set of lockpicks. In short, I could not have looked or been behaving more like a burglar if I had tried.

As I loitered in that shrubbery, awaiting the moment I would make my move, my mind drifted back to the conversation with Holmes I have just related. I recalled the little thrill of apprehension that had run through me as my friend asked me to perform what can only be described as a felony – apprehension only somewhat mitigated by his insistence that it was all in the name of the greater good.

"I have, as Langdale Pike," he said, "had little chance to explore The Three Gables. The Cultured's meetings are orderly, circumscribed affairs, taking place exclusively in the common parts of the house. Yet I cannot forget how Douglas Maberley spoke of a room. 'I have seen what's in that room. That room!' It is no stretch of the imagination to suppose that the room in question lies within The Three Gables. When Maberley mentioned it, after all, he had just returned from a rendezvous with Mrs Klein. Therefore I made an attempt to look round the premises."

Holmes told me how Langdale Pike had briefly excused himself from the dinner table, left the conservatory, and hastened along the house's mazy corridors. From earlier visits, he knew the layout of the ground floor fairly well, but there were two entire wings he had not ventured into, and the upper floors were likewise terra incognita. He did not have much time. An absence of longer than five minutes would arouse suspicion. That meant he must try only the doors to rooms he had never entered.

These afforded access to perfectly normal-looking chambers: a study, a scullery, a boot room, and so on. All too soon, his five minutes elapsed, and he returned to the conservatory none the wiser.

That was at one dinner party. At the next, he again excused himself from the table and sought out more doors he had not previously tried.

Somewhere in the north wing, he found one that was firmly locked. He had less than a minute left before he would have to return whence he had come, so there was no question of picking the lock. He put an eye to the keyhole. It had a cover, but he hoped that there was just the one on the outside of the door. Unfortunately, there was one on the inside as well, and so he could see nothing. He did, however, catch a faint smell coming from within. It was the odour of chemicals.

He was on his way back to the conservatory when, around a corner, Steve Dixie abruptly appeared.

"Mr Pike," said the prizefighter.

His flat, neutral tone made it hard to decide if this was just a greeting or if Dixie had been actively looking for the absentee. A vaguely knowing glint in his eyes suggested the latter.

"Mr Dixie!" Holmes declared. "You startled me, looming out of nowhere like that."

"You seem to have strayed from the party."

"It's a very large house. I got confused." He gave a sudden lurch towards Dixie, and saw the boxer's huge hands instinctively clench into fists. "I am also," he said confidentially, "rather drunk. Shh! Don't tell Isadora."

Dixie glanced past Holmes's shoulder, as though checking the way he had come. "Drunk or not, it don't do to go wandering, Mr Pike. This ain't your home. You got me? You should keep to the places you're meant to keep to."

"Please don't be so stern with me," Holmes said, swaying

now, as an inebriate might. "You're very fierce looking, and you're scaring me."

"Good," said Dixie. "Now, answer me straight. Why are you here, so far from the conservatory?"

"I told you. I'm drunk. I got confused. It happens to drunk people. Although," Holmes added, with a tremulous glance at Dixie's fists, "I am staring to sober up quite fast."

"I don't believe you. I think you were snooping."

"Why would I do that?"

"You're a gossip man. Maybe you're looking for dirt on Mrs Klein, something you can sell to the press."

"On dear Isadora? Never! I swore to her I would keep her secrets, hers and everyone else's here. I'm a loyal Cultured."

The boxer leaned closer to Holmes. "You're lying. I know liars. Just like in the ring, when the bloke you're fighting is pretending he's hurt worse than he is, so he can lure you in and surprise you. I can *smell* fakery, and you reek of it."

Holmes had the feeling that, come what may, this confrontation was going to end in violence. Steve Dixie seemed hell-bent on roughing him up, and while Sherlock Holmes would happily have responded in kind, giving as good as he got, this option was not open to Langdale Pike. If Dixie dealt out punishment, Langdale Pike would just have to take it, in order to preserve the imposture.

"Pray don't hit me," he said. "Isadora wouldn't like it, would she?"

"Mrs Klein has told me I should always go with my instincts when it comes to her wellbeing," Dixie replied. "That's what she pays me for. And my instincts are telling me I should pummel the truth out of you."

Dixie raised one of those fists. Its knuckles resembled knots in the wood of an oak. Holmes braced himself.

Then a voice rang out. "Steve Dixie! What in heaven's name are you doing?"

It was the housemaid, Susan. She had arrived on the scene

unnoticed by either man, and now she stood, hands on hips, arms akimbo, staring down her narrow nose at them.

"You lower that arm this instant, Steve," she said. "What has got into you? Threatening one of the guests!"

"Mr Pike ain't where he ought to be," said Dixie. "He was acting all suspicious like."

"Not suspicious," said Holmes. "Drunk, perhaps, but not suspicious."

"It's not up to you where people can go in the house," Susan said to Dixie.

"I'm looking out for Mrs Klein's interests."

"Maybe you are, but I'm sure that hitting Mr Pike won't serve those interests. Now, you back away from him, Steve. I shan't tell you again."

He rounded on her. "And what if I hit you instead, Susan? Snooty old witch that you are. Maybe you need putting in your place."

Susan did not flinch. "You just try it, Steve Dixie. Lay one finger on me, and you'll regret it."

There was a brief standoff, the prizefighter glaring at the housemaid, the housemaid defiantly returning the glare.

Then Dixie dropped his fist. "Ah, to the devil with you, woman. You're not worth the bother. You." This was to Holmes. "You come back with me to the conservatory right now. I'll make sure you get there and don't go wandering and 'getting lost' again." The inverted commas around "getting lost" were clearly audible.

As Dixie stalked away, Holmes murmured, "Thank you," to Susan.

The housemaid merely sniffed. "You're in his bad books now. You had better watch yourself."

"Oh, I will, Susan. I will."

"Mr Pike!" Dixie made a beckoning gesture, one that did not brook refusal.

As he escorted Holmes back to the conservatory, Holmes

contrived to stumble against Dixie once or twice, to reinforce the impression that Langdale Pike was drink-impaired. Dixie being so solidly built, colliding with him was, Holmes told me, akin to bumping into a brick wall. It also did little to improve the fellow's enmity towards him, but then he doubted anything could have.

"Langdale," said Mrs Klein as Holmes re-joined the dinner party. "We were starting to wonder where you'd gotten to."

"I'm so sorry," Holmes said with a bow of apology. "I took a few wrong turns. Luckily Mr Dixie was on hand to steer me straight. He was a godsend."

For the rest of the meal, Steve Dixie's scowling gaze seldom strayed from Holmes. It was clear that the prizefighter had it in for Langdale Pike and would be watching him like a hawk from then on.

That meant Holmes would find it hard, if not impossible, to investigate the locked room, and therefore someone else must do the job. Hence my nocturnal sojourn in the shrubbery, which lay some fifty yards from the house across a patch of lawn.

Over the past nine days Holmes had given me an intensive course in lockpicking and drawn me a floorplan of The Three Gables, sketched from memory. I had committed the map to my own memory, and my lockpicking skills, while no match for Holmes's own, had developed to the point where I could make a passable cracksman.

Finally my watch told me it was ten o'clock. It was traditionally around then that Mrs Klein initiated contact with Glaw Za-Jooll. The servants would be in the kitchen, occupied with washing up the dinner things. The guests' attention would be focused fully on their hostess, as would Steve Dixie's. There would not be a better time.

Steeling myself, I crept out from my place of concealment and tiptoed across the dew-damp lawn. The north wing lay at the opposite end of the house from the conservatory. Here, few windows were lit. The darkness was thick. I approached a door, the upper half of which held a grid of inset windowpanes. Holmes, from his explorations, knew this door was likely to be bolted as well as locked, with the key left in place.

From one pocket I took a sheet of brown paper and a small pot of treacle. Smearing some of the latter liberally over one side of the former, I pressed the paper to the windowpane nearest the handle. The treacle adhered it in place. Then, with my hammer, I gave the pane a firm tap. The glass broke but the treacle-coated paper both muffled the sound and prevented the shards from falling. Then all I had to do was peel it away, the shards coming with it. A few remained fastened in the putty, but picking them out was no trouble. This was an old burglar's trick Holmes had taught me. With the frame of the pane now empty, I reached through, turned the key, and slid back the bolt. The door opened soundlessly, and I crossed the threshold.

I stole through the house, my every sense on the alert. My breathing seemed inordinately loud, to my ears. Same with my footfalls, no matter that I trod as softly as I could. I listened out for voices, the sound of a door opening, a step on a stair.

A sudden burst of distant laughter sent me scurrying for refuge in the narrow gap between an armoire and an ornamental plant on a table. I remained there for a full three minutes, and in all that time I did not, I think, breathe once. The laughter was not repeated, and at last I emerged and continued on my stealthy way.

I located the locked door. Holmes's map had been accurate to the last detail, even depicting the Persian rug that ran the length of the corridor I was on.

Kneeling before the door, I fetched out the set of lockpicks. I raised the keyhole cover and inserted a torsion wrench into the bottom of the lock, exerting a slight downward pressure with it. I then inserted a rake pick above it, which I gently slid back and forth in a roughly circular motion. By this means I could bounce the pins of the lock to the shear line one after another in succession, while keeping each in place with the torque wrench.

"You have a doctor's steady hands, Watson, with a dexterity honed by delicate work such as suturing," Holmes had told me. "Think of it as a kind of surgery."

To practise lockpicking at Baker Street was one thing; to pick a lock at a house I had no business being in was quite another. Under those circumstances my hands were, in fact, neither steady nor dextrous, and after several frustrating minutes I was coming to the conclusion that the lock was never going to budge.

Then, just when I was convinced all was lost, through the torque wrench I felt a slight but significant give. The final pin had set. The lock had yielded to my ministrations.

Holding the torsion wrench in position to keep the lock undone, I turned the knob and pushed the door an inch ajar. Then I stowed the lockpicks away, opened the door fully, and stepped through.

Pushing the door to behind me, I took a moment to collect myself. My task was half complete. Now all I had to do was see what was in this room, and I could then, by God's good graces, leave the house undetected and unhindered.

The air smelled thickly musty, with a sharp undernote that reminded me, for some reason, of my sojourns at Barts and Netley, although I could not quite put my finger on why just then.

I took out the dark-lantern, struck a match and lit the wick. I swept its beam around, and gasped in surprise.

*

Perhaps I should not have been startled. After all, Douglas Maberley had effectively provided a warning. I suppose I'd been hoping that the room he had been referring to was not this one.

There were three tables lined up in a row. One was bare, while on the other two, men lay. Each had a sheet draped over him, covering him up to his chin. They were very still, but with both I perceived a slight rise and fall of the chest. They were, it would appear, in a deep sleep.

This was a queer sight but, in and of itself, not all that remarkable. Yet, as I played the beam of the dark-lantern over the pair, I perceived that one of the men was wearing what appeared to be a helmet. Closer inspection revealed it to be some kind of bluish-grey fungal growth, snugly encasing the top of his head. Tendrils from the fungus dug into his skin around its rim, causing a puckering effect. It was as though the fungus had knitted itself into place.

As for the other man, I had to look twice. My first impression was that there was something wrong with his head; that it was misshapen, perhaps owing to some congenital deformity. On second glance I learned that there was something much more seriously awry.

The top of the man's skull had been removed, sheared off just above the temples. His entire scalp was gone, and with it his brain.

That was when I identified the smell which had reminded me of my medical student days. It was the tangy odour the human anatomy gives off when its insides are opened, when blood and viscera lie exposed.

Ghastly as the man's missing cranium was, ghastlier still was the fact that he still breathed!

I approached the table with trepidation, stunned by the inconceivability of what I beheld. The surgery had been performed very neatly. Veins and arteries were sewn shut. The brain stem, at the bottom of the hollow, rugged bowl that was the man's cranial cavity, showed signs of neat excision.

My gaze roved to his body – his impossibly alive body – and I noticed how it was peculiarly lumpy. Little nodules and hillocks bulged against the sheet where no person should have any. I glanced over at the other man's body, but its contours looked normal.

Curiosity compelled me to reach out a nervous hand towards the man in front of me. Taking hold of the top of the sheet that covered him, I drew it back.

The fellow's torso was wreathed in knots and twists of the same bluish-grey fungus that capped the other man's head. It clung to him like the toils of some sticky vegetal web, and it was moving, apparently of its own volition. Several of its tubular strands, I saw, penetrated the man's ribcage and were connected to two largish flesh-like sacs which sat on either side of him and inflated and deflated in a slow, steady rhythm. Others had embedded themselves in his stomach, and ripples were passing along their length in a manner I can only describe as peristaltic.

A dreadful truth dawned.

The fungus was keeping this man without a brain alive. It was helping him respire and feeding him via a surrogate digestive system.

If this was what Maberley had seen, no wonder it had made such an appalling impression on him. Nonetheless, in the professional part of my mind, I marvelled. Was this fungal apparatus a Mi-Go offering? It could only be, in which case the Outside Things had presented the people of Earth with one of the greatest gifts of all time. If life could be sustained in a body which by every right should be dead, the applications for medical science were manifold. Complex surgical procedures, the healing of near-lethal injuries, patient survival prospects: all could be radically improved.

While chewing over these thoughts, I trained the dark-lantern around the rest of the room. There were shelves and racks around the walls, laden with boxes and glass phials. These appeared to be containers for various chemicals. There were shallow trays, too, lined with compost from which several different kinds of fungi budded. Further fungi were contained in sealed glass flasks, many of which had condensation beading their interiors.

Most notably there were a trio of hatbox-sized metallic cylinders sitting in a row. Their design was familiar. Holmes had one such at Baker Street, sporting a similar porthole and array of knobbly protrusions.

That cylinder, however, differed materially from these in certain respects. I went over for a better look and descried that, as I had thought, they were not made from the same metal as the one from Carey's toleware box, with that uncanny nacreous sheen. These were plain old brass, forged and riveted. The protrusions on them seemed cruder, too. It was as though the cylinders had been fashioned in emulation of the Mi-Go version, by earthly hands.

Two were filled with a clear, viscous liquid. I bent to peer through the porthole of the first and saw that it contained a hairy, hemispherical mass. To my disgust, I realised I was looking at a human scalp. The scalp, without question, belonged to the man on the table.

The other cylinder contained something even worse, and doubtless of the same origin. It was an entire human brain.

There the organ sat, yellow-grey and corrugated, suspended in the liquid. Everything about it – the various lobes, the longitudinal fissure, the pons, the medulla oblongata – was perfect and intact, all the way down to the truncated stem.

But there was an addition. Perched between the frontal lobes was a bright red blob about the size of a tomato. I at first thought it might be an unusually large blood clot, but closer scrutiny led me to understand that it was a type of fungus. It seemed firmly attached to the brain, its lower portion merging with the gyri and sulci of the cortex. Meanwhile a half-dozen strands extended outward from its upper portion, connecting it to the interior of the cylinder, as though the fungus was anchoring itself, and thus the brain, in position.

A sudden rustling behind me set me pivoting round.

Beneath the watch cap, my hair stood on end.

*

One of the men on the tables – the one with the fungus on his head – had sat bolt upright, the sheet slipping off his upper body to pool around his waist. His eyes were wide open below the brim of that fungal helmet, and he was staring at me with evident wariness and perplexity.

"Why...?" he said. His voice was scratchy and thin, like the sound made when one turns the spigot of a water tap that has grown rusty from long disuse. "Why are you?"

My heart was in my mouth. All I could think to say in reply was, "'Why'? Don't you mean 'who'?"

"Yes. Who. Forgive me. I got my words muddled. Who are you?"

"I am a doctor," I said. It was the most innocuous answer my flustered brain could conjure up. It was also the only one.

"Doctor." He pronounced the two syllables separately, carefully. "Yes. Doctor. A healer. One who treats the sick."

"That is me. Who are *you*?" As an interloper, I had less justification in asking him that question than he did me, but it might be helpful to know whom I was dealing with.

"I am... I am Dysart," he said. "Octavius Dysart. I write plays. Are you here to help me, Doctor? That's what doctors are for. To help."

"Indeed," I said, pulling my scarf down and fixing a reassuring smile on my face. I recalled Holmes mentioning that one member of The Cultured was a playwright. "What has happened to you, Mr Dysart? Your disorientation and mild aphasia suggest to me you have perhaps been in a coma for some time. Is that the case?"

Octavius Dysart passed a hand across his eyes. "I... think so," he said. "It must be."

"Was it an accident?"

"No."

"Then who is responsible? The Cultured?"

"The Cultured? Yes. They are the ones."

Dysart swung his legs over the table's edge and tried to stand. He wobbled, and I hastened over and took hold of him.

"You must lie back down," I said. "You are clearly very weak, and I don't think standing is a good idea."

"No," Dysart said. "I can manage."

His second attempt met with greater success. He teetered for a moment, but steadied. I picked up the sheet, which had slipped off him entirely and fallen to the floor, and proffered it, in order to allow him to preserve his modesty. In his state of confusion he didn't seem to know what to do with it, so I helped, fastening it around his waist as one might a bath towel.

"Are you one of them?" he asked. "Is that why you are here?"

"Them? The Cultured?"

"Yes. Did they engage you to watch over me?"

It seemed prudent to lie, in hopes of gaining Dysart's full confidence and dispelling any notion that I did not belong here. "Yes. Yes, that is it. The Cultured thought it advisable to bring me in, as a doctor, to ensure your wellbeing."

"You are of their number?"

"Yes. Assuredly yes."

"Then you know what has been done to me."

"In broad terms." I extemporised as best I could. "You have been subjected to a certain procedure. A highly experimental one. The, er, the fungus on your head is there to – to facilitate that procedure."

With its signal lack of detail, the statement did not sound very convincing even to my own ears, but Dysart seemed persuaded.

"Very good," he said. "And in the process of discharging your obligations, Doctor, what comes next?"

"Next?" My growing belief was that Dysart had been subjected to some kind of experiment, against his will, by his fellow Cultured members. Therefore it was incumbent upon me to get him out of the house to safety, which just so happened to accord with my own desires. But how was I to achieve that, when I had already established I belonged to The Cultured myself? It would jeopardise his trust in me if I appeared in any way to be working counter to them.

An idea struck me. "I must take you to a hospital," I said. "You can rest there and be tended to. There, too, with all the necessary equipment to hand, we can go about removing that fungus from your head. Whatever it's doing to you, it cannot be healthy."

"A hospital. I see."

"And I think we should leave straight away."

"But what about him?" Dysart gestured at the man on the other table.

"Him? I will come back for him later. Getting you proper medical attention is my foremost concern."

"Very well then."

I shut off the dark-lantern, took Dysart by the elbow, and shepherded him towards the door. I peeked out into the corridor. The coast was clear.

"This way," I said, making every effort to sound casual.

We walked for several dozen yards, and all the while I feared that one of The Cultured, or else a member of the domestic staff, might stumble upon us and the game would be up.

Then, on a sudden, Dysart went stock still.

"Come along, Dysart," I said. "This is no time to hesitate. The sooner we reach that hospital, the better."

"No."

I fought to stifle my frustration. "What is the matter?"

"The matter, Doctor, is this," said Dysart. "You are not what you say you are."

"I beg your pardon?"

He held up his arm, and I spied a small, circular rash on it. The mark of The Cultured. I had not noticed it before.

"If you were truly a member of The Cultured, you would

have one of these on your person," he said, "and mine would be tingling and changing shape, as would yours. Mine is not, and I do not think you have one yourself at all."

I thought fast. "Well now, when I said I was one of The Cultured, I misspoke. What I should have said is that I am… affiliated with them. Not a full member, as such. But close enough. I aspire to joining their ranks in due course, if they'll have me."

Dysart eyed me circumspectly. "'Doctor' has two meanings. One is to work as a healer. The other is to tamper or falsify."

"I am aware of that. Now please, let's move."

"You, Doctor, may be a healer but you are also a falsifier. Help!" He yelled the last word at the top of his lungs.

"Quiet!" I hissed. "What do you think you're doing?"

"Calling for help," Dysart said simply, then yelled again: "Help!"

Distantly I heard voices, the first stirrings of a commotion.

I was frozen with indecision. I knew I had grievously misread the situation with Octavius Dysart. It was a blunder of epic proportions, and the penalty could well be my life.

*

The hubbub was growing, getting louder, coming closer, even as Dysart kept calling for help.

Self-preservation overrode all other considerations. I began to run, making for the entrance I had come in by.

Up ahead, a man appeared. He was dark-skinned and enormous. He took one look at me and broke into a loping jog, making a beeline for me.

This could only be the fearsome Steve Dixie, and I immediately skidded to a halt and about-turned.

Running the other way, I saw Dysart move to block my path. I lowered my shoulder, as one does on the rugby pitch when carrying the ball and driving towards the opposition. Dysart I thought I could barge aside, unlike the bulky Dixie.

The playwright, however, was more determined than I had thought, and although I was able to push past him, he contrived to trip me up. I went sprawling to the floor. I was on my feet again in a flash. Dysart tried to grab me. I shook him off and resumed running.

The delay, however, allowed Steve Dixie to catch up with me. He seized hold of my arm and spun me round. The next thing I knew, I was on the floor again, on my side, doubled over, heaving for breath. Dixie had delivered a vicious jab to my solar plexus, a blow so swift, I had not even seen it coming. I wheezed and gasped, feeling as though I would never be able to draw a breath again.

Just as my lungs began to work once more, I was hauled upright. Dixie, holding me by the collar, put his leering face just inches from mine.

"Don't try nothing, my friend," said he. "'Less you want the stuffing knocked out of you."

I was hardly able to stand, let alone fight. My belly was afire from his punch, and my head swam. I was aware of people gathering around us. Faces hovered in and out of my vision. Voices murmured.

A very beautiful woman leaned towards me and said, in an American accent, "Doctor John Watson, I presume."

This had to be Isadora Klein, but even if I had not still been winded, I would not have known what to say in reply. The only clear thought I had, in the dazed tangle that was my mind, was how did she know who I was?

Another face appeared, next to Mrs Klein's. It was Langdale Pike.

"Good heavens," said he. "Dr Watson? *The* Dr Watson? As in, the aide and confidant of Sherlock Holmes? Is it really him?"

"He was present when I awoke, after my Palimpsest Process," said Octavius Dysart. "He claimed to be working for The Cultured. But I... What is the saying? Smelled a rat."

"You were right to," said Mrs Klein. "The presence of Dr Watson on the premises spells trouble. It means Sherlock Holmes is meddling in our affairs. You don't get the one without the other."

"But why?" said Langdale Pike, betraying not the least indication that he was talking about himself. "Holmes investigates crimes, and we Cultured are doing nothing wrong. Are we, Isadora?"

She ignored the question. "Steve, keep a tight hold on him. He may be just Holmes's sidekick but he is wily in his way."

"He ain't going anywhere, Mrs Klein," said Dixie, "don't you worry."

She cast her gaze around The Cultured. "The rest of you, back to the conservatory. I will handle this. Not you, Octavius. But everyone else. Go on!"

The Cultured shuffled obediently away. I watched as Langdale Pike, with some reluctance, turned to accompany them, and my heart sank. I had thought Holmes might concoct some excuse to remain. I could only hope that, even as he departed from the scene, he was thinking up a plan to rescue me and would put it into action as soon as he was out of sight.

Then Mrs Klein waylaid him with a hand.

"Stay, Langdale. I may need an extra pair of hands."

"Very well."

My relief was enormous. Without realising it, Mrs Klein had just dramatically improved my chances of emerging unscathed from this predicament.

Once it was only her, Dixie, Dysart and me left – along with Holmes, of course – Mrs Klein ordered her bodyguard to frisk me.

"Dr Watson often carries a pistol," she said.

Dixie emptied out my pockets, finding the dark-lantern, lockpicks and small hammer. "That's all," he said, tossing the items to one side. "No gun."

"Fine." Mrs Klein motioned with her hand. "Let us go to the Palimpsest Chamber. We can have some privacy there, and you, Octavius, can continue to heal. I don't think that fungus is ready to come off just yet."

"As you wish, Isadora," said Dysart.

We moved off in a procession, Mrs Klein leading the way, followed by myself, with Dixie right behind me, frogmarching me along with one arm up behind my back in a half-Nelson. Holmes and Dysart took up the rear.

"Palimpsest?" Holmes enquired as we went. "That's the second time I've heard that word in the past minute, and it is not a commonly used one. Palimpsest Process. Palimpsest Chamber. What does it refer to, Isadora?"

"You'll find out soon enough, Langdale. You are about to be initiated into the final mystery of The Cultured."

"Really? Consider me honoured and excited."

Presently we were in the room with the tables, the fungi and the cylinders. Mrs Klein shut the door and lit the gas jet, while Dixie thrust me into a corner and took up a guarding stance beside me. I had no doubt that any attempt to escape or resist would be met with immediate and overwhelming force. I bided my time, waiting for Holmes to come through with some ingenious resolution to our quandary. I still had no idea how Mrs Klein had identified me. I wasn't *that* well known, was I? I supposed she might have recognised me from Paget's illustrations in *The Strand*, but his likenesses of Holmes and myself, while close, were not picture-perfect.

"What are all these things?" Holmes said, looking around the room wonderingly. "Who is that on the table there? And why... My God! How revolting!" He did a very good impersonation of a man struggling to hold down his rising gorge. "His head. Part of his head is missing. What on earth is going on here?"

Isadora Klein had a little snub-nosed revolver in her hand.

I am not sure where she produced it from, probably a pocket of her evening gown. Now it was trained unwaveringly upon Holmes.

"'What on earth' indeed," said she. "The simple answer, Langdale, is that the jig is up. You can stop all this flimflam of yours now."

Holmes looked nonplussed. "Flimflam?"

"And I, in turn, can stop calling you Langdale Pike," said Mrs Klein, "when I know perfectly well that you are Sherlock Holmes."

*

"I've known it for weeks," Mrs Klein went on. "I knew it even before Langdale Pike set foot in this house. You may have been dissembling, Mr Holmes, but I have been dissembling too, and one of us is far better at it than the other."

I expected Holmes to put up at least a token protest. He seemed to decide, however, that there was little to be gained by that.

"Good for you, madam," said he, straightening from Pike's stooping, slope-shouldered posture to his own habitually erect one. His voice, at the same time, adopted its customary crisp, clear intonation. "Well played. It did occur to me that Langdale Pike's promotion from outsider to insider was going rather smoothly, but I elected not to look that particular gift horse in the mouth. I was sure that if you 'rumbled' me, to use the vernacular, I would see the signs and be able to extricate myself in time. Plainly I was wrong. Remind me never to take you on at cards."

"How droll," said Mrs Klein. "You are behaving with remarkable insouciance for a man looking down the barrel of one of Mr Colt's finest."

"This is not the first time I have been held at gunpoint and it will not be the last."

"The latter portion of that remark may prove untrue."

"I hope not," said Holmes. "Tell me, Mrs Klein, if you knew all along who Langdale Pike really was, why permit him such intimate access to The Cultured's secrets?"

"You make it sound like a ridiculous tactic."

"Isn't it? Ah. Come to think of it, perhaps not. You wanted me where you could see me. Indeed, you all but admitted that that was what you were up to. 'I reckon it's a good idea to have you right here at my side,' you said, 'where I can keep my beady eye on you and, if need be, use my considerable influence to curb you.'"

Mrs Klein nodded, smiling. In other circumstances, I might have found that smile captivating.

"Moreover," she said, "I could ensure that you knew only as much about our activities as I felt safe with you knowing. I dripped just enough information into Langdale Pike's ear to keep Sherlock Holmes's intellectual curiosity sated, but not a drop more. When 'dearest Langdale' disappeared from the table for an extended period, two dinners running, that was when I realised you were pushing deeper in your pursuit of discovery and I must shorten the leash."

"Hence, the second time, you had your thick-eared pet ox go looking for me."

"Thick-eared pet ox?" snapped Dixie, bristling. "Am I supposed to just let him call me that, Mrs Klein?"

"Yes, you are, Steve," came the reply.

"How did you know I was referring to *you*, Mr Dixie?" Holmes said. "I never specified whom I meant. It could have been any thick-eared pet ox."

Dixie shook a fist at him – an alarmingly large fist, whose ability to incapacitate I knew all too well. "Oh, really now!" he said. "You keep that up, I'm going to fix you, Sherlock Holmes. Fix you good and proper."

"Fix me like your bout against 'Gypsy' Jim Acosta was fixed?"

"I won that fight fair and square!" Dixie bellowed. "Anyone

who says I didn't is a liar. Third-round knockout, and Acosta wasn't faking being flat out on the floor."

"Oh, for pity's sake, Steve," Mrs Klein sighed. "Restrain yourself. Mr Holmes is trying to rile you. Doubtless he reckons that if he can push you far enough, you'll lose control, a ruckus will ensue and, amid all the chaos, he and Dr Watson will make a miraculous escape. I'm sure it is a ploy that has worked in the past. It shan't today. But only if you don't give in to your baser instincts."

Dixie grumbled and huffed, rolling his shoulders, but his temper subsided.

"We're here now," said Holmes, "in what I presume to be The Cultured's inner sanctum – the hub of its operations. Might I advance a theory or two as to what goes on in this room? Then by all means feel free to deal with Watson and myself as you see fit. Torture us, kill us, exact whatever grisly fate you have in store for us."

Mrs Klein shrugged her shoulders. "Go ahead. It makes little difference as far as I'm concerned. It won't change the outcome of events. In fact, I'm curious to see just how much the mighty Sherlock Holmes has figured out."

It was patently obvious to me that my friend was stalling, playing for time. I would have been surprised if the shrewd Mrs Klein didn't know it, too.

"Besides," she added, "you love nothing more than to pontificate in front of an audience. Sherlock Holmes is, at heart, an incorrigible show-off. Even if that weren't common knowledge, thanks to Dr Watson's stories, the proof is there in the lengths you have gone to with your Langdale Pike persona. And who am I to deny you the pleasure of one last hurrah?"

"The Palimpsest Process that takes place in this so-called Palimpsest Chamber," Holmes said, "is the transfer of a mind from one place to another. The places in question are Yuggoth and Earth. More specifically, they are the body of a Mi-Go and the body of a human."

"How have you arrived at that conclusion?"

"The brain in that cylinder, there, can only belong to that partially decapitated body, there. Each is being kept alive in discrete ways, the body by means of the fungus wreathing it, the brain through that liquid it floats in, which I presume to be some kind of nutrient-rich preservative solution. The same holds true of the scalp in the adjacent cylinder. All the cylinders I see here, incidentally, are of human manufacture."

"Built to specifications provided by Glaw Za-Jooll."

"They lack the smooth elegance of the Mi-Go's own."

"We had to make do."

"You are using one of them to store the scalp for the sake of convenience only," Holmes said. "The other, however, serves a more complicated purpose. The brain within it sports a fungal attachment which, if I don't miss my guess, fulfils much the same function as the fungus you use to communicate with Glaw Za-Jooll on Yuggoth. It is a conduit that permits a sentience to travel between worlds. Am I right so far?"

"Go on," said Mrs Klein, which I took to mean *yes*.

"The difference in this case is that the journey is one-way and permanent. The sentience overlays itself on the sentience already extant in the brain. One personality supplants another, just as in a genuine palimpsest the text of the original manuscript is effaced so that the sheet of paper may be reused for fresh text. Octavius Dysart here, to take a handy example, is not Octavius Dysart at all. Not any more. He looks like him, has his voice, to all outward appearances *is* him. But in fact, Dysart is now just a vehicle for someone else to move around in."

"What makes you say that?" asked Dysart.

"Logic argues inexorably for it," Holmes replied. "You spoke of awakening after your Palimpsest Process. Until not long ago, you were like that fellow there." He pointed to the man on the table. "Your brain was separated from your body and placed in one of those cylinders to receive the transmission of a sentience from Yuggoth. Once the process was complete, your brain was reinstalled in its rightful place, as was your scalp. Why else would you be carrying that fungus on your head? It is a type of fungus with extraordinary curative properties. If it can keep a man without a brain alive, as we see before us, then it can surely perform remarkable feats of healing too. In time, doubtless, it will be removed, and there will be no visible scarring and your altered brain will sit comfortably within your skull as though it was never absent. Nobody will be able to tell the change you have undergone, at least not by looking at you."

"This is untrue," said Dysart. "I am Octavius Dysart. That is who I am."

"You keep insisting on that," I chimed in. "You have ever since you came round on that table, and the more you do so, the less I am inclined to believe it."

"Well put, Watson," said Holmes. "Granted, you are the semi-successful playwright Octavius Dysart. But what is your real name? Your Mi-Go name?"

Dysart looked to Mrs Klein, who gave him a nod of assent. "Tell him. Like I said, none of it is going to make a difference. Mr Holmes is only ensuring that he and Dr Watson cannot be allowed to go free. Every word he utters is, in effect, another nail in their coffins."

"I am Ranax Za-Ko," said Dysart. "Or rather, I was. From now on I am Octavius Dysart. I shall go by no other identity."

Holmes bowed. "Pleased to meet you, Ranax Za-Ko. You have come far. I hope the journey was not too onerous."

"I thank you, but as I said, I am Octavius Dysart now and I would have you address me accordingly."

"How many more times are you going to use Dysart's full name? It is quite an odd habit and, I may say, not very human-like."

"He is me," said Dysart, "and I am human."

"If you really hope to convince people of that, it will take some practice, Ranax Za-Ko."

Dysart's head twitched. "You are being quite a pest, sir."

"He is," said Mrs Klein. "He's trying to get a rise out of you, Octavius, just as with Steve, and I offer you the same advice. Don't let him. Ignore him."

Holmes tapped fingers to lips for a moment, pondering. "You cannot have perfected the Palimpsest Process without first performing trial runs. That is where Shinwell Johnson comes in. He provided you with specimens to experiment upon. Human specimens."

Mrs Klein's face hardened somewhat. "And if he did?"

"That, madam, marks the point at which your actions go from understandable to unpardonable. You took receipt of three young women from Johnson. He brought them to you, unconscious and helpless, and you paid him for them, then used them as a scientist uses rats in the laboratory. It was in order to prove that you could safely remove and reinstall a brain, wasn't it? That this healing fungus worked properly?"

"It was necessary."

"Three young women, all with some social standing. That was a risk. Why not a street urchin? Why not a vagrant, or a lady of ill repute? London is riddled with lost souls whose disappearance would hardly go noticed. Why choose three who might actually be missed? After all, it was their trail that helped lead me to your door."

"I requested Johnson to do just as you say," said Mrs Klein, "to show discernment and bring me only insignificant people. He, however, was greedy and came to an ancillary arrangement with an associate of his."

"Baron Gruner."

"Why go to all the fuss and hazard of snatching somebody at random off the street when you have access to a reliable supply? Gruner was handing those women to Johnson on a plate, and also paying to have them disposed of, meaning that Johnson was making money twice over, from both me and Gruner. I entreated him to stop using Gruner as a source, but

Johnson refused, saying that if I didn't like what he had to offer, I could always go elsewhere."

"But there aren't many Shinwell Johnsons around," said Holmes. "There isn't even *the* Shinwell Johnson around any longer."

"Besides, those girls were good material," said Mrs Klein.

"Material!" I ejaculated.

"Young, healthy, liable to withstand the rigours of the process. They proved nicely biddable, too. There's a certain type of girl, from a certain type of background, who is easy to control if you cow her sufficiently. They're bred that way."

"They were human beings," I said. "They had done nothing wrong, and you – what you subjected them to is tantamount to vivisection."

"By all means vent your indignation, Dr Watson. It means little to me. You have no idea of the sacrifices and compromises I have had to make in order to get this far. I do, and have made my peace with it. If the cause is noble, anything is justified."

Behind that beautiful face, those dazzling eyes, evil lurked. I saw it now. Isadora Klein was a fanatic who did not care what depths she must stoop to or whom she must trample over in order to achieve her ends.

"Where are they now, these 'nicely biddable' victims of yours?" Holmes said. "Did they survive your sadistic experimentation?"

"Two did. One did not."

"And the one who did not is, I would hazard, buried somewhere in the grounds of this house. I would also hazard that same holds true for the other two. They may have lived, but you could not have let them go free, not after what they had been through, not with them knowing what they now knew."

"As I said, Mr Holmes: sacrifices." There was a hint of remorse in Mrs Klein's voice, but so slight as to be barely detectable. "I made it quick and painless."

"I am sure that was a great comfort to you, if not to them."

"Is it me you are trying to irk now? Having failed with Steve and Octavius, am I next on the list?" She laughed scornfully. "You must be desperate. Is it not obvious that I am impervious to shame or insult or goading?"

"A lot of things are obvious," said Holmes, "including your sheer lack of conscience and your deep-seated depravity."

"You seem to forget who is holding a gun on you."

"Oh, you aren't going to shoot me, Mrs Klein. Nor Watson."

"Who says?"

"Logic again. You keep asserting that we are doomed, that nails are going into coffins, but I note a certain caginess in your language. I think you want us alive."

"How would that be to my advantage?"

"Would Watson and I not make excellent subjects for your Palimpsest Process?" Holmes said. "Would we not be two very suitable vessels for Mi-Go sentiences to occupy?"

Mrs Klein looked at him askance. "I would be lying if I said that has not occurred to me."

"You already have Dysart there, carrying Ranax Za-Ko within him. On the table lies Ezra Woolfson, the philosopher, whose brain is even now busy being commandeered by an Outside Thing. What do the two men have in common? They are both representatives of the intelligentsia, as indeed are all of The Cultured. Watson and I are also, in our way, representatives of the intelligentsia. Killing us means having to get rid of our bodies and laying yourself open to the possibility that the police will come knocking. There are several redoubtable Scotland Yarders who might wonder what has become of us and begin making enquiries. There is also my brother, who would find my sudden, unexplained vanishment sufficient reason to apply his great brain to finding me. Why bother with all that when you can instead make good use of us? When you can turn us back out into the world alive and well, if no longer quite our former selves?"

A chill ran through me. Was that her intent? Were Holmes and I destined to become vessels for occupation by alien sentiences?

Mrs Klein's silence was answer in itself.

"What I am uncertain about," Holmes went on, "is whether your fellow Cultured know what the Palimpsest Process truly implies. They heard Dysart use the term a short while ago, and none seemed puzzled by it or queried it, so I feel safe in assuming that they are familiar with the concept. Nor, for that matter, did any of them bat an eyelid at the sight of a half-naked man with a head crowned with fungus. Indeed, some of the glances they directed towards him were admiring and envious. Do they realise, though, that the procedure necessitates the erasure of one's own personality in order to accommodate that of a Mi-Go? Have you withheld the full truth from them, in order to ensure their compliance when the time comes? Or do you have to force them into it, perhaps at gunpoint? Is that how it went with Dysart and Woolfson?"

"It's heartening that you don't know everything, Mr Holmes."

"I do know that Douglas Maberley was in on the secret, and it drove him to such a paroxysm of despair that he took his own life."

"Douglas. Poor, sweet, beautiful Douglas." Again, Mrs Klein was exhibiting a hint of remorse, but again, too little of it to be worth anything. "In hindsight, I should not have allowed the closeness between us to develop to the extent that it did. I wanted that young man as one of The Cultured almost as much as I wanted him for myself, but my romantic feelings towards him blinded me to his shortcomings."

"By 'shortcomings' you mean his sense of morality."

"I showed him this room. There was a girl in it at the time, Kitty someone-or-other, halfway through the healing part of the process."

"Her name was Kitty Winter," I said.

"I explained everything to Douglas. I thought he would understand. But seeing the Winter girl and learning what purpose she served – it was too much for him. He fled before I could stop him."

"But the letter you sent coaxed him into returning," said Holmes.

"Back he came," said Mrs Klein, "but he was no more sanguine about the situation than before. If anything, the opposite. I understood then that I would have to find some way of securing his silence. Given the wretched state he was in, it was easy. 'If we really cannot come to some sort of accommodation, Douglas,' I said, 'then I no longer have any need for you. Go. Imagine life without me. Imagine your future and how empty it is going to be. It will be no future at all.'"

"You knew exactly the effect those words would have on him," said Holmes. "They would tip him over the edge, and by killing himself he would save you the bother of having to do the job."

"He left me, a broken soul, sunk in misery. News of his death reached me a day later. I was devastated."

"Of course you were."

"I did love Douglas. I thought he had a lot to offer, and it was a pity things ended how they did. But still…"

Even as these callous words left her lips, Mrs Klein was reaching for the doorknob with her free hand, while still keeping the gun in her other hand aimed unerringly at Holmes. I did not understand what she was up to, until all at once she snatched the door open.

Immediately outside the room stood the housemaid, Susan. She was half bent over, looking startled.

"Susan," said Mrs Klein, coolly. "How long have you been standing there?"

"I don't know what you mean, ma'am. I was just passing."

"Don't take me for an idiot. You had your ear to the keyhole. It's quite obvious. I heard the faint creak of a floorboard directly outside the door about a minute ago, and another a half-minute after that. Come in."

"I have work to attend to, ma'am. I should be on my way."

"I said come in. That's not a request."

Nervously Susan stepped across the threshold. Her eyes widened as she took everything in, from the body on the table to the fungus on Dysart's head to the Colt in her mistress's hand.

"You have been very foolish, Susan," Mrs Klein said. "Your nosiness has brought you to dire straits."

"Mrs Klein, please, I am frightened." Susan's hands fluttered like birds. "That gun. This room. I meant nothing by listening at the door. It was mere curiosity. I heard voices within, and knowing the room is normally locked and we staff are forbidden to enter, I gave in to my worst instincts. I am very sorry. Please… Please can we pretend this didn't happen? I should not want to be sacked."

"Being sacked is the least of your concerns. You have seen more than you ought, more than is safe for you to have seen."

"Dear Lord!" Susan wailed. "I hope you do not mean what I think you mean. Oh, madam!" She fell to her knees before Mrs Klein and clutched her mistress's skirt, abject in her terror. "I will say nothing. I vow it. You can count on me. Only, I beg you, spare my life."

Isadora Klein looked down at her employee with utter pitilessness.

"You have been a decent enough housemaid, Susan," said she. "You carry out your duties diligently, if with little flair. Against that, you are a dull-witted thing, and there is a haughtiness about you that ill befits your station. On balance, I don't think I shall miss you greatly."

Susan tottered to her feet and started backing away from Mrs Klein. Her hands were raised defensively. "You would shoot me?" she said in a plaintive but also slightly petulant manner. "Kill me in cold blood?"

"I don't see that I have a choice."

"Before all these witnesses?"

"They, for one reason or another, are guaranteed to keep mum."

Susan found herself butting up against the shelves of chemicals. "And there is nothing I can say that will make you change your mind?"

"Not a thing."

Mrs Klein had yet to switch the snub-nosed revolver from Holmes to Susan. She must still be judging my friend the greater threat of the two. But it would only take a split second to swing the weapon towards the housemaid, fire the fatal shot, and swing it back to Holmes.

"Well then." Susan straightened up and fixed her mistress with a defiant glare. In that moment of finality, she seemed to have discovered some backbone. "Queen takes king, it would appear."

"A chess analogy?" said Mrs Klein. "From you, Susan?"

"I have hidden depths, ma'am."

"Not that deep. I take it I am the queen, but how do you reckon yourself a king? You are, if anything, a pawn."

I darted a glance at Holmes. His eyes met mine and I saw, visible even beneath his Langdale Pike makeup, a look I recognised. It said, *Be prepared. Something is about to happen.*

The mention of "queen takes king" had told me that Susan the housemaid was more than she seemed. I sensed that Holmes had known it all along. Now, assuming I was right, I had the distinct feeling that events were about to take a turn for the dramatic.

*

Susan's hand groped for the shelves behind her and fastened onto a flask containing a blotchy purple fungus. She snatched up the flask and held it aloft.

In a flash, Mrs Klein's expression went from complacent to appalled.

"What do you think you are doing, woman?" she snapped. "Put that down at once. You have no idea the danger you are putting us all in."

"I have every idea," said Susan. "If I smash this flask on the floor, the fungus inside it will also break open and will release a deadly infection."

"How can you know that?"

"Does it matter? What you ought to be asking is how willing I am to imperil my own life as well as everyone else's in this room. The answer, by the way, is perfectly willing."

Mrs Klein turned the revolver on her. "And if I shoot you before you can throw the flask down...?"

"Then I will drop it anyway. It and the fungus will still break, and you shall be as dead as I am. Your death will just take much longer than mine and be considerably more unpleasant."

"This is a bluff. You are not suicidal."

"Can you afford to test that theory?"

"Then what do you want?"

"I want you to allow Mr Holmes, Dr Watson and myself to go free."

"I don't think I can do that."

"A pity," said Susan, brandishing the flask. "Then we all perish."

Unless I was much mistaken, the fungus in the flask was the same kind that had killed three crewmen aboard the *Sea Unicorn*, as related by Peter Carey in his logbook. They had died in feverish agony. I did not relish going the same way myself.

Neither, it seemed, did Isadora Klein.

"You have the upper hand, Susan," said she. "I think I now know who you are, and if I am right, then I would be wise not to challenge your determination." She lowered the revolver.

"I thought you might see sense." Susan gestured to Holmes and me. "Gentlemen, if you will make good your exit..."

As I moved, I saw Steve Dixie out of the corner of my eye preparing to stop me. Mrs Klein gave a shake of her head.

"Let him go, Steve," she said.

"But, Mrs Klein…"

"They have got the better of us, thanks to Susan-who-is-not-Susan. They have won the round, but that does not mean they will win the fight."

With Susan keeping a wary eye on Mrs Klein, Holmes and I filed towards the door.

"I never even suspected," Mrs Klein said to her erstwhile housemaid. "You have been in my employ for half a year, and all that time you were hiding your true identity. Why have you rebelled against the Mi-Go? What has made you a turncoat?"

"One might ascribe it to a conflict of loyalties," Susan said. "Something a monomaniac like you would never understand."

Mrs Klein feigned offence. "Monomaniac. I am wounded to the quick." Her lip curled as she added, "You should know that your betrayal will not go unpunished."

"Do you think I am intimidated, Mrs Klein?" said Susan. "I have been living under your roof all this time, undetected. You hadn't the least clue who I really am. Punish me? How easy do you think it will be even to find me when you have the entire world to search?"

"It will happen. Be in no doubt about that."

By this time, Holmes and I were in the corridor, and Susan was backing out of the room, the flask still held above her head.

"It's a shame," she said to Mrs Klein. "If you hadn't just threatened me, I might have shown mercy. As it is, you have forced my hand."

Grabbing the doorknob, she hurled the flask into the room and slammed the door shut behind her.

"Run," she said to Holmes and me. "If you value your lives, run!"

Holmes and I needed no further urging. We all three

sprinted down the corridor, even as screams of rage and terror issued from the Palimpsest Chamber. Behind us, I heard the door open. A gunshot rang out. A bullet ricocheted off a wall and whined past us. We rounded a corner and kept running. Holmes barged through a door, and Susan and I followed him. We entered a library. Holmes crossed straight over and thrust open one of the French windows. We emerged onto the lawn, and onward we ran, beneath the starlit sky. A boundary wall appeared ahead, and Holmes scrambled to its apex, leaning down to offer a helping hand to me and then to Susan. When the three of us were over the wall, we resumed running. We stopped only after a mile or so, once we were sure nobody was pursuing us. I bent to catch my breath and allow my racing heart to settle.

We were on a lane somewhere in the forested depths of Harrow Weald, and by unspoken mutual consent we began walking, looking for a highway that would take us back to London proper.

*

The three of us had been plodding along in silence for several minutes until Holmes said, "Thank you, Irene."

"You're welcome," said Susan.

"Are you not going to revert to your usual form?"

"Not yet. Call it vanity, but Susan's frame is more robust than mine. Her dress does not hang well on Irene Adler. I imagine the same is true of you and Langdale Pike's clothing."

"At least I shall now no longer have to wear this outfit, or the padding and theatrical makeup," Holmes said with feeling. "I cannot say I am sad about that."

"It was a good disguise. Worth the effort, I reckon."

"Yet you saw through it at a glance," said Holmes. "'Lofty but not insurmountable, those mountains are,' Susan the housemaid said, talking about the Langdale Pikes. 'They look like they're hard to penetrate, but really there's less to them than meets the eye.' You might as well have just pointed a finger at me and cried, 'Sherlock Holmes! I know you are Sherlock Holmes!'"

"It wasn't simply your eclectic choice of character name," said Irene Adler. "I know disguise. It is what I do. It is who I am. There is nobody who can fool me with one, not even you, Sherlock. Besides, I wasn't only telling you I knew who you were."

"No. You were announcing your own identity too. I suppose I should be thankful that you did not betray me to Mrs Klein." Holmes's eyes narrowed. "Or did you? She told me she knew all along who Langdale Pike really was."

"Not my doing. Which isn't to say that the thought of debunking Langdale Pike did not cross my mind. I was worried you might queer my pitch. I thought, however, that if I revealed myself to you, you would immediately perceive that I was engaged in a scheme of my own and leave me to it."

"I did, although I wasn't wholly certain I could trust you. Not until you, as Susan, defused that contretemps between Langdale Pike and Steve Dixie."

"What is this 'scheme of my own' you mention, Miss Adler?" I asked. "Not that I am ungrateful to you for getting us out of the tight corner we were just in, but I've always understood you to be in league with the Mi-Go, which would mean, by extension, with Mrs Klein and The Cultured as well. Have you changed sides, and if so, how come?"

"Simply put, Doctor, my participation in Mi-Go activity on Earth was always half-hearted at best. As I'm sure your friend will have told you, I was more or less blackmailed into working for them. It was either agree to High Priest Glaw Za-Jooll's stipulations or die. I have done various 'favours' for the Outside Things over the years, out of a sense of obligation more than anything. Yet that sense of obligation has worn increasingly thin."

"Would one of those 'favours' have been aiding Josiah

Amberley in his revenge plot?" said Holmes. "A plot which, I might add, nearly cost me my life."

"You were never in any real danger, Sherlock," said Miss Adler reprovingly. "I had every confidence you would outwit Amberley. Cunning though he was, he was hardly your match."

"But why embroil me in his plans at all?"

"I think you know why. I hoped you would believe you had defeated the conspiracy of which I was a part and would thus devote yourself to other things. I was trying to keep you out of harm's way."

"Out of harm's way, or out of *your* way?"

"Both. By then – what was it, five years ago? – I was coming round to the idea that the Mi-Go might pose a threat to us, even if I had no clear notion how or why. Their actions could easily be construed as ill-disposed towards mankind. As for the Cultured, the Mi-Go's tame thralls, they struck me as fanatics and thus also potentially dangerous – Isadora Klein especially so."

"She whom you yourself had introduced to the Mi-Go in 'eighty-six."

Miss Adler nodded. "Mrs Klein would convey the Mi-Go's instructions to me, and I would act upon them. It was she who organised the extortion campaign I put into action back in 'eighty-eight."

"Professor Mellingford and the rest," I said.

"Yes. The more I consorted with her, however, the more I grew disenchanted with her. For one thing, she does not blink enough. Word to the wise: never trust anyone who does not blink enough. For another, her behaviour has become increasingly immoderate as time goes by. From being a convert, she is now a zealot."

"Was," I corrected. "Was a zealot. She is dead now, or as good as."

"I suppose so, assuming that purple fungus is as virulent as I understand it to be. She, Steve Dixie, Octavius Dysart –

or should that be Ranax Za-Ko? Ezra Woolfson too. All doomed."

"Thus, in light of your concerns about The Cultured," said Holmes, "you took it upon yourself to spy on them, in the guise of Susan."

"Six months ago Mrs Klein's then-housemaid came into an unexpected legacy, some five hundred pounds," said Miss Adler.

"Courtesy of you, no doubt."

"Naturally she quit, and I, knowing that a sudden vacancy had come up among the domestic staff at The Three Gables, applied for the job and got it. Or rather, Susan did. She came with excellent references."

"Immaculately forged, I should imagine."

"They were, even if I do say so myself. I had to be very careful in my spying. I couldn't be sure the Mi-Go would not realise that their tame shapeshifter was, in shapeshifted form, snooping around in the home of their primary human agent. The consequences of being discovered would no doubt have been dire."

"You put yourself at great risk," said Holmes. "Yet you did not want me exposing myself to the same risk." He sounded – a rare thing for Sherlock Holmes – puzzled.

"Is that so unreasonable?" Miss Adler said. "There are some things we would rather do ourselves than leave to those whom we – we admire."

I could have sworn she had been about to use a verb other than "admire", a much more emphatic one.

"I should be flattered," said Holmes.

"You should. At any rate, there I was, making progress, and who should come blundering onto the scene, swathed in stage makeup, but Sherlock Holmes?"

"Blundering!" my friend expostulated.

"All I could do was look on, at arm's length, and hope that your investigation would not interfere with mine."

"But you did get involved on that one occasion," I said. "That 'contretemps' Holmes just referred to."

"I knew Pike would have to take a drubbing from Dixie in order for the imposture to be preserved," she said.

"And you could not bear to see Holmes badly beaten?"

"There is that, but more importantly, I was afraid Dixie would realise, during the course of the pummelling, that his victim was wearing stage makeup and sporting a fake paunch. I didn't know then that Mrs Klein was already wise to Sherlock Holmes's game. By stepping in I redirected Dixie's ire onto me, confident that not even he would hit a woman."

"The upshot of all this," Holmes said, "is twofold. First, if Mrs Klein has indeed received a fatal infection from the purple fungus, then The Cultured are done for. Without her to guide them and spur them on, they will fall apart. By the same token, the Mi-Go will have lost their principal agent on Earth. Their plot has unravelled. Second, we know what that plot is: the systematic replacement of certain prominent individuals with Outside Things."

"They were trying to infiltrate British society," I said, "using Mi-Go sentiences occupying human bodies."

"And 'trying' is the operative word there, Doctor," said Miss Adler. "Messrs Dysart and Woolfson were the first Cultured to undergo the Palimpsest Process. The first and, as it transpires, the last."

"All in all, a decent night's work," said Holmes. "However, we still have to ascertain the Mi-Go's motives. If Mrs Klein is to be believed, they wish to bring about positive change in the world."

"But if that's the case," I said, "why not be upfront about it? Why all the subterfuge?"

"Precisely, Watson. It may simply be because people do not always want what is perceived to be 'good' for them. They resent it as meddling or nannying, and kick back against it. The Mi-Go understand this and would prefer to avoid it.

We must, furthermore, be open to the possibility that they have other allies besides The Cultured, and other plans in motion."

"You could usefully apply yourself to that problem, Sherlock," said Miss Adler.

"I? And not you too? Now that you have shown firmly where your allegiances lie, Irene, do you not feel it incumbent upon you to resist the Outside Things further? There is a certain pleasing irony in you deploying the talents they gave you against them."

"No," was the adamant reply. "I am done with all this. It is time I moved on to other things. I have been at the Mi-Go's beck and call for fifteen years. I would like to start living my life wholly on my own terms again."

"That," said Holmes, "is a shame."

Miss Adler brushed a hand against his cheek. "I have every faith in you, Sherlock. You too, Dr Watson. And now I shall take my leave of you. Good luck!"

So saying, she got down on all fours, and next moment underwent a transformation so startling, I can scarce put it into words. Her face contorted, her nose elongating, her eyes growing round and yellow. Her limbs shrivelled. Her back arched. Her entire body writhed and distended. Hair appeared on her skin where no hair had been. Her dress slithered off her like a tent whose guy ropes have been severed. Within seconds, in place of Susan the frowsty housemaid there was a fox, standing with a puddle of feminine garments around its feet.

The fox – a rather handsome specimen, with alert ears, thick brush and lustrous marmalade-orange coat – looked at both Holmes and myself. Its eyes were amber-coloured and seemed infinitely wise. Then, with a decisive flick of its tail, the creature turned and loped off into the woods at the side of the lane.

It was a full minute before I found my voice.

"That was… remarkable," I said, still staring off in the direction the fox had gone.

SHERLOCK HOLMES and the HIGHGATE HORRORS

"Memorable, I'd say," Holmes opined.

"Well, I can now add housemaid and fox to the forms I have seen Irene Adler in, and yet still I have not met her as she normally is. At this rate, perhaps I never shall. I can't help but wonder, though, why someone who has made a point of saying she does not wish to be hunted would choose to transform herself into, of all things, an animal that is routinely hunted."

"I am sure she will be fine, Watson," my companion said tersely.

"I was just making light of the situation."

"Well, kindly do not."

With that, Holmes bundled up Miss Adler's discarded clothing and disposed of it amid a clump of brambles. Then we continued on our way.

Soon we could make out the lights of London, shedding their glow against the bowl of the heavens, and not long after that we were on the Harrow Road, an arrow whose unwavering course would take us into the heart of the capital. Throughout the journey, Holmes was sunk in silence, and I, sensing the depth of feeling that had given rise to this brown study, chose not to intrude upon it.

*

All the next day, and the day after, Holmes scoured the newspapers for reports about Isadora Klein and The Three Gables. He expected headlines declaring that a noted society hostess had been taken severely ill, had been ferried to hospital, and had died despite doctors doing their utmost to save her. None appeared.

Eventually, frustrated by the lack of information, Holmes took himself back up to Harrow Weald. I accompanied him. I felt no little trepidation as we passed through the gates of The Three Gables and approached the house. If Mrs Klein was alive and well, I doubted she would receive us cordially, and I did not much look forward to another confrontation with

Steve Dixie. My service revolver was in my pocket, however, which helped allay some of my concerns.

In the event, the house was empty. There was no answer to Holmes's knock, and through the ground-floor windows we saw rooms whose furniture was draped in dustsheets. Going round to the back, we got in through the same door I had used the night before last. The broken windowpane had not been replaced.

Our footfalls echoed hollowly through the corridors. There is a peculiar kind of stillness that falls over a property when it is abandoned, an almost forlorn hush, and just such a hush now filled The Three Gables. Everyone had vacated the place, from the lady of the house down to the lowliest servant.

"Where?" I said to Holmes. "Where have they gone to?"

"With Mrs Klein's resources," came the reply, "it could be anywhere."

"So she lives."

"Maybe, or maybe, ravaged by sickness, she has taken herself off somewhere to die, bringing the similarly afflicted Steve Dixie, Ezra Woolfson and Ranax Za-Ko along with her."

We tried the Palimpsest Chamber. The room had been cleared out. Only the tables and shelves remained, all bare. The smell of bleach hung in the air.

"Someone cleaned up here," I said. "Scrubbed it thoroughly to get rid of any trace of the purple fungus."

"So it would appear."

"Then this has been a wasted journey."

"Not entirely," said Holmes. "We may at least be able to bring some resolution to the families of three missing girls."

We searched the grounds, and eventually, in an overgrown corner behind the walled kitchen garden, we found a patch of disturbed earth. Some cursory digging revealed a silk-clad arm, and we knew we had found the last resting places of Kitty Winter, Cornelia Waunchope and Abigail Roxbury-Trent.

Back in London, Holmes contacted Scotland Yard to

report our grim findings: three graves at The Three Gables. To Sir Hartley Winter he conveyed, in person, the tragic news about his daughter's demise. He also tried to get in touch with Morley Babington, but the prepaid reply slips with his telegrams were returned blank. Visiting the theatre impresario's house in Bloomsbury, he was told by a manservant that "Mr Babington has been called away unexpectedly on business." The fellow said that his master had given no indication when he might return, and he had no knowledge where he had gone.

Holmes made enquiries into the whereabouts of other members of The Cultured, with similar results.

"They have scattered to the four winds," he said.

"Is that a good sign, or a bad one?" I asked.

"You mean have they fled in terror, never to be of concern to us again, or have they gone to ground in order to regroup and retrench? I wish I could say."

"So this is not over yet."

"At the very least, we must keep on our guard," said Holmes. "And not just in the conventional manner, either, such as looking out for ambushes or watching for spies."

"Explain."

"If Mi-Go can inhabit human bodies, Watson, they can impersonate anyone. You could secretly be an Outside Thing, for all I know."

"You don't suppose for one moment that—"

"No, my friend. No. I am not suggesting you are a Mi-Go sentience masquerading as John Watson."

"I am glad to hear it."

"Although, having said that, you were away in France for a goodly length of time. Could it be that Mrs Klein or some other Mi-Go agent got to you there and subjected you to the Palimpsest Process?" Before I might object again, Holmes wafted a hand as though batting the thought aside. "It is a serious concern nonetheless, broadly speaking. The Palimpsest Chamber at The Three Gables might not be the only one in existence."

"So we must be careful."

"Very careful," said Holmes. "We cannot be certain that the people around us, even people we know well, can be trusted."

That night, as I ate supper with my wife, I looked across the table at her. She smiled back at me in that winsome way of hers, head on one side, eyes bright. I recalled how we had met: her near-accident with the pantechnicon, my saving her. Could it have been staged?

"What is it, John?" said she.

"Nothing," I replied. "Nothing at all, my dear. I was just thinking how fortunate I am to have met you."

She smiled again, and I resumed eating, and the food tasted like coaldust in my mouth.

PART VII

Summer 1903

OFTEN I HAVE BEEN ASKED BY MY READERS WHY Sherlock Holmes retired to Sussex when he did. He left London in the autumn of 1903, just shy of fifty and in excellent physical and mental condition for a man of that age. One might even say he was still in his prime and had many years of productive professional life ahead of him. What prompted him to give it all up and move to the south coast to keep bees? Was there some drastic catalysing incident? That is what these people want to know.

In answer to such queries I tend to say that Holmes simply grew tired after a long and storied career and fancied a change of scene. He had accumulated sufficient funds to live off comfortably and felt that his twilight years would be better spent in the fresh air and open spaces of the countryside, rather than the teeming, smoky cloisters of the capital. Besides, he did not abandon crime-solving altogether, merely became selective about which cases he pursued, taking only those that piqued his interest or had unique qualities he had not encountered before.

That is the response I give, but it is not the truth.

This is the truth, and it happened a couple of months after the adventure just previously recounted, on a humid, damp day late in the summer of 1903. Many will remember that particular season as being unusually rainy and inclement, for the entire world's weather had been adversely affected by three large volcanic eruptions around the globe earlier in the year. Sherlock Holmes was alone in his rooms at Baker Street when an illustrious caller came. I, for the record, was not present for any of the following events and am reproducing them here from Holmes's own very detailed account.

*

The caller's name was Count Negretto Sylvius, and he did not come unaccompanied. With him was a fellow called Sam Merton, and although Sylvius introduced him as "my legal representative", Merton – from his perpetual scowl to his thick neck and the coarse stubble on his chin – was a henchman through and through.

Billy showed both men in, then offered to stay. "If you need some company, Mr Holmes…" he said with a significant glance at Merton.

"Thank you, Billy. I'm sure I shall be fine. The count's and his colleague's purpose here is purely social, I am quite confident."

Billy withdrew, and the two visitors faced Holmes across the room. The pair could not have formed a greater contrast with each other. Where Merton was pallid and lumpen, Sylvius was swarthy and lithe. Where Merton was clad in hobnail boots and brown tweed, Sylvius wore a sleek tailored suit and patent leather dress shoes. Where Merton was a sullen, brooding presence, Sylvius was all sparkle and flamboyance. A ring adorned practically every one of the count's fingers, while his outfit was enhanced by a diamond-stud tiepin and silver cufflinks, and the glitter of all this jewellery was matched by his eyes, which had the darting watchful brilliance of a jackdaw's.

"Well, well, well," said Holmes. "I suppose I should consider myself honoured. I was expecting just the one visitor, not two. I shall regard you, Mr Merton, as an unlooked-for bonus. Might I enquire which law firm you work for?"

"I am 'ere, Mr 'Olmes," said Merton, "in a purely hadvisory capacity. Should matters become 'eated, then I shall step in and offer the benefit of my hexpertise." The last word was accompanied by the grinding of fist into palm, leaving no doubt as to the nature of the "hexpertise" being referred to.

"And does your advisory role encompass the correct usage of aspirates?" said Holmes. "Or should that be 'haspirates'?"

Merton's piggish little eyes looked at him with equanimity. "I am not known for taking humbrage easily, but be in no doubt, sir, that if the circumstances dictate, my 'ostility is both swift and fierce."

"Noted. I shall be at pains not to rouse your 'atred, lest I be on the receiving end of marked haggression."

Merton's fist stopped its grinding for a moment, then recommenced, this time more intently.

"Gentlemen, gentlemen," said Sylvius. "There is no need for discourtesy. I am here to do business, that is all, and I have every hope that we may comport ourselves peacefully and with civility throughout." The count's accent churned all consonants to gravel, betokening his roots in an eastern European principality. "You, Mr Holmes, have something which I want and which is rightfully mine. I would like to know your terms for returning it to me. Is it money you are after, perchance? My chequebook is at your disposal. Name the sum."

"Tempting," said Holmes, "and yet money is not a motivating factor for me."

"Then what other form of inducement might I bring to bear?"

"Not the sort your colleague Mr Merton has in mind, I should hope. No, Count, I am quite prepared to surrender the item in question to you without any financial recompense."

Sylvius's eyebrows rose towards his slicked-back hairline. "You are letting me have it for free?"

"Free. Gratis. Not a penny."

"This is not at all what I expected."

"How pleasing it is to have wrongfooted you. What you're after lies on that shelf over there, covered with a tea towel."

Sylvius directed Merton to go and look where Holmes was indicating. Merton removed the tea towel to reveal a metal cylinder with a glass porthole, visible through which was a brain suspended in liquid. The cylinder was of the chunky manmade variety, not the stranger and sleeker Mi-Go original.

The brain sported a bright red fungus at the front, its tendrils tethering it to the cylinder's interior.

"Take it, by all means," said Holmes with a magnanimous wave of the hand. "The tea towel too, if you like."

"I do not understand," said Sylvius as Merton covered the cylinder again and removed it from the shelf. "You went to a great deal of trouble, I should imagine, stealing the thing. Now you return it to me, for no reward? Why?"

"I did not say for no reward. I said for no financial recompense."

"Ah. I see. You want something else."

"Nothing much. Just a few minutes of your time, Count."

"That is all?"

"Can you refuse me? Your man already has the cylinder in his hands, demonstrating my good faith. Why not reciprocate?"

Sylvius shrugged his shoulders. "I see no reason not to sit and, as you English say, have a chinwag."

"But on your own," said Holmes. "Without your hadmirable legal representative present."

A frown creased the aristocrat's smooth brow. "I am not so sure."

"What do you fear? That I might attack you? I would have nothing to gain from it. But if it's reassurance you seek, how about this? Mr Merton can remain outside, on the landing, with his booty. He will not be privy to our conversation, but should anything untoward occur, you may summon him with a cry and he can be back here in a trice."

"I'm not sure it's a good idea, sir," Merton said. "Mr 'Olmes might 'ave ways of silencing you as 'e hassaults you, so you cannot call out."

Sylvius studied Holmes carefully. "No, Merton. I think our friend here is sincere. I think I will not even need you to sit outside the room. Go downstairs. Take the cylinder with you. Wait in the carriage for me."

Merton hesitated. "If you're quite certain…"

SHERLOCK HOLMES and the HIGHGATE HORRORS

"Quite certain. But in order to allay your concerns... Mr Holmes, do you give me your word, as a gentleman, that no harm shall come to me if I stay?"

"You have it."

"There," said Sylvius. "Englishmen never break their word. They are famous for it the world over. Off you go, Merton. I shall see you shortly. And, Merton?"

"Yes?"

"Look after it, I beg you." The entreaty was solicitous to the point of being plaintive. "It is very precious."

Sam Merton exited with his burden, and Holmes invited Sylvius to take a seat.

"Cigar? Cigarette? A drink?"

The count shook his head. "Not that I don't trust you, Mr Holmes, but..."

"But my offer of hospitality may disguise something more sinister. Poison, for instance."

"You'll forgive my caution."

"Did you not just say something about Englishmen never breaking their word?"

"Ha ha! I only told Merton that in order to convince him to leave. I think there are any number of people in your nation's colonies and protectorates who can justly claim that the English are as untrustworthy as you can get."

"A harsh assessment but not an unfair one," said Holmes.

"So, while I am prepared to give you the benefit of the doubt, I remain on my guard."

"Understandable. If nothing else, you are new to that body and it would be a shame to ruin it so soon. Akin to scratching a gramophone record with the needle the first time you play it."

"I don't follow," said Sylvius. "'New to that body'. My English is not perfect. Is this some popular saying I do not know?"

"Your English is immaculate," said Holmes, "and you know exactly what I am getting at. You, sir, are not Count Negretto Sylvius, not as such. I am, rather, in the presence of a member of the Mi-Go race. Furthermore, I do believe I am in the privileged position of conversing with none other than Glaw Za-Jooll, High Priest of Shub-Niggurath."

Count Sylvius said nothing for a moment, then gave a low chuckle.

"This is preposterous," said he.

"No," said Holmes, "'preposterous' would be to maintain the pretence when there is nothing to be gained by doing so. I have lured you here to Baker Street precisely because you are who I have just said you are – namely Glaw Za-Jooll – and I wish now to discuss certain topics with you in the hope of us arriving at some sort of understanding."

"And what if I don't wish to have such a discussion?" said Sylvius. "What is to stop me simply standing up and walking out of here? I'll tell you. Nothing. You no longer have your bargaining chip."

"You said you would give me a few minutes of your time."

"And I have."

"Hardly."

"Enough that I feel no compunction about leaving. Especially since you have started referring to me by some sort of absurd nonsensical name, as though we are children in the nursery. High Priest... What was it? Glow The Jewel? Ridiculous."

"Glaw Za-Jooll," said Holmes. "High Priest of Shub-Niggurath. If, as seems plausible, Mi-Go society is run along theocratic lines, that would make you a highly placed individual indeed. Might I even suggest you are a ruler?"

"That's it," said Sylvius. "I am leaving."

He half-rose from his chair. Holmes, without stirring from his own chair, said simply, "You don't have the brain."

"I beg your pardon?"

"I said you don't have it. The brain I stole from your hotel room."

"I do. Merton took it out to my carriage."

"What Merton took out," said Holmes, "is a confection of modelling clay, sculpted by me, and very nicely wrought, if I do say so myself. There is an artistic streak running through my family – my great-uncle was a French portraitist of some note – and it comes out in me from time to time, when the situation demands. The cylinder is the one from your apartment, but the brain and the fungus attached to it are mere replicas, as is the liquid they float in, a confection of water, gelatine and food dye which looks indistinguishable from the original nutrient-rich solution. I have the real items and am keeping them safe. My bargaining chip remains in my hands."

"No," said Sylvius.

"Go down to your carriage and check, if you like. A bit of rending and tearing of the simulacrum should do the trick, although what a pity to destroy such a sculptural masterpiece. Alternatively, if you'll allow it, I shall fetch the actual brain for your perusal."

The count gave a slow nod of assent. "Very well. Get it. Prove you are not lying."

Holmes went to his bedroom and came back with another cylinder. This was one of the Mi-Go's own; indeed, the one Peter Carey had brought back from the Arctic. There was a brain inside, with red fungal adornment.

"The cylinder came into my possession a few years ago," Holmes said. "I deposited the real brain from your cylinder into this one, fungus and all, along with the nutrient solution, of course. So far, in spite of their relocation, both brain and fungus appear to be thriving."

"How do I know this is not a fake too?" said Sylvius.

"Easy." Holmes raised the cylinder above his head. "I shall dash the whole lot onto the floor. I wonder how long the brain will survive when deprived of its life-preserving 'womb'. Not long, I should imagine."

"No!" said Sylvius sharply, and then, more softly, "No. Please."

"Not willing to risk it, eh?"

"I do not know quite how ruthless a man you are, Mr Holmes, but you seem sufficiently of that persuasion that I must believe you."

"Wise." Holmes set the cylinder down on the table beside his chair, then re-seated himself. The cylinder lay within easy reach. Knocking it to the floor would be no trouble, requiring a mere sweep of his arm. "Now then, where were we? Oh yes. You were busy denying you are Glaw Za-Jooll. If you like, you may keep up the whole rigmarole of objecting, or we could just skip past that and get to the part where we talk matters over, man to man. Or rather, man to Mi-Go. Which is it to be?"

Count Sylvius deliberated for a fair while before at last, seemingly with a heavy heart, making his decision.

"Very well. Yes, I am Glaw Za-Jooll."

Holmes clapped his hands in delight. "How gratifying! I was far from being certain. I put my chances of being right at about fifty-fifty."

"You mean you tricked me into the admission," said Sylvius coolly.

"If you are ever to pass convincingly as one of us humans, Count, you must learn that we often fabricate. Some do it for sport, some for personal gain. When I do it, I do it professionally, in pursuit of my enquiries, knowing that the one sure way of eliciting the truth from a person is getting him to think he has no alternative but to admit it."

"But what led you to suspect my true identity?"

"For that, let me take you back a few weeks," said Holmes. "I had just put an end to The Cultured's operations at The Three Gables. Mrs Klein was gone without a trace, and The Cultured themselves appeared to have disbanded. Yet I knew who most of them were, having ostensibly joined their ranks in the guise of Langdale Pike, and I began to put feelers out. Telegrams flew from this room like snow, blizzarding throughout the country, and indeed, throughout Europe. Police stations and private investigators were contacted. Numerous favours were called in. Soon enough I had pinned down the whereabouts of approximately half of the people I sought. A few remained on these shores, in the remoter parts – the Scottish Highlands, the Cornish moors. A handful had gone to France. The great majority, however, were in Germany, in the west of that country, not far from the French border. They were clustered around Heidelberg, formerly the hometown of Mrs Klein, all of them staying in rented accommodation or hotels. In other words, there was the illusion of dispersal, but only the illusion. The Cultured had not disbanded so much as reconvened."

"I see."

"I realised then that the Palimpsest Process scheme would be resumed. The necessary materials and equipment had been taken from The Three Gables. All I had managed to do was delay The Cultured's plans, not avert them. Further Mi-Go sentiences had doubtless made their way across space from Yuggoth to Earth and been installed in human subjects, and more were coming. I began monitoring The Cultured's activities in and around Heidelberg, by means of various paid agents. In the dispatches those agents sent me, one name kept cropping up. Yours, Count Sylvius. You were consorting regularly with The Cultured, and indeed, were found to be travelling extensively across the Continent and also, on occasion, to England. I intuited that you were a go-between, liaising among The Cultured in their diverse boltholes. When next you came to this country, I was ready for you and contrived to follow you, in a range of disguises, as you went about your business."

"You spied on me."

"Spying implies distance," said Holmes. "I was next to you practically the whole time. You may recall you handed me a parasol I dropped in the Minories."

"That was an old woman."

"The very parasol," Holmes went on, "which sits in that

corner over there. See? You may also recall how you passed a pleasant ten minutes with a sporting man in Hyde Park, discussing the merits of Shropshire and Staffordshire as the best places for pheasant shooting."

"He was you? Like the old woman? But wait. I have this." Sylvius rolled up his sleeve to reveal the fungal mark denoting membership of The Cultured. "And you do too, do you not? It was bestowed on you when you were posing as Langdale Pike. Mine would have tingled when you were close by. How come it did not? How come, for that matter, it isn't now?"

"Mine has faded." Holmes, too, rolled up his sleeve, showing bare, unbesmirched forearm. "See? The mark was never renewed, and now is gone."

"Of course. That explains it."

Holmes buttoned up his sleeve again. "To your credit, Count, you proved really very engaging company. On every occasion our paths crossed, you could not have been more pleasant. I noticed, at times, that you stumbled over a word or phrase, and you seemed unaware of certain customs, as though discovering them for the first time. Anyone else might have thought this just the awkwardness of a foreigner, unfamiliar with our English ways. Not I."

"It is strange, because I know everything that Count Negretto Sylvius ever knew. I have access to his memories and to his habits and peccadilloes. I am just not at home with them yet. I feel as though I am walking around in a suit of armour, and every move I make requires concentration and effort. It is becoming easier as I grow more accustomed to being human. In time, I hope, it will be second nature."

"Wear a mask long enough and you cease to realise you are wearing a mask," said Holmes. "Speaking of masks, my final coup was posing as a fellow guest at the hotel where you are staying. Remember that baronet with the withered arm, the one you played gin rummy with one evening?"

"You."

"Me. By the way, you made a couple of errors during the game. You discarded a card you had just drawn from the discard pile, and once, you made an invalid declaration. I refrained from drawing attention to either."

Sylvius shook his head. "I had a hard time keeping the rules straight."

"Another man might have thought you were cheating," said Holmes. "I, though, saw a Mi-Go trying to be human and not quite succeeding. Of course, as that palsied baronet I was able to observe your comings and goings at the hotel, and when you brought a woman up to your suite one afternoon I understood that you might well be conducting a Palimpsest Process. You claimed that she was your wife, but I knew her to be the Most Honourable Xanthe Dudderidge, Marchioness of Kilminster, another Cultured. The next morning, you went out for a stroll alone, having given the chambermaid strict instructions not to enter the room to clean it, for your 'wife' had a headache and wished not to be disturbed. I, feeling unconstrained by that injunction, picked the lock. Within the suite I found Lady Xanthe lying athwart the bed, minus the top half of her head, her body swathed in life-sustaining fungus. In the wardrobe, what should there be but two cylinders, one with a scalp in it, the other a brain. I purloined the latter, and smuggled it out of the hotel in my suitcase."

"Whereupon you sent me a note, arranging this meeting."

"And here we are, Glaw Za-Jooll."

"Please. I much prefer it when you address me as though I am Count Negretto Sylvius. It is who I am destined to be for the remainder of my days."

"You could hardly have been granted a better vessel to be transferred into," said Holmes. "A young, healthy man, handsome, moneyed, well connected. It is equivalent to being a saloon passenger on an ocean liner, travelling in the utmost luxury, and entirely fitting for an august personage such as your Mi-Go self was."

"I am curious," said Sylvius. "When you told me you knew Glaw Za-Jooll was a ruler, you also said the principal form of government on Yuggoth is theocracy. How did you know that?"

"From the account given of a psychic journey to your planet by a certain Irene Adler. She described being met by you at a temple presided over by an enormous statue of Shub-Niggurath. It is usually only in cultures where church and state are indissoluble that religious icons of such size are erected. Add to that a high priest acting as spokesman, and theocracy is the likeliest probability. It is thanks to Miss Adler's account that I think I know, too, why you Mi-Go have gone to all this trouble journeying to Earth. For some time I have vacillated over the answer. My friend Dr Watson is of the opinion that you come in peace and want to help us. He has experienced war first-hand, and that has made him dovish, for I do not think he wishes anyone to experience it again. I, being of a more hawkish bent, have been inclined to regard you as an occupying force, gradually and clandestinely insinuating yourselves into our midst with a view to taking charge. On reflection, however, I have come to the conclusion that the truth lies somewhere between the two poles. You are not philanthropists and you are not invaders, but something else."

"What are we, then?" said Sylvius.

"Refugees," said Sherlock Holmes.

*

Count Sylvius's response to this assertion was a while in coming. At last, he cocked his head to one side and broke into a wry smile.

Holmes had his answer. His surmise had been correct.

"The Mi-Go race is dying out," said he. "Miss Adler reported seeing apparently empty cities on Yuggoth, and the large metropolis that was her final destination was distinctly underpopulated. Its streets were unswept, its public gardens unkempt. The impression she conveyed was of a barren, ailing world, once home to myriads, now practically devoid of inhabitants."

Sylvius said, "Do you know, I would like to take you up on your offer of refreshment after all. A whisky and soda, perhaps?"

Holmes served him from the decanter and the gasogene, and helped himself to a drink too. The frosty atmosphere that had attended Sylvius's arrival had thawed, and the two interlocutors now regarded each other, if not cordially, then with a marked lack of hostility.

"I am learning about human bodily pleasures," said Sylvius after taking a few sips of his drink, which he did clumsily, with a certain amount of slurping. "Whisky ranks high among them. On Yuggoth there are fungi that serve as inebriants. They none of them, however, generate quite the same sense of warmth and comfort as a good single malt. I feel ready now to relate the terrible tale of our race's demise, Mr Holmes.

"It began a few generations ago, when there came the first signs of a noticeable decline in our reproductive rate. The eggs in our hatcheries were not developing in the usual numbers. Out of every clutch laid, which would average a dozen in total, one might expect half to fail. That was the customary level of attrition. Of the hatchlings that emerged, half again would die within a short period due to sickliness or frailty. It was simply the way of things, and parents, by habit, did not become emotionally attached to their offspring until they had passed their first larval stage and become nymphs. However, all at once the level of attrition had begun to rise steeply. Now we were seeing only a single viable hatchling in every dozen, and sometimes not even that.

"Our scientists and doctors put their minds to the problem. Their conclusion was that a bacterial plague was devastating the embryos *in ovo*, fatally weakening them. Cures were attempted. None succeeded. The contagion spread and strengthened. The Holy Council sent out a decree stating that the only recourse was for parents to breed more prolifically, in order to compensate for the plummeting birth numbers. This, alas, bore no fruit. It resulted only in greater quantities of stillborn eggs.

"Naturally, we prayed. We prayed to Shub-Niggurath night and day, asking for intercession. Was she not a fertility goddess? A divine mother, famed for her fecundity? We made burnt offerings of the finest fungi we could cultivate and begged her to deliver us from the plague and reverse the population decline. Shub-Niggurath did not hear, or if she did, she did not listen.

"Years passed, and our elderly died off and precious few young arose to replace them. Faith in Shub-Niggurath waned. Our priest class retained power, and worship continued, but only because no better alternative suggested itself. Every '*Iä!*' we uttered was a reflex act, ingrained by tradition. We knew that we were doomed. There would come a time when no more of us were being born and those who remained were fated to be the last of our kind. To them would fall the tragedy of watching their fellows perish one by one until, in the end, nobody was left.

"I belong to that final generation, having been among the last batch of hatchlings where any survived. My father was High Priest Jooll Za-Trid, and I followed in his footsteps and joined the priesthood myself. I married, and my wife Wael Cha-Yor duly produced eggs over several mating seasons in succession. None hatched, and this was what spurred me to devise a plan. We whom you call Mi-Go could not continue on Yuggoth as before, that much was clear. Our extinction was inevitable. But could we live elsewhere? Might a different world not only provide a refuge but, being plague-free, allow us once more to procreate and thrive? And so we built ships…"

"Ships?" said Holmes. "Plural?"

Sylvius nodded. "Grew them from fungus, equipped them

with tendrils that could catch the solar winds like sails and propel them along, crewed them with volunteers, and despatched them into space. A ship flew to each of the planets in the solar system. But these scouting parties met with calamity. None of the worlds could support any form of life – save one."

"Earth. But Earth could still not support Mi-Go life. Its gravity is too much for your race's insectile frames."

"Nonetheless, we knew now that an inhabited planet existed, which offered a solution to our predicament, if a radical one. We might not be able to survive physically anywhere, but perhaps we could mentally. Our racial essence would not die out."

"On the proviso that you could find bodies for your sentiences to occupy," said Holmes. "That is where Dr Ulrich Felder and his fungal reanimates fit in to all this. Under Isadora Klein's auspices, Felder thought he was curing cancer. In fact, without realising it, he was conducting an experiment on your behalf, to see if the dead could be brought back to life as vacant vessels into which you could transfer yourselves."

"Just so," said Sylvius. "To inhabit the dead would be a tidy solution, like a hermit crab adopting a discarded shell. We did not foresee, however, that the fungus we instructed Mrs Klein to give him would create monstrosities."

"Perhaps, in time, Dr Felder would have overcome the problems in the process and made it work," said Holmes. "But he perished before he got the chance, in part due to my intervention. At the time, all I knew was that I was investigating a case of corpses coming back to life. Things went awry."

"It was a first attempt," said Sylvius philosophically. "We took a fresh tack."

"And so the Palimpsest Process was born. Mrs Klein started assembling her Cultured around her, selecting them for naivety and biddability, in order to give you a supply of host bodies."

"You speak of it as though we are the only ones who had something to gain."

"Indeed. You come bearing gifts."

"With our various fungi and our other technologies, we have much to offer the human race."

"My friend Watson has noted that your life-sustaining fungus, for instance, could be of immense benefit in the medical sphere."

"And that is not all," said Sylvius.

"Yes. Communications. Transportation. Recreation. All could be substantially enhanced through Mi-Go knowhow. It could be a Golden Age."

"The offer is there. *Quid pro quo*, I believe the saying is."

"Armaments, too," said Holmes, sounding a more sombre note. "At least some of your fungi are fatal to humans. They could be utilised for political assassination and, in quantity, with devastating effect on the battlefield."

"Or it could be a deterrent. Have you considered that? The mere threat of such a weapon might have the effect of preventing conflict from breaking out in the first place."

"If you think that, Count, you do not understand human nature. But in light of your proposed munificence, I now see why you had Irene Adler run her campaign of extortion against the British establishment. It was not to undermine this country. It was a gesture of goodwill directed towards The Cultured. You were demonstrating to them that you Mi-Go want a more peaceful world."

"The British Empire is currently the most powerful political entity on the planet," said Sylvius. "It is not, however, unquestionably a force for good. It wages wars. It subjugates nations and loots them of their treasures and natural resources. Think of the violence with which it suppressed the Indian Mutiny. Think of its treatment of China, forcefully selling opium to that country's people, causing addiction and untold misery. Think of the Boers who are even now being kept in squalid concentration camps, their settlements having been burned to the ground by British troops. Your empire purports to bring civilisation to the uncivilised parts of the world but itself behaves with barbarism."

"I've already indicated that I am not ignorant of the less savoury activities of my countrymen abroad," said Holmes. "I like to think that on the whole the empire does more good than harm."

"All we did, through Miss Adler, was attempt to clip its claws," said Sylvius. "What looked like sedition was actually an exhibition of common decency. The Cultured needed that in order to be convinced of our sincerity."

"And again, my intervention nipped the thing in the bud."

"Mr Holmes, you have constantly been – to use another botanical metaphor – a thorn in our side. I say that both with exasperation and a certain grudging admiration. Every way we turn, there is Sherlock Holmes, meddling, foiling, thwarting."

"It's a failing of mine."

Sylvius indicated the cylinder. "Even now, you incommode us."

"You cannot blame me for believing that you are an enemy," said Holmes. "Every one of your actions can be interpreted as antagonistic."

"Could it be that you are so accustomed to chasing and catching criminals, everything looks like a crime to you?"

Holmes mused on the matter. "I still have to be convinced that The Cultured are quite as blameless an organisation as they would like to make out. Mrs Klein seemed to have bent the other members to her will. A Golden Age cannot be built on the backs of dupes and thralls, with a fanatic as their leader."

"But don't you see, Mr Holmes?" said Sylvius. "The Cultured are not deceived or deluded. Far from it. The Cultured may be regarded as some of the bravest and most virtuous humans around."

"In what way?"

"In their capacity for self-sacrifice." He thumped his chest. "This body – that of Count Negretto Sylvius – was given voluntarily. Sylvius submitted to the Palimpsest Process knowing full well that he would be surrendering his sentience to mine, that he would in effect be dying."

"You mean…?"

"In return for the promise of a better world, the original Sylvius, and all the other Cultured, have bequeathed their existences to us Mi-Go. It reflects well on them, does it not?"

Holmes took a minute to digest the import of this revelation.

At last he said, "I am a fool. A blinkered fool. That interpretation – a form of martyrdom – never occurred to me. I thought either The Cultured would be acting under duress or else Mrs Klein had lied to them, or some unholy combination of the two. I never dreamed they were participating of their own free will. And it is done? Every one of The Cultured is now a Mi-Go? The transference of sentiences is complete?"

"Save for that brain there, yes. That is the last."

Holmes stood and paced the room for a while. Sylvius watched him, his gaze straying more than once to the cylinder. Finally Holmes stationed himself by the window, further from the cylinder than before but still only a couple of swift strides away. He did not think Sylvius would make a grab for the thing, but he remained close to it just in case. Outside, a soft, thick rain had begun to fall, its drops landing on the panes with metronomic insistence, like a slowed-down clock.

"Before you came, Count," Holmes said, "I had a certain course of action in mind. Our conversation has almost diverted me from it."

"Almost, but not wholly?"

"What it comes down to is self-determination."

"Whose self-determination?"

"Ours. Mankind's. If forty or so Cultured have given up

their bodies to house forty or so Mi-Go sentiences, that was their choice. I cannot change that."

"I sense a 'but' coming," said Sylvius.

Holmes fixed his gaze on him. "I cannot and will not allow you to alter the path of human progress through your so-called gifts. Your fungi, your technology – these may bring us on in leaps and bounds. They may indeed usher in a Golden Age. Equally, they may cause untold disruption and upset the equilibrium of the world. Progress happens at its own pace. When the time is right for gunpowder, gunpowder is invented. When the time is right for steam locomotion, steam locomotion is invented. I am not implying some divine plan. I am simply saying that progress is a natural process, like evolution. It cannot be hurried and should not be interfered with. And that, I fear, is what the sudden introduction of a whole slew of innovations, courtesy of you Mi-Go, would do: it would interfere with progress, dangerously. Like handing a loaded gun to a monkey."

"I take your point. If, though, the introduction was not sudden, but gradual, in measured stages…"

"Can you guarantee it? I think not. Then there is the fact that the distribution would not be even. It would be most likely concentrated within a single nation, namely Great Britain, that being where the majority of The Cultured hail from and whither, as was once the case with Rome, all the world's roads lead. Britain, as you have so cogently argued, is not an unalloyed force for good. Our empire is not saintly, any more than any other empire in history has been. Were it to obtain ways of consolidating its power even more firmly, there is no telling what it might do. Empires wax and wane. That is another natural process. Even the mightiest of them must fall in the end. Imagine if the British Empire were able to colonise the entire globe, though. Imagine if, with the panoply of Mi-Go devices and fungi at its disposal, it overcame all the other great powers. Its rule might last indefinitely. There would be stagnation, corruption, stasis. Whether one likes it or not, rivalry between nations is one of the main drivers of progress. It keeps things fresh."

"I am sure we could come to some sort of accommodation whereby our technology is parcelled out globally."

"Then there is the question of it falling into the wrong hands," said Holmes. "There are villains out there, Count, who would happily seize on it in pursuit of their nefarious ends. From criminal mastermind to tin-pot dictator, they would stop at nothing to control this new resource from outer space and reinforce their dominion over others with it. We, mankind, simply cannot be trusted with what you're offering us. That is what it comes down to. The gift is not the problem; the recipient is."

"I would hope that we could recognise the bad among you and avoid them."

"If only it were that easy. I have known many a malefactor whose smiling face and reasonable speech are a façade for the most despicable personality. Now, there is one final issue to consider: the simple fact of aliens living secretly in our midst and the consequences should their presence be discovered. However smoothly you Mi-Go slip into the pool of human civilisation, there is always the chance your true natures could become publicly known. The chance becomes greater if strange, unfathomable technologies emerge and can be traced back to any of you. People tend to treat outsiders with suspicion and hostility. I myself have been guilty of that with your race. You would not want to become the focus of the world's enmity. It could prove your undoing."

"For our own safety, we must keep a low profile, is that what you're saying?"

"The lowest. By all means conduct yourselves in a manner appropriate to your rank and standing. Just do nothing to draw untoward attention."

"You seem quite resolute in your stance," said Sylvius. "Is there nothing I can say that would sway you?"

"What I am telling you is that you Mi-Go must lead quiet, modest lives and leave us natives to get on with things in our own way."

"You make it sound like a *fait accompli.*"

"It is," said Holmes.

"And if I were to lodge an objection…?"

"This brain." Holmes moved over to the cylinder. "It is important to you, isn't it? I saw how fretful you were when Merton took the other brain out of here, which you did not know to be a fake. You can scarcely tear your eyes away from the real one. Lady Xanthe, Marchioness of Kilminster, has forfeited her life in order that the sentience of someone close to you can occupy her body. I submit that that someone is none other than Wael Cha-Yor."

Sylvius sighed. "So. That is how it is."

"I am right, am I not? The mind transfer must be complete by now, and here she sits, your wife, ready to take up residence in Lady Xanthe's body."

"I am not denying it is my wife. What disturbs me is that you are holding her life to ransom. I must agree to your demands, and ensure that my fellow Mi-Go do likewise, otherwise you will destroy her."

"You misconstrue my intentions," said Holmes. "I would not harm her. I was, in fact, on the point of inviting you to pick up the cylinder and take it with you."

"Oh."

"But before you do, there is someone you must meet. His carriage has just pulled up outside, and even now I hear his tread upon the stair."

Shortly, an elderly, cantankerous-looking man entered the room, shaking rainwater from his mackintosh. It was Lord Cantlemere, in all his hatchet-faced, whiskery glory.

Holmes made introductions. "Your Lordship, this is Count Negretto Sylvius, formerly Glaw Za-Jooll, High Priest of the Mi-Go."

Lord Cantlemere briskly shook the other's hand.

"Alien, eh?" he said, peering hard at Sylvius, as though the latter was a piece of crockery that had been broken and repaired and he was looking for the joins. "Wonders will never cease."

"Lord Cantlemere belongs to an elite body known as the Dagon Club," Holmes said to Sylvius. "He and his colleagues have, at my instigation, taken on the task of monitoring all Mi-Go on Earth. Their reach is extensive and their resources unlimited. Believe me when I tell you that nothing any of you does will escape their notice. At the same time, I am proposing that this be a relationship founded on mutual openness. You, Count, will liaise with the Dagon Club on a regular basis, keeping them informed of your people's movements and whereabouts. This will save the Dagon Club the trouble of having to have all of you watched and will help foster trust. Should that trust be betrayed in even the slightest degree, there will be consequences, and Lord Cantlemere will see to it that they are rigorously enforced. Is that not so, Your Lordship?"

"I am not a man to be trifled with," said Lord Cantlemere. "Remember that, Count Sylvius, and all shall be well."

"What about those Mi-Go who yet remain on Yuggoth?" said Sylvius. "Not all of us wish to come here. Some would rather stay on their home world to the bitter end. They do not think they could adapt to life in human form. I do not condemn them for that decision. I quite admire it. However, there are many who wish to make the crossing and live on as Earthmen."

Holmes pondered this. "If," he said, "you can find individuals willing to give up their bodies to house those Mi-Go migrants, as The Cultured did, then it is permissible. The act must be entirely voluntary, however, and the Dagon Club will invigilate to make sure that is true in every case. Should they adjudge that pressure has been applied – the least hint of arm-twisting – then the transference will not be allowed to go ahead and steps will be taken to prevent further Palimpsest Processes ever taking place. Does that sound workable, Your Lordship?"

Cantlemere nodded.

"But if we cannot promise to better your world in exchange for their sacrifice, what reason would people have to volunteer?" said Sylvius.

"That is your problem," Holmes said. "I have set out the terms of your leave-to-remain. What say you?"

The count looked from Holmes to the gaunt, fierce-eyed peer, and back again. "This *fait accompli* of yours," he said, with a bitter laugh, "is a choice that leaves no room for choice at all. What else can I do but accept?"

"Good. You and Lord Cantlemere can thrash out the details between you. You'll find this arrangement is best for everyone, Count."

"I hope so, Mr Holmes," said Sylvius. "I hope very much that you have not made a mistake and deprived mankind of a great opportunity."

"I hope that too," said Holmes.

At a gesture from Holmes, Sylvius gathered up the cylinder and its precious cargo.

Just as the count and Lord Cantlemere were leaving, Holmes said, "One last question, Sylvius."

"Yes?"

"Isadora Klein. Is she dead?"

Sylvius nodded. "The infection from the purple fungus took its toll. She and all those who were with her in that room perished."

"Irene Adler is not to be held accountable for that," Holmes said. "There will be no repercussions. Do you understand me?"

"Is this another *fait accompli*?"

"Very much so."

"Then yes."

"Let me hear you say it."

"No repercussions will be visited upon Irene Adler."

"You swear?"

"I swear."

"Thank you," said Holmes. "And, Count Sylvius?"

In the doorway, Sylvius turned. "Yes, Mr Holmes?"

"Welcome to Earth."

*

No sooner had the two men departed than Holmes rang for Mrs Hudson. The landlady duly appeared.

"Tea, Mr Holmes? It's about that time of day."

"That would be most kind. Set it for two, would you?"

Minutes later Mrs Hudson returned with a laden tray. "Whom are you expecting?" said she as she placed the tray on the dining table. "Someone important? Or might it by any chance be Dr Watson?"

"Are you excluding Watson from the category of important?" said Holmes.

"You know what I meant. He is long overdue a visit, and I miss his cheery face."

"I am expecting no one, not even the 'unimportant' Watson. Take a seat, would you?" Holmes indicated a chair at the table, then occupied another himself.

"I am having tea with you?" said Mrs Hudson, smoothing down her skirt. "This is unexpected. To what do I owe the honour?"

Holmes's expression turned sombre. "We can dispense with the niceties, my good woman. I think you well know why I might wish to talk to you."

The landlady's face ran a gamut of emotions, from apprehension to guilt to fear to resignation. At last she said, "You know, then," adding, "Of course you know. You are Sherlock Holmes. When does Sherlock Holmes ever *not* know?"

"Mrs Hudson," said Holmes, "I have lived under your roof since 1881. Twenty-two years, and in all that time you have been nothing but steadfast, loyal and long-suffering. I cannot be the most congenial of lodgers, what with visitors coming and going at all hours, and the strange smells from my chemistry experiments, and the occasional bout of violence."

"Not to mention the target practice," Mrs Hudson said, glancing at the V.R. bullet-pocks. "No, it has not always been plain sailing, Mr Holmes, that's for sure. Set against that, Dr Watson was charm itself when he was here, and was ever ready to smooth my ruffled feathers. He more than made up for your... drawbacks. And in recent years, as your practice has become so much more successful, you have been paying over the odds in rent. Don't think I am not grateful for that."

She made to pick up the teapot, but Holmes got there first. "I shall be mother for once," he said, and filled both of their cups. "Milk? Sugar? There we go. All of this preamble, my dear lady, is leading up to an apology."

"You," said Mrs Hudson, taken aback, "are apologising to me? But——"

"I am aware that you have an apology of your own to make. Let me get mine out of the way first. I regret to tell you that I am giving you notice. I am leaving Baker Street, and indeed, London. I am relocating to Sussex. I have already put in a bid on a very attractive smallholding atop the cliffs near Eastbourne. I should hear within a day or two whether my offer has been accepted, but the vendor is keen and the estate agent is optimistic."

"That is quite a step. Are you sure you will be happy, away from the capital?"

"I think I will be deliriously so. London's attraction has palled somewhat, and your behaviour is part of that."

"Yes. I can see why. When did you realise?"

"That you had been informing on me to The Cultured?" said Holmes. He gave a rueful shake of the head. "Really, I should have spotted it straight away. That's the trouble with people in whom you have implicit faith. They are the ones who can fool you best. The truth did not dawn until after Isadora Klein admitted she had known all along who Langdale Pike really was. There are only two individuals who could possibly have clued her in. Only two were aware that I was gadding about in that disguise. One is Watson. The other is you. Knowing Watson, he would rather die than betray me. That forced me to the uncomfortable conclusion that the guilty party must be you."

The landlady's eyes were moist, and she pressed trembling knuckles to her lips.

"Oh, Mr Holmes," she said. "I meant to tell you. Several times I came close to throwing myself on your mercy and confessing all. They had me in a bind, they did. The Cultured. They sent me a letter, about a year ago. You know my sister in Margate? The one I stay with from time to time? The letter threatened her. Her and her daughters. Nothing explicit, just a vague implication that if I didn't do as asked, my sister and nieces might no longer enjoy the best of health."

"You should have come to me," Holmes said. "Immediately. I would have dealt with it."

"The letter said that I was to say nothing to you, on pain of the same penalty. If it had been *me* they'd threatened, I would have told you all. I would not have cared. But my family..."

Now tears spilled from her eyes. Holmes was not moved to comfort her, but did proffer her his handkerchief.

"I presume," he said, "that The Cultured required you to report on my activities."

"I was to make notes and hand them, every Saturday, in an envelope to a man on a street corner in Covent Garden, where I go to buy the weekly flowers for the house. One time I was held up and arrived late to the rendezvous, only by a few minutes, but the man was not there. I was in a dreadful panic, and I wired my sister to check on her. She said all was well, although she mentioned that just that morning one of her daughters had had an encounter with a strange, menacing fellow. He had followed her home and made some appalling insinuations. My niece was left very shaken."

"A cunning stratagem. Doubtless the whole thing was prearranged. Your liaison was never at Covent Garden that day and it would have made no difference whether you had turned up on time or at all. The Cultured were toying with you, reminding you of their power over you."

"Well, it worked," said Mrs Hudson with a shudder. "And now I have made myself a Judas."

"Hardly that, madam. You caused me some minor inconvenience, that is all."

"Perhaps so. You are still here, are you not? Still alive and well. Nonetheless, it has been eating me up inside ever since. All this time, I have barely slept. I have dreaded us having this very conversation. But now that we are, I am relieved. The secret is out in the open at last."

"I am only sorry that I did not get around to broaching the topic sooner," said Holmes. "I have been very preoccupied lately."

"Is this what has persuaded you to abandon London? My betrayal? In which case, I beg you to reconsider. I shall never let such a thing happen again, I swear. In hindsight, I should have put the matter in your hands. I should have been confident you could resolve it. My instinct was to protect my family, and that overrode all other considerations."

"You are not the cause of my departure, Mrs Hudson. You are, rather, the justification."

"How so?"

"Your family were endangered through your association with me. That is unacceptable. Watson is different. He volunteered for this life of ours and is perfectly capable of looking after himself and, for that matter, his wife. You and your nearest and dearest, however, should not suffer simply because you happen to be my landlady. Therefore I am taking you out of the equation. On my own, in the wilds of Sussex, I put nobody but myself at risk."

"But, Mr Holmes..."

"I shall hear no more, my good woman. My mind is made up."

Mrs Hudson began crying again, more softly this time. Her tears were not of bitter self-recrimination now, but of sorrow.

"I shall be sad to see you go, Mr Holmes," said she.

"Not as sad as I am to be leaving your house, Mrs Hudson," came the reply. "I have never considered anywhere home but 221B Baker Street, and to my dying day, I never will."

He helped both of them to more tea, and they sat and drank together in silence, while the rain continued to tick and tock slowly, gently against the windowpanes.

*

Holmes broke the news to me via a letter. "You will be aware of Dr Johnson's maxim that when a man is tired of London, he is tired of life," it said. "I am neither. I find myself nonetheless compelled to seek the sanctuary of the countryside, where I mean to reside in perpetuity. I do not consider this the end of our partnership, and you are welcome to visit me whensoever you wish. In fact, I insist that you do."

As soon as I read the missive, I hurried over to Baker Street, although whether to remonstrate with my friend or simply to verify the situation for myself, I cannot say. Holmes was not there. He had packed up and left the same day he posted the letter. He had not seen fit to inform me of his intention in advance or in person, and this should have irked me, but I felt compassion more than anything. Presumably he had feared seeing me upset or disappointed. Matters of the human heart were not Sherlock Holmes's forte. Here was a man who would run headlong into a hail of bullets but shied away from emotional scenes.

474

I gazed wistfully around the no-longer-tenanted set of rooms. Gone were Holmes's books, including his library of arcane volumes, *Necronomicon* and all. Gone his chemistry bench, the Persian slipper with his tobacco in it, the violin and music stand. Gone, too, Peter Carey's toleware box and the modified orrery. All that remained were the furnishings, which were Mrs Hudson's own, and the V.R. on the wall, the one enduring mark left by Holmes upon the place.

A melancholy mood fell over me. Whatever Holmes might say about visiting him in his rural retreat, he was no longer here in town, no longer a short walk away. Would I ever again receive the call to arms? Would I ever again be summoned to his side with the promise of adventure? Would I ever again hear those thrilling words "The game is afoot"?

The phrase "the end of an era" is an overused one, but this felt like that to me.

Mrs Hudson's spirits seemed no less depressed than mine. "I am selling up, Doctor, and moving to Margate to be near my sister," said she. "Mr Holmes has only been gone a day, and already I know I shan't get used to his absence. I could easily find another lodger, but who could replace him? It is simpler if I go elsewhere and start afresh."

"I sympathise entirely," I said. "He is unique."

"That is one word for it. He did tender Billy a very generous severance. The lad tells me he is planning to emigrate to Canada. I shall miss him, too. I shall miss all of this."

At the time, I took Mrs Hudson's sadness at face value. Only later did I learn how instrumental she had been in Holmes arriving at his decision. When he told me that she had been blackmailed by The Cultured, I recalled her unwonted nervousness on that occasion when I surprised her in the hallway, while the business surrounding The Three Gables was in full swing. She had deflected my solicitude by saying she was concerned about Holmes's behaviour, whereas in truth her concerns must have centred around her family's welfare and the ramifications her actions might have for Holmes.

The revelation about Mrs Hudson formed part of a second letter I received from Holmes later that same week. This one, headed with the address of his Sussex homestead, was a lengthy epistle setting out the sequence of events I have detailed above in this section of the book, from Count Negretto Sylvius's arrival to Holmes's farewell tea with Mrs Hudson.

"I felt you were owed a fuller explanation of my reasons for leaving town," the letter concluded. "You will also see that the Mi-Go affair has reached some kind of terminus. I have every faith in the combined efforts of the Dagon Club and Glaw Za-Jooll to ensure that the Outside Things settle comfortably and, more important, unobtrusively here on Earth. Should that not be the case, I – and, I hope, you – stand ready to act."

My wife noticed a distinct lightening of my disposition once I had read the letter. I had been harbouring doubts about her – vague, nameless doubts – ever since Holmes had warned me that "the people around us, even people we know well" could not necessarily be trusted. The reference, it turned out, had been to Mrs Hudson, and I was elated to have my wife exonerated of suspicion.

"Why are you smiling at me like that, John?" she asked. "What has come over you?"

"Nothing, my dear," I said, embracing her. "It's all fine. Everything is going to be fine."

As a brief postscript to this chapter, I readily acknowledge that the depiction of Count Negretto Sylvius in my published tale "The Adventure of the Mazarin Stone", which appeared in 1921, differs considerably from his depiction herewith. The reason why I chose to portray Glaw Za-Jooll's human identity in a rather unflattering light will become clear in the next – and final – part of this book.

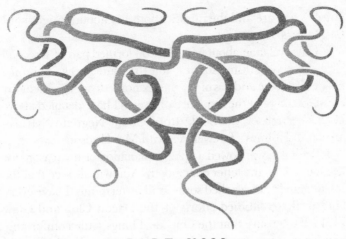

PART VIII

Autumn 1918

I WRITE NOW OF AN EXHAUSTED MAN IN AN EXHAUSTED nation in an exhausted world.

That world was the world that was reeling after four years of gruelling, brutal conflict. That nation was Great Britain, which had played a major role in the war and paid a huge price for it, losing nearly a million of her native sons and around as many again from her colonies, with hundreds of thousands more left wounded and crippled. As for that exhausted man, he was I.

Having reached my mid-sixties, I had all but given up medical practice, continuing to see just a few of my older patients who had been with me all their lives and could not bear to take their ailments to a new GP. I was wrenched out of semi-retirement, however, by the arrival of the Spanish 'flu pandemic that gripped our country just as the Great War was in its final throes. Physicians were needed to tackle the huge surge in cases, and age was no bar to involvement. Thus I found myself putting in long hours, going to whichever of London's hospitals required an extra pair of hands.

Ward beds were already in short supply, for wounded soldiers from the front occupied many of them. The 'flu-stricken were put wherever space could be found. They lined corridors. They huddled in cupboards. Some even sat in stairwells. It is hard to convey what conditions were like in those congested hospitals. Everywhere one turned, there they were in their droves: the suffering, the dying, and the dead. The staff themselves were stretched thin, their ranks depleted through sickness and sheer fatigue, not forgetting the number of doctors who were still overseas, embroiled in the fighting. More than once I came across a nurse sobbing in a corner, overwhelmed by the demands being imposed on her, and I am not ashamed to admit that I myself came close to weeping on several occasions. Doctor and nurse alike, near to breaking point, stumbled around in a kind of stuporous daze, fulfilling their duties as best they were able and hoping, praying, for a swift end to it all.

But the plague persisted. The statistics are staggering. The tally of dead worldwide is estimated at somewhere between 50 and 100 million, more even than died during the preceding global hostilities. In Britain alone, some 250,000 people perished, many of them otherwise healthy individuals. Today, looking back from a perspective of over a decade later, I still find the figures appalling.

Yet living through it, being exposed to the horrors the pandemic threw up on a daily basis, was even more appalling. The hellish scenes at the hospitals put me in mind of the worst excesses of Bosch or Brueghel the Younger. Repetition did not inure me to the sights I saw. Patients of all ages, from grey-haired grandparents down to infants, lay prostrate, coughing, wheezing, gasping for breath, their skin turning blue as they slowly suffocated on the fluid in their lungs. There was no curing them. Their lives were in the hands of a higher power. Those who were innately able to combat the infection would recover. Those who could not were consigned to a prolonged, dreadful end. All we medics could do was make each of them as comfortable as possible, offer whatever palliatives were available, and wait for the disease to run its course.

There was many an occasion when I wondered what we might have been capable of, had we had the Mi-Go's life-sustaining fungus to call on, or some other, similar extraterrestrial wonder. I understood Holmes's rationale for denying mankind the Mi-Go boons, and to a point endorsed it; but surely, with a fungus like that, we could have at least mitigated the death toll, if not eliminated it altogether.

It was during November of that year that I observed a new set of symptoms in several of the afflicted. This was at the height of the second wave of the pandemic, whose effects were markedly deadlier than those of the first, during the spring, had been. One of my private patients – the barrister Lionel Axton, KC – had come down with the disease, and when I received a summons from his wife by telephone shortly after breakfast, I went round to the Axton house in Hammersmith fully expecting to find the fellow feverish, shivery and short of breath. I did not expect to find him dead. Nor did I expect to find his airway and lungs occluded, not with the pleural effusion commonly arising from influenza, but with blood.

"When did the infection start?" I asked his wife.

She, poor woman, was too distraught to answer, but Axton's valet was more collected and told me that his master had complained of a headache and sore throat the previous evening and had taken paregoric for it and gone to bed. In the morning, he had awoken feeling, in his words, "utterly wretched", whereupon he had begun to cough violently and hadn't stopped. Between the telephone call to me and my arrival at the house, Axton had started retching up blood and, within minutes of that, was dead.

I would have thought this haemoptysis simply an idiosyncratic, more violent reaction to the 'flu germ and dismissed it as a one-off. However, while working at St Thomas's, to which I had been seconded for a week, I discussed Axton's death with a colleague, and when I described that the cause had been a rupturing of the lungs rather than a build-up of fluid, he told me that he had heard of a spate of similar deaths at the Royal Free Hospital.

In due course I spoke to a senior consultant at the Royal Free, who confirmed an outbreak of what he termed "bloodier fatalities" there. He expressed concern that we were seeing the nascence of a third strain of the influenza, one which had developed hot on the heels of the second and whose effects were not only rapider but more savage. He hoped he was mistaken but feared he was not, and we both agreed we would monitor the situation and, if we thought it warranted, would alert Sir Arthur Newsholme, the Chief Medical Officer.

I confessed to my wife the dread I felt, anticipating the havoc and devastation such a novel strain might wreak. I said much the same in a letter I wrote to Sherlock Holmes. In those days he and I kept in touch sporadically, always by post, exchanging news and views in that way of old friends who have long been apart but still feel strongly the bonds that once tied them. I would travel down to Sussex to visit him perhaps once or twice a year, and would find him, in person, as frail and decrepit as ever. He had been left that way owing to his great exertions in 1910, as chronicled in my manuscript *The Sussex Sea-Devils*; when he had prevented a great evil from being unleashed upon the world, but at serious and permanent cost to his health. His mind remained sharp and lively, for the most part, but physically he was diminished, a straw effigy of Sherlock Holmes. Were it not for his Scottish housekeeper, Martha, who had come to live with him in late 1911, he would scarcely have been able to look after himself and would probably have given up the ghost. She, a doughty, tenacious creature, fed him, cared for him and was responsible for restoring at least some of his former vigour.

I mentioned the possibility of a new strain to Holmes just as a passing reference, in amongst complaints about my burdensome caseload and general expressions of despair about the progress of the pandemic. I did not think that he would remark upon it, and in the normal course of events he would not have written back to me for at least a month. As it happened, a reply came by telegram the morning after I posted the letter, and it was brief and its tone was urgent.

SYMPTOMS SINISTER STOP COME TO SUSSEX AT ONCE STOP

*

Wintry winds rolled in across grey seas and heaved themselves up over the clifftops to batter Holmes's villa. As the Renault taxicab that had transported me from Eastbourne station puttered off along the coastal road, I gathered my trench coat around me and walked through the gates and up the chalk path to the front door. Every fresh gust of wind seemed dead-set on tearing my hat off my head and sweeping my legs out from under me. The hawthorn trees that served as hedgerows for the smallholding were bent almost double, waving their branches in distress.

Martha answered my knock and ushered me indoors without a word. After a brief struggle she managed to close the door, and only then, with the howl of the wind subdued, were we able to converse.

"Welcome, Doctor. Braw weather we're having, no?"

"Only a Scotswoman would consider turbulent skies and heavy gales braw."

"Aye, well, where I'm from, this is a balmy summer's day."

I had a great deal of time for Martha, and not just because she had proved such a tonic for Holmes. She combined a finely tuned sense of irony with a no-nonsense attitude, all this enhanced by delicate Caledonian features and long, curly hair which, save for the occasional white streak, retained its innate auburn hue. Had Holmes been the marrying kind, he could have done a lot worse than wed this intelligent, forthright lady, who matched him in wit as well as years. As things stood, he was fortunate to employ a live-in helpmeet who diligently tended to his needs and refused to tolerate him when he was at his most cantankerous and irascible.

"Mr Holmes is in the living room, by the fire," said she. "You come through and get cosy there too."

My friend was sunk in an armchair with a tartan blanket around his legs. "You'll forgive me if I don't get up, Watson," said he. "My legs are unusually bad today. The arthritis, you know."

I clasped his slender, gnarled hand lightly in mine. His face was sallow and liver-spotted, riddled with wrinkles, and yet his eyes, though rheumy, retained their old spark.

"You are looking well," I said.

"You are a liar," he replied, "and a poor one at that. But I accept the sentiment. You, for your part, seem in the pink. Do you not get old?"

"Now who's lying?"

Holmes chuckled dryly. "Martha? Something warming for Watson. Whisky?"

"'Please'," chided Martha.

"Please," said Holmes, with a sigh.

"Coffee, if you don't mind, Martha," I said. "I have had to cut back on the alcohol. It thins the blood, and my aged blood is thin enough already."

"Coffee it is, Doctor."

"Thank you."

Martha aimed a look of rebuke at her employer. "You see, Mr Holmes? Your friend has manners. You could learn from him."

"There was always much I could learn from Watson," came the reply. "I just was never an attentive pupil."

When we two were alone, Holmes said, "I wish I had invited you here for purely social reasons, old fellow."

"I wish so too. Your wire, however, left little room for doubt. My description of the possible new strain of Spanish 'flu has set your alarm bells jangling. Why? What about it is so sinister? Beyond the obvious, that is – its virulence, its vileness."

"First, tell me in detail your experience of it."

I related the circumstances of Lionel Axton's death and the instances of other 'flu sufferers who had died the same way.

"The outbreak was at the Royal Free Hospital, you said?"

"Fifteen dead, last I heard. Anyone showing the symptoms is whisked to a special ward, and there, alas, more or less left to expire."

Holmes indicated a small stack of newspapers by his side. "Have you seen the afternoon edition of the *Times*?"

"I have not."

"It's reported that a mews in Kensington has seen several households succumb to 'a deadly lung sickness of a bronchitic nature', whose primary symptom is coughing up blood. The remaining residents have voluntarily shut themselves up in their houses and closed off the street, with police enforcing the quarantine."

"Ghastly. It feels like something from the days of the Black Death."

"So far no connection has been made with the Spanish 'flu, nor any association drawn with the cases you have identified."

"It is surely only a matter of time. All it takes is one enterprising journalist to do some digging."

"Do you know of the Duchess of Lomond?"

I frowned. "No. Why do you ask?"

"She is a wealthy widow who spends most of her time on the Continent," said Holmes. "She cuts an eccentric figure, going about veiled in public and speaking only in a whisper. It's rumoured that she has been blighted by some disfiguring ailment, hence the veil and perhaps, too, the whispering. When war broke out, she took up permanent residence in London, and in recent months she has been a regular donor to various of the capital's hospitals, supporting their care for our wounded troops. Often she will tour the wards, sitting at soldiers' bedsides and offering them comfort."

"She sounds like a saint. I am surprised I have not heard of her, but then I don't keep up with the chatter in medical circles as much as I used to."

"What if I told you that only last week the duchess paid a visit to the Royal Free?"

"If you are suggesting some kind of correlation between that and the outbreak of the haemoptysic variant of the 'flu…"

"You would think it too coincidental to be likely," said

Holmes, "and I would agree. But what if I then told you that the duchess held a dinner party at the weekend at which one of the guests was your patient, Lionel Axton?"

"No!"

"It is in the society columns. You may also be interested to learn that she lives on Brompton Square, a stone's throw from the address in Kensington I just mentioned, Princes Gate Mews."

I passed a hand across my face. "The only conclusion one can draw is that this Duchess of Lomond is a carrier of the new strain. She is going about like a new Typhoid Mary, heedlessly disseminating it. This is a public health emergency. We must notify the police and the General Medical Council at once and get her sequestered somewhere."

Holmes held up a forefinger made crooked by arthritis. "Not so fast. I have been keeping an eye on the duchess for several years now. I have reason to believe she is an old acquaintance of ours, going by another name. She met the Duke of Lomond while he was holidaying in Germany. Visiting the Black Forest, to be exact, near her home. They were introduced by a mutual friend, Count Negretto Sylvius. There was a whirlwind courtship, followed by marriage, and then the couple settled down in Heidelberg and lived there in relative seclusion until his death in 1912. A year later, as it became more and more indisputable that Germany and England would be going to war, the duchess felt it prudent to move to this country."

"The Black Forest. Sylvius. Heidelberg. Why, if I didn't know better, Holmes, I would assume you were talking about Isadora Klein. But she is dead."

"No, Watson," said Holmes. "Glaw Za-Jooll, a.k.a. Count Negretto Sylvius, *said* she was dead. It would seem that when I taught him about the human capacity for fabrication, he learned the lesson quickly."

"He lied."

"To my face. Somehow Isadora Klein survived her encounter with the purple fungus, although apparently it has left her beauty and her vocal cords ruined."

"And now she is at large in London," I said, "deliberately sowing disease? It beggars belief. Why on earth would she want to?"

"I cannot speak to her motives. All I can do is try to stop her. Help me up, would you, old friend?"

I took Holmes's arm and assisted as he rose effortfully, with much creaking of joints, from the chair. He swayed for a moment and I had to steady him until he managed to regain his balance.

"Thank you," said he. "Now we must venture outside into the teeth of this gale. The potting shed awaits."

*

Holmes's potting shed leaned against the back wall of the house, adjacent to his collection of beehives. The house itself afforded some protection from the wind's onslaught, but on our way to the shed we still walked hunched over, staggering somewhat and clutching each other for support, and it was a great relief to reach shelter.

I should perhaps have predicted that a potting shed, for Sherlock Holmes, was not merely a place where gardening tools were stored and seedlings nurtured. His own currently fulfilled an additional function. Its windows were covered with blankets, and once he lit a lantern I saw that he had been propagating certain fungi in trays of compost, in the dark. There were scores of them, all a deep crimson colour and plumply glossy, like large blood blisters.

"I have been developing these for the past month," said he, "as a contingency measure."

"A contingency measure for what? You mean to say you foresaw that Mrs Klein – rather, the Duchess of Lomond – would embark on a campaign of mass murder by contagion?"

"I had a strong suspicion that something of the kind might occur. We are in the middle of a pandemic. If one wished to instigate a plague of one's own and not be found out, what better time to do it than while another plague is already raging?"

"And how better to do it than under the guise of a philanthropic hospital visitor?"

"The Royal Free was just the start of it. I am sure the duchess has her eye on other hospitals. Even now, she could be swanning through Guy's or St George's, acting like Lady Bountiful, while covertly leaving a trail of death."

"And the dinner party Lionel Axton attended? The mews?"

"Given that nobody else at the dinner fell ill," said Holmes, "my assumption would be that Axton alone was exposed to whatever the source of the infection is, perhaps inadvertently. As for the mews, its proximity to her home – practically on the duchess's doorstep – makes it a conveniently placed site for an outbreak, where she might observe events unfurling at first hand and assess their success or otherwise. But it is in hospitals where her efforts will prove the most effective, perhaps not surprising given that in a hospital you have hordes of people gathered under one roof, cheek by jowl."

"Most of whom are already very unwell, with weakened resistance. How fiendish of her. What are these, then?" I pointed to the crimson fungi. "The antidote?"

"Well done, Watson. Right first time. Or at least, I hope they are the antidote. They should do the trick, if the duchess is using what I think she is using."

"Namely…?"

"The same fungus, that verdigris-coloured puffball mushroom, with which Josiah Amberley dispatched his wife and her lover and tried to dispatch me. I spied one of them among the assorted fungi in the Palimpsest Chamber at The Three Gables. Given that the room had been cleared out when we returned there, the erstwhile Mrs Klein could only have taken it with her when she fled the country. The turquoise fungus would be a deadly weapon in anyone's arsenal, not least that of a woman who is exercising a grudge of some sort and is evidently not in her right mind."

I peered at the fungi in the trays. Each was as large as my fist, and there was something quite repugnant about their redness, glossiness and fleshiness.

"So you were able to develop an antidote for the puffball mushroom from scratch?" I asked.

"Actually, 'from scratch' sums it up rather well," replied Holmes. "You will recall that I immunised myself against the puffball's effects. My blood retains that immunity still. These fungi are a breed of the puffball grown in compost fertilised with copious quantities of my liquid lifestuff. It took a few attempts to get right, but they now carry spores that are able to counteract the puffball's spores. I have tested them out on rats, giving the rodents spores from these fungi to inhale, then making them inhale spores from the original puffball mushroom. All the rats survived the latter exposure unharmed, and not only that but proved able to pass their immunity on to other rats, much as bacteria can pass from one organism to another through simple proximity. I'm pleased to say that, in addition to being a prophylactic, the antidote spores also work as a remedy, and I am convinced that by releasing them upon London, I may put paid to the Duchess of Lomond's mad scheme. That is where you come in, Watson."

"Say no more. These things shall be got up to town as soon as possible."

"I knew I could count on you. I have arranged for a car to pick us up in an hour or so."

"Us?" I said. "But—"

"You think I am in no fit state to make a hundred-mile round trip by car? Let alone conduct business up in the city? Well, you may be right. But I must do what I must do. The pain and discomfort are a small price to pay for forestalling a terrible crime."

"Even if I say it goes against all medical advice, I doubt that will make any difference."

"I will just respectfully ignore you."

"Then what choice do I have?" I said. "A last hurrah. Sherlock Holmes and Dr Watson to the rescue, one final time."

"Well put, old man."

*

As we emerged from the potting shed, we were met by Martha.

"So this is where you two have got to," said she. "Your coffee is waiting indoors, Doctor. Oh, and a car has just pulled up out front, Mr Holmes. I presume it's the one you hired."

"If so, it is early," said Holmes. "What sort of car?"

"A long limousine."

"Not a Wolseley Colonial? Wright's of Eastbourne only have a Colonial and a Humber tourer to hire out, and I always ask for the Wolseley. The Humber's suspension is rougher."

"Neither," said Martha. "It's a Daimler, I believe."

The wrinkles on Holmes's brow doubled. "Hum! Let us go and see who has come to call. I daresay it will be a well-heeled individual, if the Daimler is his own."

We ventured round the side of the house, to be greeted by the sight of a burgundy limousine purring by the gate and a chauffeur in cap and uniform helping his passenger to disembark.

The passenger was a woman in black, her face veiled. She moved slowly, with her head bowed, a small embroidered reticule dangling from the crook of one elbow. The wind tore at her dress, making her skirts flail about her like a raven's wings.

Beside me, Holmes stiffened, as did Martha. I myself felt my breath catch. Surely this could not be who I thought it was.

"Sherlock…" said Martha softly.

"Speak of the devil," said Holmes.

So distracted was I by the apparition before us, I only vaguely registered that Martha had used Holmes's forename and not the customary more formal mode of address.

The woman hobbled up the path, escorted by the chauffeur. Was this what had become of Isadora Klein? Was this bent-backed, stiffly moving creature all that remained of that beauteous and vivacious virago?

She halted in front of us and disengaged herself from the chauffeur's solicitous hand. "Go back to the car, Frederick," she said in a voice so low and hoarse that I could barely hear it above the wind.

Frederick the chauffeur did as bidden.

"Her Grace the Duchess of Lomond, unless I'm much mistaken," said Holmes.

"Mr Holmes," came the whispered reply. Through the veil I glimpsed a face whose contours were unnatural, somehow stretched and twisted. "Aren't you going to invite me in?"

"I most certainly am not. I do not think it is safe to be in an enclosed space with one such as you."

The duchess cackled, a sound like autumn leaves on a bonfire. "I did not doubt that you would have figured out my little scheme by now. Nor that you would have brought in Dr Watson as reinforcements. Indeed, I was rather relying on it."

"Your 'little scheme' is causing misery and death," Holmes retorted. "I would ask you to desist, but things are too far gone for that. Instead, I intend to halt it, and you, by any means necessary."

"Including killing me?"

"If it comes to that."

Again, there was that dry cackling from the duchess, although this time it was mirthless. "You are too late, Mr Holmes. Far too late. I am already dying. Of cancer, as it happens."

"Ah," said Holmes. "The same disease that took away your first husband. The same disease whose cure Dr Felder attempted, with your sponsorship and assistance, only to wind up creating something worse. Is that poetic justice? I don't know. It certainly has an ironic ring about it."

"Easy for someone to say who is not suffering as I am," said the Duchess of Lomond. "But then suffering is something I have been familiar with for many years. Ever since the summer of 1903, to be precise, when a certain she-devil tried to kill me."

"And evidently should have tried harder," said Martha.

The duchess flapped a dismissive, black-gloved hand. "Oh, be quiet, you. Whoever you are, this conversation is between me and the two gentlemen alone."

Martha bridled, but Holmes shook his head at her. "Just a moment. Let us hear the lady out."

"There isn't much to tell you," said the duchess. "You have probably deduced most of it anyway."

"You were infected by the purple fungus which Irene Adler hurled at you in the Palimpsest Chamber," said Holmes. "You, along with the three men in that room. You were nearest the door, and you hastened into the corridor to loose off a shot at us as we ran. For that reason, you would have received a lesser dose than Steve Dixie, Octavius Dysart and Ezra Woolfson, all of whom remained in the room longer. They were beyond saving. You nonetheless took them with you when you fled the country for Germany."

"Steve died on the ferry over to Calais. The other two, thanks to the healing fungus each wore, lasted longer, but succumbed before we reached Heidelberg. That fungus has the power to mend flesh but even it cannot neutralise the insidious effects of the purple fungus once it has invaded the body's system. I arranged for the remains of all three men to be immolated at the crematorium in Gotha, and awaited the same fate myself. I had the feverishness and the purple swellings and fully expected that my days were numbered. Imagine my surprise when, after a few days, the symptoms began to abate. At first I thought it just some temporary reprieve, a false dawn before the inevitable occurred. As time went by, however, it became clear I was going to live. If you can call it living."

"Your body was left irrevocably damaged."

"Exactly so. I retained most of my faculties but only a trace of my voice and none of my former dynamism. I was able to wed again, and my husband, a kindly and forgiving man, bore with my infirmity throughout our marriage, short though it was. Yet even he found it hard going at times, and who can blame him?"

Her hands went to her veil.

"Look at me," she said. "Look at what was left of me."

She raised the netted shroud, to reveal a vision of horror.

Very little of the Isadora Klein I had met remained. Most of her face hung lumpenly down, as though made of melted tallow. What had been the left side of her forehead now dangled over the eye below, half covering it, and what had been two shapely cheeks sagged into pendulous dewlaps. Her skin was wan and lustreless, with here and there faint mauve patches that showed the places where, one presumes, buboes had once blossomed.

"No need to comment," said she waspishly. "Your expressions say it all. I am hideous. Picture the rest of my body in a similar condition, and you will have some idea what I have had to put up with for the past decade and a half. I repulse myself. Rarely can I bring myself to look in a mirror. Added to that, I am in constant pain. To be honest, I am glad that cancer now has me in its grip. For too long I have been living as a grotesque cripple, and now that the end is drawing nigh, I welcome it. The torment will soon be over."

"But you have decided to take others with you," I said. "Why? As some kind of petty recompense? How does killing innocents make things better?"

"Oh, it's not that, Doctor. It's to show Mr Sherlock Holmes that he cannot get everything his way. He interfered with the work I was doing on behalf of the Mi-Go. His meddling resulted in this." She jabbed a finger at herself. "And now, in retaliation, I am presenting him with a situation he is helpless to resolve. I have sown death."

"Starting with those who have perished at the Royal Free and Princes Gate Mews," said Holmes, "and also with Lionel Axton."

"Yes, poor Lionel. An incorrigible plant fancier. Giving in to his own curiosity, he poked his nose into my conservatory and touched something he should not have, and I was too late to prevent him. However, he and the others are only the first of what is sure to be a multitude. I have left death all across London, Mr Holmes. It is cached in dozens of different places, and you will never find them all. What has already begun will soon escalate. I estimate the final toll will run into the hundreds, if not the thousands."

That whispering voice had risen to a furious hiss, like an angry snake's.

"And all those fatalities will be on your head, Mr Holmes!"

"Now listen here," Holmes said. "I grant you, the outcome of my investigation at The Three Gables did not end well for you. That was not deliberate on my part. In the broader scheme of things, though, you got what you wanted. Mi-Go now dwell among us. I permitted that."

"Did we humans get everything that was promised us?" said the duchess. "Do we live in a world enhanced by everything the Mi-Go could have done for our race? No! You saw to that, Mr Holmes. You presented Glaw Za-Jooll with a set of strict conditions, and you told him he and his fellow refugees would go unmolested on Earth as long as they complied with those conditions. In doing that, you deprived the human race of so much."

"I had my reasons, and I stand by them. The recent hostilities have been terrible enough. Imagine how much worse they could have been, had Mi-Go weaponry been implemented. That is but one example."

"Who gave you the right to choose for the rest of us? Who appointed you spokesman for the whole world?"

"You did," Holmes replied simply. "As long as individuals like you exist, Duchess, with your ruthless extremism, your overweening certainty, your willingness to take life in the name of your beliefs, then individuals like me must stand in opposition to you. Individuals like me must take the hard decisions, in order that individuals like you do not dictate the future."

The Duchess of Lomond lowered her head. "I thought you might say something like that. It seems I have no choice, then. I cannot allow even the possibility that you might thwart me. I came here to crow, I freely admit that. I came to look you in the eye one last time and see if there was a scintilla of remorse in your soul. There is none, and so I have no regrets about doing what I am going to do next."

With that, she delved into her reticule and pulled out a fungus. It was thin and fluted, completely jet black, with a trumpet-shaped "mouth" at the top.

Holding the fungus up to her face, she squeezed it. A tiny dark cloud of spores erupted from within, and the duchess inhaled hard.

What followed next was as appalling as it was astonishing. The duchess's entire body began to mutate. It started with her head, whose distorted features further deformed, swelling, darkening. Her neck ballooned, as though afflicted with a host of goitres. Her shoulders and arms bulged within her dress, ripping the sleeves at the seams. Her torso and legs followed suit, all of her expanding and distending to the accompaniment of ghastly creaks and cracks and wet sucking noises. Before our very eyes, her skin and musculature became a mass of large, horrendous lumps and growths, until what stood in front of us was a bulbous, hulking parody of a human being, clad in a few tattered scraps of black silk.

Eyes glared out from beneath beetling brows. They burned black with hatred.

Coarse, fattened lips moved to form words.

"A woman... with cancer," the duchess growled thickly, "is now... nothing but... cancer." Every syllable seemed an effort, having to be torn from her throat. "I am... invulnerable. I am... unstoppable. I can tear you apart... with my bare hands... and I will... relish every minute."

She raised two huge monstrous paws. I took an involuntary step backward, wishing I had my revolver with me, and at the same time thinking that even a bullet would not impede this thing the Duchess of Lomond had become.

As the behemothic creature loomed menacingly over us, I saw Martha place a hand on Holmes's chest and move in front of him.

"Leave this to me," she said.

"By all means," my friend replied. "You are far better equipped than I to deal with her."

Martha looked small and fragile compared to the duchess, and I could not imagine how she hoped to mount any kind of resistance against such an abomination.

Then she too began to mutate.

Her face elongated and smoothed, her eyes sinking into their sockets until they disappeared. Her fingers stretched into talons. A pair of devilish horns sprouted from her forehead. The back of her bodice split open and two enormous batlike wings unfurled. A tail snaked out from under her skirt. Her skin assumed a black, rubbery sheen. In the space of a few heartbeats, Martha was gone, and in her stead was a nightgaunt.

My mind reeled. I struggled to comprehend the whys and wherefores of this transformation. Holmes and I had met one of these blind beasts once before, in the marshes of Essex, and I would gladly have gone through life without ever encountering another. This one was different, however, in as much as it was Martha in an altered form and therefore, presumably, on our side. More to the point, Martha was clearly no mere Scottish housekeeper and could only be a certain former opera singer from New Jersey.

"Irene Adler," I breathed. "She is… That is…"

"Close that gaping jaw, Watson," said Holmes, "and join me in beating a retreat. This fight is between Irene and the duchess, and Irene has enough to worry about without us getting in her way."

As he and I made for the shelter of the front doorway, the nightgaunt launched itself at the duchess. Talons flailing, it tore strips of flesh off the cancerous creature. The duchess shrieked and fought back, fetching the nightgaunt a sidelong, swiping blow that sent it flying. The nightgaunt rolled and regained its feet, only to find the duchess charging for it, arms outstretched. The nightgaunt beat its wings and took to the air, but gained only a few feet in height before the duchess snatched it by one ankle. She swung the nightgaunt down onto the ground as though cracking a whip. The impact resounded. The winged black thing had no mouth but surely would have screamed in pain if it could. The duchess, still gripping it by the ankle, now flung it hard against the side of the house. Knapped flint cracked as the nightgaunt struck. I watched in dismay as the monster that was Irene Adler slumped to the earth, clearly stunned.

"Holmes, we must do something. Miss Adler is losing."

"A nightgaunt is resilient, Watson, and so is Irene." Holmes sounded confident but his expression betrayed doubt.

The nightgaunt hauled itself up into a crouch, surveying the duchess with its eyeless face. Miss Adler, it seemed, had underestimated her opponent and was reassessing her tactics. As the duchess lumbered in for a fresh assault, the nightgaunt bent low and darted for her legs. A slash of talons was followed by a roar of agony from the duchess. She stumbled, her left leg coming apart at the knee. The nightgaunt delivered a second blow from behind, raking its claws down the muscles of the duchess's back. Flesh as lumpy as cobbled paving tore open, weeping blood. The duchess roared again.

Yet, even as she writhed in pain, I saw the wounds in her back knitting together. Her half-severed leg reunified, tissue growing with uncanny speed to seal up the gap. I now knew what she meant about being invulnerable. The black Mi-Go fungus had turned her into a walking tumour, with a tumour's ability to thrive against all odds. I feared that even a nightgaunt was no match for a woman whose body could repair any amount of harm inflicted upon it.

Miss Adler, however, was undeterred. The nightgaunt renewed its assault on the duchess, latching on to her with its feet and hacking and rending with its hands. The duchess hammered her fists down on the nightgaunt's back but could not dislodge it. The black monster carved away at her with its talons, sending out sprays of gore to left and right. Howling, the duchess wrenched at her assailant, trying to rid herself of it, but the nightgaunt was unrelenting, and at last the duchess's efforts started to slacken. The nightgaunt was demolishing her body faster than it could mend itself.

The duchess tumbled to the ground, and the nightgaunt pressed home its advantage. The lawn in front of Holmes's villa became an abattoir as fragments of gristle and muscle and viscera and bone were scattered in all directions. Feebler and feebler grew the duchess's efforts at defending herself, while the nightgaunt kept up its frenzied carnage. Eventually there was no fight left in the duchess at all. Her limbs went limp. Her head lolled back.

"Irene!" Holmes called out. "Irene!"

The nightgaunt's gouging talons slowed. It turned its head to one side.

"She is done, Irene," Holmes said. "It's over. You may revert to your usual self."

The nightgaunt appeared to gauge Holmes's words, and for a dreadful moment I thought that there was no Irene Adler in that creature any more, that she had lost herself and only the nightgaunt remained. In that case, Holmes and I were apt to be its next victims, and facing a beast as fearsome as this, with nothing to protect us against it, we stood no chance.

The nightgaunt seemed to come to a decision and crawled off the horribly mutilated remains of the duchess. All at once, its limbs shrank. Its wings receded. The horns shrivelled down to nothing. The tail was gone.

Squatting on the grass was a woman in her sixties, with the remnants of a housekeeper's uniform draped about her. This was not Martha now but rather the Irene Adler I knew from the photograph Holmes had of her, older here, a little more weathered, but still undeniably lovely looking. She tottered to her feet, dripping with the duchess's blood. She had bruises all over, and from the way she favoured one leg I could tell that her ankle was either dislocated or badly sprained.

She limped towards us, almost collapsing as she reached us. I caught her, taking her weight.

"Thank you, Doctor," she said.

"Miss Adler. Not a formless spawn, or a fox, or even a Scottish housekeeper. The real Miss Adler. We meet at last."

She half smiled. "I wish the circumstances were better. I am in bad shape, as you see."

"Not as bad as the Duchess of Lomond."

She looked round at the butchered carcass. "I thought she was never going to die."

"I feared *you* were," said Holmes.

"Nightgaunts are made of stern stuff, Sherlock, and so am I. Having said which, I am feeling rather cold and my foot hurts like Hades. Doctor, would you help me indoors?"

I made her comfortable by the fire and examined her ankle. "Ah yes, it *is* dislocated. I will have to perform a closed reduction. I shan't lie, this is going to hurt."

Throughout the procedure, as I manually realigned the joint, Miss Adler bit her lip and cried out only once. When it was over, I advised her that she must not put weight on the foot for several days and get plenty of rest.

"You will have to look after me, Sherlock," she said. "That'll make a change."

"I shall be happy to," Holmes said. "However, Watson and I have urgent business to attend to in London first. The Duchess of Lomond may be dead but she has left a legacy of potential massacre that only we can prevent."

"I understand. Go."

"You will be fine?"

"Yes, I'll be fine. Go!"

*

Rather than wait for Holmes's hired car, we commandeered the duchess's Daimler, chauffeur and all. Poor Frederick had looked on as his employer, in mutated form, engaged in battle with a nightmarish winged entity, and understandably he was shaken to the core.

"There is no simple explanation," Holmes told him. "Suffice it to say that your mistress was a monster, in more ways than one. Do you feel capable of driving?"

"I d-don't know, sir," the fellow stammered. "I can't... I can't seem to make sense of anything any more."

"You will have to. Believe me when I say that lives depend on you getting us to London as quickly as possible. Many lives. Can I count on you to do the right thing, Frederick?"

The chauffeur collected himself, and soon he was helping us load the trays of red fungus into the back of the limousine. Then, with Holmes and myself ensconced in the Daimler's back seat, he cranked the starter handle and the car rumbled into life. For the first few miles of the journey he drove with timorous caution, as though he scarcely trusted himself to keep the vehicle straight. In due course, as the distance between us and Holmes's house grew, his confidence returned. By the time we joined the Brighton-to-London road the Daimler was sailing serenely along near its top speed of 70mph, and Frederick was whistling a tune to himself.

"So," I said to Holmes, "the duchess has turquoise fungi stashed around the city, ready to erupt and release their deadly spores. We surely cannot hope to find them all in time. We shall just have to go around distributing your antidote fungi wherever they're needed. It will be cure rather than prevention, and I fear there will still be deaths."

"Not necessarily," Holmes said. "There *is* a way we can utilise the spores' preventative properties. It all depends on wind direction." He slid open the glass partition between the passenger and driver sections of the car. "Frederick?"

"Yes, sir?"

"In a previous life you were formerly a Royal Marine."

Frederick glanced at Holmes in the rear-view mirror, his eyes narrowed in curiosity. "How did you know, sir?"

"You were just whistling 'A Life On The Ocean Wave', the Marines' regimental march. In addition to that, on the inside of your left wrist the letters 'PMPT' are tattooed, which can only stand for the initial letters of the Marine motto, *'Per Mare, Per Terram'*."

"Very perspicacious, sir."

"I try to be."

"Took part in the storming of Fort Fao in 'fourteen, and I was there at Gallipoli too. I had a busy war."

"Sounds like it," said Holmes, "and I am grateful to you for helping defend the nation in its hour of need. Now it is *our* hour of need, and your help is required again. As a man familiar with shipboard life, you would surely have noticed which way the wind was blowing when you left London this morning with Mrs Klein."

"From the north, sir," said Frederick smartly, "about five or six on the Beaufort. There may be a southerly blast back there on the coast, but up in town it's not as strong and definitely blowing the other way. Nippy with it, though."

"Very well. Thank you. Keep driving. Aim for Hampstead." With the partition closed again, Holmes said to me, "I was thinking we might go to Box Hill, near Dorking, because the prevailing wind across London is west-southwest. However, if Frederick is correct, we shall need to go to the north of the city instead."

"Box Hill, where your parallel career as a supernatural investigator began," I said. "There would have been some symmetry in that."

"There will be some symmetry still," Holmes said, "for my goal is Highgate Cemetery, where began our long and sporadic interaction with the Mi-Go. We need a vantage point, you see. A summit."

A couple of hours later we were nearing the cemetery. A half-hour after that, Holmes, Frederick and I were threading our way through the necropolis to a point where we had a commanding view of London. Each of us carried trays of fungi.

Halting on the hillside amid rows of graves, we set the trays down. A strong breeze blew. Holmes licked a finger and held it aloft.

"That should do," said he.

"Why are we here?" Frederick asked. "I'm not sure I understand any of this."

"I don't expect you to. You will be able to tell your grandchildren, however, that you assisted in an endeavour that saved countless lives. Just watch."

Taking out a penknife, Holmes knelt beside one of the trays and cut open a blood-red fungus. Immediately, spores burst forth from its interior and were whisked away by the wind, towards the city.

"If you two would care to do likewise…" he invited us.

Frederick and I sliced open more of the fungi, releasing countless spores that had been nourished with Sherlock Holmes's own blood. The wind carried them out over the massed headstones and monuments and mausoleums, and beyond, into the city, from necropolis to metropolis. With them, the spores bore hope – hope that people would breathe them in, that the effects of the turquoise fungi would be negated, that all the Duchess of Lomond's plotting and scheming would be for naught.

We watched the spores go, each little cluster spreading out in the wind, thinning into invisibility. In Holmes's face I saw satisfaction. I saw the look of a person who had done his best to undo another person's act of inhumanity. I saw the closing of a circle.

If this was the last time Sherlock Holmes ever righted a grievous wrong, he could not have done it on a grander scale, nor in a more apposite location. Here, from a place of death, he was sending out the promise of life.

*

That London did not see vast numbers die of lung haemorrhage is testament to the effectiveness of Holmes's antidote fungus. The spores settled upon people in the environs of Highgate and propagated within their bodies, fostering immunity. They passed this immunity on to others, and those others to others still, neighbour to neighbour, stranger to stranger, kin to kin, a spiralling exponential progression. In a crowded, populous city like our capital, with its constant churn and press of inhabitants, the spread was rapid. Thus, the turquoise fungi which Isadora, Duchess of Lomond, had salted away in various locations like timebombs did detonate, but their toxicity was largely nullified.

I say "largely" because, sad to relate, Holmes's counteraction was not an unqualified success. There were two incidents whereby groups of people perished choking on their own blood. One was at a hospital, the other at a convalescent home. The death toll was twenty-six, not trivial but nonetheless far from the widespread slaughter the duchess had wished for. The General Medical Council later determined that the cause must have been latent tuberculosis, which gained the upper hand in an unfortunate few whose resistance to disease had already been badly compromised by the Spanish 'flu. The deaths were deemed statistically insignificant and became lost amid the welter of casualties wrought by war and the pandemic.

Holmes returned to Sussex and Irene Adler, and there he stayed for the remainder of his life, which amounted to a handful of years. While Miss Adler kept up the pretence of being housekeeper Martha when other visitors called, she would drop the disguise whenever I came by. I got to know her as the woman she normally was, and found her brilliantly clever and delightfully mercurial. Sherlock Holmes had met his match in her, and I am pleased to think that his last days on earth saw him married, to all intents and purposes, and contented.

With regard to the Mi-Go among us, there has so far been no indication that they have overstepped the bounds imposed on them by Holmes. That said, just last year my friend and correspondent H.P. Lovecraft recounted to me an episode in Bellows Falls, Vermont – where, of course, that Mi-Go meteorite landed in 1885 – which hints that some Outside Things on Yuggoth are attempting to establish rapport with people on Earth, and from the sound of it these ones are not so benign as Glaw Za-Jooll and his circle. It must be that there is a faction on that dying world, perhaps driven to desperation, who wish to achieve by compulsion what Glaw Za-Jooll attained more peaceably.

Lovecraft proposes to write the matter up as a short story, to be entitled "The Whisperer in Darkness", and I wonder what kind of reception the tale will receive. Perhaps it will be dismissed as mere fantasy, but its import should not be belittled, especially since astronomers are now firmly convinced a ninth planet exists and are actively searching the skies for it. What will happen when, inevitably, they find it? Will it presage an era of communion between our two races, or will it precipitate antagonism and bloodshed? Are we, *pace* Wells, looking at a potential war of the worlds?

These questions trouble me and I shan't be around to learn

their answers. At the end of this lengthy narrative in which cancer plays a significant role, it turns out that I myself have contracted the disease. I have not troubled to see an oncologist in order to have the diagnosis confirmed. I know my own body well enough, and I know the signs. I estimate I have another five or six months ahead of me. I have not told my wife yet. I wanted to get all of this down on paper first, the last of these *Cthulhu Casebooks* and my final ever Sherlock Holmes story.

The future holds, for me, little but pain and misery, and, for my wife, the hell of caring for an invalid whose deterioration will be messy and wretched to behold. My trusty revolver sits in a drawer of my desk as I write. It has not seen use in years, but with a good cleaning and oiling it can be made functional again and perform one last service. I could, just by pulling a trigger, spare both my wife and myself the ordeal to come. What difference does it make if I end things now or later? The result is the same either way.

The choice is whether to close the book of my life now, or trudge through its few concluding pages even though they hold no pleasure. At some point I shall have to make the decision. For the time being, I shall set down those two small words which are the inevitable terminus of everything, and leave it at that.

THE END

AFTERWORD BY JAMES LOVEGROVE

I, LIKE DR WATSON, AM FINISHED WITH THIS PROJECT, having turned his manuscript into what I hope is a readable book. Watson was a fine writer, but *The Highgate Horrors*, in its original form, had all the hallmarks of a man whose powers were failing and whose judgement was starting to become faulty, and given that he was dying and knew it, this is hardly surprising. I have tidied and trimmed, topped and tailed, and it has been a labour of love but a labour nonetheless, and now it is done.

An author is often at the mercy of their life. I have definitely found that, when writing one of my own books, small synchronicities and coincidences crop up that inform the work in progress. It can be a phrase you overhear, which you find incorporates itself neatly into the storyline and gives you a defining line of dialogue for one of your characters. It can be an insight prompted by something mundane like a newspaper headline or a song lyric that turns the plot wonderfully on its head. It can be a stray thought that strikes you out of nowhere – usually at an inconvenient moment, even more usually during the wee small hours – and provides the key to a passage you were struggling with. When it happens, you just have to go with it. They are omens. The universe or your subconscious – take your pick – is nudging you, offering you a helping hand. Pay attention. Accept it.

During the year or so while this particular book was occupying my headspace, I went through several life-altering experiences. A close relative died of cancer. A good friend died of cancer. I myself nearly died of cancer. More broadly, there has been a pandemic, its effects still lingering. A long-reigning queen has passed away and a new king crowned. There is political turmoil both at home and abroad. Migration has become a hot media topic. The ground seems to be shifting beneath everyone's feet, but I mostly notice it happening beneath mine because, well, they're mine. I look back over these pages from a century ago and see reflections – too many – of the world immediately around me. Something that came to me by chance is offering omens of its own.

Those omens suggest that it's time to step away from the *Cthulhu Casebooks* and more broadly from Sherlock Holmes. It's time to look elsewhere, try new things, seek new challenges. Nothing is permanent. Life is short. Change is healthy (and health is changeable).

No doubt there are countless more of Dr Watson's manuscripts waiting to be discovered and published. I will leave that joy to other writers. If they are enthusiastic Holmesians, then the great detective and the good doctor, those eternal steadfast companions, are safe in their hands.

JAMES LOVEGROVE

ABOUT THE AUTHOR

JAMES LOVEGROVE IS THE *NEW YORK TIMES* BESTSELLING author of *The Age of Odin*. He has been short-listed for many awards including the Arthur C. Clarke Award, the John W. Campbell Memorial Award, and the Scribe Award. He won the Seiun Award for Best Foreign Language Short Story in 2011, and the Dragon Award in 2020 for *Firefly: The Ghost Machine*. He has written many acclaimed Sherlock Holmes novels, including *Sherlock Holmes and the Christmas Demon*. As well as writing books, he reviews fiction for the *Financial Times*. He lives in Eastbourne in the UK.

THE CTHULHU CASEBOOKS

SHERLOCK HOLMES AND THE SHADWELL SHADOWS

James Lovegrove

It is the autumn of 1880, and Dr John Watson has just returned from Afghanistan. Badly injured and desperate to forget a nightmarish expedition that left him doubting his sanity, Watson is close to destitution when he meets the extraordinary Sherlock Holmes, who is investigating a series of deaths in the Shadwell district of London. Several bodies have been found, the victims appearing to have starved to death over the course of several weeks, and yet they were reported alive and well mere days before. Moreover, there are disturbing reports of creeping shadows that inspire dread in any who stray too close.

Holmes deduces a connection between the deaths and a sinister drug lord who is seeking to expand his criminal empire. Yet both he and Watson are soon forced to accept that there are forces at work far more powerful than they could ever have imagined. Forces that can be summoned, if one is brave – or mad – enough to dare…

"With its canny reflection of the modern metropolis…
the Cthulhu Casebooks is a lot of fun."
Times Literary Supplement

"The pastiche is pitch-perfect; Lovegrove tells a thrilling tale and vividly renders the atmosphere of Victorian London."
The Guardian

THE CTHULHU CASEBOOKS

SHERLOCK HOLMES AND THE MISKATONIC MONSTROSITIES

James Lovegrove

It is the spring of 1895, and more than a decade of combating eldritch entities has cost Dr John Watson his beloved wife Mary, and nearly broken the health of Sherlock Holmes. Yet the companions do not hesitate when they are called to the infamous Bedlam lunatic asylum, where they find an inmate speaking in R'lyehian, the language of the Old Ones. Moreover, the man is horribly scarred and has no memory of who he is.

The detectives discover that the inmate was once a scientist, a student of Miskatonic University, and one of two survivors of a doomed voyage down the Miskatonic River to capture the semi-mythical shoggoth. Yet how has he ended up in London, without his wits? And when the man is taken from Bedlam by forces beyond normal mortal comprehension, it becomes clear that there is far more to the case than one disturbed Bostonian. It is only by learning what truly happened on that fateful New England voyage that Holmes and Watson will uncover the truth, and learn who is behind the Miskatonic monstrosity...

"A geuninely enjoyable read that fits remarkably well with the Holmes characters and canon."
The Crime Review

"Incredibly fun, frightful mysteries."
Barnes & Noble SFF blog

TITANBOOKS.COM

For more fantastic fiction, author events,
exclusive excerpts, competitions, limited editions and more

VISIT OUR WEBSITE
titanbooks.com

LIKE US ON FACEBOOK
facebook.com/titanbooks

FOLLOW US ON TWITTER AND INSTAGRAM
@TitanBooks

EMAIL US
readerfeedback@titanemail.com